Also by John Dalton

Heaven Lake: A Novel

The Inverted Forest

A Novel

John Dalton

Scribner

New York London Toronto Sydney

SCRIBNER

A Division of Simon & Schuster, Inc.

1230 Avenue of the Americas

New York, NY 10020

First SCRIBNER hardcover edition July 2011

SCRIBNER and design are registered trademarks of The Gale Group, Inc., used under license by Simon & Schuster, Inc., the publisher of this work.

For information about special discounts for bulk purchases, please contact Simon & Schuster Special Sales at 1-866-506-1949 or business@simonandschuster.com.

The Simon & Schuster Speakers Bureau can bring authors to your live event. For more information or to book an event contact the Simon & Schuster Speakers Bureau at 1-866-248-3049 or visit our website at www.simonspeakers.com.

Designed by Carla Jayne Jones

Manufactured in the United States of America

2 4 6 8 10 9 7 5 3 1

Library of Congress Control Number: 2011005574

ISBN 978-1-4165-9602-8
ISBN 978-1-4165-9818-3 (ebook)

This novel is for my brother and sisters:
Jim Dalton
Judy Dalton Sellmeyer
Peggy Zundel
Jean Dalton Young
Joan Dalton
Carla Meyer

Part One

Shannon County, Missouri
Summer 1996

Chapter One

A night breeze lifted the dark skirts of the forest. The usual riot of insects fell quiet. Into the well of this new silence came a sudden peal of laughter—a bark of laughter, exuberant, righteous, feminine.

Hahhhhhyeeeee!

The sound of it at 2:16 A.M.: half raucous cheer, half squeal of delight, borne like a tumbling feather across the wide, night-screened meadow of Kindermann Forest Summer Camp.

On the opposite side of the meadow, in a one-room cedar cottage joined to the camp office, Schuller Kindermann looked up from his drafting table.

He considered his wristwatch. His kindly shopkeeper's face, known for its paternal softness and for the mildness of its expressions, assumed a disappointment that was sharp and private. In his unsteady right hand he held a surgeon's scalpel, the tip of the scalpel pressed into a sheet of heavy Italian-made paper, the paper to be cut millimeter by millimeter, fiber by fiber, then prodded, molded, expertly creased, until, like a pop-up book or the ribs of a paper lantern, it would rise up and assume the shape Schuller intended.

He called his creations Foldout Paper Cards, a hobby of his own invention, though recently an art supplies wholesaler had visited camp and surveyed Schuller's cards, which had been set out in a display case, and declared them examples of kirigami, a Japanese art form. Schuller wanted to scoff at this pronouncement. *Kirigami.* Imagine that. To be told he is a kirigamiist! He'd begun making Foldout Paper Cards some eight years earlier, near the time of his unofficial retirement and the gradual handing over of daily camp operations to the program director. Tonight, Schuller had hoped to cut and bend and coax from the paper a three-dimensional outline of the Basilica of San Lorenzo in Milan, Italy. Too bad then that, at this late hour, the basilica would not rise, would not reveal itself, thanks to the bark of laughter and his lack of concentration and the palsied tremor—mild, to be sure—quivering the wrist of his right hand. What a shame. If he'd had his window fan on, he might not even have heard it.

He rose and slipped his bare feet into a pair of loafers. Before stepping out the door, he switched on the porch floodlight—a marbled brightness, a low, buzzing hum. In an instant there was a mad spiraling of gypsy moths and enough gauzy light for him to shuffle ahead a few timid steps and descend the porch's sagging pine board stairs.

It was much better once he felt the rich meadow grass beneath his loafers. He had his bearings. His night vision was reasonably good. If he concentrated, he could recall, or rather *rehear,* the laugh, its upward feminine lilt, its open claim of privilege, too.

At once he had a sure-voiced intuition as to which direction the laughter had come from, and he set out along a path that would take him across the meadow toward the sleeping cabins and sandlots and recreation courts and swimming pool. A lengthy enough hike, especially at night, but so be it. He was used to crossing the meadow—three acres long, two wide, the largest clearing in all of Kindermann Forest Summer Camp. Over the course of the summer the meadow would serve as assembly and parade ground, capture-the-flag field, parking lot. It never failed to draw the eye of each visitor. To parents the meadow looked *safe,* a happy accident of geography amid an otherwise rugged Ozark landscape. (No accident. The meadow had been cleared of cedar trees in 1957, and every spring since then Schuller and the maintenance staff had collected and carried off thousands of stones that pushed through the skin of the grass.)

There was a soft freckling of light along the scrubby southern edge of the meadow, the clustered winking of fireflies. In time he made a measured and mostly confident descent along a mild, dew-slick slope to a volleyball court and a row of tire swings. At the swings a brick walkway began and in the span of a few careful steps became something else: a burrowed path into the woods, a long sweep of tunneling darkness.

From this point on, it would be a more painstaking journey. With the soles of his loafers, he felt his way forward, one brick to the next, a meticulous and sure-footed tap, tap, tapping, until, after much time and blind probing, he arrived at a large, partially lit swimming pool built into the thick of the woods.

So they'd been bold enough to turn on the shower-house lights and let the soft gleam spill out across the deck and the pool's lapping surface. A few dim shapes moved in the water. He could see the red glow of cigarettes, could hear a kicked bottle rolling across the concrete deck. All of this an unwelcome surprise, a disappointment, truly. But a satisfaction, at least, to know that his first hunch had been correct. And a relief, a consolation, to remember this: the campers had not yet arrived; the start of the first session was still, thankfully, two days away.

Even so, he marveled at the trespassers' sense of entitlement, of which he'd seen no sign during the past week of counselor training. Not that he knew what to look for, exactly. In Schuller's experience each generation of summer camp counselors adopted its own awkward and always veiling brand of etiquette while in the company of the camp director. This group had shown him nothing but a bright and vaguely cloying eagerness. *Carry your satchel, Mr. Kindermann? Will there be a campfire this evening? Oh, good, Mr. Kindermann. And will we be doing "Lights of the City" on the guitar?*

Such agreeableness. And yet, here they were, his earnest counselors, ignoring the midnight curfew and wading about the pool like guests at a spa. He stepped up to the fence.

They were pale and chubby, these trespassers and curfew breakers. They had lined up at the diving board, most of them. And in the matter of swimsuits, they seemed to prefer—

He squinted, blinked.

What he'd first thought to be two paunchy and shirtless young men were, on second glance, two bare-breasted young women, naked young women, edging along the length of the board. He knew them by assignment rather than by name: an archery instructor, a petite arts and crafts attendant, her hair cut in a girlish bob. Both young women moved as if they were treading the windblown ledge of a high building, and yet, unmistakably, they were grinning and laughing and pretending to unbalance one another with a sudden push or turn. Upon arriving at the end of the board, the first girl did a brave hop and fell a few short feet onto what looked to be a very narrow plastic raft that someone had floated in her direction. No surprise that the raft buckled and shot out from beneath her. She somersaulted forward and revealed the dark cleft of her ass.

The raft was floated back out in range of the diving board. The second young woman took her leap. Only then did Schuller recognize the raft for what it was: a large, absurd blow-up hot dog nestled in a fat, inflated bun—a ridiculous pool toy, but also an advertisement for the Oscar Mayer Company. Tonight it was being put to a different use—as a sight gag for the girl counselors of Kindermann Forest.

And the boy counselors? There were several lined up at the board. They, too, walked their naked walk. One difference: the hot dog was held back and an ordinary black inner tube was floated out to the center of the deep end. Each boy leapt toward it. The goal, apparently, was to land dead center and penetrate the tube with a dive or feet-first jump. None of the boys could manage it. But what a scene they made, under- or overshooting their target, then hoisting themselves up naked onto the inner tube, sprawling across it, writhing for control. For this they received whooping cheers of encouragement from an unseen audience treading water in the pool.

Schuller, his fingers curled through the wire diamonds of the pool fence, understood he was seeing an elaborate game or joke acted out: the lurching Oscar Mayer hot dog for the girls, the drifting inner tube for the boys. He wasn't blind to the implications.

The front gate was open and swinging on its hinges. Schuller passed through it and, having descended the first of eight wide steps, looked out and saw a host of young men and women strutting about the shallow end. For all he knew, his entire staff of counselors had gathered here. They were, without exception, unclothed, naked by consensus.

Of course he'd have to pass along news of what he was seeing to other members of the Kindermann Forest senior staff. There'd be the presumption that Schuller took pleasure in this spectacle. After all, the counselors were young. He was old, seventy-eight years to be precise. Wasn't it arousing for an old man to look upon a young woman's naked body? His most honest answer: no, not women's bodies, nor, for that matter, men's. Not children's, either.

He took a step down, this one rushed and uneven, and found himself swaying to the left, not far enough to fall, but enough to get his heart racing and to draw the attention of someone nearby, a young woman standing beside the open shower-house door. Even in his precarious state he recognized her: Wendy Kavanagh, head lifeguard and swimming instructor, an exceedingly tubby girl with large round hips and buttocks, enormous clapping thighs. He'd had reservations about hiring her. But what objections could he offer? Her credentials had been first-rate. And she'd easily outswum the competition. At present she was moving toward the steps, her gaze trained on him, her manner oddly commiserative. A lifeguard's whistle dangled between her breasts.

Did she think she was beautiful without clothes? Was she not embarrassed? There was a time, not so long ago, when young women of her size and odd shape would not dare appear—even clothed—at a public swimming pool.

She raised her bare arm up to him.

Only then did her intentions become clear. She meant to steady him as he descended the steps. She meant to guard him against falling. As courtesies went, this one was unforgivable.

He managed the last six steps on his own, crossed the deck to the shower house, and flipped on, one by one, the full complement of outdoor pool lights. At once a nimbus of hazy yellow light, a dome of light, materialized over the pool and drew—or were they there already?—a thousand whirring insects.

A naked diver leapt from the board. A dozen or more swimmers began to splash and cry out. "Lights off! Lights off!" they shouted. They raised their hands against the glare and recognized him. "Mr. Kindermann?" There was the proper ring of astonishment in their voices, though not the shamed panic he would have liked. Before long they were scrambling from the water, padding about the deck naked, towel-less, snatching up whatever hastily flung garments they could find. Somewhere in their ranks a young man laughed. A friend shushed him. Too late though. By then the hilarity had traveled to others, and soon they were all laughing aloud, several of them hysterically so, as they tried to wrestle underwear over their wet limbs. When this failed, they simply held their balled-up clothing to their chests and ran laughing for the gate.

Because there was but one exit, Schuller had time to recognize each counselor as he or she passed, if not by name then by camp assignment. Wrangler, arts and crafts attendant, canoe instructor. Thirteen, no, fourteen counselors in all.

The pool they'd left behind was a ruin of gaudy debris: beer bottles and clothing and side-turned lounge chairs and, in the middle of it all, Wendy Kavanagh, who by now had covered herself, armpit to thigh, with a large beach towel and was stooped over the deck, gathering up stray kickboards and stacking them, as she'd been taught, beneath the lifeguard's chair.

The sight of her, bent to work, aggravated him. He found his voice. "Oh, for Christ's sake, Wendy. Get back to your cabin."

She labored on.

"Do you hear me, Wendy?"

She nodded while stacking boards. "I'll just be a minute, Mr. Kindermann."

"You will not," he ordered. "Find your swimsuit and *steer* yourself back to your cabin."

She stood straight and weighed the instructions given to her. Some element of what he'd spoken, the tone perhaps, appeared to baffle her. "I can let the boards go till morning," she said. "But the filter's off and the—"

"LEAVE THEM BE!" he shouted, and she stared back openmouthed, amazed. A June bug alighted on her damp hair. She shook it off, surveyed the cluttered deck, winced in sadness or regret. Then she rummaged beneath a lounge chair, found her flip-flops, though not her swimsuit, and marched her way up the steps and into the cavernlike blackness of the walkway.

Schuller meant to follow her, yet once he'd tuned off all the lights, he found the boundary between deck and stairs impossible to locate. He stepped back, flipped on the shower-house switch.

The sudden flickering of light caught an unclothed woman stranded halfway between the shower stall and the bay of lockers behind which she'd been hiding.

They both jumped. Schuller's heart did a queer double thump before settling back into a more sensible rhythm. The woman appeared even more startled, struck dumb, too overwhelmed to catch her breath.

"Oh, for heaven's sake!" he insisted.

Her mouth hung open. She raised a hand to her lips and fanned her fingers about, as if she'd just tasted something blazingly hot. An absurd gesture, certainly, and, for Schuller, a familiar one. He had a younger cousin, now twenty years dead, who, when frightened, would fan her mouth in the exact same motion. Odd that this long-forgotten gesture should reveal itself in, of all people, this naked woman, a black woman no less, the first Kindermann Forest Summer Camp had ever employed.

"Really," he said. "I—"

She found her breath, suddenly, in one deep and rather noisy inhalation. Her shoulders heaved.

"What would your people think of this?" Schuller asked.

She would not look him in the eye. Instead she let her gaze wander the shower room. She reached out, pulled a deflated beach ball from the locker shelf and, after a moment's consideration, decided to hold it over her lap rather than her chest. "I don't think they'd be very happy about it," she said.

"They'd be furious, I'm sure. And your son. What would he think?"

"He's so young, Mr. Kindermann. I don't think he'd have an opinion, one way or the other."

"He'll grow up fast though, won't he? Then he'll have all sorts of opinions." He squared himself for the task of climbing the pool steps. "After I'm gone," he said, "you will dress and you will turn off the lights. Do you understand me?"

She nodded.

"I won't forget this," he said. "The disappointment. The shock of seeing you."

It seemed he'd spoken persuasively on the matter. Fortunately, he didn't undermine his message by teetering on the steps or, once he'd located the brick walkway, losing his way amid the utter darkness.

The meadow, when he reached it, was awash in humid air. Nearby the tree branches raked against one another. The grass beneath his feet felt spongy and alive. From the valley behind him came a soft rumbling thunder and the distant hiss of rain moving in his direction. He picked up his pace. In time he could see the glow of his cottage window. Fifty yards closer and he could make out the crown of soft lamplight shining down on his drafting table.

At worst he would make it back to his cottage with a few thick raindrops puddled in his hair. But what if he didn't make it back at all?

Sometimes, not often, it made him unaccountably happy to think of the curtain swinging shut on his life. To be taken in an instant. To have a lightning bolt find him and leave for the staff of Kindermann Forest a stirring artifact: his half-charred loafers steaming in the meadow grass.

Nothing of the sort happened. The remaining events of his night were small and ordinary. He brushed his teeth (real teeth, not even a crown or bridge). He went to bed. Three hours later he woke to a muted gray dawn and a steady drizzling rain against the cottage window.

He had every right to feel groggy and drained. A pleasant surprise then that he should feel such unexpected vigor in exchange for so little rest. He washed and dressed. Then he passed from his cottage into the much larger camp office, where he brewed a pot of coffee and sat behind the director's desk.

At six-thirty he called Meadowmont Gardens Nursing Home and spoke to Mrs. Davenport, the shift supervisor on Hall 2A, regarding what progress, or lack thereof, had been observed during the previous week. While they talked, a nurse's aide helped Schuller's brother, Sandie, shuffle from his room to a lavishly furnished yet sterile parlor, to a leather armchair, to a telephone receiver placed in Sandie's left hand and guided to a resting place between his neck and chin.

This was a ritual carefully followed each Saturday morning for the past eleven months, since Sandie's release from the hospital and his admittance to Meadowmont Gardens. Impossible to know whether these phone calls lifted Sandie's spirits; on the whole they left Schuller feeling glum. And it wasn't so much Sandie's disabilities, his pivoting shuffle and withered left side, his grossly slurred and often impenetrable speech, which eleven months of therapy had done little to improve. No, it was a certain dullness that Schuller had detected in his brother several years before the stroke, a slackening of interest in camp activities, in his model railroad sets, in himself. Difficult to share a life and a cottage with someone so annoyingly *mild*. All the more troubling because they were twins. Not identical, but fraternal twins who happened to look a good deal alike. *Not identical,* they'd explained to the unobservant thousands of times during their seventy-eight years as siblings and four decades as codirectors of Kindermann Forest Summer Camp, during their long and unbroken bachelorhood—though, of course, few people would mistake them as identical now.

"There's some weather headed your way," Schuller began. "We got it last night. Wind and showers and whatnot. Nothing dire, but if you're going out to Holy Infant this afternoon, you'll want to have Theresa bring along an umbrella."

To this a curt reply, not so much a word as a breathy huff of acknowledgment.

"And you're adjusting very well to the new blood medication. No dizziness with this one. At least according to Mrs. Davenport. That's good news, I would think."

From Sandie a murmur, a kind of elongated "huuurrummm-mmph."

They were abrupt and one-sided, these Saturday phone conversations. One always hoped for the solace of family connection, but then again, one was frequently disappointed. At least today Schuller had an interesting topic. He began describing last night's spectacle, the shock of it, the willfulness involved, and a question came to him: he wanted to know what would cause young women to undress and behave that way. Schuller had grown up in the world of boys and men and knew their tendencies. But women? It was widely known they didn't have the same appetites as men. So what pressures had been brought to bear on them? Was it alcohol? When it came to the conduct of women, Sandie's experience extended beyond his own. Certainly, Schuller would have liked to have known, but instead he talked about the strewn clothing and cigarettes and beer bottles, and at last he received a prolonged response, sibilant and damp and plain-tive-sounding. Without recognizing a single word, he understood the sum and substance of Sandie's reply, his primary objection: the loca-tion of the swimming pool. Years earlier Schuller had insisted the pool be built twenty yards into the woods, and he was now willing to concede that it wasn't worth the extra expense, or years of leaf-clogged filters and root damage, not to mention the after-hours enticement a secluded pool presented to young counselors. So, yes, Schuller admitted, an unwise choice all around. He should not have been so stubborn. The problem at hand, though, was the violation of camp rules that had occurred the night before. Schuller had a specific penalty in mind, and when he shared this, he was surprised by both the vehemence of the response and by the fact that he'd not made sense of a single word.

"All right," he told his brother. "I'll certainly take that into consideration. We may just be of the—"

Another forceful reply, of which Schuller understood the words *you* and *anyway*.

"Very well, Sandie. You're still my codirector after all. I remind everyone here of that. I do. All the time."

"Sal-waze dun hut-chu-like."

"I think so, yes. I'm inclined to agree. Now then, Mrs. Davenport says the van to Holy Infant leaves at three this afternoon. That's an hour early. Theresa knows this. She'll have everything ready. So, give my best to Father Ed and, well, everyone. Goodbye, Sandie." He hung up the phone and watched several beaded drops of rain commingle and slide down the office picture window.

At seven-thirty he convened an emergency meeting of the senior staff: Program Director Linda Rucker, Head Cook Maureen Boyd, Head of Maintenance Reggie Boyd. Normally, a senior staff meeting would have included the head lifeguard and camp nurse and several others. Not so this meeting, which Schuller decided to limit to just himself and the three others: Linda, Maureen, Reggie, each of whom had worked at Kindermann Forest more than fifteen summers.

They arranged their chairs in a half circle around the director's desk and then went straight to the strong pot of coffee Schuller had brewed, filled their cups and grimaced at the first sip.

He said it as plainly and forcefully as he could: "There's been an incident that requires our immediate attention." The somber tone he'd used and the careful way he'd assembled his words made Linda Rucker slump down into her chair and then lift her broad face up to Schuller with a wince of trepidation.

He recounted for them the events of the previous night, along with the pertinent details: the drinking, the discarded clothing, the inflatable hot dog and inner tube. Reckless behavior to be sure. More reckless, more vulgar than the usual indulgences of a summer camp staff. When Schuller revealed his recommended penalty for last night's violations, he could tell it was not to Linda's and Maureen's liking. Quiet, uncomplicated Reggie Boyd, Maureen's nephew, looked as if he wished he were back in the oily kingdom of his maintenance shed.

"Let's think a moment, Schuller," Linda said. "Let's slow down just a minute and make sure this is the right step for us to take."

He assured them he had thought it through. And it was the right step. No use trying to sort out all the different offenses: curfew, alcohol, trespassing, nudity. Much simpler to apply the same penalty to everyone.

"But we have to think about the timing, don't we?" Linda asked. "Is it the best thing to do *now*, with the training nearly done? With the first and most difficult camp session still ahead of us?" Between Linda and Maureen there was a certain glance, pained and knowing, as if his involvement in this matter was an ordeal to be endured.

But what could they do, really—except exchange their glances and ask their patient questions? It was up to Schuller to determine what was necessary. He was still founder and owner of Kindermann Forest. The camp bore his name. The fact of it was so obvious it couldn't be spoken aloud.

After the meeting, he walked with his senior staff across the meadow to the mess hall for breakfast.

At least they, his truant counselors, had managed to bring themselves, bleary and uncombed, to the mess hall tables. Schuller stood for Morning Prayer. Afterward platters of scrambled eggs and pancakes were passed from table to table. When breakfast was done, he rose and walked among the benches and finally motioned to a petite, freckled young woman, an arts and crafts attendant. He believed her name was Stacy. "Would you be kind enough to walk with me to the camp office?" he asked. And she nodded and strolled beside him, patiently, as he traversed the length of meadow.

Inside the office he sat her on the opposite side of the director's desk and without preamble told her that her employment at Kindermann Forest had ended and she should make arrangements to be gone by dinnertime, if not sooner. She stared at him coolly from across the reach of the desk, a red-haired, pixie-faced college freshman who could pass for fifteen. Perhaps she thought of herself as brave. If so, she would need to revise her opinion. When he slid the phone across the table, when she dialed and spoke the first words to her father, her voice caught in her throat and she let out a loud, blubbering sob. Her father's remarks seemed to make matters worse. She hung up the phone and cried harder. After a while she stopped. Schuller sent her to her cabin to pack and set out across the meadow to the mess hall.

It was a round-trip journey he made fourteen more times. Odd, but you could never tell in advance how a counselor would receive the news. Those who trembled and stuttered with anxiety during the walk over sometimes found a well of self-possession to draw upon when the phone was passed to them. Some who were aloof broke down. Kenny Cossman, unit leader for male counselors, cried. Schuller had spotted burly Kenny the previous night bouncing up the pool steps with his clothes in his arms (his penis half-erect and bouncing along with him). Too late now, of course. Nothing could be changed, senior staff member or not. But how odd it was, truly, to observe

Kenny and several of the other large young men. They pleaded. They begged his pardon or cursed under their breath. Yet when the phone was handed to them, they huffed and sputtered and wept. Was there a particular frailty to large men when it came to being dismissed? One had to wonder.

He called upon Head Lifeguard Wendy Kavanagh last. By then, of course, the news was out. As they walked toward the camp office, she asked if it was mandatory that she be packed and out of camp by dinnertime.

He said it was.

Because her mother, she explained, would have to drive down from Chicago and wouldn't reach Kindermann Forest until after dark.

"Then you may wait on the bench outside the front gate," Schuller told her.

In the office she went straight to the phone and placed her call. "Swimming," she said to her mother. "Swimming at night. After curfew. Oh yes," she said, as if just now remembering. "Swimming naked. Yes, Mom," she said. "Right. Wait a minute." She held the receiver to her chest and turned her gaze across the table toward him. "Why?" she asked.

"Why what?"

"Why are we being fired?"

He nearly laughed. What a ridiculous girl! Was the whole world a puzzle to her? "As a counselor," he said, "you have responsibilities, yes? For example, you are in charge of campers. And what if they were to sneak from their cabins—such things happen all the time—and see you and other counselors drinking and parading naked about the pool? What sort of lasting impression would that make? And what would it do to Kindermann Forest's reputation if they were to return home and tell their parents or guardians?"

"But there *are* no campers," Wendy said. "The campers don't arrive till Monday."

In his mind's eye he reviewed what he'd seen of her the night before: her paunchy belly and enormous buttocks and thighs, the whistle dangling between her heavy breasts. Of the many reasons he had for firing her and her fellow counselors, the first was simple outrage. Outrage at the stupidity of the young. There was an old-fashioned name for this stupidity: callowness. What they'd been celebrating last night, these callow young men and women, was the oldest and most tedious joke—the penis, the vagina, the spectacle of intercourse. If they couldn't feel shame at their own callowness, then let them at least feel the humiliation of being fired.

"Even so," he said. "Campers or no campers. The principle remains the same."

As it turned out, they'd inherited a muggy and slate gray morning. Schuller would have liked to have settled down in his cottage for a nap. Yet to do so would deny his remaining staff an essential loyalty: after all, if he were principled enough to make the truly hard decisions, then he should be equally mindful of helping to deal with the consequences. Inside the mess hall he found what remained of his senior staff in a desultory huddle around the director's dining table: Linda Rucker, Maureen and Reggie Boyd, Camp Nurse Harriet Foster.

Of course, it wasn't anywhere near as hopeless as they thought. He told them so. No time for discouragement, he said. Yes, they had two days to assemble a new staff of counselors before the campers arrived on Monday afternoon, but they would not be alone in the enterprise. He knew of more than twenty professional acquaintances who would begin working at once on their behalf. For instance, a list of potential lifeguards could be obtained from the YMCA. Counselors might be hired from the highest ranks of the Boy Scouts and Girl Scouts or from seminaries or from more than a dozen midwestern charity organizations. Not so impossible after all, he said, and for the benefit of a defeated-looking Linda Rucker, he raised his soft eyebrows in an expression that he hoped was measured and wise and determined. Nearby, Nurse Foster's five-year-old son—fatherless, lighter skinned than his black mother—sat on the floor and let an old-fashioned wood top spin inside the corral of his legs.

Just outside the mess hall, on the pathways leading to and from the cabins, cliques of expelled counselors gathered to commiserate. No one, it seemed, could travel more than a few paces without receiving a prolonged embrace, a teary farewell. Schuller couldn't help but marvel. What camaraderie, what solidarity of feeling, when, in fact, all they had done was endure a week's worth of first aid and program training—and perhaps groped one another in the darkened woods.

And on the patio adjoining the mess hall sat the three counselors who, the previous night, had obeyed camp regulations, honored curfew, and remained clothed and sober in the cabins. They were—it had to be noted—an ungainly bunch, the two girls bony, anxious, unlovely; the boy pale and cloddish and otherwise hopelessly bland. What a shame, too, because these inadequacies were always obvious to the campers' parents. Even with the tumultuous events of the morning, these three couldn't seem to manage among them any sort of spirited conversation. Nevertheless Schuller strolled by and gave them a nod of encouragement.

But inwardly he brooded. Too bad, really. If it were possible, he would dismiss them all and start the summer from scratch.

Chapter Two

At that age—nineteen and twenty or a few years older—it was best not to think too hard about the assignments to which they committed themselves.

They came from towns in Missouri and Arkansas and Illinois, and throughout winter, especially the dismal midwestern months of February and March, they imagined with startling clarity all the bright components that would make up their summertime lives. To think of it! The leisurely jobs they would hold. The weekend road trips taken with friends. The one unforgettable summer party at which they would do or say something daring and hilarious and thereby attract the notice of someone special, someone a mark or two wiser and more beautiful than they deserved. At that age they were the deepest and truest of romantics.

By the second week of June it was clear that none of this would happen as they'd imagined. It probably wouldn't happen at all. They couldn't get over it, this chasmlike difference between their brightest imaginings and the sodden feel of their actual lives.

But at church Sunday morning or on a flyer stuck to the door of their YMCA or in an out-of-the-blue phone call from a former teacher or scoutmaster they learned of an extraordinary opportunity.

Needed Immediately. 12 Summer Camp Counselors. 2 Lifeguards. 1 Horse Wrangler. Work with children and others. Kindermann Forest Summer Camp, Shannon County, Missouri.

A summer camp job. It set their minds racing. They could picture it all so clearly: the quaint, tree-shaded sleeping cabins, the rowdy and adoring children, the sudden camaraderie of other male and female counselors—the possibilities this entailed for tenderness, for sex.

Beguiled, they called Kindermann Forest and spoke to Program Director Linda Rucker. They were given only a few hours to decide. That was part of the attraction. They paced around their backyards or up and down their parents' driveways, and once they'd decided, they rushed back inside and made the announcement to their families. *I'm going to camp. Yes, sleepaway camp. For the whole summer.* It was all a mad rush after that. They had to first untangle themselves from various obligations—their dull summer jobs at the nursery and grocery store and drive-thru restaurant, which, embarrassingly, they had to quit after just a few weeks of training. Yet it was harder still, or trickier, to break free from their hometown boyfriends and girlfriends, whom they relied upon but did not love, at least not passionately. *Yes, I know. I know. We had plans for the summer. Sure we did. But I guess I've changed my mind about those plans. I'm going away to camp.*

They spent their last evenings at home talking with close friends on the phone. Given the suddenness and haste of their departure, they could get by explaining themselves with simple platitudes. They were bored, they said. They were ready for a change. So why not give summer camp a try? They didn't bother asking themselves where this new sense of adventure had come from. Their public reasons for going were all the same. Their private reasons were a different matter altogether.

Marcy Bittman accepted a lifeguard position because after just a week at home she found the sight and especially the sound of her mother, Coco Bittman, almost unbearable. She had no idea why. They adored each other. While away at college Marcy talked with Coco once or twice a day. They were known in Marcy's sorority as the daughter and mother so young and lively they could pass as sisters. When Marcy took the job at Kindermann Forest, she told her weeping mother that without the services of a certified lifeguard the camp would have to shut its doors and turn away hundreds of heartbroken children.

Veronica Yordy went to camp because her friend and sorority sister Marcy Bittman was going.

Wayne Kesterson signed on at Kindermann Forest because he'd been tried in Missouri State Court and found guilty of possessing five and a half ounces of homegrown marijuana. He'd be sentenced, probably to jail time, on the second Monday of September. The Big House. The Slammer. He could joke about it to family and friends. But inwardly he felt a long, steady surge of panic. It was agonizing, really. He needed something to fill the long summer days.

Stephen Walburn took a job as wrangler because he overheard his drunken aunt Marie say that a skinny man could only be attractive to women if he was seen in full command of a galloping horse.

Carrie Reinkenmeyer took a counselor position because everyone in her small Arkansas town knew she'd made love to the stupidest and least attractive boy in her high school senior class. The teasing she received, most of it from female friends, was constant and frequently cruel. But the experience itself was tender and not at all unsatisfying—and, if she didn't leave right away, likely to be repeated.

Christopher Waterhouse went because those in charge of Kindermann Forest seemed to have changed their minds about him. He'd applied for a lifeguard position in April. After three weeks and no word, he called to see if they'd received his application. They had, a woman said. You'll just have to wait for your letter. Ten days later the letter came. No thank you. They hadn't even invited him down for an interview. To hell with them, he thought. He'd work at a better camp. Or start his own.

Now, when he called to ask about a possible job, the only question put to him was, How soon can you get here?

There were a dozen others, among them Kathleen Bram and Daniel Hartpence and Ellen Swinderman and Gibby Tumminello and Michael Lauderback and Emily Boehler, all of whom were not in the habit of weighing their private reasons for anything they did. For them it was simple. The offer came to them. A voice inside said, *Go.*

A clear voice inside Wyatt Huddy said, *Go.* But an equally clear and probably wiser voice said, *Better stay put. Better stay exactly where you are.* It was exhausting to be caught between these two opposites. Yes and No. Go and Stay. A needling ache settled into the corner of his stomach. Throughout the night he flitted in and out of sleep—his thoughts urgent and full of raw feeling.

It was as if the summer months ahead were being divided into two distinct regions: the land of staying put and being exactly who everyone knew him to be. Or the land of going away and presenting a version of himself that the children and counselors at camp might find agreeable.

A strange and precarious place, this second land.

Chapter Three

Toward morning the ache in his stomach dissolved. His thoughts slowed. For several hours he slept a grateful, unbroken sleep. When he woke, his mind was steady and clear—unstirred by worry. This seemed to Wyatt like a minor miracle. How on earth had he managed it?

From the window of his back room—a former woodshop and now a bedroom of sorts—he watched the morning light, slanted and grainy, flooding over the depot yard and revealing, in small increments, the long gravel driveway, the donations trucks parked side by side, the twin Dumpsters, the stone fountains and secondhand playground sets, the gifted (and tarnished) camper shells and tractor equipment; all of it settled atop a scrubby, brown lawn. Nothing rare or beautiful about this landscape, except that for a few minutes every day—in the early morning and again in the late evening—what went on outside his back room window was Wyatt Huddy's to behold, exclusively so.

He rose from bed and dressed for the coming day: blue jeans, a stretched and spotted XL T-shirt, his socks and work boots. He pried his retainer from the roof of his mouth and placed it, hideous and wet, into its plastic holder. Then he paced down the hall and at the showroom entranceway flipped on every other switch and waited patiently while the long bars of fluorescent lights popped and sputtered and threw their white glare over the center's enormous showroom floor.

Lampshades and scuffed bedroom furniture and picture frames and racks of neatly hung dead men's trousers: it went on forever. Because each item carried some residue, some intimacy, from its former owner, Wyatt had to convince himself that it was all ordinary enough to mark and sell or eventually throw away in one of two mammoth Dumpsters parked in the depot yard. He'd grown used to tossing out toys, particularly dolls, but sometimes the most inconsequential items could provoke him: a shoelace, for example, made in 1953 and perfectly sealed inside its paper and cellophane wrapper. What modest hopes its maker had once had for it. A shoelace. And what a sharp pang of regret for Wyatt to toss it forever unused into the Dumpster.

Each morning—and this morning was no exception—a caravan of large, canvas-sided bins holding yesterday's donations was lined up along the center aisle. Wyatt took a moment to rummage through them. No real treasures, of course. A stainless steel desk lamp, a flower vase, a glass certificate frame. To turn such shiny objects over in his hands was to be allowed an elongated view of himself. Impossible to explain this to others, but it was perfectly all right to go about the center's showroom at 6:17 in the morning looking large and unkempt and Wyatt-like. For nearly two hours he would have sole use of the employee washroom and kitchen. He'd make breakfast and then begin sorting the bins. At eight Mrs. Barnett would come in and help him with the pricing. They'd work until the clerks, Mindy and Janet, arrived and counted up their cash drawers. By then a few bargain hunters might be waiting outside the sliding glass doors, which was fine if they were regular customers or friends of Mrs. Barnett. He would stay where he was and keep on with the pricing and shelving.

But if they were strangers, especially mothers with small children, then the easiest and most pleasurable part of his workday was over, and he would hurry back to the loading dock, where, for the remainder of the morning and afternoon, he would unload and repair whatever heavy furniture the trucks brought in.

It was taxing and sometimes hazardous work, which was why he felt such contentment now to stand in the employee kitchen pouring cereal and watching waffles cook in the blistering slots of a donated toaster. At the break room table he set out a magazine to read, a bygone issue of *Popular Mechanics*. This morning's article: "Build Your Own Watercraft of the Future!" The illustration was certainly handsome, though the assembly instructions thwarted him at every turn. *Align the aft portion of the chine and sheer clamp carefully to allow for the thickness of the transom. The coamings should be cut from 1/2-in. mahogany and rabbetted to the top edge of . . .*

When he glanced up from the magazine, he heard a steady *thump-thump-clink, thump-thump-clink* that couldn't have been the ventilation or any of the center's innumerable objects settling on the shelf. He stood and cocked an ear toward each corner of the showroom. Then he made his way down the center aisle and out the back door to the loading dock.

There was Captain Throckmorton trudging away atop a rickety treadmill that the donation trucks had brought in the day before. A crown of sweat had beaded around the captain's bald head. Every few seconds a drop would plunge down his cheek or the back of his neck. He seemed not to know what to do with his arms and, finally, to keep them from bouncing at his sides, rested them on the shelf of his belly, a high-set belly, firm-looking and comically round. From time to time he glanced at Wyatt and rolled his eyes as if to say, *I know I look ridiculous. I know I'm a spectacle.*

Maybe others might have thought so. Not Wyatt, who a few years earlier had been rescued by Captain Throckmorton from a steadily worsening family situation. If there was anything truly unusual about the captain, it was that, unlike the other Salvation Army captains or other men who worked at the center, he didn't appear to have stumbled shaken and pale and weak out of a ruinous past life. He lived across the street and shared an apartment with his best friend, the barber Ed McClintock. They both sang tenor in the St. James choir. Each Wednesday evening they invited Wyatt to their apartment for dinner and board games. Just before they began their game—usually Risk or Yahtzee—Ed McClintock made coffee and poured a single shot glass of Irish Cream into his and the captain's cups. This would be the only alcohol they'd consume all evening, perhaps all week, and, before raising the cup for his first sip, Ed McClintock would say, "Here's to our glamorous lives, Captain."

Eventually Captain Throckmorton slowed his pace and stepped off the treadmill. He consulted a stopwatch hanging from his neck. For a while he did nothing but breathe deeply. "Eleven minutes," he said. "And from what I've heard some people will torture themselves on these things an hour a day? Could that be true?"

Wyatt said that yes, he thought it could.

"Hard to believe," Captain Throckmorton said. He studied the treadmill as if it had reneged on an extravagant promise. Then he produced a handkerchief and wiped sweat from his brow and chin. "How'd the *watch* go last night, Wyatt?"

"Fine."

"Nothing out of order?" he asked. "No cat burglars? No safe-crackers?"

Wyatt couldn't help but grin. It was a joke he'd come to enjoy, that the captain paid him to watch over the depot yard and showroom at night rather than unload the donation trucks during the day. That was part of the joke. The other part, which he'd not quite understood at first, was that few, if any, thieves would be interested in secondhand furniture and clothing in a Salvation Army depot on the outskirts of Jefferson City, Missouri. "No safecrackers," he reported. "But I was thinking about it some, and I wanted to ask . . ."

"Yes?"

"Is it a rule, do you think, that everyone has to swim? Everyone who works at a summer camp?"

"I wouldn't think so," Captain Throckmorton said. He squinted in concentration. "No," he said. "Probably not."

"Because it seems like it would be a rule. Every time you see a show about a summer camp on TV, people are always swimming."

"I'm sure it's not a rule. I'm sure there are counselors who don't swim at all."

"Yes, maybe," Wyatt said. From the wide concrete lip of the loading dock he looked out across the depot yard at the donation trucks and Dumpsters, the swing sets and yard fountains, the same fixtures, mostly, that he'd studied a short while earlier, upon waking, from the uncurtained window of his back room. There wasn't anything he could say by way of explanation. It wasn't as if he'd been able to *reason out* a decision. Yes or No. Go or Stay. The best he could do now was take a deep breath and decide on a whim. "All right then," he said. He filled his lungs with damp morning air. "I'll go ahead and do it," he said. "If it's all right with you, I'll go ahead and start working at the summer camp."

It was rare to see Captain Throckmorton taken by surprise. There was a sharp focus to his gaze. His coloring deepened into something like a blush. "You will?" he said. "I'm very glad to hear that, Wyatt. Very glad. It would have been a mistake, I think, to waste your summer here."

"Yes, maybe so."

"I'll get on the phone right away and let Mr. Kindermann know you're coming. And I'll have one of the ladies from the St. James auxiliary drive you down." He smiled hugely. "This is good news," he said. "You've changed your mind. Was it about the swimming all along?"

Wyatt hardly knew how to answer. "Not just swimming," he said. "It's always hard, isn't it? When you have to go someplace new. And settle in. And introduce yourself a hundred times."

"I guess it is, yes."

"Especially for me," Wyatt said. "Plus, I've never tried working with children."

Once his word had been given, it couldn't be taken back. He knew that. He packed his clothes and towels and soaps and the retainer he wore at night and a book about American presidents he didn't much enjoy reading. Mrs. Barnett brought him a flashlight and canteen she'd gathered from the store shelves. She told him to spray for insects and not to stand in direct sunshine. The clerks, Mindy and Janet, who rarely talked to him, stood unseen in the hallway outside his room and called out together in the same tepid voice, "Have a good summer, Wyatt." Captain Throckmorton hurried to Sears and bought a new sleeping bag. He said, "Choose a bunk bed near a window." He said, "If you get a cold or sunburn or poison oak rash, go straight to the camp nurse." He said, "A good way to begin a conversation is to say, 'Excuse me. I'd like to introduce myself. My name is Wyatt Huddy.'"

By now the center, which had been entirely and exquisitely Wyatt's at 6:00 A.M., was alive with the clamor of phones and earnest customers. Both Mrs. Barnett and Captain Throckmorton had matters to attend to. Their goodbyes were rushed and clumsy. "Take care and . . . be careful." The truck drivers, hard-pressed and often bitter older men, considered Wyatt's leaving a desertion. *Why summer camp?*

they asked. *What's the point when there are upright freezers and heavy office desks to unload?* Wyatt couldn't think of a reasonable answer, and so, to escape their sourness, he waited out back beside the gravel lane that led from Highway 54 up to the loading dock.

Ten minutes later a white Ford Galaxie turned into the lane and made a halting progress toward the depot building. It rolled past him. It braked. It backed up. "Excuse me," a voice called from the driver's window. "I'm looking for Captain Throckmorton."

"He's in his office," Wyatt said. "But he's . . . Are you from St. James?"

The driver, a middle-aged woman in a sleeveless checkered blouse, had climbed from the car and was rounding its front end. "I've been assigned a job," she said. "And I was wonder—" She stopped in her tracks.

"I'm Wyatt Huddy," he said.

She noticed his duffel bag and turned the whole of her attention toward it. All the features of her ruddy face were pinched in concentration. She furrowed her brow. She grimaced. After a while she said, "The back driveway to the depot, it's not very well . . ."

"Known?" he offered.

"Marked," she said, still scrutinizing his duffel bag. "I passed the signpost a few times before I saw it and then . . . I don't know . . ."

"Then you found it."

"Yes. I'm Barbara McCauley from the St. James auxiliary."

"Thank you for driving me."

"Oh," she said and waved her hand to and fro. "It's not any . . ."

"But it is. It's a long way, there and back. Would you like me to ride in the backseat, Barbara?"

She appeared to consider the offer, tilted her head in thought, reached a conclusion. "Up front is fine," she said.

Yet once they'd buckled themselves in and set out, she seemed unnerved by his close proximity. She gripped the wheel and fixed her gaze on the road ahead. What he felt for her then, what he always felt in these strained circumstances, was a tenderness so acute it nearly pierced his heart. Who better than he to understand her discomfort, her embarrassment? He was, after all, well acquainted with the many flavors of distress people felt upon first seeing him. In Barbara McCauley's case it wouldn't improve matters to explain that the displacement of his features—the left half of the face higher than the right, the eyes offset by nearly an inch, the nose a bit mashed, the right side of his mouth sloping down—had a name, and that those unfamiliar with the disorder always assumed its sufferers were mentally retarded, when, luckily or unluckily, they were often of average intelligence.

He wasn't retarded, a fact to be carefully and painfully imparted to every stranger he met. Not disabled. Not handicapped.

But not the equal of other young men or women his age, either. He'd earned a high school equivalency diploma from a technical school. He could assist in the repair of lawn mowers and certain automobiles and might have gone further in this career were it not for the machine manuals, which proved either too difficult or too poorly written. But he could weld. He had a good memory. In the two and a half years he'd lived in the depot, Captain Throckmorton had taught him to keep track of stock and pay utility bills and answer telephone inquiries.

They rode with the windows down to the outskirts of Jefferson City. Once the highway traffic opened up, Barbara McCauley let one hand drop from the wheel and braved a glance in his direction.

"I bet you're an athlete," she said. "I bet you play football. Does the Salvation Army have sports teams?"

"They don't, no. Not sports teams."

"But you've played some football, haven't you?"

"Not really. We play field hockey on the dock sometimes, me and one of the other loaders."

"Oh, but you should talk to the other boys you work with and get them all together for a football match. You'd be great at it. A young man your size. You'd smash right on through and score a goal."

"Thank you, Barbara. I'll think about doing that."

She turned her attention back to the highway, which was arrow-straight and sided by long-drawn fields of squatty soybeans, wavering corn.

Certain things about the Salvation Army depot he was glad to have escaped. No, not things. Certain people. The register clerks, Mindy and Janet. Wyatt didn't enjoy their company, though he wasn't able to share this opinion, since everyone else at the depot—employees and customers alike—thought Mindy and Janet were wonderful. They'd been inseparable best friends since childhood. Between them they'd developed a repertoire of code words and outrageous expressions. Often they goaded one another into hysterical laughter. (Unless, of course, either Mindy or Janet was in a sour mood, and then they would sulk and ridicule and make each other miserable.) But it was widely known that both young women had wild imaginations. For example, they could reach into a donation bin and pull out a random object, a pencil holder say, and pretend it was a blind man's begging cup. For the rest of the afternoon, Mindy would teeter about the showroom calling out to Janet, *Please, madam, please. Spare a nickel for a wretched blind man!*

One afternoon the previous fall the trucks brought in a load of cast-offs from an estate sale, and there, buried in a pile of old accounting ledgers, was a river otter, stuffed and mounted atop a varnished oak board. It was a strange-looking creature, this otter. When extracted from the water, stuffed and mounted, it looked different than you might expect—not playful or cute but flat-headed and fierce with a mouth full of crooked teeth. This otter was dead, obviously, its gaze dark and intense, its sleek body frozen in an unattractive forward lurch.

Mindy and Janet couldn't get over it. "Well for goodness' sake," Janet said. "Take a look at this, Wyatt. A stuffed otter. It's just what you need."

He squinted at her doubtfully.

"A furry friend. You could use a furry friend, couldn't you?"

For the rest of the day all their talk was about the stuffed otter and Wyatt. Wyatt and his furry friend. The adventures they would have! They'd wear matching sweaters and travel about the country in one of the depot trucks. Hilarious. Wyatt and the otter would check into expensive hotels and order their meals from room service. *And a cup of French onion soup for my furry friend.*

The next evening, a Friday, the showroom phone rang. The depot had been closed for hours. Wyatt wasn't obliged to answer.

"Excuse me," a male voice on the telephone said. "I've been calling all the stores in Jefferson City because I'm looking for a very special item. A very hard-to-find item. A river otter. Do you happen to have one?"

The voice was sincere and inquiring. To Wyatt it seemed that an honest answer was required. He said that yes, they did have an otter, but that it was stuffed.

"Stuffed is perfect. I already have a stuffed beaver." Through the phone line Wyatt could hear a swell of merry chatter. The man might have been calling from a party or a crowded restaurant. He asked that the otter be set aside in his name. He'd come to the depot and pick it up first thing Monday morning. The man's name was Harry S. Truman.

And so Wyatt wrote out and taped the man's name to the animal's soft belly and placed the otter behind the front counter. Even as he performed this task, it occurred to him that Mindy and Janet might have arranged this phone call. Which wasn't so terrible, really. The things that set Mindy and Janet alight with laughter, the things that sent them shrieking and reeling about the depot showroom, didn't always make sense to Wyatt. But they didn't offend him, either.

It wasn't a great surprise to learn on Monday morning that the phone call had been a prank. Everyone at the depot seemed to enjoy it. Hilarious. A stuffed otter with the name Harry S. Truman taped to its fur.

"But you must have known," Captain Throckmorton said to him. "The name must have tipped you off, didn't it?"

Wyatt could only nod vaguely. He could tell he'd missed something important. Harry S. Truman. It was a name he was supposed to recognize.

"Yes," Wyatt said. "That's right. I knew it. I knew that name." But he could tell from the wincing expressions of those around him that he hadn't been believed, and finally he shrugged and shuffled away. Later, once the depot was crowded with customers, he wandered to the far corner of the showroom and consulted a set of donated encyclopedias. Harry S. Truman was an American president. The thirty-third. He'd come from Missouri, from the not-so-distant town of Independence. To understand this was to feel a sudden flood of humiliation. To be drowned in shame. It required a painful adjustment. He'd had to refigure his opinion of himself, to lower his estimation of what he was capable of.

They stopped at a drive-in for lunch, and Barbara McCauley bought him, over his objection, two king-size hamburgers. She sipped a coffee and told him that several years back, when her son and his friends had played high school football, they would practice at a nearby park and then tramp right into her kitchen looking for food. She made them remove their jerseys and pads before serving them hamburgers. But what a mess and commotion they made, these sweaty, shirtless teenage boys gathered around her kitchen table. She said she wanted to spank their butts and send them straight to the shower.

It seemed to cheer her, this story, and once they'd climbed back into the Galaxie, she had lively opinions to share on other topics: for instance, the Lawrence Welk singers and dancers, who could teach young people a lot about how to behave, and a hooded sweater she'd mail-ordered and was waiting to receive, and finally and at great length she talked about a Shetland pony she owned that was more perceptive about her moods than her husband or children or, for that matter, any person she'd ever known. By then the landscape had changed from cropland to gentle, shrub-covered hills. A half hour later Barbara was urging the car up one steep and winding incline after another, only to let it swoop down the opposite side. It was for Wyatt an unfamiliar terrain—not just steep hills but small mountains eroded and ancient-looking and separated by craggy valleys, nearly all of which contained deep hollows or clear, gurgling creeks.

Kindermann Forest was set back three miles from the highway along a well-tended gravel road, the camp's entrance gate fronted by a bench made of split logs. Beyond the gate stood a weathered office and cottage—nothing particularly welcoming about either of these buildings. The same was true of the camp grounds, which, like the countryside in general, looked ancient and weedy. In Wyatt's view, it was not how a summer camp should be. And yet, beyond question, it was more beautiful than anything he'd anticipated, more striking and vast and real, with stone fences and a giant meadow that shone lushly green beneath the bright midday sun. The trees were either knotted hickories or tall, bristling pines. Through a curtain of such trees he could see several large cedar cabins gray with age and weather.

When he turned to thank Barbara McCauley and climb from the car, he found her ruddy face squeezed with emotion.

"Don't you dare thank me," she insisted. "This drive, this time we've spent together, Wyatt, has been a great opportunity for me.

It's *really* made me think." She looked, for the time being, too over-whelmed to report on whatever conclusions she might have reached. She dropped him off with his duffel bag at the mess hall steps and sped away.

Inside the mess hall a meeting was under way. To attend he must pass through screen doors and take his place among a gathering of what could only be other newly arrived counselors. This, more than swimming, was the dread he had tried to describe to Captain Throck-morton. But perhaps it couldn't be described. Perhaps it was Wyatt's burden to own each second of what happened next: the slow creak of the screen door opening, the clap of it swinging shut, more than a dozen strangers turning their bright faces toward him, their gaze expectant, then startled, then troubled. And then, of course, the moment of recognition—the sizing up and the swift classification. Maybe too swift. Had Captain Throckmorton called? Had they been told in advance? Because they seemed to recognize him or at least expect his arrival.

A sturdy, middle-aged woman led the meeting. She gave Wyatt her name without any indication as to what her position might be. Linda Rucker. She flipped through a three-ring binder and, with a satisfied nod, seemed to find the proper notation. "Wyatt Huddy?" she asked.

To this Wyatt nodded. He felt keenly the purposeful way each person in the room turned their attention elsewhere.

"We've put you in Cabin Two."

"Yes. All right."

"And in a moment you'll have a list of your campers." She regarded him frankly. "Are we all set then?"

"Yes," he said. "All set." He found a bench at the rear of the hall. A paper was making its way toward him. When it arrived he found his own name and beneath it a list of campers three names long.

"I was explaining to the group, Wyatt, that at the end of the day, after the evening activity, you'll escort your campers back to the cabins. You'll make sure they wash up. You'll see that they brush their teeth and get to bed. After that you'll be off duty and can gather in The Sanctuary with the other counselors. We expect you to be back in your cabins and asleep by midnight. Am I clear about that?"

The new counselors gave her a mild nod, which seemed enough for Linda Rucker. She then explained meal procedures and nightly cabin watch duty. While she spoke, she flipped through her clipboard of papers. "Never mind," she said. "Never mind. It's too much to tell you all at once. I'm afraid you'll have to learn as you go along. The scheduling, for example, it's always—" She stopped herself. From outside came the bray of a diesel engine. A large white bus, the first of three, appeared at the far end of the meadow and rumbled toward the mess hall. Linda Rucker squeezed shut her eyes a moment, concentrated. "For now I'm only going to insist that you remember one thing. At each meal the camp nurse, Harriet Foster, will come to your mess hall table. You will identify each camper for Harriet. If they require medications, you will make sure they take them. You will do this for every meal. Breakfast. Lunch. Dinner."

The buses had drawn close, veered from the gravel lane and rolled to a halt a few yards deep in the meadow. One by one they shut down their squalling engines. In each vehicle a mob of passengers rose from their seats and thronged the aisle. The first bus threw open its door, and down climbed a truly odd-looking teacher or chaperone—a blatantly pear-shaped woman, a great ridge of fat around her waist, but a thin chest and arms and a wide, flapping, probably toothless mouth. Wyatt, who never failed to notice such irregularities, stared. What scorn she must receive from the children. Behind her was another curiosity, a very tall, lanky gentleman with a sloping forehead who limped down the bus's landing and took a few unsteady steps across the meadow. And after him came a squat little man who wore impossibly thick glasses and whose wide eyes and

myopic gaze and thick lips were all clear markings of mental retardation, of an affliction, Down syndrome, which Wyatt happened to
know by name.

Within the mess hall the new counselors began to stir and shift,
and all at once, amid their anxious muttering ("They're here already.
They're *here*!"), they rose from the benches clutching their bags.

"The first step!" Linda Rucker shouted. "Listen to me, *please*. The
first step is to hurry to your assigned cabins—and, yes, I do mean
hurry. You'll need to choose a bed. And stow your bags away. Be quick
about it. Then you'll run back here to the meadow and *find* the campers on your list. Do you understand? Get going then. Go. Go. Go."

At once they threw open the mess hall doors and hurried down
the gravel pathway toward the cabins. Wyatt stayed behind, and
when the opportunity presented itself, he approached Linda Rucker
and broached his question.

"Excuse me?" he said. "Will there be children? Is it a camp for
children?"

There was a clear wrinkling of concern in her otherwise patient
regard. All the while she held his gaze. "It is a camp for children,
Wyatt. But not the first two weeks," Linda explained. "For the first
two weeks all the campers will be handicapped adults from the state
hospital."

He could not, for the time being, sort out exactly what this meant.
No children. Instead the campers would be disabled adults. Retarded
adults. This, of course, was exactly what he deserved—for making a
decision on a whim, for being who he was. No one would appreciate
this more than the depot register clerks, Mindy and Janet. What a
reaction they'd have if they were here, if they could see the retarded
campers spilling off the buses. *The state hospital campers and Wyatt.
Wyatt and the state hospital campers.* Across Mindy's and Janet's faces
would bloom the richest expressions. They'd turn to one another
wide-eyed, joyful.

"I didn't know." Wyatt said. "Adults from the state hospital. We'll be taking care of them?" A deep crimson blush colored his face.

"That's right. You will. Night and day. Are you all right?" Linda Rucker asked.

"I am, yes. I'm fine." He hoisted his bag. "Thank you, Captain Rucker," he said and pushed through the mess hall doors and out onto the open meadow, with its enormous white buses and strewn luggage and unbearable crowd.

Chapter Four

A retarded woman—plump, middle-aged, dressed in a gray cotton sweat suit—came to the infirmary door. She didn't knock. Perhaps she was too timid. Instead she began twisting the doorknob back and forth, a steady and soundless turning.

Luckily, Harriet was inside and happened to look up from her work desk and notice a glimmer of light rolling along the edge of the knob. She crossed the room and pulled open the door.

A lot to take in all at once: the retarded woman, the glaring and humid afternoon and, across the gravel roadway atop a usually bare corner of the Kindermann Forest meadow, a commotion and thickening crowd and several enormous vehicles. School buses. (So it hadn't been the Waverly Foods supply truck she'd heard minutes earlier.) Huge bundles of bed linens were being rolled out of the ends of the buses. The men and women doing the work, a dozen sweating and uniformed state hospital attendants, were, without exception, black.

Just then the woman at the door did something curious. She pulled the loose waistband of her sweatpants down to reveal a white, fleshy patch of hip and buttock. With the other hand she held up a brown paper lunch bag for Harriet's inspection. Inside were two bottles of insulin and a cluster of disposable syringes.

"What's your name, honey?" Harriet asked.

No answer. The woman might have been mute as well as retarded. Most likely she'd missed her lunchtime injection and had been sent to the infirmary by one of the attendants.

Certainly, you could make such an assumption, but then again, you could be wrong. At Meadowmont Gardens Nursing Home, where Harriet had worked before coming to Kindermann Forest, a registered nurse had been passing through the dining room and chanced upon an elderly woman choking on her evening meds—three pills taken together, one the size of a small grape. The nurse helped the woman disgorge the pills into a napkin, then watched as she reswallowed them separately with a generous gulp of water. Of course later, when the woman was discovered frothing and unconscious, they realized she'd swiped the pills from her heavily sedated partner at the table. Such things happened. The trick was to never make assumptions—unless the patient was yours, in which case, it seemed, you did nothing but make assumptions.

As for the woman at the infirmary door, there wasn't even a glint of expectation in her eyes, just the supreme patience of the institutionalized. No trouble at all for Harriet to take her by the hand and guide her to an infirmary bed, where the woman lay on her side, her sweatpants wedged down, her bare hip exposed.

"I'm just waiting to hear from your attendant," Harriet said. "Your attendant or your nurse."

The woman stared back without blinking. She had the least imposing gaze Harriet had ever seen.

"At least we have a cool place to wait, don't we?" Harriet said and nodded toward the infirmary's air conditioner, a mammoth window unit capable of sudden gasps and long manly sighs of pleasure.

The woman ran a thick tongue across her chapped lips. She let loose a sudden gusty breath.

"Only cool place in camp. I'm surprised I haven't . . ." Harriet made herself stop. She had a hunch she was boring her patient.

On the infirmary desk was a clipboard containing one hundred and four camper health forms. For the past week Harriet had been flipping compulsively through the forms compiling lists of allergies (penicillin, nine; sulfa, eight; iodine, four; beestings, three; aspirin, one), medical conditions (cerebral palsy, thirty-nine; Down syndrome, nineteen; autism, seventeen; factor X, eight; head trauma, seven), secondary diseases (seizures, thirty-six; cardiac abnormalities, eighteen; diabetes, nine; asthma, seven; arthritis, seven; blindness, six; deafness, five; gout, four). It wearied the mind. She squeezed her eyes shut and tried to concentrate.

An absurd worry, maybe, but she didn't want to be a bore. And from this small anxiety, this trifle, she felt a much deeper wavering. Perhaps what would be demanded of her in the coming days was simply too much. Too much for Harriet. It happened of course. People overestimated their own abilities all the time.

Because the cedar walls of the infirmary were thin, it was possible to hear a wide range of commotion coming off the meadow in waves: the din of the newly arrived campers—and what a peculiar din at that, the heavy grunts and human squealing, the many slurred and off-timbre voices, the disorder of it all—and beneath these sounds the thud of luggage on the meadow grass and the wet clicks of the cooling bus engines. Soon there were footsteps, a small regiment of them, crunching across the gravel pathway toward the infirmary.

Better to meet them on her own terms, Harriet thought. She took a moment to pat down the bangs of her hair. Then she opened the infirmary door to a long line of retarded adult campers led by a swaying, prodigiously buxom woman in her fifties: a nurse from the state hospital, a black nurse no less, who put a hand to the rail and ascended the infirmary's single oak board step with a high, girlish exhalation. A tag pinned to her collar read: B. COLETTE DUNBAR, R.N. She wore a huge white leather purse over one shoulder and balanced a box in her hands, though most likely it wasn't either of these burdens that had her sweating and wheezing. It was almost certainly those enormous breasts—them and the vast underwire bra that kept her bosom lofted above her belly. Growing up, Harriet had seen a neighbor lady fitted with such a contraption. Welts and rashes and backaches and endless agonies, all of which had turned the neighbor lady into a meek child. By comparison, Nurse B. Colette Dunbar's suffering looked to have given her a stooped posture and a crimped and spiteful way of scrutinizing others. She used this crimped gaze to appraise Harriet, then the patient on the bed, then the Lysol-scrubbed tile floor. She wheezed discontentedly and said, "You get it done already?"

Before Harriet could answer, she had to first suffer a sharp pang of discomfort. After all, what awkwardness: both of them registered nurses, both black, both in the employ of whites. All this shared experience—and still they had nothing in common. It was Harriet's fault mostly. She wasn't a dependable black person. For whatever reasons, complicated or simple, she spoke differently, thought differently, formed different allegiances. Black women like Nurse B. Colette Dunbar sensed this attitude a mile away. Black boys steered clear of Harriet. Some white boys took a step closer.

"Excuse me?" Harriet said. "Get what done?"

"I'm referring to Miss Mary Ann Hornicker. The lady on your bed here. She had her insulin yet?"

"No," Harriet said. "I wasn't sure—"

"Then maybe you should get to it. Five units. Humalog. She's been waiting since lunchtime."

Inwardly Harriet bristled. But outwardly she did as she was told. She measured five units, drove the syringe into Miss Hornicker's freckled hip (not a stir or even a blink from her patient). Nurse Dunbar stood close by and supervised the injection—it seemed only to bore her—and then began rooting through the box she'd carried in. She pulled out a prescription bottle and summoned into the infirmary the first of her charges: a wiry little man who swiveled forward. His left side appeared withered and useless, his right side incongruently strong. He let out a raw-sounding grunt.

"This would be Mr. Talbot. M for Marcus. Takes Dilantin in the morning. Suffers from asthma—mild compared to some of the others. You'll need to keep his inhaler or else he'll lose it or treat it like a toy. Won't you, Mr. Talbot?"

Mr. Talbot froze, as if a spotlight had found him in a moment of great indiscretion.

"Won't you?" she repeated, her tone part teasing, mostly scornful.

He shifted from his left to right side, then gave a quick jerk of his head, which might or might not have been a guilty nod.

Satisfied, Nurse Dunbar dismissed him with a wave. Another man, this one tall and rail-thin, stepped forward in his place. "Now Mr. Jarman here can't have products with sugar and sometimes, most of the time, uses Senokot for help with his BMs. He used to take lithium, but not anymore . . ."

Harriet reached for her clipboard of forms.

"Leave the forms go and listen to what I'm tellin' you."

It was probably best for Harriet not to reply. At least not yet. Besides, she'd endured this sort of bullying from other nurses. It sometimes happened that those who knew their patients the best liked them the least, and were the most tyrannical when it came to passing on their knowledge to others.

More campers were called forward and their ailments listed aloud. Mrs. Tamerack's swollen feet. Mrs. Petterson's inflamed hemorrhoids. Mr. Henley's memory loss and seizures, the severe, age-yellowed binder he wore to keep his hernia pressed against his abdomen. Some twenty campers paused for Harriet's inspection. She'd seen some extreme variations of the human body while working in a nursing home. And yet, there was something outlandish about these state hospital campers. How had the women managed to grow fat in such striking ways? Not just bottom-heavy but with sudden shelflike ridges of fat that jutted out from their hips. They had either no breasts to speak of or hard-looking, conical breasts that looked too high-set and pointy to be real. With the men it was most often the opposite problem: a remarkable thinness, gangly arms, concave chests. A comic gauntness. You saw them from a medium distance and thought of old cartoons, the slouching, cross-eyed idiots with their awful haircuts and shortened trousers, their mouths full of sprawling teeth.

But up close you noticed how each man or woman had gone inward and found a perch—unsteady maybe, or tilted, but still a perch—from which to peer out past the spasms and tics and whatever odd shapes their bodies had grown into.

Last in line was a stiff-postured little man with thick black glasses and enormous woolly sideburns. He tottered rather than walked, as if the bones of each leg and been locked into place and fused shut. "And this is Leonard Peirpont," Nurse Dunbar said. "Seizures. Some bad. Most of them light. You tell whoever . . ."

Thus far Leonard Peirpont was one of the few campers to seek out and hold Harriet's attention, the first to address her directly. He had a prim, wide-eyed face and a shrill voice. "Up in Kingdom City they won't allow it," he announced. "They've got rules you ain't heard of . . . rules for driving and for . . . and rules for hunting quail."

"Quiet down now," Nurse Dunbar chided him, mildly. "You tell whoever takes care of Leonard to hold him here at the elbow and take it easy because—"

"—They won't wash windows, either, without you give 'em an extra fifty cents an hour."

"He's liable to pitch forward at any minute."

"—Or mop the floors. They won't allow it."

"And he won't stop once he gets started," Nurse Dunbar said. "Will you, Leonard?"

At the sound of his name, his broad expression tightened and a look of something like clarity passed across his features, passed and faded. "I suppose I'll do . . . what I have to do," he said.

A short while later attendants carried in a duffel bag containing, improbably enough, fifty cartons of cigarettes. It would be Harriet's duty to supply the counselors, who would ration out cigarettes to the campers. Last, from the deep pouch of her leather purse, Nurse Dunbar produced a medium-size brown paper bag. The top of the bag had been rolled down and stapled shut. Schuller Kindermann's name was written in thick black marker on both sides. "For Mr. Kindermann," Nurse Dunbar said and let the bag plop down onto the countertop. "He told me to leave it in the infirmary and that he'd be by soon to pick it up."

"I'll see that he gets it."

Nurse Dunbar leaned against the medicine cabinet and set her face in a tight-lipped pout. Everything she glared at with her hooded eyes seemed to either weary or annoy her. "He's a peculiar man, Mr. Kindermann. A peculiar type, isn't he?"

Harriet shrugged. "I guess so."

"Guess so? He a friend of yours? You owe him favors?"

"No," Harriet said. "No, I don't."

"Well, I hope not," Nurse Dunbar said. "Mr. Kindermann's got some old-fashioned ideas. Old-time Catholic Church ideas. This paper bag I brought in? Mr. Kindermann wants what's inside the bag kept separate from the other medications. He wants things his way. But that don't mean you can't make your own *arrangements*."

"Arrangements?" Harriet asked.

"There's a lot Mr. Kindermann don't understand about retarded people—about the way they are. So each summer when we come on the buses, I meet with the camp nurse. I say, 'Pay attention.' I say, 'Make your own arrangements if you have to.'"

All Harriet could do was nod slowly, as if she understood the implications of this conversation, as if she were well acquainted with the ways of retarded people.

"I do what I can," Nurse B. Colette Dunbar said. "But each summer it's a new nurse here at camp. Never the same face. It's not the kind of job you want to come back and do again," she said. "And it's these two weeks with the state hospital patients that does it. Pushes you to your limits." With her thick eyelids half lowered, she seemed to be conjuring a picture of Harriet pushed to her limits. "Two weeks," Nurse Dunbar said. "How you going to manage?" She didn't wait for a reply. Instead she reached for Leonard Peirpont's elbow and directed him toward the infirmary door. By now the rest of her charges had deserted her. The moment they were beyond her jurisdiction, they let out sharp squawks of happiness and resumed their odd mumblings, their bodily tics and contortions, and staggered off toward the chaos of the meadow. Yet Nurse Dunbar was obliging, even tender, with Leonard Peirpont, coaxing him down the infirmary step, talking to him in a soft voice. "Easy, Leonard. Easy."

Inside the infirmary Harriet was left holding her clipboard of health forms. She stood dumbfounded flipping through the forms: a myriad of diseases and disorders and medications. There were brief personal histories, too. Leonard Peirpont, she read, was not born retarded. He'd been brain-injured ten years earlier, at age twenty-seven, in a farming accident.

When she glanced up from her papers moments later, she noticed that the side door leading from the infirmary to her living quarters was cracked open an inch or two. Into this gap a face was pressed, or a portion of a face, a boy's round cheek, a boy's focused and wary eye.

Her son, James.

Other people tended to remark on her son's demeanor, his terse way of speaking, or not speaking at all, his habit of slipping unnoticed into the room and listening in on adult conversations, his brow furrowed, the corners of his mouth pursed, as if in judgment. Her white friends called him bashful, her black friends, sly or secretive. Inevitably, both groups asked the same question: Was he always this quiet?

Not exactly. In private James could be a bully for her attention. He sometimes screamed if, while they were speaking, her attention strayed to the TV or radio. Or he might sulk openly if she showed the slightest interest in other boys his age. (Such jealousy didn't extend to the attention she paid little girls.) He was five years old. *Five.* It amazed her, this number. He was small for his size. At five he'd retained a few passionate interests that might be said to belong to younger children. Staring contest, for instance, with her, with his mother. He still liked to set his boy-face a centimeter before hers, to fix her with a deep and unblinking gaze. It was either a phase—and she'd seen many distinct phases in his five years—or the solidifying of his true personality.

She believed he'd enjoyed his time at summer camp thus far. During training week several of the male counselors had made a point of including James in a hike to Barker Lake, in a lazy game of catch before dinner. What a special brand of happiness for Harriet to see her son at play with these young men, professional camp counselors no less. Had these moments been meaningful for James? Hard to say. A few days later he'd shown little reaction when she told him these same counselors had been fired. Though he did want to know why they'd been let go.

"For swimming at night," she said.

"But why?"

"It's dangerous, swimming at night. You could hit your head and drown."

She'd been equally tactful when preparing James for the sight of a hundred and four retarded adult campers. A few weeks before they'd left their St. Louis apartment for Kindermann Forest, she'd brought home a book on Down syndrome, and together they had looked through the pages. "Not so different, really," she'd said. She told him he should not be afraid. "True," she said. "On the outside they would look . . . unusual, their faces and bodies and their behaviors."

To this James blinked in agreement. "But they're normal inside, right?" he asked.

"Yes," she said. "They're good people. They have good, normal hearts."

Of course she'd said these things to lessen the strangeness and dread of the moment—this moment, in fact—when James looked upon retarded men and women for the first time. He appeared awed by what he'd just seen. It was a daunting task, maybe, to try to match their misshapen bodies to their supposed good and normal hearts.

"James," she said. "Next time, you don't have to stand in the doorway and stare. You can come in and meet them. You can say hello."

He gave her a quick nod and blink.

"You don't have to be afraid." She waited. "Are you afraid?"

"No," he said. "Why do they swing back and forth like that when they walk?"

"They were born with a disease. Or a defect. Or they had an accident. The man who just left, Mr. Peirpont, fell off his tractor and hit his head."

She wasn't beyond inventing a cautionary tale, at least the part about the tractor. She'd seen James turn his eager boy-gaze toward the maintenance staff's tractor and brush hog, a roaring and violent contraption. If her falsehoods were casual enough and attached to something James knew to be true, then she could make him reflect. She could guide his thoughts a bit. No doubt he was presently thinking about the sharp blades of the brush hog or Leonard Peirpont's tottering walk or the hazards of swimming at night.

He was a handsome and determined thinker, the way he raised his chin and half-squinted. His hair was dark brown and would have fallen into loose waves if she didn't cut it short. His complexion shone a few shades lighter than Harriet's—not just lighter but composed of different tones. People looked at her son and wondered.

"I've got medicines to organize," she said. "If only you could help me. But I bet you're busy, aren't you? What are you doing in there?"

"Building bridges."

"Yes," she said. "I thought that's what you might be doing."

She returned to her charts and medicines and he settled back down onto the floor of their living quarters and resumed work on his bridges. Bridges to islands. Bridges across chasms and rivers. Bridges to other bridges.

Twenty minutes later Maureen Boyd from the kitchen came by with two very large oven pans, or muffin trays to be exact, industrial-size, sixty-four muffin holes in each tray. Harriet looked up from her desk, puzzled.

"For your medications," Maureen said.

She still didn't understand. But once Maureen explained, Harriet realized that muffin pans were perfect. A camper's name could be taped into each muffin well. She could sort and arrange breakfast, lunch, and dinner meds. At mealtimes she could go from one mess hall table to the next with her muffin tray balanced in one hand.

After Maureen left, Harriet practiced walking waitress-style around the infirmary beds. She stopped at the window, pulled back the curtain. The crowd of campers had thinned. Across the meadow Schuller Kindermann had just stepped out of the camp office and was making his way toward the infirmary. She wasn't at all panicked.

Given his methodical pace, there was plenty of time for Harriet to turn her attention to the folded paper bag and conduct whatever investigations she thought necessary.

She weighed the bag in her hand. The sides of the bag had been expertly folded down and stapled shut, meticulously so—a neat row of three tight staples.

The first of these Harriet removed with a hemostat. But this method proved too painstaking. The remaining staples she simply cut in half with a nail clipper.

Inside the bag were stacked sheets of birth control pills, dozens of sheets, one for each female state hospital camper of childbearing age. Their names were taped to the edges of the sheets. MRS. RAMONA KAISER, MISS BLANCHE NAGEL, MISS MARY ANN HORNICKER.

Because these names had been neatly handwritten on adhesive labels, you might think that each woman had pondered her circumstance and then made a practical choice. But of course that wasn't it. Someone at the state hospital had decided—wisely—on their behalf.

Could it be that Mr. Kindermann had misunderstood these intentions, or misunderstood the workings of birth control pills?

Or did he plan to hold back these pills for the duration of the state hospital session—the act of an old-fashioned Catholic, a principled man?

It was hard, if not impossible, to know his intentions. At that moment all Harriet could do was dump the birth control pills into the bottom drawer of her work desk and searched for a reasonable replacement. Seltzer tablets? Gauze bandages? Stool softeners?

In the end she chose throat lozenges, twenty or more sheets' worth. A ridiculous substitute. She placed the lozenges in the bag, folded down and restapled its sides.

Maybe the real difficulty of reading Schuller Kindermann's intentions had to do with his age and appearance. At first glance he looked properly, reassuringly paternal. Grandfatherly. His face was pale and kind, his hair vibrantly white. He had the fussy manners people seemed to approve of in the elderly. (Easy to imagine a man like Schuller Kindermann fixing clocks or cobbling shoes in some quaint Bavarian village.) If you looked close, you could see an age-softened version of the child he'd once been: a tidy, well-mannered boy of ten or eleven, a boy not so very interested in other children or in pleasing adults, but not at all troublesome, either, just wholly devoted to his own interests and pursuits—self-sufficient, determined, a bit aloof. You looked at seventy-eight-year-old Schuller Kindermann and expected a grown boy's sly humor, or at least a willingness to be playful.

What you got was altogether different.

The infirmary door creaked open, and Schuller hoisted himself inside. A carefully placed step. A slow turn. He carried with him the expectation that each of his slow and deliberate movements was somehow interesting for others to watch. "Well," he said. "Linda Rucker tells me we have one hundred and four campers. Eight more than last year." He glared at the infirmary floor, waiting, it seemed, for Harriet to take his simple statement—a hundred and four campers—and turn it into a lively and inclusive conversation. Several tepid moments slipped by and he lifted his face and took a squinting glance out the window at the buses and the bright afternoon. "These attendants from the state hospital," he said. "They really ought to do a better job unloading the buses."

Again Harriet was struck by the oddness of it. The incongruity. To be so primly lectured to by such a seemingly mild and kindly old man.

"But it always looks like pandemonium at first," Schuller added. "There was a summer four years ago when a dozen of the state hospital campers arrived with the stomach flu. By the next day we had an epidemic. All the infirmary beds were full. We lined up cots in the mess hall. But I probably told you about that, didn't I?"

"Yes, Mr. Kindermann. You did."

"Awful for the nurse that year."

"Yes," she said. "Awful."

"These new counselors. Have you met any of them?"

"I haven't had a chance."

"Well, they look good. They're frazzled, of course. Who wouldn't be? But they'll catch on. Say, did a nurse from the state hospital, a Ms. Dunbar, drop off a package for me?"

Almost funny, the effort he made to act as if this request were of no importance. When she pointed the bag out on the counter, he picked it up as if it were an afterthought. "They'll do Salisbury steak and potatoes for dinner," he said. "And I wanted to drop by and make it clear that you and James are welcome to join us at the director's table." He waited.

"Thank you."

"But I'll let you get back to your business," he said. He took a few carefully measured steps and was out the infirmary door.

He had not, during the entirety of his visit, looked her in the eye. She'd never sensed in Schuller the bashful unease some white people had in her presence. Nor did she think he'd been made shy by having seen her naked a few nights earlier in the swimming pool shower room. He hadn't indulged in the sight of her. He wasn't interested in her that way.

Hard, if not impossible, to imagine what he was *interested* in. He was an odd man, Mr. Kindermann. He almost certainly wasn't a good camp director. He might even be a fool.

And yet, in the three days since she'd been discovered at the pool, she found it difficult, even painful, not to address Schuller Kindermann directly, to seek his pardon by saying, "Look here, Mr. Kindermann. I'd like to explain myself . . ." But what could she say? None of her reasons were noble.

Look here, Mr. Kindermann.

Best to start at the Meadowmont Gardens Nursing Home. (That was how Harriet had come to work at Kindermann Forest; Schuller had approached her one day and asked if she and her son might like to spend the summer at camp.) In the very back of Meadowmont Gardens, in the oldest and longest wing of the building, was a corridor called Special Unit C, where the patients—mindless or insensible or, better yet, cataleptic—thrashed away or trembled or simply weighed down the mattresses with their comatose bodies.

The human body, in its last phases, could fall apart in such dreadful and astonishing ways. To be a nurse was to see it up close and, over time, grow accustomed to the dread and wonder.

But all this was just a potent reminder, not the lesson itself.

For the lesson Harriet had to spend time caring for an entirely different class of Meadowmont Gardens patient—different corridor, different world altogether. They called themselves the Garden Ladies because their rooms were private, with little parlors and kitchenettes and French doors leading to the Meadowmont flower gardens. They were all ladies of a certain type: elderly, white, meticulous dressers, absorbed in books and crossword puzzles, particular about tablecloths and butter pads and hairdressing appointments. They could be trusted to operate a toaster oven but not to self-administer medication. Each evening they brought their own silverware to the dining hall and, after the meal, returned to their rooms and scrubbed the tines of the forks and the dull blades of the knives in their kitchenette sinks.

No surprise that the Garden Ladies were great traffickers of gossip. Certain details—book titles, recipe ingredients—eluded them.

But how keenly they remembered stories of a personal nature: the ill-timed remark, the cheap gift, the wrong dress, or Mrs. Perrault on Hall 1B, who drank too much wine and slept through her stepson's wedding reception, or Mrs. Decker, who, during a twelve-city bus tour of Europe, developed an unseemly crush on her Swiss tour guide (while her husband dozed in the bus seat beside her). Even now, Mrs. Decker still wrote the tour guide effusive notes and made her dull husband carry them to the front desk for mailing.

As for the Garden Ladies themselves, their lives had been much tidier: one marriage (inevitably a portrait of a dead husband, a mild-looking man, propped on a dresser top), one career (a homemaker, a grade school teacher, a city clerk), a small family (a child or two so carefully reared and independent they were now fulfilling important career duties three states away).

You learned these details over time if you were their nurse. And eventually you watched the Garden Ladies falter. They fell or stroked out or succumbed to a weakened heart. For some there were a few days of clarity before they died or were moved to Special Unit C. It wasn't as if they wanted Harriet to listen while they reviewed their lives. But they did hold her hand, even those who, upon first meeting Harriet, had gone to the front desk and wondered why they'd been assigned a "negro" nurse. Now they called her "dear" and asked about her home life. They wanted to see photos of her son. Such a handsome little boy, they said. She was brave to raise him alone, though, surely, it would be an easier task with the right man at her side, wouldn't it? Why not marry and give the boy a father? There were several nice young men in housekeeping. Not that she shouldn't set her sights higher, because she was pretty and there were a few eligible doctors who saw patients at Meadowmont Gardens each week. Why not Dr. Marshburn? He was married, of course, but everyone knew his wife lived in Columbus, Ohio, and the two rarely occupied the same residence. Or why not Dr. Silverman, only thirty-three and rumored to be a playboy, but if he took Harriet to dinner or away for the weekend, it would almost certainly be someplace very nice.

The Garden Ladies never mentioned the fact that all these possible suitors for Harriet were white men. Had the picture of James tipped them off? Or did these distinctions no longer matter?

Probably they no longer mattered. Because at this late hour in their lives, with the mindless and the comatose of Special Unit C waiting just a few hallways away, the Garden Ladies were no longer interested in judging the personal choices other people made. If anything, they were warning her not to deny herself a worthy experience.

And so on the last day of counselor training, Kenny Cossman, unit leader for male counselors, came to the infirmary and told Harriet there'd be an after-hours bonfire in one of the horse pastures. Already the beer had been bought and iced, and there'd be music and something good to smoke, and, who knew, maybe later they would all sneak down to the pool for a swim? He hoped Harriet would join them. Most likely he was hoping for more than that. During the course of the week, he'd made a few small overtures. One evening before dinner the counselors had played a stupid game. They'd tossed around a soccer ball, and the person who caught it had to name a famous person whom they wouldn't mind spending time with on a deserted island. Kenny had said he'd like to spend time with R&B singer Toni Braxton, an offering meant for Harriet—a nice offering since Harriet liked to think that her best features were more Toni Braxton–like than Mariah Carey–like or Whitney Houston–like. At least Kenny was paying attention. He was only twenty-two, though his friendliness and his husky build made him seem a bit older. He didn't inspire in Harriet the hopes for any great romance, but if he were funny and modest, which he usually was, she wouldn't mind going to the bonfire and getting a bit drunk and letting him lead her to some quiet corner of camp for a kiss. Nothing more than that. Or maybe a little more. It was pleasant enough to think of treading water beside him in the pool. All that male yearning just a few watery feet away.

The Garden Ladies would have been the first to tell her, yes, go ahead, even if it meant leaving James—truly the soundest of child sleepers—alone in the infirmary for bits of time while she joined the party. She could always run back to check on him. Was that irresponsible?

It probably was, but she'd gone anyway. The gathering in the horse pasture was the very best kind of party, because a week of first aid and program training and side-by-side living had made them intimate enough to know who could be teased or flirted with, who could be counted on to act outrageously.

At some point it was decided that they should go for a swim. *A midnight dip* the boys called it, though by then it was well after midnight. *Straight to the pool,* they said. *No time to stop by the cabin for your suits.* Such weak logic: the girls didn't argue too hard against it. There'd been rumors the night would end like this, with everyone peeling off their clothes. No doubt, like Harriet, the girl counselors had chosen their underwear carefully when dressing for the party.

She'd stopped by the infirmary and checked on James. He was fine, coiled in his bedsheets, unaware. And yet some of the spell of the bonfire had been broken. She was a mother, after all. She was five years older than most of the counselors. She was black. They were white and, by and large, considerate, even welcoming, people. Yet they thought of her as having lived a reckless, even desperate, urban life. In truth she'd grown up in the countryside west of Durham, North Carolina. Her father, college-educated, worked in the earth sciences labs of Duke University. Her mother trained Sunday school teachers for the Baptist Church.

By the time Harriet got to the pool, nearly everyone had undressed and gone in or lined up at the diving board. They seemed to be acting out some sort of prank or challenge or drunken dare. Of course Harriet felt ungainly disrobing alone in the shower room, but for a foolish reason: she'd been teased about her name in grade school and thought that somehow it might be true, she might be, well, *hairier* than most young white women. But this wasn't the case, at least not judging from Eileen Haupt, who ran to the woods to pee, or from Wendy Kavanagh, who patrolled the pool deck naked, sober, and unshy.

How might it have felt to leave the shower house and pad naked across the pool deck with others watching? Awkward. Maybe even humiliating. Or delicious. Hard for Harriet to be certain. She never got that far. Schuller Kindermann appeared at the top of the steps, made his unsteady descent. A sobering moment, but what Harriet felt—and what many of the laughing counselors must have felt, too—was a sense of extreme dislocation. All night long they'd worked hard to create a cabaret atmosphere of sexual daring. Then to see Schuller Kindermann, and be reminded that there were those—the elderly, the soon-to-arrive state hospital campers—who weren't in on the joke. The night's rowdiness and camaraderie seemed to deflate all at once. The Garden Ladies, who'd been Harriet's confidantes, turned their backs on her and resumed their rigid ways.

The next morning Schuller fired fifteen counselors, two of them members of the senior staff, though not his camp nurse. Not Harriet Foster.

Chapter Five

No time to dawdle. On the gravel pathway, with their belongings for the summer balanced on their shoulders or dragged roughshod at their heels, the new counselors fell into a loose, half-jogging regiment. Enough like an army regiment for someone in the back ranks, a jokester, to shout, "Sound off! One, two. Sound off! Three, four."

They all laughed, just as the pathway veered into the woods. From high above, a canopy of evergreen branches threw down its shade. An entirely pleasant surprise to be under the roof of this woods, with its dewy air and a spaciousness that felt intimate and many-chambered. Dogs could be heard, panting and furrowing in the underbrush. One moment the pattern of tree trunks looked endless; the next, it was possible to recognize, crouched almost shyly behind a scrim of trees, several hulking, gray cedar buildings: sleeping cabins one through four.

Here the regiment of new counselors broke apart. Young men to the right and up the walkways leading to Cabins One and Two, young women a hundred yards deeper into the woods, to the walkways and creaking porch doors of Cabins Three and Four.

Later they'd learn that each cabin interior was identical: a screened porch, two long sleeping barracks, a large fluorescent-lit bathroom— a latrine really, with latchless toilet stalls and musky wood showers. There were no counselors' quarters. Or maybe there had been, but the room for these quarters was now occupied by dismantled bunk beds, worn mattresses, wool blankets. Where then would the new counselors sleep? In the sleeping barracks, apparently, on bunk beds, above or beneath the campers.

Wyatt chose a bottom bunk in the far corner, near a window. There wasn't time to take stock of the accommodations or negotiate introductions with the other male counselors hurrying past him. He unrolled his new sleeping bag. He placed his travel clock and retainer box on the shelf beside his bunk. From his shirt pocket he withdrew his list of campers:

1. Gerald (Jerry) Johnston
2. Leonard Peirpont
3. Thomas Anwar Toomey

Through the screened window he could hear counselors regrouping on the gravel pathway. The jokester, whoever he might be, was shouting again, "Sound off! One, two. Sound off! Three, four." By the time Wyatt joined the group, the women counselors were hurrying from Cabins Three and Four—the quick bounce of their steps lovely and painful to look at—and soon the whole regiment was in a full jog toward the heat and bright light of the meadow.

They seemed to have arrived at a crucial moment.

The crowd of campers had disbanded, straying from the white buses in wobbly little groups of three and four to the long open porch of the mess hall, or to the shade of the picnic tables, where they stood about, each of them in a private reverie of body movement and what looked to be a slowly dawning awareness of the grass and warm air and sunlight. Other campers were not so patient. A dozen men and women, solo wanderers, had, for whatever their reasons, set a zig-zagging course out to the very periphery of the meadow. The state attendants, burdened with luggage and bedclothes, could not hold all of these wanderers back. Several had crossed the border and stepped into the shrubby edge of the woods.

Linda Rucker, her bangs stringy with sweat, waved at the counselors with her three-ring binder and shouted, "Go! Go! Go! Bring 'em back! Bring 'em back!"

So this would be their first assignment, to race after these wanderers, to latch on to a belt loop or wrist or shirtsleeve and tug them, step by step, back into the fold. In Wyatt's case it turned out to be rough work. The man he'd gone after was bullishly large, with a bald head and rolling, half-closed eyes. He seemed to have a single-minded wish to tromp through the underbrush. "Yop, yop, yop," he panted. When he saw Wyatt coming, he pushed twenty yards deeper into the forest and wrapped his fat arms around a tree trunk. "Yop, yop," he groaned. There was a bellowing sound to these panted breaths, as if he were a rutting animal.

He was strong. Wyatt was stronger. But was it acceptable to grip the man's wrists—his flesh felt oddly spongy—and pry his arms from the trunk and then mostly drag him through the brush and back to the center of the meadow? The state attendants didn't object. Nor did Linda Rucker. So it seemed it was acceptable, given that the campers might be lost in the woods, given that the meadow was in a state of chaos.

All around the buses were small piles of strewn luggage and bedsheets and the remains of paper bag lunches—baloney sandwiches, fruit cups, wax paper bags holding clutches of broken Oreo cookies.

Nearby one of the few younger campers, a skinny teenage girl, set out running from the picnic tables at full tilt. But then her legs wobbled. Her arms windmilled from side to side. She made it twenty yards before a seizure brought her down and she flailed and trembled upon the thick meadow grass. Her counselor, a portly young woman named Emily Boehler, crouched beside her. "Can someone help me?" Emily pleaded. "Oh, my goodness. Can someone *please* help me?" Other campers and counselors hurried by undaunted. A few minutes later the teenage camper came to her senses, rose, and lurched into another stumbling run. Another twenty yards. Another seizure.

"Find the campers on your list," Linda Rucker called out. "Check with the attendants. But you must make sure you have the right person. Don't just ask the camper. Check the clothing tags, if you have to. That's right, *yes,* step up behind them, peel back their shirt collars or the hems of their pants, and look for their names."

An awkward practice, this looking into strangers' shirt collars. Some of the men whose clothing Wyatt looked inside reacted with a dazed and dreamy regard. They craned their heads around to look at him. What rich expressions they had—wide-eyed, addled, incredulous.

But others jumped at the violation of his fingers and turned on him, shrieking, gnashing their crooked teeth, ready to lash out.

What else could Wyatt do but press on with the search? He squeezed through throngs of sweaty men and women. Those who squatted down on the grass or those who lay clutching their duffel bags and bedclothes, he stepped over.

"Can anyone help me find Jerry Johnston?" Wyatt called out. "Does anyone know Leonard Peirpont?"

Several of the attendants merely waved him off. But when he called Leonard Peirpont's name, he caught the attention of a stout and ferocious-looking woman in a nurse's uniform. She carried her mammoth bosom low on her stomach, clutched her purse while stomping toward him across the meadow.

"*Leonard,*" she repeated, as if she'd been startled out of a gloomy daydream. She glared at Wyatt. "Who told you to ask for Leonard Peirpont?"

"He's on my list."

She wanted to see this list. But even after she'd read the names of Wyatt's campers, she didn't appear to approve. More so, she seemed to begrudge him for some personal failing, perhaps the whiff of inexperience he gave off. She said, "When you're talking to me, you look me in the eye and say, 'Yes, Nurse Dunbar' or 'No, Nurse Dunbar' or 'Leonard is on my list, Nurse Dunbar.'"

He raised his gaze to her.

She said, "You as dumb as you look?"

"No, ma'am," he said. "No, Nurse Dunbar."

"*Christ,* I hope not." She pointed to the mess hall porch. "Leonard's up there, in the shade, where I left him. The one with the glasses and checkered shirt. See him?"

"Yes, I do . . . Nurse Dunbar."

"You hold him by the elbow, understand? Wherever you go. You hold Leonard's elbow and walk beside him."

"Yes, Nurse Dunbar."

"And you make sure that, when you're not walking beside him, you got him parked next to something sturdy he can hold on to."

"I will, Nurse Dunbar." Then, thankfully, she was through with him, had turned her broad back and was treading a few heavy paces to the nearest white bus. Up the steps she went, hoisting herself and her dangling white purse. She slumped into the first bench, where she sat waiting, glumly, for the attendants to finish and the bus to whisk her away.

Wyatt set a course for the mess hall porch. The person she'd pointed to was an odd-looking man—but weren't they all odd-looking?—who gripped a porch column and swayed to and fro atop his stiff little legs. He was middle-aged with woolly sideburns, but his startled, blinking eyes, windowed behind sharp-cornered glasses, made him look newly hatched.

"Leonard Peirpont?" Wyatt asked.

The man set his squinting gaze on Wyatt. "I'm not supposed to cross this early in the year," he said.

"Yes? Not supposed to cross what?"

"Not supposed to cross till July or August. Depends on the weather."

Wyatt placed a hand on the man's shoulder, peeled back his shirt. L. PEIRPONT. "All right then. I'd like to introduce myself. My name is Wyatt Huddy."

"Weren't you one of them boys that got the call to come up . . ." Whatever came next seemed to elude Leonard Peirpont. He closed his eyes and concentrated, pursed and unpursed his lips, as if he were taking tiny, toothless bites of an imaginary fruit.

"Come up?" Wyatt offered.

". . . up onto the stand . . ."

"To come here to camp, you mean? To Kindermann Forest?"

"Up onto the judge's stand and get your ribbon."

"No, no. Not me."

"Your name on the ribbon and your name in the county ledger."

"I don't think so. Not my name, no."

It was a minor shock to discover that Thomas Anwar Toomey was a gaunt old man. Did they let gaunt old men come to summer camp? Apparently, they did.

Thomas Anwar Toomey had a thick head of closely cropped, black-gray hair and deep hollows in both cheeks that suggested some type of dental collapse. He'd arrived at Kindermann Forest dressed in his pajamas and had found his way from the bus to the wide trunk of an oak tree shading the camp picnic tables. He stood with his sagging face just a few inches from the trunk, as if he and the tree were exchanging intimacies.

"Thomas Anwar Toomey?" Wyatt asked.

The old man turned from the tree. His full name was stitched onto the pocket of his pajamas. He kept rearranging his jaw and mouth as if readying to speak, though no words came out.

A mute, Wyatt thought, though this turned out not to be so.

Thomas Anwar Toomey had a pillowcase stuffed full of clothing and toiletries and, wedged beneath one arm, several blankets and bedsheets tied together in a knot. He dipped a hand into the loose pocket of his pajama bottoms and pulled out a pack of cigarettes. Lucky Strikes. He held a single cigarette out to Wyatt. "Please," Thomas Anwar said.

He wanted fire, of course. Wyatt had to flag down a passing attendant and borrow matches. When he set fire to the tip, Thomas Anwar sealed his lips over the cigarette, sucked and gulped, sucked and gulped. A minute later there was nothing left but a wet nub. Thomas Anwar pulled out a fresh Lucky Strike. "Please," he repeated.

"No, no," Wyatt said. "We have to find Jerry Johnston and move to our cabin."

"Please," Thomas Anwar begged, but there was already a mark of defeat in his expression. With his baggy pajamas and knot of bedclothes, he looked like a man accustomed to disappointment, a refugee turned away at every border.

Along a stretch of gravel pathway, near the opening to the woods, a group of campers had come together in a private little clique. There were seven of them in all, and they could easily have escaped into the scrub. Instead, they stood together in the shade. One of them would speak and the others would nod in recognition, a very stiff and exaggerated nod that required the bowing of their heads, necks, and shoulders. It took time for Wyatt to reach them—to hold Leonard Peirpont by the elbow and allow him his fraught and minuscule steps. Thomas Anwar Toomey shuffled behind. Once they'd drawn close, Wyatt could see the group was made up entirely of Down syndrome campers.

He asked for Jerry Johnston, and several in the group turned toward a potbellied and middle-aged man in blue jean overalls. His brow was deeply creased, and his hair shot up from the crown of his forehead in a bristly, blond wave. Like the others in his group, he had thickly lidded eyes and a plump tongue that seemed always on the verge of sliding forward between his cracked lips.

"Are you Jerry Johnston?" Wyatt offered.

The man smiled in reply.

"He's saving up all his stars," one of the Down syndrome women explained, and whatever this might mean, it set off a chain of raucous laughter.

"Jerry will trade his stars in for peanut butter cups."

"Or TV magazines."

"Jerry's on vacation now."

Each of these remarks, voiced by a different camper, drew a round of laughter.

"Are you Jerry Johnston?" Wyatt asked the man. "If it's all right, I'll look at the tag inside your shirt."

It made Jerry Johnston laugh to be asked such a question, laugh even harder to have Wyatt peer inside the collar of his white T-shirt. He said to Wyatt, "I've been to camp three times in a row, but I haven't seen you."

"I'm new this year," Wyatt said. "We're all new."

"Do you know my friend, Denny Ballantine?"

"I don't think so. Is he here at camp?"

"He's here in my pocket," Jerry Johnston said, and from one of the many folds of his overalls he produced a photograph: a rotund middle-aged Down syndrome man in a bright red life vest crouched rather proudly before a canoe.

"Denny Ballantine," Jerry Johnston explained.

Wyatt considered the photo and nodded, and it was then passed on to each member of the group, who did exactly the same thing, considered it and nodded, until it made its way back to its owner.

"Will we have chocolate milk for bedtime snack?" Jerry asked.

"I'm not sure," Wyatt said. "Was there chocolate milk last year?"

"No."

"I don't know then. Probably not."

"Can we choose which grace we say at breakfast?"

"I guess so," Wyatt said. "We should go to our cabin, Jerry. We should choose a bed before they're all taken."

This was warning enough for Jerry to grab his bag and set out for the cabins at a fast clip. The rest of them—Wyatt, Leonard, Thomas Anwar—followed behind. They must have made a peculiar sight. Wyatt couldn't help but wonder which of them was the oddest looking. No easy contest given that the standard had changed: all around them were countless other odd and misshapen campers stumbling toward the sleeping cabins. And as for judges, Wyatt's fellow counselors looked too harried and miserable to offer an opinion. The same was true of the state attendants, a regiment of lean, uniformed black men who were bearing the last of the bags and bedlinens to the cabins. You could see in their eyes how eager they were to be back aboard their buses, minus their patients, rolling clear of the camp gate. A moment of celebration.

In preparation for dinner the kitchen staff had swept and mopped the mess hall floor and set out thirty-five heavy wood tables that ran in neat rows from the center of the mess hall out to two adjoining screened porches. On each table fresh-cut dandelions had been placed in paper coffee cups. Beside the cups, folded index cards bore each counselor's name, pink cards for female counselors, blue for male.

Platters of food were set out on the enormous metal counter that separated the kitchen from the mess hall, and it was Wyatt's duty to retrieve dinner—Salisbury steak in brown gravy, real mashed potatoes, canned sweet corn—and bring it to the table for Leonard Peirpont, Thomas Anwar Toomey, and Jerry Johnston to enjoy. Jerry proved to be the only enthusiastic eater, dredging his steak and potatoes through the gravy and chewing with a tempo that made his stiff head and shoulders bob up and down and his free hand tap, tap, tap against the table. Thomas Anwar hung his head over his plate. Once or twice he bent down close enough to touch his food with his nose or lips but then backed off, as if, on principle, he'd decided to deny himself.

Leonard Peirpont had to be fed by hand. It wasn't a matter of physical disability. He could grip a spoon and raise it shakily to his lips. It was just that, in the journey between plate and lips, he forgot his intentions. Midway, he might shake his head, blink naïvely, and say, "She was the one that expected you could grow carrots alongside summer melons." Each of these musings caused Leonard Peirpont to marvel in wonder. And after his wonderment passed, he tried to reassess whatever action he might have been in the middle of. He gaped, dumbfounded, at the spoon in his hand.

But there were far stranger happenings unfolding at other tables. There were men and women from the state hospital whose diseases left them in states so pitiful and rare that they could not, on first glance, be believed: a man whose tumored head had doubled in size and whose face had begun to sag and droop as if it were made of melting wax; several creatures, perhaps women, who were small, pale, nearly hairless, and darted about with the energy and nimbleness of monkeys. By far the most striking, or rather the most horrendous, were two elderly twins, the Mulcrone sisters, whose malformation was so astounding it could not be stared at directly or even properly acknowledged. The new counselors of Kindermann Forest, Wyatt included, looked at the sisters and turned away. Later, maybe, he and the other counselors would come to believe and accept. But for now it was better to think that what they saw must be a trick of the sisters' intense homeliness and the hall's bad lighting.

Of course they were not all monstrous. Among the campers were scores of men and women whose syndromes and conditions had rendered them childlike in appearance, and a dozen others who could pass as normal until they drew near and one could see a troubling unevenness in their gaze.

To be sure, though, they were all of one tribe. There were many of them and few of the counselors. As a tribe, they could do what they pleased. More than a few had risen from the benches, their mouths crammed with food, and stumbled to the nearest porch screen. Step by step, they began feeling their way along the screened perimeter of the mess hall. It was no use at all for their counselors to shout or make threats. These wandering campers couldn't easily be called back to their tables.

Wyatt spotted, in the crowded center of the hall, bobbing above the campers' heads, a large serving tray—a muffin tray held aloft by an upraised hand. The young woman who carried it was slim and dark haired, dark-skinned, too—alert-looking, pretty. She wore an expression of severe concentration that was all the more striking for the mayhem erupting around her.

Easy enough to guess who she might be: Harriet Foster, the camp nurse. Her muffin tray was filled with medications.

She went from table to table, from camper to camper, placing pills in their hands, sometimes waiting long minutes until each pill found its way into the cavern of their mouths and was flushed down with

water. At Wyatt's table she had lithium for Thomas Anwar, phenobarbital for Leonard, digoxin and Tagamet for Jerry Johnston. Before
they swallowed their pills, she had Wyatt verify and re-verify their
names.

"Do you take any medications, Wyatt?" Nurse Foster asked him.
"Did you bring any pills to camp—prescription pills from the doctor
or over-the-counter pills from the drugstore?"

It confused him, this question. For a while he thought Nurse Foster had mistaken him for a camper. "I'm a counselor," he explained
meekly.

"I know you are," she said. "I'm asking all the counselors the same
question. Did you bring any medications to camp?"

The only pills he'd brought were fiber tablets to aid his digestion.
"Yes. Stomach medicine," he said to Nurse Foster, and she nodded
and told him to bring his stomach medicine to the infirmary for safe-
keeping. "Thank you, Wyatt," she said, and before she turned and
moved on to the next table, she placed her free hand lightly, briefly,
on his shoulder.

He'd not expected this: the settling of her warm hand on his
shoulder—a remarkable happening, at least in Wyatt's experience.

Program Director Linda Rucker had scheduled a different activity
each evening, and this being Monday, the first evening, she'd made
preparations for the Kindermann Forest Welcome Parade. An unusual
parade, since the entire camp walked and there was no one to wave
from the roadside. Two of the oldest and most tolerant mares were
bridled and brought down from the stable to lead the way. Sashes and
batons were handed out. The camp tractor was hitched to a flat-top
trailer, and those, like Leonard Peirpont, too unsteady to walk the
length of camp, were allowed to ride atop the trailer, waving as if from
a parade float.

By nightfall they were back in their cabins, though nearly every-thing about the cabin interiors—the light and smell and calm order of things—had undergone a vivid transformation. In sleeping Cabin Two, the bunk beds were askew and draped in strewn clothing. Shambling retarded men wandered the aisle ways and porch, some of them half-dressed or undressed. They pressed their faces to the window screen and sent their gruff squeals and barking laughter out into the night. It took courage to step inside the cabin bathroom, breathe the steamy and rank air, make your way past the line of toi-lets and showers, each with its own pitiful scene to look upon. Worse even to discover what services would be required of the male counsel-ors. Some campers could not wash their own bodies. Others couldn't wipe themselves after a bowel movement. Wyatt and his fellow male counselors performed these duties, did them quickly and often badly. While in the jurisdiction of the bathroom, they made a point not to look one another in the eye or in any way acknowledge whatever task they'd just performed. They'd been told to have their campers show-ered by nine, dressed in pajamas and in their beds by nine-twenty. In theory, a sensible plan; in reality, all but impossible because the male campers of Cabin Two were more awake, more charged with the new-ness of their surroundings, than they'd been at any time throughout the day.

On a square of concrete just outside the cabin porch, Thomas Anwar Toomey had found a place to do his frantic smoking. He studied the woods as he smoked, leaning one way then another and squinting at some dark shape lodged among the tree trunks and shrubbery. Never once did he step off the square of concrete. After each vanquished cigarette, he'd enter the cabin and trail after Wyatt, sometimes clutching the hem of Wyatt's T-shirt with his bony fingers. "Please," he said, meaning another lighted match, another cigarette.

"But remember," Wyatt said. "You only have one pack of cigarettes for each day you're at camp. If you smoke them one after another, you'll run out. A few days from now you won't have any cigarettes left at all."

This warning settled over Thomas Anwar in crushing increments. His hands trembled. In his stricken demeanor Wyatt glimpsed a life of quaking anxiety.

"Ahhh!" Thomas Anwar sighed. "But what can I do?"

"You'll have to save your cigarettes. Instead of smoking one after another, smoke one each half hour."

And so, beginning at nine, Thomas Anwar stood on the porch studying his wristwatch. At nine-thirty, and at ten, he came looking for Wyatt. Thomas Anwar was back again at ten-thirty. Once more they stepped outside onto the square of concrete and Wyatt struck a match. A peculiar sight to watch Thomas Anwar gulping at his cigarette with the desperation of a landed fish. All the while, he kept peering out at the woods, especially at the slanting boundary where the cabin's floodlights ended and a curtain of deep shadows began.

"What is it you keep looking for?" Wyatt asked.

There was no sign that Thomas Anwar had heard the question. Or that he intended to answer it. But then several moments passed and he shook his head mournfully and said, "He's followed me here."

"Followed you? Who?"

"I told them at the hospital that he'd follow me, but they wouldn't believe it. And now here he is, sneaking up on me from behind the trees. Ahhh! Right there, yes? *Right there.* Do you see him?"

"I don't," Wyatt said. "See who?"

Clearly it was a source of discomfort, of genuine embarrassment for Thomas Anwar to provide a name. He cringed. His cheeks sagged pitifully. "He is Thomas Anwar Toomey. He has followed me here from the hospital."

"I don't think so," Wyatt consoled him.

"He's waiting for me to fall to the floor and die."

"Oh, I don't think so," Wyatt repeated. "You don't need to worry anyway. You *are* Thomas Anwar Toomey. You're right here. You can't be two places at the same time."

Almost certainly Thomas Anwar had heard such advice before. He smiled a thin and patient smile, an indication that he'd received a lifetime's worth of similar counsel, all of it worthless. He pulled deeply on his cigarette with trembling lips.

At a quarter to eleven word passed from cabin to cabin that all counselors should convene in fifteen minutes for a staff meeting.

This news set in motion a rush of activity. The campers of Cabin Two were sent and, in some instances, dragged to their beds. They wouldn't stay put for long, of course; they seemed to know this new urgency would be short-lived. Of Wyatt's three charges, only Leonard Peirpont could be counted on not to stray. He lay on his bunk with the same bolt-straight, fused posture he used when standing. His arms were at his sides. He'd forgotten to remove his glasses, and even when this was done for him—the glasses carefully folded and placed in his pajama pocket—he lay perfectly still, blinking up wide-eyed at the bunk above him.

Two Kindermann Forest maintenance men appeared on the porch landing. Normally they'd have ended their shift at 7:00 P.M. and gone home. Tonight they had been told to stay late and perform cabin watch. They were hard-looking, scrappy young men, yet the prospect of being left to rule the cabin, with its barracks of noisy retarded men, appeared to fill them with dread.

The meeting took place in The Sanctuary, an oak board cottage that decades earlier had housed the camp office and was now a refuge where off-duty counselors might smoke and gossip and buy cold soda pop from a wobbly vending machine. The furnishings were meager: a pay phone, a refrigerator, three torn and dusty couches. Most of the girl counselors had arrived and settled in. They'd brought with them a climate of distress, of grievance. Counselor Emily Boehler, who'd attended to her camper's seizures most of the day, had claimed the phone and was curled up on one arm of the sofa, head against the receiver. She seemed to have exhausted herself in describing the day's ordeal, and whatever advice she was receiving only made her sigh dispiritedly and mumble, "Yes, all right, all right, yes," into the phone.

But they were all harried and distraught, especially the young women counselors of Cabin Four. It seemed there'd been an incident. An obese but otherwise docile female camper had, when led into the shower and sprayed with water, gone into a frenzy. She'd turned and seized two tight handfuls of her counselor, Kathleen Bram's hair and pulled Kathleen down until she was curled up with her face pressed roughly against the shower floor. Then the camper, naked and furious, had sat on her and screamed.

Kathleen Bram was the one wearing the cheek bandage. At dinner she'd looked sturdy and capable. At the moment, slouched on a dusty couch, she appeared drawn and timid. Her fellow girl counselors hovered around her. They'd come to her rescue in the shower and now, when she repeated the details of her story, they were stricken on her behalf. It was awful, they said. Awful what had happened to Kathleen. She should have been warned about what this camper might do. They put their arms around her and helped her sit up straight. *Here, drink this, Kathleen,* they said and offered her sips of Fresca. When she cried, they pushed her long brown bangs aside and wiped her forehead and the corners of her eyes with a cool cloth.

This was, for Wyatt, a startling sight. He couldn't help but stare. How had they managed it, these girl counselors? To have gone from strangers to *confidantes,* all in the course of a few hours?

His fellow male counselors were not on such intimate terms. They did, however, share a moment on the way to the meeting. This had happened after they'd filed from the cabins and onto the dark pathways and were plodding through the thick sand of the volleyball court. They stopped. Together they turned and looked back into the black scrim of the woods from where they'd come. All they could see was the splintered gleam of the cabin porch lights. But they could hear, with a shrill clarity, the howls and grunts of their male campers, sounds that spilled from the cabins' screened windows and made their way to them through the woods.

There at the volleyball courts half of the boy counselors lit cigarettes. "Jesus H. Christ," one of them said. "Can you fucking believe what we've got ourselves into?"

No answer to this, because they couldn't believe it. So they stood there exhausted, looking back into the woods in numbed wonder.

At The Sanctuary they had time to take stock of one another: the men sneaking measured glimpses of the women, the women sizing the men up in return. In the corner of the room, sitting primly on foldout chairs, were three unrecognized individuals, a young man and two young women. An unhappy trio. It took a moment to realize these three were all that remained of the original Kindermann Forest counseling staff. They were together but not, apparently, on friendly terms. No one yet knew their names. Everything about them—their closed postures and wooden expressions, their downcast gazes—made knowing them an irksome chore. So much easier to appraise them from across the room and then choose a sly nickname: the Lonesome Three.

A few stragglers wandered in. The crowd within The Sanctuary had swelled to standing room capacity: sixteen counselors, two lifeguards, one wrangler. Still no sign of Linda Rucker or Mr. Kindermann, and this allowed the murmur of complaint to grow in volume and particularity. Everyone had a point to make: *If only they'd known what to expect. If only they could have read their campers' files ahead of time. If only the state hospital attendants had stayed long enough—a few hours at the very least—to see that the campers had properly settled in.*

Someone said, *But they kept the truth from us. On purpose. So we'd show up. You understand that, don't you?*

The mood in the room darkened by a degree or two. Yes, they were beginning to understand. They were ready now to consider a more serious charge, something beyond mere incompetence.

At that moment a young man stepped into the center of the room and raised his hand in an appeal for quiet. His name was Christopher Waterhouse. Most of those gathered knew him, in part because he had the lanky swimmer's build and brown-skinned boyish handsomeness befitting his name and assignment, a lifeguard, but also because rather than sneak away to the quiet of the closed swimming pool, as his fellow lifeguard had done, Christopher Waterhouse had spent his first day helping with the state hospital campers—chasing wanderers, carrying luggage, attending to fits and seizures and the unpleasantness of the showers and toilets, the sort of help that left you stinking, scratched, and shaken.

"Excuse me," Christopher Waterhouse said to those gathered. He had a fresh-faced, earnest gaze that might, in other circumstances, have discounted anything he had to say. "Excuse me," he repeated, and when those who'd been whispering or fidgeting in their chairs fell quiet, he gave a small, half-embarrassed shrug. It wasn't his intention to be a spokesman for the group. His little shrug made that perfectly clear. "I don't think anyone who runs this place—Linda or Mr. Kindermann or whoever—has done a very good job preparing us," he said.

Around him the new counselors sighed in weary agreement.

"But it's worth remembering they're in some kind of bind. I don't know what exactly, something serious I'd guess. Serious enough that they'd fire most of the staff."

With that the collective interest turned away from Christopher, to the corner of the room, to the Lonesome Three. They wilted noticeably under this scrutiny. It seemed possible they might curl up on their chairs and shrink away to nothing at all. At last one of the three, a bony, inelegant girl, lifted her glum face and said, "Sex games. Sex games at the pool."

There was a moment of hushed silence while the new counselors contemplated this news, as strange as anything they'd seen or heard that day.

"That sounds pretty serious to me," Christopher Waterhouse said. "The point is that when Mr. Kindermann and Linda Rucker spread the word about this job, they didn't really make it clear who we'd be taking care of the first two weeks. They said *state campers* to some of us, but they didn't explain what that meant. A minute ago I heard someone say it would serve them right if we walked off the job. Probably would. But the ones who'd pay for it would be the campers. They'd get bused right back to the state hospital."

To this several of the new counselors groaned in protest. It wouldn't be their fault, they said, if the campers got bused back to the state hospital. Besides, would the campers even realize they'd been away?

"Some of them wouldn't," Christopher said. "Most would. I mean, this may not look so great to us, but this is their two weeks' vacation. It's their idea of fun—walking in a parade, staying up half the night driving us batty." He surveyed the girl counselors huddled around Kathleen on the couch. "I'm sorry for what happened to you, Kathleen."

From behind her tilted gauze bandage, Kathleen Bram looked up. Christopher's apology, if that was what it was, had sounded *personal* enough to make her bow her head in acceptance.

"I'm guessing that tomorrow they'll behave better," he said.

"Or worse," Emily Boehler replied. "By tomorrow we'll be exhausted. Then they'll push us to the limit."

"No, I don't think so," Christopher said. "What we're doing is training them, aren't we? To get used to camp and get used to our schedule. They'll catch on, I think. We'll have much better days than today. That's all I'm going to say about it." With that he took his place against the wall with the other young men. He lowered his head and concentrated, as if he were a stranger at a bus stop wrestling with a weighty dilemma.

By the time Linda Rucker arrived, the grievous mood within The Sanctuary had lifted somewhat. She'd brought along a thick sheaf of papers to distribute—none of the new counselors had yet filled out an application, a tax or staff health form—and she paused more than once to look about the gathering with a puzzled expression.

"Is everyone all right here?" she asked.

A chorus of dull murmurs. A few careful nods.

Still, something had taken place in her absence. She appeared to sense it, without having any notion of the grievances spoken or the deepening resentment from which she'd been spared.

They were back in their cabins by midnight. What exactly had the meeting taught them? That it was their duty to stick beside their campers through all manner of seizures, fits, and rages. That they were never to hit back. That they would be paid once a month at the rate of one hundred and sixty-five dollars per week. Wyatt had learned the names of the other male counselors with whom he shared the responsibility of Cabin Two: Michael Lauderback, Gibby Tumminello, Christopher Waterhouse. The four of them made a weary and reluctant return to their cabin. They brushed their teeth at the bathroom sinks and treaded lightly to their beds—Michael and Gibby in the right barracks, Wyatt and Christopher in the left.

Most of the campers had fallen into an exhausted state of repose that wasn't exactly sleep. Their eyelids were closed or fluttering, and they seemed to be rocking back and forth in their narrow bunks, drawing their heavy breaths and snoring with an unnerving shrillness.

This would be the last and perhaps most difficult task of the day: to crawl into their bunks and try to sleep in the close company of retarded men. It was as intimate as any of the other duties they'd performed that day. Best not to listen too closely. Or steal a glimpse of the campers' collapsed and unguarded faces. One way for Wyatt to escape was to close his eyes and imagine himself in the showroom of the Salvation Army depot in Jefferson City, the racks of clothing and shelves of small kitchen appliances, all the innumerable objects that, if pictured clearly enough, might lull him to sleep.

And he did sleep, for a while at least. At 3:00 A.M. he woke to Thomas Anwar's rough knuckles grazing his cheek. "Please," Thomas Anwar said. "Fire for my cigarette."

"No, no. Back to bed. Back to bed," Wyatt whispered, and Thomas Anwar gave a slumped bow of resignation and shuffled away.

An hour later another disturbance. Christopher Waterhouse had half-risen from his bunk and was shouting toward the far corner of the barracks. "Back to your beds! Now! Back to your beds!" Ten minutes of relative calm. *"God damn you!"* Christopher Waterhouse cried. He was out of his bunk, stomping up and down the aisle, wild-haired, frantic, utterly unlike the composed young man he'd been at the staff meeting. *"Back to your fucking beds!"* he screamed. His voice had gone hoarse in a yelping, childish way. He stepped toward Wyatt's bunk. "You have any idea what they're doing back there?" he demanded. "Fucking animals. Fucking disgusting," he said. "I don't have to put up with this. I don't have to stay here another minute." He had his clothing and sleeping bag balled under one arm, and he rushed from the barracks out to the porch. The screen door slammed, and he could be heard stomping loudly along the gravel path.

In the corner of the barracks, not far from where Christopher had been sleeping, a group of campers had congregated between bunks. They were standing close together, as men might do in a baseball dugout or the back of a crowded bus.

"Back to bed!" Wyatt demanded of them. He rose and stumbled barefoot down the aisle. Without expecting to, he came upon Leonard Peirpont's bunk. Poor stiff-bodied, wide-eyed Leonard, just a few feet from the congregation of men.

Wyatt reached down and lifted him from his bunk, hoisted him sideways onto his hip, as one might do a large child, and carried Leonard up the aisle and placed him in the bunk beside his own.

"Back to your beds," Wyatt called out.

No acknowledgment from the huddle of men. They'd unfastened their pajama bottoms. In the darkest corner of the barracks they were squeezed together reaching for one another.

He did not have the determination to bully them back to bed. They were disgusting, he told himself, though it wasn't exactly disgust he felt. Rather he was deathly afraid of the evidence being shown to him. This was what the unfortunate of the world made do with. This was their tenderness. This or nothing at all.

Chapter Six

Here was a new fact of parenting for Harriet to consider: the things she would obscure for her son, James, the half-truths and sentimental fabrications he would eventually pay for. Sooner rather than later.

Case in point: he was a powerful magnet for the retarded campers from the state hospital. They saw him and let out long, wailing shrieks—shrieks of amazement, shrieks of ferocious longing. Easy enough to understand their reasons for wanting to be near him. James was small and alert and perfectly formed. He was the child they would never be allowed to conceive or raise. They saw in him a version of their own arrested selves.

All credible explanations. Not one of them mattered when, during the first camp breakfast, Tuesday morning, a gangly female cerebral palsy camper had stood up from a nearby bench, gone into a stumbling run, and seized James as he sat beside Schuller Kindermann at the director's table. One moment the boy had been spooning jelly onto his French toast, the next he was hoisted up and clutched sideways to her hard bosom while she shook her head violently from side to side and let out a keening screech. Harriet, dispensing meds on the other side of the mess hall, handed off her muffin tray to a counselor and came running. Bad enough if James had burst into tears and cried for his mama. Instead, he'd crossed his hands over his face, closed his eyes, and let the rest of his body go slack—a state of surrender agonizing for Harriet to behold.

A counselor and lifeguard had stepped in to help Harriet pry the boy loose. But what an effort it had been, and what a dire impression the cerebral palsy camper had made, with her shrill voice and spastic energy. Afterward Harriet had wanted to sit James down and amend her earlier advice: *Forget their good hearts, honey. If they come for you, race toward the first normal-looking adult you can find.*

Luckily, the boy seemed to intuit this advice without having to be told. At meals he was ready to duck and fold himself beneath the director's table at a moment's notice. If he was playing beneath the apricot trees outside the infirmary, he would carefully track each approaching and departing camper. Whenever a camper broke from the pathway and lurched toward him, he would pivot on his heels and break into a run, a sly little move, almost funny were it not for the boy's terrified concentration and frantic speed.

The yard outside the infirmary was a meeting place of sorts. Counselors used its shaded benches as a way station where their campers could rest a few minutes and slurp water from a cast iron drinking fountain. Maureen and Reggie Boyd sometimes took their morning coffee breaks on those same benches, and soon enough Harriet, eager for camaraderie, set up a small first aid station at the yard's picnic table and treated those who came to her with an assortment of lotions and bandages and stomach remedies. If the problem was more complicated or required disrobing, she would lead her patients inside, but not before she assigned James to sit beside a capable adult guardian.

Usually this person turned out to be Linda Rucker. Solitary, sturdy, hardworking Linda Rucker. She oversaw every significant detail of daily operations, double-checked every schedule, signed every invoice and check. It had taken her just a day to know all the new counselors and an astonishing number of campers by name. For the State Hospital Session, she organized each evening's campwide activity: the parade, the talent show, the camp Olympics, the farewell dance. A sizable portion of her mornings and afternoons was spent in the infirmary yard, on a bench near two gravel pathways, where she did paperwork and chatted with each group of campers as they stopped to rest. Whenever she noticed a counselor at the breaking point, she stepped in to relieve them of their most difficult camper for an hour or two.

For James she'd made possible a rare and considerate privilege. The boy couldn't step inside the gates of the swimming pool without being mobbed and terrified. But from four-forty to five o'clock each afternoon, once the pool had closed and the lifeguard staff got busy with cleaning and maintenance, Linda arranged twenty minutes for James to splash about the shallow end with his kickboard and water wings.

Too bad that most of Linda Rucker's generous acts went unrecognized. She wasn't necessarily loved by her staff. For one thing she didn't have the spry, athletic energy and sunny demeanor of a proper camp director. Perhaps there wasn't a gracious way to describe her physique. Rugged? Bulky? Her legs were straight and thick, her hips square. From the waist up she was remarkably stout, broad in the shoulders and in the arms. She tended to swagger when she walked. She had a slumped way of lifting her head and looking about. But her eyes were a clear and lovely hazel, and their deep intelligence sharpened a face that might otherwise have seemed too wide and dull in its expressions. Women like Linda—women who carried the burden of an unladylike demeanor—were often the ones you saw working in the back corridors of warehouses and restaurants and nursing homes. They didn't often rise to the position of camp program director.

On the shaded benches outside the infirmary, there was time and opportunity for Harriet and Linda to trade, somewhat stingily at first, a few details of their lives. A confidence seemed to be springing up between them, perhaps the makings of a real friendship. A small surprise to learn that Linda had started at camp eighteen summers earlier as a kitchen girl and worked her way up. For the past ten years she'd stayed on during the fall and winter and spring, when the grounds were deserted and Schuller and Sandie Kindermann had relocated to their town house in St. Louis. During the off-season, she kept the office open and twice a day loaded the tractor with hay and grain and took it out to the horses in the pasture. In the coldest stretches of winter these same horses had to be corralled and in the stable by nightfall. The next morning she'd be up by five to make sure their water supply hadn't frozen.

"Winter," she said. "My favorite time of year."

There wasn't any sarcasm in her voice or, more important, in the direct bearing of her gaze. Apparently she meant it. She was a woman who'd prefer to be up before sunrise in January chipping away at a water trough with an ice pick, the long off-season her reward for all the unacknowledged work she put in during the summer months.

"But don't you get lonely?" Harriet asked.

The question made Linda Rucker sigh deeply and screw one corner of her mouth shut. She didn't at all appear offended, but she didn't reply to Harriet, either. *Don't you get lonely?* The sigh, the crimped grin seemed to say there was no single or simple way to answer.

But the next afternoon, sitting opposite Harriet at the picnic table, Linda Rucker, who was gluing together award medals for that evening's camp Olympics, raised her head and said, "It's not as if I go the whole winter without seeing another soul. There's always the town of Ellsinore twelve miles away. There's a place there for pizza and a saloon I like to go to on Friday nights."

Harriet nodded thoughtfully and went back to sorting meds.

"I'm known in Ellsinore," Linda said. "I have a friend I meet at the bar. Sometimes this friend of mine will come stay with me here." She smiled wryly. "A gentleman caller."

"I see," said Harriet. So that explained something significant about Linda Rucker, the aura of experience that hung over her. But you'd expect the opposite. You'd expect that she'd be the sort of person who would close herself off, protectively, from the world of love and sex. Instead she seemed entirely aware of the various lies and disappointments and stolen pleasures involved in that world. When she'd said *gentleman caller,* she'd done so in a voice weighted with both fondness and trepidation.

Some things, personal things, Harriet was willing to offer in return. The very fact of James made it clear she'd had her own experience with a gentleman caller. At the time she'd been a first-year student at the state university in Durham, North Carolina, and she'd held a work-study job in which she helped shuttle supplies some thirty miles outside Durham to the university's agricultural research farm. She could tell Linda Rucker, truthfully enough, that her gentleman caller had been a recently married graduate student with whom she'd worked. He'd driven a large gray university van. It was in the back of this van where he'd done his calling.

She didn't bother mentioning that he was a white man. Linda Rucker could figure that out. She could know the bare outline of Harriet's story and jump to her own conclusions: Harriett had been young and naïve. The gentleman caller had seduced her. Once she was pregnant, he'd abandoned Harriet and returned to his unsuspecting wife. All of this was generally true, though not specifically. Did it matter now, six years after the fact, that they'd loved each other? Maybe it didn't matter. She had to use all her powers of forgiveness to remember that her gentleman caller was modest and kind and very smart. For a married man, he was surprisingly unworldly. He blushed sometimes if she looked at him too directly. How strange and wonderful it was to have a man crave her opinions the way he did. He'd say, "I've been wondering what you'd think of this all weekend, Harriet. I've been itching to tell you." He brought her small, perfectly chosen gifts, unaware of their implications. In the end, though, he needed a little encouragement from Harriet to take the first step. They found a secluded corner of the university farm where they could park and talk and hold one another. Initially they'd decided only to bend the rules of monogamy. But, of course, their resolve didn't last. Several times they were hasty and reckless in their lovemaking. Five months after they'd begun she was pregnant.

The fallout, for Harriet Foster, was nearly unbearable. She'd had to withdraw from the university and return home. In her hometown the Fosters were known as a moderate and accepting family. Yet once she was pregnant, she learned that this leniency toward others came from a belief in their own impeccable behavior. Her mother assumed—falsely—that they were being shunned by the community. Outwardly her father seemed unfazed by the news. But his misery had turned inward. After a fifteen-year abstinence, he was found drunk and inconsolable one afternoon in the family garage.

Two months before James was born Harriet moved to St. Louis and into the home of her aunt Marie, whom the rest of the family had pegged as moody and lonesome. They'd misjudged her. Marie was only irritable when visiting North Carolina. In St. Louis she led a lively and successful life. She had a large house and a wide array of interesting friends. In Aunt Marie's neighborhood there were other young black women who shared Harriet's situation, which was to say that, like Harriet, they were pregnant and single and angry. They made elaborate plans to punish the men who'd abandoned them.

Unlike Harriet, they were scalding, even violent, in their anger, and yet she carried the notion, rightly or not, that her betrayal was somehow more painful, more personal than theirs.

James, when he arrived, was a thousand times better than any notion she had of herself as a wronged woman. He was such a good boy. But it wasn't easy to explain or describe his goodness. She might say that as a person he ran deep and true. He'd almost certainly grow up to be a thoughtful and generous young man. Whatever this quality was, it was neither simple nor common. And to see it present in her son brought her a radiant new happiness.

She'd reconciled herself to the fact that her gentleman caller's suffering had been minor compared to her own. By now he and his wife might have a child of their own. She wouldn't begrudge them if they did.

Of course it took years of living and raising James to accomplish this perspective. One thing still troubled her. Before leaving Durham she'd discovered something significant about her gentleman caller's wife. During the course of the affair, he'd said very little about her except that she was an overworked and driven medical student. He never mentioned she was black—a black woman, a black wife. It was still a rarity to be a white man with a black wife, to be part of an interracial marriage, even in a North Carolina college town. He'd chosen to keep this crucial fact about his wife to himself.

But knowing it distorted everything Harriet thought she understood about her gentleman caller, especially his reasons for loving her. It was the part of her story she always kept secret. Six years later it still had the power to unsettle her.

On Wednesday a cool front passed over the Missouri Ozarks and graced Kindermann Forest with the season's first lovely June afternoon. The glaring heat lifted. An eighty-four-degree, low-humidity crispness fell across the valley. Sunlight, warm and pure, shivered the dogwood leaves and made the cedar buildings and gravel pathways appear soft-edged and perfectly arranged.

Such fine weather raised the counselors' spirits. Harriet's, too. Once siesta ended and the campers and counselors were set loose from their cabins, she put a note on the infirmary door and headed south across the meadow. But she stopped halfway to consider her surroundings. It really was a beautiful place. A summer camp. A kingdom unto itself. There wasn't a single television in any of the camp buildings—Mr. Kindermann wouldn't allow it—and therefore no news of Unabombers and mad cow disease and African civil war. The world was elsewhere. Harriet had to concentrate to locate it.

She pressed on, into the yawning mouth of the woods, along the gravel pathway bordered by railroad ties, up the walkway to Cabin Four and through the screen door, where Linda Rucker stood waiting beside an impossibly fat and entirely placid woman named Ms. Peacock. The other residents of Cabin Four—some two dozen campers and five female counselors—had been sent away, most of them to the swimming pool.

It had been decided that Ms. Peacock, the obese camper who'd forced her counselor to the bathroom stall floor and sat on her, should have a proper shower during her time at camp. At the moment Ms. Peacock, eyelids half-closed, was swaying to and fro on her heels. She breathed through her nose in long, slow draughts of air. Was she deeply relaxed or asleep on her feet? Either way she was an exemplary patient, easy to lead into the latrine's shower bay, unperturbed when her expansive sundress was tugged over her head and her sagging underwear fell to the floor.

But the spray of water across Ms. Peacock's freckled back sent her into a frenzy. Her eyes flew open wide. She reached for them with her meaty hands. "No, no, no, no, no," she cried. "No. You. Won't." Her voice, clear and exacting, was an instrument of authority. "You will not," she insisted. "You will not." Linda and Harriet blinked at one another in surprise. It was as if they were being chastised by someone with a lucid mind and enough administrative power to have them fired. They wetted sponges in soapy water and began a lunging dance in which they washed under Ms. Peacock's enormous arms and hanging belly and hips, between her legs. Then they doused her with buckets of clear water. She screamed until the water rolled off her and whatever it was that had been angry and *awake* in Ms. Peacock shrank away. She was herself again, an obese woman—listless, slovenly, more than a little sad. She allowed them to pat her dry with towels and dress her in fresh underwear and a sundress.

Then they led her along the pathway to the swimming pool and told her to sit in the shade of the shower house. Ms. Peacock, who held no grudges, did just as they asked, sat with her back against the shower house, licking the callused skin on her knuckles and watching her counselor and fellow campers slap a beach ball back and forth across the shallow end of the pool.

Harriet waited at the gate while Linda Rucker went about her director's duties: a quick tour of the pool deck, a sober appraisal of the maintenance schedule. She chatted awhile with Christopher Waterhouse, who sat alert in his lifeguard's chair, his eyes shielded by Wayfarer sunglasses, his face—and presumably his gaze—trained on the deep-end swimmers. Now and then he tilted his ear toward Linda and nodded in recognition of whatever she'd said. Afterward she climbed the stairs and joined Harriet at the gate, where they stood looking out at the whole of the pool, its rowdy swimmers and shrieking energy, its waves of sloshing water.

"Harriet," Linda said. She seemed to have readied her thoughts with exceptional care. "How about our two lifeguards? What do you . . . *think* of them?"

Harriet shrugged in reply. She wasn't at all sure what she was being asked to evaluate. "They're good," she offered. "So far they seem to know what they're doing."

"And what about Christopher Waterhouse?"

Again there was an air of uncertainty. Was she being asked about his competence as a lifeguard? Or was it something else? An invitation to crack wise about his good looks, his sexiness? Because Christopher Waterhouse was probably the most attractive male member of the staff. For one thing he had strong and shapely legs, swimmer's legs, masculine in their way, but really not so very different from a female dancer's or woman athlete's legs. He seemed to like sitting above everyone in his lifeguard's chair and stretching those legs out in front of him, flexing his handsome ankles and feet. To watch him do this was, for Harriet, one small perk of coming to the pool each afternoon with James. You could see the direction Christopher Waterhouse's handsomeness was heading—toward a rougher and manlier presence. But this summer there was still a fresh-faced, boyish edge to his looks, something that Harriet found interesting but that the white girl counselors of Kindermann Forest might easily swoon over. If there was room to speculate about Christopher Waterhouse, it was to wonder which of the girl counselors he would end up partnered with. The easy assumption was that it would be his fellow lifeguard Marcy Bittman. The two of them were tan and elegantly shaped in a way that placed them in a category above the other counselors. In all likelihood they'd wind up together.

"He seems all right to me," Harriet said.

"Do you trust him?"

She could only say that she had no reason *not* to trust him. At the mess hall he'd been the first to jump to his feet and help rescue James from the grip of the cerebral palsy camper. For that act alone she'd give him the benefit of the doubt.

They left the gate and walked the tunneling pathway out into the meadow, and Linda, who'd been studying the progress of her feet as she walked, stopped and folded her arms across her broad chest. She squinted in concentration. "About Christopher," she said. "I have a few things—well, maybe just one thing—that worries me."

"What's that?"

Linda Rucker offered up a rueful half smile. "I don't even know if I can describe it. All I can say is that there's something about him, his sincerity maybe, that I don't quite trust."

"But you don't know anything about him for certain?" Harriet said.

"I don't, no. It's just a feeling I have. And I had this feeling the instant I met him, even before he opened his mouth and we had our first conversation. I don't know what it is about him, but I have an intuition that he's not a good person. And so I'm wondering, Harriet, if you have the same intuition."

This wasn't coercion, not exactly. Still, if Harriet wasn't careful, she could wilt under this delicate pressure. She said, "The few times I've been around Christopher he's been fine. Helpful. So he seems all right to me."

"Does he?"

"Yes."

From Linda a complicated response: she bowed her head and weighed the answer given to her, and then she pretended—Harriet was sure it was pretense—to reach some private understanding, a revised opinion of Christopher Waterhouse. Her expression brightened. "Well, this is good for me to hear," she said. "It's really just a feeling I had. Thank you, Harriet," she said, her voice cheery but unemphatic, as if they'd just met and were bringing to a close their very first conversation "I'll see you around," Linda Rucker said and headed off, in her heavy-footed way, toward the Kindermann Forest camp office.

But what did Harriet know about other people's private natures? Their deepest intentions? Her family had once considered her a sound judge of character. (They'd changed this opinion once she'd become pregnant.) But perhaps it was true. It also had to be said—though she would never say such a thing to Linda Rucker—that she was less confident in her appraisal of white people. Easier somehow to recognize a black schemer or narcissist or Good Samaritan than it was to distinguish their white counterparts. With white people the motives were more deeply buried, the disguises less familiar.

She knew certain things, however. As camp nurse, she sometimes opened the infirmary file cabinet and read the staff health forms for no better reason than the itch of curiosity. And she dispensed medication to the staff. It was a strictly held camp rule that employees of Kindermann Forest turn over all their medications to the nurse. (Far too dangerous to have bottles of pills lying about the cabins for children or state hospital campers to discover.) So the counselors came to Harriet each day for their aspirin and Benadryl and laxatives. Pretty Veronica Yordy used prescription ointment for an odd, yellowing toenail fungus. Marcy Bittman and Carrie Reinkenmeyer and Emily Boehler and Ellen Swinderman arrived each morning for their birth control pills, but so, too, did a member of the Lonesome Three, a deeply shy, spindly, and mournful-faced young woman. Was it a matter of controlling her menstruation, or was this homely young woman hoping for love?

Wyatt Huddy came to see her after dinner each evening for his stomach medication—a stool softener. He preferred to wait on the steps rather than enter the infirmary. He was invariably shy in her presence, more so, Harriet felt, than with any other staff member at camp. Why should this be? Perhaps it was the fact of her race. But it might also be that he sensed her deep interest in him and backed away as a result.

As it happened, she knew the name and terms of his disorder without the need to consult his health form. Apert syndrome, a genetic disease in which the bones of the skull fused shut and gave the head and face a distorted appearance. There were other effects as well, though one of them wasn't, as people expected, a diminished IQ. She knew this not because of nursing school or any research she'd done on genetic disorders, of which there were thousands. She knew because a family in her North Carolina hometown had twin boys—one with Apert syndrome, one without. She'd see them about town and, from a distance, she'd dreamed up a sad life for the Apert syndrome boy.

Then she came to know both boys. As a high school junior, she was asked to babysit for Taylor and Eddie. Taylor, the afflicted one, had a pointy crown to his head and a sunken, uneven quality to his eyes and nose. But at age three, what did it really matter? His appearance might be striking at first, yet soon enough you saw the beauty and ordinariness of a young boy. Taylor, it turned out, was bright and eager and more outgoing than his twin, Eddie, who tended to stand back and learn from his brother's successes and failures. The first day Harriet had arrived at their home the boys were out in the backyard trying to shape the scattered remains of a March snow into a convincing snowman. After an hour of play she'd brought them inside, removed their jackets and mittens. Taylor's hands took her by surprise. The index, middle, and ring fingers were fused together like the three-digit hands of a stuffed animal or cartoon character. She was sentimental about those hands. She liked to cup them in her own hands and feel the contours of those fused fingers. A few months later, when he turned four, a surgeon separated his fused fingers into five better-functioning but decidedly less beautiful digits.

Now, each evening when she placed pills in Wyatt Huddy's hands, she saw that he had undergone the same procedure.

Among the counselors of Kindermann Forest, Harriet noticed a shift in morale, a lightening of attitude. They were not so moody. Not so ready to throw up their hands in disgust or defeat. They'd been on duty seventy-two hours and were showing signs of a wry humor and toughened nonchalance, as if in the course of three days they'd witnessed in their state hospital campers the full range of unruly behavior.

In The Sanctuary, where Harriet went each afternoon to buy a cold bottle of Coca-Cola, she came upon off-duty counselors doing boisterous imitations of the campers they cared for. Perhaps the most celebrated and oft-impersonated state hospital camper was Mr. Terrence J. Stottlemeir. Mr. Stottlemeir was an odd case. Just fifty-seven years old and he seemed to have lost his mind. His arms and hands were in a wild and constant state of agitation, darting up out of his lap, flailing about. For this reason the counselors had begun calling him "the mad drummer." He looked, with his thin, regal face and balding pate, like a straight and narrow tax accountant who'd let himself go to seed. His cheeks were thick with stubble. (It was hard to shave a man so intent on slapping anyone who tried to assist him.) He cursed loudly and with an eccentric vocabulary. Everyone at Kindermann Forest considered him the camp's crotchety old man.

Any decent impersonation began by mimicking Mr. Stottlemeir's single rich expression—part outrage, part horror at the ruined world. Then the cursing: *God damn you to hell eternal. God damn you, I say. God damn you. I'll kick you, you jizzy bastard. I'll kick you shitless.*

From there the counselors spun out improvised skits: a rock band named Stottlemeir and the Jizzy Bastards. Or an incensed Stottlemeir sharing a White House dinner with President Clinton. *God damn you, Billy Boy. God damn you to hell eternal.* Or Grampa Stottlemeir reading storybooks to five-year-olds at the local library. *God damn you, spoon. God damn you, room. God damn you, cow jumping over the moon . . .*

Was it cruel? An observer who stumbled into camp might think so. Harriet was less sure. Maybe after a long day of close proximity to the retarded, the counselors needed this release. They brought themselves to tears with these skits. They collapsed onto The Sanctuary's dusty couches, clutching their sides and howling. The best lines they repeated in every corner of camp, especially in the presence of Wayne Kesterson, Mr. Stottlemeir's counselor. Poor Wayne. By now it was public knowledge that he'd be sentenced in the fall for marijuana possession. His days were numbered. Hard to picture Wayne behind bars. He was such a gangly, forgetful, good-natured young man. Mr. Stottlemeir treated him with particular scorn. If Wayne got too near, Mr. Stottlemeir would shout, *Don't touch me, you stinking puddle of piss!* Of course the counselors found this richly hilarious: *stinking puddle of piss,* an insult Mr. Stottlemeir seemed to reserve exclusively for Wayne. Naturally, it caught on.

Hands off that last pancake, Wayne, you stinking puddle of piss.

Wayne, your mother called. She wants you to remember to wear your clean jammies and to never forget—you're a stinking puddle of piss.

He laughed along with them, gamely, merrily. It was pleasure, maybe, for Wayne to see those around him roused into such high spirits. He wasn't the true brunt of the joke after all. Mr. Stottlemeir was. They were laughing at his crotchety demeanor, at the clever mimicry.

But one afternoon in the infirmary Harriet was audience to the real thing. She'd had to give Mr. Stottlemeir a dose of Benadryl for an outbreak of hives. To do that she and Wayne had needed to pin Mr. Stottlemeir in a chair and hold down his flailing arms. The scalding look he gave: all the features of his face, once elegant and now mangy, were pinched into an expression of intense hate—a hatred that felt long-held and personal and aimed solely at Wayne Kesterson.

"You stupid knob," Mr. Stottlemeir said, wet-lipped and sputtering. "Get your filthy hands off me, you stinking puddle of piss!"

To this, mild-mannered, hapless Wayne Kesterson lowered his head and shuddered.

Certainly Harriet had seen her fair share of startling behavior. She'd had campers shriek out strange songs during examinations. One gentleman had crumpled to the floor and played dead while she bandaged his scraped knee. Another woman, in the middle of an oral exam, had leaned forward and wetly licked Harriet's cheek.

The most remarkable thing said to her had come from Leonard Peirpont. His counselor, Wyatt Huddy, had noticed Leonard walking slower and with a more pronounced limp than usual and had brought him to the infirmary yard. She'd taken Leonard inside and removed his shoes and socks. An easy enough problem to diagnose; his toenails had grown long and sharp. She trimmed them and then washed and dried his feet. She put his socks and shoes on and helped him stand.

"Better?" she asked.

He stood gripping her forearm, swaying atop his stiff legs. There was always a look of wide-eyed surprise about him. At the moment his amazement seemed especially acute. He studied her intently, leaned close. "How 'bout I take you back to Higbee with me," he said.

Higbee? This may or may not have been Leonard's hometown. The funniness of the name and the intensity with which he said it made her laugh. "All right," she said. "Let's go to Higbee."

"You can come stay in my house and be my little blackie."

She was too stunned to do anything but blink in surprise. If only there was another black employee at camp. She'd seek them out and tell them of this offer. To be Leonard Peirpont's little blackie. With the right black person, she could pass an entire evening repeating this remark and laughing until she cried. (No good sharing it with Linda Rucker or any of the white counselors, since they'd first have to register their shock and disapproval. To them it would be a jolting surprise. Imagine that. Leonard Peirpont had been racist before he injured his brain.) What was more amazing, at least to Harriet, was that he'd been looking at her rapturously when he said it. *You can come stay in my house and be my little blackie.* She doubted she'd hear another offer this tender all summer long.

Chapter Seven

If he had rested well the night before and if the mood so struck him, Schuller liked to set out early from his cottage, a veil of soft light and dampness hanging over the countryside, and walk the camp's gravel roadway from where it began at the weedy front gate and slipped past the office and open meadow and eventually ran beside the infirmary and mess hall, on past the maintenance shed and parking lot (the two unsightly regions of Kindermann Forest), and then into a long, lovely stretch of cedar and elm trees before dead-ending at the horse stables. That was the journey's reward: to lean against the wood fence and watch the old mares stomping about the water trough, snorting, raking the ground with their cracked hooves, a liveliness that would be hard to locate once they'd been blanketed and saddled for the day.

This morning, Thursday morning, walking back from the stables, he happened to survey the parking lot and notice a green pickup truck with a black camper shell. At the moment the rear hatch of the shell was opening so that someone—just a figure from this distance—could climb unsteadily over the tailgate and step down onto the pavement. It was just after 6:30 A.M. The figure stretched: a male figure given that he strolled a few yards to the edge of the lot and peed standing up into a line of scrubby bushes. Afterward he plodded down onto the gravel roadway.

That's where Schuller had paused to meet him. The figure turned out to be the lifeguard Christopher Waterhouse. His clothes and hair were sleep-tousled. No need to ask what he was up to. The implication was perfectly clear: Christopher had passed the night in the back of his pickup truck rather than in the cabin to which he'd been assigned.

At least he didn't try to pretend otherwise. He bowed his head a moment, a boyish admission that he'd been caught bending the rules. Then, much more cheerfully, he wished Schuller a good morning. "I'm starving," he said. "Any chance we'll have biscuits and gravy for breakfast?"

"No chance whatsoever," Schuller said. Among other fastidious habits, he was a careful reader of the weekly camp menu.

"How 'bout hash browns then? That'd be my second choice. With fried—"

Schuller brought up his raised hand until it was just inches from Christopher Waterhouse's face. Sometimes, when addressing the young, a gesture like this could save Schuller valuable time.

"Why is it, do you think, Christopher, that we ask our counselors to stay in the cabins at night?"

Instead of a reasonable answer, Christopher Waterhouse bit his lower lip and brooded.

"Because we need you there," Schuller said. "Your presence in the cabins at night, whether you're sleeping or not, is every bit as important as the work you do for us during the day."

"I understand."

"Do you?"

"Yes."

"Then can I take it that we have an agreement?" Schuller said. "You'll be sleeping in the cabins from now on, because if not . . ."

But the young man's attention had drifted up and beyond Schuller, a rather dreamy scanning of the treetops and pale morning light.

"Christopher?"

"Do you know what goes on in the cabins at night, Mr. Kindermann?"

"I know it's not always pleasant. It's difficult to sleep, I'm sure."

"The men in the cabin . . . I mean the retarded men, sneak out of their bunks and congregate in the back of the sleeping barracks. They get together back there, four or five of them, and then . . . they have sex with one another."

Until now Schuller had anticipated each of Christopher Waterhouse's remarks. Not this one. What a horrible picture it painted in his mind. More distressing yet, the very thing he had gone to such lengths to rid Kindermann Forest of had returned in a different and worse form. "Oh, Lord," he said. "Are you sure?"

"The other counselor in my barracks, Wyatt Huddy, can back me up."

"Then this is *awful*," Schuller said. "This is . . . You should have come to us the very first time it happened, you and Wyatt. We can do something about this."

"I don't see how," Christopher Waterhouse said, almost sadly. "They're more determined than we are. It's not like we can stay awake all night."

"We can separate the ones who . . . the instigators. If we have to, we'll send them back to the state hospital. But we can't begin to fix a problem like this, any problem for that matter, unless we know what's happening. You really should have come talk to us sooner."

For the moment Christopher Waterhouse seemed willing to accept a small part of the blame. His hair was uncombed, his face unshaven. If he had an answer for Schuller, he appeared to be assembling it in private. "It's not always easy . . . ," he said at last. He shook his head. "From our perspective, it's not easy to know if a problem like this will be taken seriously."

"Well, for *heaven's sake* why wouldn't it?"

"Because from our perspective, the perspective of the counselors, it doesn't always seem like things here at camp are in control."

Schuller blinked in surprise. "How so?" he asked. "How are things *not* in control?"

"From the moment we arrived there didn't seem to be any planning or any preparation. It's something we felt right away, and, well, some of the counselors, more than a few, were pretty upset about it. I had to talk to them and get them to calm down. It's better now, but that's just because we're all starting to get used to the way things are."

"The way things are," Schuller repeated, skeptically.

"I'm not talking about you, Mr. Kindermann. If I understand how things work around here, you're in charge, but you don't do the planning and the preparation."

Schuller pretended to consider this. Nearby, there were squirrels running in the tree branches and tiny finches hopping along the railroad ties that bordered the gravel roadway. He could actually hear the soft scrape of their clawed toes against the ties. He said, "This has been an unusual summer for us, Christopher. We haven't been able to plan and prepare as much as we would like. I'm sure you know why. The word must have gotten around by now. Are you telling me we made a mistake by letting our first counselor staff go? It may be worth remembering that you have a position here at camp because of that decision."

A small pleasure to see Christopher Waterhouse squeezed by an argument he did not anticipate. He ran a hand through his tangled hair. "I'm very glad to be here, Mr. Kindermann. I really am. But when it comes to something that serious—people having a naked pool party, or what's going on in the cabins now—then maybe me and the other counselors need to feel like someone's in charge."

It was almost enough to make Schuller smile wryly in appreciation. To be offered this frank appraisal, one that carried with it a prickly thorn of criticism. And to know that it had come from a young man who'd been on the job less than four days and had already broken an important camp rule.

And yet an appraisal worth considering.

"These are weighty topics, Christopher. But they're not part of the discussion I intend to have with you right now. So let's make it very simple. Do the things you're expected to do. Or leave camp and find another job for the summer."

"Yes. All right. But it's—"

"Now go to your cabin."

For Christopher Waterhouse, there was a moment of wavering. Beneath his baleful expression you could sense a carefully weighed calculation taking place—a wish, maybe, to amend his comments. Or to press his point further.

Wisely, he turned on his heels and did as he was told.

And so Schuller returned from his walk to a camp office and cottage made shabbier by what he'd learned from Christopher Waterhouse. It was too much really.

Retarded men pressed together like animals in some dark corner of the cabins. You couldn't shake such a picture from your head; some scenarios were so appalling they sprang to life and crashed lumbering and wretched through every neat boundary of your mind.

In truth he'd always held an ambivalent view of the state hospital campers. Surely other members of the Kindermann Forest staff were of two minds on the matter. But who could argue against it? The idea was generous and moral and Christian. If you had any imagination at all, you could picture the institutions where these retarded men and women lived out their thin lives and know what two weeks outside in the natural world might mean to them.

It had, for Kindermann Forest, a very practical meaning as well. The past decade had been an era of declining enrollment at camp. It hadn't always been so. Throughout the seventies and much of the eighties, they'd run ten straight weeks of children's camp, from mid-June right to the end of August. But in the last ten years they'd begun cutting two-week sessions from the end of the summer. Ten weeks to eight weeks to six weeks. Seven years ago Schuller's brother, Sandie, had brokered a deal with the state hospital to bring retarded adults to camp for a two-week session. It wasn't a moneymaker (or a loser for that matter), but it did lengthen the dwindling camp season by two weeks.

Still, though, when Schuller saw these campers each summer shambling about the gravel pathways or clustered outside the cabins doing their manic cigarette smoking, or when he heard of the awful mess they left in the bathrooms for the cleaning women, he tended to forget the act of charity and feel as if a purer quality of Kindermann Forest—its pristineness maybe—had been offered up in sacrifice.

He sat behind his director's desk and waited for Linda Rucker.

They had fallen into the habit of calling the fifteen minutes they spent together each morning a meeting, but in truth it was mostly the ritual of coffee and a chance for Linda to share with Schuller whatever details regarding the day-to-day running of camp she saw fit. To her credit she didn't burden him with problems whose solutions were either simple or obvious. If a horse had not eaten in twenty-four hours, the vet was called in. If one of the kitchen girls quit or didn't show up for work, an employment ad was placed in the Ellsinore *Gazette*. Hard sometimes for Schuller to explain to outsiders his precise role at camp. He was retired. Or semiretired. In most instances camp business went forward without his participation.

Through the office picture window he could see an otherwise pleasing stretch of the camp roadway and a few older cottages, mainly The Sanctuary, from which Linda Rucker had emerged and was strolling toward the office with a bundle of yesterday's mail under one arm. She nodded to Schuller upon entering the office and went straight to the coffeepot. There she poured and sugared her coffee and then sat before the director's desk, her cup balanced on one knee, the mail in a sorted pile on her lap. It wouldn't be fair to declare Linda Rucker a peculiar person. But often, like this morning, she sat for long minutes in Schuller's presence without speaking a single word. Wasn't that peculiar?

He resolved not to speak until she'd lifted her gaze from the stack of mail. Finally she did. "Linda," he said. "The men of Cabin Two, the retarded campers, are having sex with one another." He paused to allow Linda her moment of distress: a low gasp, a straightening of her slumped posture or, perhaps, a sudden, sharp creak from the wheels of her office chair. "From what I've heard," he continued, "they wait till the lights go out at night and then congregate in the back of the barracks. A group of them."

Again he waited for a startled reaction. Sometimes, in the sullen cast of her expression and in her closed demeanor, she reminded Schuller of a man; not men in general, but a particular type of stubborn and inward tradesman that was somehow more numerous here in the Missouri Ozarks. Occasionally these tradesmen were called in to do work at camp. There wasn't anything chatty or charming about these men. Nothing about them invited you into their lives.

And yet, like Linda, they were meticulous and extremely knowledgeable about their work. (Whatever her faults, she was not, as Christopher Waterhouse implied, unprepared.) But they did lack something significant: a certain openness or personal allure that made you glad you'd hired them.

"What kind?" she asked.

"What?"

She took a sip of her coffee. "What kind of sex?"

"I don't know exactly. I don't care to know. Homosexual sex. Beyond that, does it really matter?"

She eased back in her chair and released a long, ponderous sigh. It might have been one of several patient gestures she used exclusively with him. She said, "I've seen the men be very . . . affectionate, very physical with one another sometimes. Same with the women. So that's one thing, isn't it? But it's another if they're taking things further than that."

"I believe it has gone further. The counselors of Cabin Two say it has."

"Well, that's a big problem then. We'll have to make changes right away."

"Yes, we will. I'm wondering if we can figure out who the offenders are and send them back to the state hospital."

"I'd rather try separating them first," Linda said.

He sighed. By *try*, of course, she meant that this was the solution she'd settled on. Separation. No doubt she was ready to argue stubbornly if necessary. If he wanted to have it his way, a strenuous effort would have to be made.

"All right," he said. "Separation then."

"I hate to send anyone back. And at least when it's between men we don't have to worry about anyone getting pregnant."

He would have to let this remark pass. But it irked him nonetheless. There was a reasonable chance she knew his strong opinion on this matter. "The main thing," he said, "is that the counselors understand this absolutely can't go on anymore. I don't want there to be any doubt in their minds. We're taking the problem seriously. We're in charge of things. Both of us. I'd like to gather them all together and talk about it directly."

"I don't know that we have to do that, Schuller."

"Oh, I'm sure we do. As soon as we can arrange it. And I'd like you to talk to the counselors of Cabin Two before then. Right after breakfast is over," he said. "Start with Christopher Waterhouse. Figure out which campers need to be separated."

"Why Christopher Waterhouse?"

"He's the one who let me know. I ran into him this morning. He's so put off by what's happening in the cabins at night that he's been sleeping in the back of his pickup truck."

Here now, at last, were the signs of distress he'd been looking for: she tightened her grip on her coffee cup and shifted forward all at once so that the metal wheels of her chair let out a piercing squawk.

"What?" Schuller asked.

"I wish we were getting word of this from someone else. Not Christopher Waterhouse. I'm not sure about him, Schuller."

"What exactly does that mean?"

She shrugged. "I don't know what to think of him yet."

"We have quite a few new counselors here at camp. Are you saying you already have an opinion about each of them?"

"Yes," she said. "Mostly, I do. I know enough not to worry too much about them. But Christopher Waterhouse . . ." She grinned as if masking a pain prickly and familiar. "Christopher applied for a lifeguard position last spring. We didn't call him in for an interview. He never made it that far and I couldn't remember why. So I dug out his application yesterday. We didn't interview him because his references didn't check out. He only gave us one. Not even a name. Just his university, Southeast Missouri State, and a general phone number. I remember calling and speaking to the university operator. Christopher Waterhouse is or had been a student there. One of ten thousand. No way for her to put me in touch with anyone who knew him."

"And?" Schuller said. "So?"

"I'm just saying I wish we could speak to someone who knows him."

"He's not the first Kindermann Forest employee to leave lines blank on his application. I'm sure of that."

"My main worry," she said. She appeared to be choosing her words with exceptional care. "What worries me, Schuller, is that he may be a very selfish and destructive person. The very worst kind to have working at camp."

"And what do you think we should do about this worry you have, Linda?"

He didn't much care for the look she gave him, its seriousness, its open appeal.

"You think we should let Christopher Waterhouse go based on a bad feeling you have about him?"

Until this point she'd been leaning forward in her chair, her eyes sharp and features tense. She wet her lips and sighed and, after turning her unhappy gaze across the room, focused on the deep polish of the director's desk. She said, "If you're asking the question seriously, then I'd say, yes, we should fire him. You said he spent at least one night away from the cabins, didn't he? That would be enough to terminate him and get him out of camp as soon as possible."

What could he say? He was in no small part astounded by her reaction. "That strikes me . . . I have to say, Linda, that strikes me as an extreme reaction. An overreaction."

"We've fired people for less," she said.

"I hope you're not trying to compare your bad feeling about Christopher Waterhouse with the drinking and trespassing and stupidity that began our summer."

To this no answer. She had gone into a quiet sulk, and after a moment she rose from her chair and turned toward the coffee machine.

"Linda?" he said. Unfortunately, there were times when he had to step away from his role as retired or semiretired director and assert himself more directly. "I'll say it again. I hope you're not—"

"No," she said, her back to him. "There's no comparison."

That, of course, was part of the problem of working relationships that went on for years; eventually they became as contentious—and as sustaining—as family relations. With Linda Rucker some of the blame for her contentiousness could be laid at Schuller's and Sandie's feet. They'd indulged her. In the last decade they'd come to overrely on Linda as program director and winter caretaker. Like family, they'd grown used to the sight and sound and everyday fact of her, and they'd overlooked the compartments within her private life that had sharp corners and the power to startle.

Several years back, two and half years to be precise, in the off-season, they'd gotten a glimpse into one of these compartments. It began with an out-of-the-blue phone call that reached Schuller and Sandie in their St. Louis home, a two-story redbrick town house in an elegant and pristinely kept neighborhood known as St. Louis Hills. It was early Saturday morning in March. At the time they were both active and in good health—Sandie, too, a fit, lucid man of seventy-five—and immersed in the world of their choosing, which is to say that they were in their town house basement, perched on rolling metal stools, inching their way around a giant wood platform twice the size of a Ping-Pong table. On the platform was a sprawling model railroad set, backed by a rolling pastureland and set with roads and sidewalks and all manner of miniature homes and buildings, including a model-size baseball park, the tiny mesh-wire fence of which Schuller and Sandie were painting with thin, little brushes and careful daubs of silver paint. The basement phone rang. The call was from Officer David Pressy, chief of Ellsinore, Missouri's, three-man police department. He had astounding news.

Linda Rucker had been arrested and had spent the night in the holding cell of the Ellsinore Police Station. She was waiting for someone—she had no dependable relatives—to pay her eight-hundred-dollar bond so that she could be released.

Schuller, who'd answered the phone, passed along this information to Sandie. Afterward they set down their paintbrushes and stared at one another dumbfounded.

Then they withdrew eight hundred in cash from their bank and set out in their Impala station wagon for the town of Ellsinore. It was a cold and molted gray morning. The highway on which they traveled, an embanked interstate, offered views of other people's scattered backyards, their stuffed and rusting storage sheds, their listing playground equipment. A first-time traveler to the state might mistake all this for wintry, midwestern dreariness, but they wouldn't see, as Schuller did, the satisfying openness of the countryside and, farther south, the rolling hills and winding, tree-bordered two-lane highways that led to the towns of Farmington and Arcadia and eventually Ellsinore, with its single stoplight and fading main street, its police station housed in a modest cinder-block building.

They'd had dealings with Officer Pressy in the past and found him, on the whole, to be fair-minded and honest. A man of tidy habits and mild temperament, he donned his glasses and read for them, in measured voice, the charges against Linda Rucker: harassment and trespassing. "It's worth adding," he said to Schuller, "that Ms. Rucker was very *nearly* charged with resisting arrest." This was the extent of what Officer Pressy was willing to divulge.

They paid her bond. They waited. Twenty minutes later Linda Rucker entered the station waiting room, where she seemed, to Schuller, to have adopted the clothing and quaint manners of another person, a woman whose look, though eerily similar to that of Linda Rucker, came from a different well of experience. This other woman wore a wide black dress and a dark gray winter coat with a fur collar.

Her feet were squeezed into a pair of maroon pumps. She'd applied makeup to her full chin and cheeks and especially her eyes and, even after a night spent in jail, her made-up face looked, if not exactly nice, then at least tastefully done. All of this was remarkable and strange.

On the ride to Kindermann Forest she sat in the backseat of the station wagon, her face to the window, respectfully interested in the passing scenery. They asked if she was hungry, and she said, no, she wasn't. Coffee then? they asked. No, no, she said and shook her head sadly and with a calm grace that was, for Linda, strangely feminine. Schuller asked if anyone had checked on the horses this morning, and she told them that the first thing she'd done at the police station was call Jerry Boyd and beg him to drive to camp at sunrise and water and grain the horses. They drove the rest of the way to Kindermann Forest in a puzzled silence. When they pulled up outside the camp office, she said she'd make sure that Schuller and Sandie got every penny of their bond money back. She opened her car door. "Thank you," she said again, as if in farewell.

"Hold on a minute," Schuller said.

She stopped, one foot out the car door.

"Look here," he said. "This can't be easy for you, Linda, but we need to have some idea of the trouble you've gotten yourself into."

She sank back into the fur collar of her coat. She looked ready to endure a long silence.

They could feel the chilled March air seeping into the car. Beside Schuller, Sandie had begun stirring in his seat. "You know what?" he said to no one in particular. He pried open his car door and stepped outside, stretching his shoulders and legs as if readying himself for a jog across the meadow. Instead he strolled around to Linda's open door.

"You know what I think I'll do," he said. "I'll go ahead and walk Linda to her cottage, Schuller."

"What now? I don't think that's necessary."

"How 'bout you go and take a drive round camp and come back and pick me up?"

"Well, what could I possibly—"

"How 'bout it, Schuller?" It wasn't exactly a request. He'd cast an altogether unsparing look at his brother.

And so Schuller relented. What else could he do? He knew all too well what Sandie was up to. They'd bickered about this very situation more than a few times over the years: the way Sandie tended to make himself a confidant of the employees, especially the women. Years earlier, when he'd been a middle-aged codirector of camp, he'd befriended several female counselors. Timid Jennifer. Sweet but peculiar Marion. There were probably others. Eventually these young women had courted and married men their own age. Over time they became moody housewives and mothers, and at least once a year, sometimes more, they'd feel in need of something—pity or compassion—they weren't getting from their husbands and children, and they'd contact Sandie—quiet, unsuspicious Sandie, with his bottomless patience for other people's problems. He could waste entire evenings on the phone with these women. He wrote them long letters full of intimate understandings.

Schuller set the car in gear and pulled away. In his rearview mirror he could see the two of them—Sandie with his old man's stoop, Linda in her elaborate coat and wobbly pumps—treading arm in arm across the meadow patched with ice.

Because there was a haze and cold weight to the air, everything a hundred yards beyond the windshield looked watery and half-formed. A few large, ratty crows had fixed themselves in the branches of nearby elm trees. Ahead Schuller could see the infirmary shuttered up for the winter and beyond that the mess hall, where the windows were glowing with light. A bright, warm, extravagant light.

He stopped the car and went inside.

Ridiculous. Someone had dragged one of the heavy wood dining tables to the center of the mess hall floor (the rest were stacked away in the corner of the hall awaiting summer) and covered it with a lace tablecloth and then set out candles, fine china, a bottle of wine. Two places at the table had been set, each with silverware and glasses and a domed meal that had long gone cold. Schuller lifted a dome: a glazed trout fillet, rosemary potatoes, a neat pyramid of asparagus spears. All the lights in the hall and in the kitchen blazed away.

He went from switch to switch turning them off. Then he drove to the end of the road, where, from his car window, he could see the mares grazing dry clumps of grass in the pasture and steaming the air with their warm breath.

Driving back, he found Sandie waiting near the road outside the camp office. It wasn't often that he got to look upon his twin brother from this vantage point, from the perspective a stranger might have in a passing car. How unusual. They were almost always in one another's company and, though they rarely argued outright, so much of their time together each day was spent on shrewd remarks and subtle gestures meant to remind the other just how predictably he behaved. *See there, Sandie. See there! More evidence that you are unreliable, childish, easily manipulated by others.* Or, in Schuller's case, overbearing, insensitive. Cold of heart. It seemed they could go on like this for decades more, neither happy nor particularly unhappy. But as Schuller approached him now in the station wagon, there was something in Sandie's posture, a strength and modesty, a willingness to tackle difficult dilemmas, that made it clear that none of the flaws they'd tagged one another with was exactly right.

Together they drove out through the camp gates and onto Highway 52 and eventually through Ellsinore and onto the interstate. Miles went by without either of them speaking. At last Schuller said, "If I feel like it, I'll go back downstairs after dinner and paint the rest of the ballpark fence. Maybe a few of the bleacher seats, too."

In the seat beside him Sandie gave a quick, judicious nod.

"I'd sure like to get that ballpark looking right before the weekend's through."

"I know you would."

Schuller relaxed his grip on the wheel. Then he told Sandie about the lighted mess hall and the neatly laid table and the trout fillets. "I guess she was arranging a romantic dinner," he said and glanced from the road long enough to see his brother's expression tighten into a frown, a sure sign that this was, for Sandie, a matter of divided loyalties.

"I suppose she was," Sandie said. He buried his hands in the pockets of his coat and turned his face to the window. "I don't know that it's any of our business, Schuller."

This remark Schuller would have to ignore. But inwardly it was worth noting that they'd paid Linda Rucker's salary for eighteen years. Ever since she'd become program director, they'd provided her a year-round place to live. More so, they'd entrusted her with the care and running of Kindermann Forest. By Schuller's reckoning, Linda Rucker's record of arrest was very much their business. "What strikes me," he said, "what I'm most confused about, is Linda's state of mind. The way she's dressing and behaving. I don't know what to make of it."

"She's going through a rough time."

"I'm sure she is. I'd like to understand it better."

"Would you?" Sandie said.

"I would. So we can help in whatever way . . . Oh, *for heaven's sake.*"

They could push you to your limits, moments such as these: to see Sandie's face lit with the secret knowledge that Schuller was more concerned with how the arrest would reflect on Kindermann Forest than he was with the pain it had caused Linda Rucker. But such knowledge would be a secret only to the simpleminded or the self-righteous. Anyone who lived and succeeded in the world would have exactly the same priorities.

"Look here," Schuller said. "You can tell me what you know or I can wait and learn what happened from the police report."

"All I'm asking," Sandie said, his head bowed piously, "is that you don't *pretend* to be concerned when, in fact, you're not."

"Fine," Schuller said. He exhaled an extravagant weary sigh. "No more pretending, Sandie. I have a heart frozen solid. Ice water flows through my veins."

It was a perfectly absurd end to their little squabble—and yet, enough, somehow, to slacken their intense and long-accumulated aggravation with one another. They both leaned back in the seat and retreated into themselves. A minute or two passed, and Sandie frowned in concentration and said, "She told me a good deal of what happened. The rest I can piece together on my own."

"All right then," Schuller said. "I'd certainly like to hear what you know."

According to Sandie, Linda Rucker had met a local man.

This had happened several months earlier in Ellsinore, at the saloon where Linda liked to socialize Friday nights. This local man lived east of Ellsinore in a trailer with a woman and her child. He wasn't married to the woman or the father of the child, but he wasn't exactly single, either. All week long he was something of a family man, but Friday nights were his own, and he liked to go to the saloon. That was where his relationship with Linda, which had begun as a simple bar friendship, intensified into something else.

"What else?" Schuller wanted to know.

"Something between a friendship and a romance, but whatever it was, it was unofficial."

"You mean secret. A secret affair. No need to make it sound better than it really is."

This secret affair went on for three months. Sometimes this local man would accompany Linda back to camp after the saloon closed and stick around long enough to help her feed the horses in the morning.

"Oh, Lord," Schuller groaned. How it aggravated him to hear this.

According to Linda, this local man was a decent enough fellow—hardworking, trustworthy. He knew how to talk and how to listen. He was handsome. Or at least she'd held these high opinions of him until last night, Friday night. She'd planned an elaborate dinner for the two of them. In her mind it marked the three-month anniversary of the start of their relationship. She sent an invitation to the lumberyard where he worked. She went shopping for clothes and a bit of makeup. She bought food and wine, and tidied up the mess hall. But, of course, when Friday night rolled around, he didn't show. So she waited a few hours and then she went to the saloon to see if there had been a mix-up. No mix-up. He wasn't there, either. She came back to camp, waited some more, called his house several times, and hung up when a woman answered. By then she was on the verge of throwing dinner in the trash. Instead she climbed in the camp van and drove to his trailer park, circling round and round until she spotted his car. All the while she was feeling wilder, more frantic. She stormed up to his trailer door and banged away. No one answered, though there were lights on. So she pulled the van right up across their tiny yard to the front steps, turned on the high beams, and began laying on the horn, over and over . . . until the police arrived.

"What in the Lord's name?" Schuller said. "What was she hoping to accomplish?"

Sandie didn't know. He said she probably hadn't been thinking rationally. And now she felt miserable about it all; mostly because when the police were hauling her away, the woman and her little girl came out of the trailer and Linda could see that she'd terrified them.

"Of course she did," Schuller said.

There was more still. As it happened, the local man wasn't even home. The police told Linda he'd gone to Springfield with friends to see a motorcycle rally. Linda said she kept going over it all in her head. He knew about the special dinner. She was certain of it. He'd just chosen to do something else that night. What galled her most was that he hadn't called or sent back the invitation to let her know he wouldn't be coming. He wasn't honest enough to tell her *no*.

She'd made this confession to Sandie while standing on the porch of her cottage, smoking a cigarette with an unsteady hand. She said that after a night in jail she'd come to the conclusion that while she may have been a worthy enough friend to drink and talk intimately with each Friday night—and to sleep with, too—she wasn't the kind of woman he wanted to think of as a girlfriend or a lover. No romance. No tenderness. Or, at least, none that could be acknowledged. In part it was her fault, she said, because she'd fooled herself into thinking it might be otherwise. But not anymore. She knew what she was. She knew how men thought of her, how little of themselves they were willing to give. She'd go back to knowing herself the way she did before this relationship. She promised she would.

For all Schuller knew, every word of Linda Rucker's confession— as told to him by Sandie—had been utterly sincere, utterly true. Were he a more cynical man, he might have suspected that her story had been softened by Sandie so that Linda Rucker could retain her posi- tion as program director. Because it had certainly turned out that way. She'd made all the proper amends, paid back the bond money, written what must have been a convincing letter of apology to the woman she'd terrorized. By summertime the charges of harassment and trespassing had been dropped.

Schuller decided to hold his staff meeting in the camp office, in the hour after lunch, known at Kindermann Forest as the siesta hour. Outside the afternoon had turned humid and hot, and much of this balminess had found its way inside the office. But the counselors and wrangler and lifeguards seemed not to notice. They'd arrived in a cheerful mood and had lined up against the walls or had sprawled languorously across the office furniture, stretching their suntanned limbs, smoothing the ragged hems of their cutoff shorts. Wherever Schuller turned his gaze, he saw the fussy and preening gestures of the self-absorbed.

"I'm afraid we have a problem," he began and then told them straightaway. "The male campers of Cabin Two have been congregating in the back of the sleeping barracks at night and having sex with one another."

Did they appear startled? Yes. Startled to have him say such a thing aloud, yet they seemed to be on familiar terms with the news itself.

"Here's what Linda Rucker and I want you to know," he said. "This absolutely will not continue. We are making plans to separate the male campers of Cabin Two, and if anything remotely like this is happening in your cabin, it's essential that you tell us at once. We are deeply concerned. Do not doubt for a moment that we're in charge and ready to take action."

He seemed now to have everyone's attention, the young women with their carefully brushed ponytails and jaunty postures, the young men, who, under the weight of the matter being discussed, had decided to fold their arms and stand up squarely.

"We began the State Hospital Session in such a rush," Schuller said. "I would have liked to talk with you right at the start. But I haven't had the chance, until now, to share a few thoughts with you. Thoughts on the state hospital campers. And so I'll begin by asking a very simple question. Who are the retarded?"

As he might have expected, the counselors were made bashful by such a question. They pulled at the seams of their clothing. They lowered their heads, frowned in concentration.

"I don't mean to put you on the spot," he said. "You can answer however you like. Who are the retarded? Please tell me."

Together they endured a lengthy silence. Schuller, who'd chosen to stand sentrylike before the director's desk, was happy to wait them out.

A young woman raised her hand. "Someone with a mental condition," she said. "A mental condition that causes a low IQ."

"Yes," he said. "That's a good start, I suppose."

"A very low IQ," someone said. "Lower than a hundred."

"And behavior problems, too," a young man offered.

Apparently they'd gotten over their bashfulness, were willing now to offer opinions like so many dull coins pitched into a fountain.

"No, no. Not lower than a hundred. Lower than seventy."

"Seventy or a hundred. Does it really matter?"

"It does if you have an IQ of ninety-nine."

"Well let's just say it's a hundred then."

"But it's not. It's seventy!"

"Oh, shut up, Wayne, you *stinking puddle of—*"

An explosion of laughter. They pitched forward in their seats and howled. Whatever this joke might mean, the counselors appeared to love it.

Eventually the room ebbed a few degrees quieter. "Let me answer the question a different way," Schuller said. "Let me answer by telling you who the retarded are *not*. They are not children, not exactly. And not helpless, either. There are many things they can and will do on their own, provided they know what's expected of them. And provided someone in authority is standing nearby ready to urge them in the right direction.

"But they're definitely not adults. I'll say it again. *Not adults.* Even though some supposed experts have complained that you insult the retarded if you don't pretend they are all independent adults." He surveyed his audience to see if anyone thought this an idea worth defending. No one did. "Imagine the questions these experts think we should be asking. For example, do the retarded want to vote and marry and have children? Do they want to sleep with one another? Some would say that they do want these things. Why? Because it is what *we* are supposed to want. We are all human, you and I and the retarded. Therefore we must all want the same things.

"But if you can find a retarded person who hasn't been influenced by these expectations, they will always be ambivalent about such matters. They don't care either way. They don't particularly share our wishes and desires. Our appetites. And yet, like children, they are very good at imitating the things we do. Think of how it is that so many of the campers smoke cigarettes. Where do you suppose they learned this? From their caretakers, of course. And if you look close at the way they smoke cigarettes—that frantic huffing and puffing—then you'll see they're acting out a habit they don't even understand."

Schuller could see Linda Rucker sunk deep into a padded chair at the back of the office. He could read her half-squinting gaze well enough: she thought he was taking too much obvious pleasure in his speechmaking. Perhaps he was. But should it be done any other way? Was he supposed to convince his audience by being stodgy and dull and fumbling with his words?

He waved off her unspoken criticism with a slow shake of the head and said to the assembled counselors, "I honestly cannot imagine what these experts in charge of the state hospital are thinking. To allow the retarded to imitate our worst habits. And then, when they are sick from smoking or hysterical from all the sex and violence they see on the television, then, these experts say to themselves, 'Oh my, it's time to cure our retarded patients with therapy or protect them with medication.' What nonsense. Wouldn't it be better to create for the retarded an environment in which these influences don't exist at all?"

A long moment passed before his audience understood he had ended his address. They stared at him, perplexed. He smiled back.

"Are you saying," a young woman asked, "that we should take away their cigarettes? Is that what you're saying?"

He told her no, he was not. "I'm talking about an idea," he said. "An idea of Kindermann Forest Summer Camp as a refuge."

She gave him a respectful yet dubious nod, an expression of reluctance he saw mirrored on nearly every other face in the room. With one exception: Christopher Waterhouse. He was still thinking through Schuller's message, still straddling his foldout chair and tipping his forehead up and down, concentrating, and then, as Schuller watched, arriving at a judgment of what he'd just heard—a judgment in favor of Schuller's message. Clearly this was the case because he rose from his seat with a look of half-grinning approval and turned to the wrangler, Stephen Walburn, one of the more dour skeptics, and pretended to exchange a series of slow-motion punches. (They were fond of acting out elaborate, balletlike slaps and punches, this group.)

"It's an *idea,*" Christopher Waterhouse said. "If you could roll back the clock and raise them from infants without influences, they'd be totally different people."

Stephen Walburn shrugged thoughtfully. Nearby other counselors listened in. It was a measure of Christopher Waterhouse's standing with the group that those who a moment earlier had been ready to argue or ridicule were now willing to stop and reconsider.

For that Schuller was grateful.

He had the rest of the day to do with as he pleased. Hours and hours indisputably his own. In his cottage he stretched out on his bed and read from a book on the castles of Ireland and Scotland. He dozed off, woke, read a few more pages, dozed again. For dinner Maureen Boyd and her kitchen girls put on one of their better meals: oven fried chicken, mashed potatoes with country gravy, fresh green beans. By early evening he was back in his cottage at his drafting table. No way to explain to others the pleasure he took—a pleasure as expansive and deep-to-the-bone as any—in the coziness and privacy of his cottage, feeling the crisp separation of good paper between the sharp blades of his scissors. His window fan thrummed softly. Through it he could hear the din of the evening activity, a scavenger hunt, coming to him from a pleasing distance.

The good meal. The finely grained texture of the paper. The airy voices.

One small matter detracted from these satisfactions: the memory of what it had been like that afternoon to finish his address and hear the dull silence and then take stock of his uncertain audience.

He was not a fool. Of course, you couldn't make a public declaration to that effect. Nor could you explain to an audience the private rationales that lay behind your strongest beliefs. But for now it was worth insisting, if only to himself, that he wasn't a fool. He didn't lack self-knowledge. Since boyhood he'd been willing to look inward and weigh carefully his private inclinations. Long ago he'd understood something singular and important: whatever it was that made people miserable or frantic or deliriously happy with longing, whatever strong compulsion made them lie down with strangers or writhe alone in their beds, whatever this was, it was not present in himself.

To be clear: not a void, not a hollowness, but a benign absence.

It wasn't a trait he'd inherited from either of his parents. His father, Theodore Kindermann, owner of a sometimes prosperous St. Louis flooring store, adored his mother. Often he lingered at the breakfast table when he should have left for work or, at his worst, followed her from room to room. Schuller's mother, Marta Kindermann, was far more fickle in her return affections. Neighbors thought them an odd pair. Handsome, endlessly patient Theodore and matronly, plain, easily distracted Marta. She suffered through fifty-five years of his affection. Yet she wasn't without tender feelings or sharp desires; they were just aimed at impossible and unacted-upon targets outside her marriage. At her most distressed, she'd plead for breathing space. She wondered, tearfully and aloud, why she couldn't be allowed to step away from this endless partnership, if just for a week or two, and have an honest-to-God, actual experience in the world. What she wanted, of course, was the experience of loving other men.

As teenagers Schuller and Sandie were aggrieved to understand this. But they had their own fraught dealings with the opposite sex to contend with. Or at least Sandie did. Like his father, he was easily stricken. A girl in the school choir they attended could undo poor Sandie by encouraging his attention as she tied her hair in a long red ribbon. Schuller wasn't so easily undone. He'd rather the girl left her affections and hair ribbons at home. And he'd have liked her better if she arrived at rehearsals on time. Which was not to say that he didn't notice she was pretty. Prettiness was far better than homeliness, certainly, but he didn't have the desire, as other boys of his age, to unwrap this prettiness and press his fingers and tongue and the most private parts of himself against it.

An odd dilemma: in many ways they were the same, he and Sandie, but in this respect they were different. And they knew it, each of them, without ever discussing the matter openly. Sandie pined for the company of girls. He composed letters—even songs—that hours later caused him to cringe in shame. He looked at photographs. He kept a hand towel wedged between his mattresses. Schuller did none of these things. When he was twenty, his parents sent him to lunch with an elderly physician uncle who asked a series of prying questions. Was he too shy to speak to girls? Was he afraid of them? Did he think it disgusting to kiss a girl? Did he prefer the company of boys? Did he dream of boys?

He was startled, of course, to have the conversation take such a private turn. No, he said. No, not afraid. Not disgusted. He didn't really keep company with anyone besides Sandie, but if he did, he'd probably choose boys since they were smarter and more capable.

As for dreams, romantic or otherwise, the answer was definitely no. Not ever. (Until this chat it hadn't occurred to him that boys could lust after boys.) His uncle gave a tenuous nod of acceptance. It was unclear what he reported back to the family at large.

Undaunted, Schuller went forward with his life and career: a college degree in business, a carpet cleaning service that he expanded into a successful venture, then sold. In 1956 he acquired a summer camp. All the while his parents and extended family thought up safe euphemisms for Schuller's situation: he was a late bloomer in his teens, an all-consumed entrepreneur in his twenties, a confirmed bachelor in his thirties. They went to their graves wondering.

He'd have liked to have spared his family this disappointment. Yet it couldn't be helped. It couldn't have been otherwise. In his later years he'd come to understand a peculiar irony at work in the world: what you lack will always be magnified by the people and events that constitute your life. A boy with no appreciation for food will be born into a family of cooks and live above a bakery. A woman who feels no kindness for her children will see, everywhere she goes, mothers and fathers fawning over their babies. So it was with him. He'd gravitated to a career as a summer camp director. All his life he'd been exasperated by other people's unwise longings.

The next morning he chose a different route for his walk: a straight trek across the meadow and onto the gravel pathway that slipped under the roof of the forest and led to Cabins One through Four. He had thought, mistakenly, that he would be a lone figure at 6:45 A.M. strolling past barracks of sleeping men and women. Not so. Already there were faces pressed against the porch screens—peculiar faces in that they were intensely homely or intensely comic or intensely naked in their expressions. Outside Cabin Two, a group of retarded men were squeezed onto the concrete landing as if it were a tiny stone island in the middle of a boiling sea. No one dared step off the edge. They were all in their pajamas and had unlit cigarettes squeezed into their mouths. When they saw Schuller, they let out a great clamor of grunts and jeers, none of it intelligible, and yet it was so cheerful and clearly aimed at Schuller that he felt obliged to answer back.

"Yes," he said. "Good morning, friends."

They crooned back at once. "Harruuuuuuummme! Arrryuhhh!"

"Yes, yes. Let's keep it down. We have people still sleeping."

The cabin door opened and one of the counselors stepped out, the big one with the disfigured face and the somewhat lumbering manner. He was in the process of setting fire to the men's cigarettes when he spotted Schuller.

"Mr. Kindermann. Good morning," he said and raised a hand to wave. How odd it was, truly, to see his distorted face among so many distorted faces and then have him bark out a clear greeting.

"Yes," he said. "Good morning . . . young man."

Schuller pressed on, and a hundred yards farther, with the women's cabins in view, he encountered another unexpected sight: the girl lifeguard, Marcy Bittman, dressed in her swimsuit and blue jean shorts, walking briskly from women's Cabin Four to women's Cabin Three with a wicker laundry basket balanced in her arms. She stepped inside Cabin Three just long enough to collect something and put it in her basket. Afterward she trotted down to the pathway and wished Schuller a good morning.

He was pleased to have remembered her name. "Marcy," he said. "Nice to see you up early and ready to go." He asked what she was collecting.

"Pot lids," she said.

True enough. Her basket contained an unruly stack of pot lids, the wide clamorous type that Maureen Boyd used in the camp kitchen.

"I'm on my way to the men's cabins to get the rest," Marcy said, by way of explanation.

"But why?"

"In case Maureen needs them to cook breakfast."

"No, no," he said. "Why would you keep pot lids in the cabins?"

She wrinkled her slender nose and grinned. A pretty young woman, Schuller supposed. She had an open face, and her enthusiasms had a way of sweeping across her petite features, sharpening her dimples and lighting her hazel eyes. "Because of what Christopher figured out," she said brightly. "About how to use the pot lids to keep the campers in line."

"And how, exactly, does that work?" Schuller asked.

"Well," she said. "Last night they tried separating the men in Cabin Two. Just like you said. Except as soon as the counselors dozed off, the campers, you know, got together in the back of the barracks. So Christopher Waterhouse snuck up to the kitchen and brought back some pot lids. The next time they tried it, he jumped out and clanged them together." She made a grand flapping gesture with her slender arms. "Like cymbals," she said, smiling hugely. She seemed to be waiting for a reply from Schuller—a response of equal exuberance.

"That's something," Schuller said. "I would imagine that . . . that would startle them, certainly."

"All it took was one big clang and they let go of each other and ran back to their beds. Stayed there, too," Marcy said. "Worked so well he went and got more lids, Christopher did, and brought a pair to each of the cabins. We used them last night in Cabin Four, with the women who like to sleep together in the same bed."

"Well, for heaven's sake," Schuller said. "I wouldn't have thought of it myself."

"It scares them," Marcy said. "It makes them pay attention."

"I'm sure it does. But maybe we should present this idea to Linda Rucker. Yes, that would probably be best. Do me a favor, please, Marcy. Tell Christopher to talk over this idea of the pot lids with Linda Rucker. To let her know what's going on."

At this she winced and let out a small, deflated sigh. "I don't know about that, Mr. Kindermann. I can ask him, but I don't think he'll do it. He and Linda Rucker, they aren't really talking to one another anymore."

This wasn't exactly news to Schuller, though he'd have liked to know more. And with Marcy Bittman, he wouldn't have to push very hard. Her reluctance was mostly pretense. The frowning, the creasing of her eyebrows in worry. What she wanted—in spite of these feigned gestures—was to share what she knew.

"Well?" he said.

"It's because she got upset with him," Marcy said. "But honestly, Mr. Kindermann, there wasn't any other way Christopher could have done it. She kept coming down to the pool, especially during the first few days of camp. She'd stand next to his lifeguard chair, talking to him while he guarded. I think she got it into her head that there was something between them. An attraction or at least a boyfriend and girlfriend kind of friendship. I'd watch her talking to him, and she looked very . . . persistent. And so she made Christopher an offer, and when he told me—"

"What offer?" Schuller said

"Not an offer, really, but a kind of request, something she'd like him to do. And I don't think it's fair for me to say what it is because it's *personal,* and it embarrassed Christopher. I'm not sure he'd want me repeating it to you. But she asked him to do something and he told her sorry, no. Maybe he said it too directly. But there wasn't any way around it. I mean, Christopher and I are friends. We talked things over after Linda made her request. He's not looking for a girl-friend. He has one back in college. And he and Linda Rucker aren't really very well . . ."

"What?"

"Matched," she said. "They wouldn't make a logical couple."

Schuller was still dazed and blinking from this news. "No," he said. "They wouldn't make a logical couple." He stared off into the ribbons of sunlight pouring through the forest canvas.

Oh, but he was disappointed. He'd heard all manner of gossip in his forty years as summer camp director. Some things, like this news from Marcy Bittman, had the ring of truth. Other things didn't. The true things always exhausted him. He took a slumped and weary step back, found his balance, stood a degree or two straighter. But really he'd have liked to have sat down with Marcy on the railroad ties that bordered the pathway and described to her the weight of his disappointment. To explain to Marcy Bittman, with her perfectly combed hair and her freshly scrubbed and eager face, the impossible irony he'd lived with all his life.

Chapter Eight

Saturday morning, holding Leonard Peirpont by the elbow and guiding him along a dirt pathway that would lead, eventually, to Barker Lake, Wyatt glanced ahead to a bend in the trail and saw someone stomping toward them. This someone turned out to be a Kindermann Forest maintenance man, a shovel balanced across his shoulder. He dragged behind him a length of clay pipe.

"Hey," the maintenance man said. He had the buoyant stride of a young man pleased with the duties assigned to him, and he filed past the four of them—Leonard, Wyatt, Jerry Johnston, and Thomas Anwar Toomey—dragging his pipe in the dirt.

It was perfectly clear to Wyatt what would happen next.

"Hey," the maintenance man said again. He'd come to a stop. "Hey, guys? Where's your counselor?"

Wyatt, who tended to hold his breath at such moments, exhaled sharply through the side of his mouth. "I'm looking after them," he said. "I'm their counselor. We're on our way to Barker Lake for a ride in the canoe."

The maintenance man wavered a moment. "Are you . . . to the lake?" he said. He was squinting as if trying to recognize them from a great distance. "Yes," he said. "To the lake. All right. Be careful."

That was the end of it. The trail took them in separate directions. For Wyatt and his three campers there was a descending pathway choked with hard gray horse turds or crisscrossed with the knuckled roots of cedar trees.

Here was a puzzle Wyatt kept turning over in his mind: while he'd been mistaken for a retarded camper numerous times by members of the kitchen and maintenance staff and even several times by his fellow counselors, the opposite had not happened. The campers had never confused him for one of their own. Not Leonard or Jerry or Thomas Anwar Toomey. Not any of the dozens of campers he'd had dealings with during this first week of the State Hospital Session. In the crowded barracks of Cabin Two, the male campers didn't elbow him out of the way or push him from behind, tactics they used generously on one another. Two days earlier, at the stables, Wyatt and his group had been feeding the trail horse handfuls of oniongrass through the corral fence, and a bee-stung horse had suddenly lurched against the fence and gone into a wild bucking stomp. The campers, even those Wyatt barely knew, had reached for him, had grabbed him by the shirttail and belt loops and looked up at him desperate to be reassured.

They knew. He was not sure how, exactly. Either they were quick to recognize the rank of those in charge or they saw in him a sharpness of mind, a capableness that they didn't see in one another.

Somewhere ahead, not far into the curtain of underbrush, there were scurrying dogs, yelping in a human pitch.

"They'll make themselves a nest in there if you let 'em," Leonard Peirpont said.

Wyatt tightened his grip on Leonard's arm. The pathway dipped. "Yes, that's right."

"You can't sort 'em out or talk sense to 'em. They'll do what they like."

"Hmmm. Yes. I guess so."

"They'll still be here a hundred years from now . . . after you and I have gone back from where we come."

"That's right," Wyatt said. With Leonard it felt like the very worst rudeness not to take part in his meandering conversations.

The trail turned sharply. Some twenty yards later they came upon Barker Lake, or rather the sandy corner of it that Kindermann Forest rented each summer and set with canoes and paddles and tree-hung racks of life vests. The lake water this morning was limpid green, the sunlight bright on the surface, the waves lapping meek against a mossy shoreline. They'd been told that, in a regular week of camp, the children and their counselors would be allowed to paddle out to the main body of the lake before turning back. For the State Hospital Session the procedures were altogether different. An aluminum canoe was hauled up onto the sandy beach. Two campers, fit snugly with life vests, were guided into sitting positions at the bow and stern. Then two mainte-nance men, Jim and Ronnie, dragged the canoe into the lake as evenly as possible and stood there beside it, up to their thighs in lake water, making sure a camper didn't rock or stand or otherwise tumble into the lake shallows. The campers floated there in place. After ten min-utes Jim and Ronnie hauled them back up onto the beach.

All of this took time and effort, and so for the State Hospital Ses-sion the activity of canoeing was a scheduled activity. Counselors put their names on a list at the mess hall and came with their groups to Barker Lake at the appointed time. Emily Boehler, 9:05. Veronica Yordy, 9:35. Wyatt Huddy, 9:55. He'd arrived with his campers fif-teen minutes early, and now, at their own peril, they had to sit in the shade and try not to watch Veronica Yordy persuade her two charges, the Mulcrone sisters, the two most astonishing and unsettling state hospital campers, to rise from the sand and don life vests.

It seemed to Wyatt that Veronica Yordy had been given an impossible burden in the sisters. But Veronica thought otherwise. During after-hours conversations at The Sanctuary, she was happy to explain herself. You had to look at both sides of the coin, she said. The good and the bad. The night and the day. For example, if you got up in the middle of the night to pee and you came upon one or both of the Mulcrone sisters in the grainy light of the bathroom, or you bumped into either of the sisters, who tended to slink around the dark barracks in their ratty pajamas, they could frighten you so completely that you might feel a part of yourself tearing away. Being that frightened, Veronica said, might be the way a person felt when he or she was on the verge of a nervous breakdown.

To Wyatt and the other counselors of Kindermann Forest this made perfect sense: because the Mulcrone sisters were as close to real-life monsters as anything they'd encountered in the world. Several counselors had been overheard on the Sanctuary pay phone describing the sisters to relatives. Their accounts were not believed. Perhaps it would have been better to start with what was known about the sisters. They were identical twins. According to Camp Nurse Harriet Foster, they'd been wards of the state hospital at Farmington for four decades. They were haggard and unkempt, though this wasn't an indication of their age. They might have been forty-five or seventy-five. Both sisters had wiry, near-transparent hair, through which you could see their scabbed and lumpy scalps. They both had faces composed of flat foreheads, noses, and square chins and, of course, the feature that amazed and terrified everyone: each of the sisters had an extra set of pupilless eyes set just above the hard ridge of her brow. These eyes were cast at a slanting downward angle so that the sisters always appeared vexed or in contemplation of a cruel act. They were formed enough, these extra eyes, to turn in their sockets, especially when the sisters slept. Among the female counselors in Cabin Four, it was considered a grave mistake to look upon the sisters' sleeping faces.

Really, Veronica had said to anyone in The Sanctuary willing to listen, you can't get over the sight of them at night. You can't shake it out of your head once it's there. So you tiptoe around hoping not to see them. It would be ridiculous, she said, if it weren't so entirely frightening.

And yet she could stand to deal with the sisters in the daytime. Mostly because what they wanted above all else was so common and so simple: coffee and cigarettes. In their waking hours they might as well have been a pair of disheveled, housebound old aunts. Each muttered a long litany of complaints too low and garbled to understand. Both sisters drank their coffee scalding hot, smoked countless cigarettes, and breathed out their sour breath. But they weren't, Veronica said, necessarily hard to manage. If they had or were about to have coffee or cigarettes, they were fairly pleasant people.

Fortunately, the Mulcrone sisters had been allowed to bring coffee in closed foam cups with them to the lake this morning. They refused to let go of these cups, even for a second, and so Veronica had to thread the various life vest straps over and around their occupied hands. In the clear air and bright morning light, the sisters looked supremely ugly. (At least, for their sake, it was an ugliness they seemed altogether unaware of.) They took seats in the canoe and were eased out into several feet of lake water. Each of the sisters was given a lighted cigarette, and they sat there floating in the canoe, smoking thoughtfully and sipping coffee.

From the shoreline Veronica Yordy called to them. "Way to go, ladies! Nice job! Look at you both, floating out there on the water." A burning cigarette was cupped in Veronica's hand. The same was true of the maintenance men Jim and Ronnie, who both smoked while standing thigh-deep in the lake. Almost everyone at camp, it seemed, had either discovered or renewed their commitment to the habit.

On the shore, not far from where Wyatt and Leonard Peirpont crouched on a log, another of Veronica Yordy's charges, a young barefoot woman in jeans and a striped blouse, languished in the dirt. Her name was Evie Hicks, and she inched forward, impossibly slow, on her elbows and knees and belly, her face a few inches above the ground. Whatever stone or twig or grassy bit of debris she came upon, she lowered her head and scrutinized with a myopic fascination. Now and then she turned her face up toward the sunlight and the voice of her counselor.

At least once every minute Veronica Yordy called out to her. "Evie Hicks, what are you doing there on the ground?" Or "Evie Hicks, don't even think about putting that dried-up leaf in your mouth." Or "Evie Hicks, you have no more clean blouses, so what are we supposed to do now, Evie Hicks?"

These were exactly the sorts of chatty remarks the counseling staff of Kindermann Forest liked to direct at Leonard Peirpont. "How is your world today, Leonard Peirpont?" Or "Leonard Peirpont, what do you make of this hot June weather? Good for growing green beans, isn't it?" Of course Leonard was incapable of a logical reply. That, Wyatt knew, was part of what the other counselors liked: to see Leonard's eyes go comically wide and his face tighten in concentration. With his thick black glasses he looked like the most befuddled college professor in the world. "What big plans do you have today, Leonard Peirpont?" they asked him, if only because he, along with Evie Hicks and several others, was considered a favorite among a hundred other state hospital campers who were so much harder to love.

But Evie Hicks was significantly different from these other favorites. She had—there was no way not to notice—an unusually generous figure, big, obvious breasts that strained the seams of her blouse, wide hips, and a round, overlarge rear end. She walked in a wobbly pigeon-toed shuffle—she had yet to find a way to properly balance those breasts and hips and her swinging rear end—and unless a counselor was there to goad her along, she would drop down on her hands and knees and begin her close examination of the weeds and tree bark and litter that covered the ground. Most often you could see Evie hunched down in the yard outside Cabin Four, working her way through the carpet of wood-chip mulch that Jerry Boyd and his maintenance men dispersed at the start of each camp season. Evie was capable of a fierce and sustained concentration. It was as if she intended to catalog each item. A twig. A crumbled leaf. An ant or wood snail. As she worked, she'd raise her full rear end each time she felt the need to scoot along.

At least the female counselors could joke about how they envied Evie Hicks her figure. For Wyatt it was a much more troubling dilemma. To let his gaze linger a moment too long on Evie's body was to be aroused. To be aroused was to hate himself. Even now, with her sprawled in the dirt near his feet, Wyatt made himself look away, and when he did he found Jim and Ronnie, standing a dozen yards away in the lake, staring back at Evie on the shoreline, their eyebrows raised in appreciation.

No comfort, really, to know he wasn't alone in this treachery. They should all be ashamed: he and Jim and Ronnie, all the male employees of camp who were tempted to look. Wyatt more so, maybe, because on the occasions he'd encountered Evie Hicks, he was as struck by her round, girlish face and her sweetly preoccupied expression as he was by her body. She seemed to be a thoughtful young woman. At least he imagined she was. And in truth he liked being around the women campers and counselors of Kindermann Forest more than the men. A better, kinder, more generous atmosphere among the women. Several times he'd led his group down the gravel pathway to the yards of Cabins Three and Four just to be on the periphery of that atmosphere, to see the women campers roaming the yard and hear their counselors calling to them from the porch landing. "Evie Hicks, what are you searching for down there in the wood chips? Have you found gold yet, Evie Hicks?"

Silly to say this—she was *retarded* after all—but she looked, with her pert, small-featured face and wide green eyes, like she might possibly be an intelligent person, a considerate person.

It was a selfish thought. He knew it as he sat there at the edge of Barker Lake with Evie Hicks sprawled in the dirt just a few paces away. Yet it seemed to Wyatt that, in the world as it ought to be, Evie should be allowed to come to him as a girlfriend, a wife, a lover. Except that wasn't enough. (He was greedy in his longings.) She couldn't be a mindless wife or lover. Evie would have to *want* to be with him. So let her at least be aware. Give her an intelligence that would allow her to know him for who he was. But at this point he realized he'd carried the fantasy too far. If she were to have this level of awareness, then she would look around at all that was available to her and not want to be with him in the first place.

It was difficult to know how much he should hold himself responsible for this disgraceful longing. His first and sharpest inclination was that in exchange for his unseemly thoughts about Evie Hicks he should be forced to endure a punishment. But what kind? For the time being he could only guess that it should be powerful. Yet that might not be right, either. Were he to discuss the matter with Captain Throckmorton, the captain would almost certainly see it differently. He would say, "These thoughts, Wyatt, are mostly beyond your control. Best not to dwell on them." Or he might say, "When it comes to accepting punishment, Wyatt, you may not have a clear notion of what's reasonable and what's not."

This, of course, would be the captain's way of referring to the life Wyatt had shared with his sister, Caroline Huddy, before he'd come to live at the Salvation Army depot. Caroline. Caroline Huddy. A real, live, breathing person, and yet he couldn't think of her without feeling oppressed and bewildered. Worse even, because he supposed he owed her. She'd taken care of him after the passing of Wyatt's father. They were not a healthy or prosperous family. Their mother had died of ovarian cancer many years earlier, while Wyatt was still a toddler. Yet by all accounts his sister, Caroline, older by fifteen years, had gown up very much in the mold of their mother: stubborn and large, unafraid, angry.

For a long while most of Caroline's scorn had been directed at their father. He was, in her view, a fool. True, he could raise a dozen chickens or pigs and manage a large garden, but a steady job outside the farm was beyond him. In terms of income he received exactly two hundred and twelve dollars a month in a government disability payment for a congenital malformed hip and a hopelessly twisted left leg. He shuffled and hopped rather than walked. He'd always been a scrawny, hunched little man, and his pairing with their strapping, hard-tempered mother was a comic mishap all of their neighbors seemed to enjoy. Of equal embarrassment to Caroline was the fact that he traveled about their community in a broken-down pickup truck trading extra produce and livestock and sometimes money for the salvageable parts of antique tractors—machines so corroded and useless that most farmers allowed them to rust away in their fields. He was a collector of these tractors and their various components and, for reasons confounding to Caroline, he brought truckloads of old tractor parts home and arranged them in a huge metal-roof shed.

Within this tractor shed, Wyatt's father had a life of his own: tools and solvents and bygone tractor manuals and secret stashes of hard apple cider and cigars. Friends dropped by to see him in the shed. They called him Hoppy, though not with the gruff bark of ridicule that Caroline brought to his nickname whenever he entered the farm-house and was subject to her rules and grievances. "Hoppy," she'd say, "don't you dare think about sitting down anywhere in this house in those greasy overalls." She'd make him retreat to the front step and undress while Wyatt fetched his father's house robe. But even the sight of him in that robe grated on her. "How can you stand to look at yourself?" she'd say. Or else she'd order him to carry table scraps out to the pigs or bundle up the trash or any one of a hundred other chores. "Get up, Hoppy. Get up and earn your keep for a change." If Wyatt had a single image of his father, it would be in the moment or two following an order from Caroline, in which Hoppy, with a subtle wincing frown he kept secret from her, would quietly calculate his options, only to rise from his chair and shuffle off to do as he'd been told.

Eventually his heart gave out. But even in the hospital's cardiac recovery unit, Wyatt's father, in the deep fog of his medication, would overhear Caroline telling a doctor about Hoppy's failure to listen or eat right and, at the sound of his nickname, he'd put a hand to the bed rail as if to rise up and do what was demanded of him.

After his passing, Caroline made it clear to Wyatt what behavior would be expected of him inside the farmhouse and what chores he would need to accomplish after school and during his summer vacations. All of this had seemed reasonable to him as a fourteen-year-old boy. Feed the chickens and pigs. Keep the tractor running. Keep his late father's sprawling vegetable garden watered and free from weeds. But Wyatt was lazy sometimes. For a while he'd had a friend or two in the remedial class at Dutton Junior High School, and he would run with them after school and sometimes forget the chores assigned to him. And so Caroline had said, sensibly enough, "If you won't look after the garden during the day, try looking after it at night." At dusk that evening she'd had him stand with his back to a huge walnut tree that faced the garden and she'd begun winding ropes around his legs and under his arms and even through the belt loops of his blue jeans and then tying off the ropes at the back of the trunk, where he couldn't reach them. He'd had to stay there yoked against the tree all night. Nothing to do but keep still and look out over the garden. Several hours after darkness a possum waddled by close enough that Wyatt could almost touch it with his shoe. It considered him with its

black button eyes, then crawled away. It was a mild night. As punish-
ments went, this wasn't so bad. He could nod off to sleep for short
periods of time. Much later the dew began to coat his sweatshirt and
hair and, after hours of trying not to, he peed himself. Even so, in
the morning when she untied him, it still seemed funny to Wyatt—
funny and exactly what he deserved.

But it didn't cure him of his laziness, especially when it came to
school. By ninth grade the energy it took to walk down a high school
hallway—to be jeered at and fake-punched and turned away from
in disgust—was too much. Too much for Wyatt. There wasn't much
energy left over that he could use to concentrate on his more difficult
school subjects. Caroline wasn't pleased. Or rather, sometimes she was
enraged and other times she shrugged it all off, wearily. For a dismal
progress report she might make him stand in a bucket of ice water.
Yet when the actual report card came several months later with its
columns of failing grades, she declared the whole enterprise of high
school a waste of time. She decided he could quit going altogether or
transfer to a technical school. Either way, she said, the schoolwork
didn't matter because he was probably an idiot.

He chose technical school, where his fellow students, if not exactly
friendly, were at least mindful of his size and strength. He learned to
weld and repair small engines. Neither of these skills mattered much
to Caroline Huddy. At thirty-two she'd grown heavyset and haggard-
looking. She spent long hours in the bathroom or in bed, where she
watched rented movies on a videocassette recorder. It amazed him,
this machine. His neighbors had been watching video movies at home
for years, and yet it was astounding that Caroline had tracked down
a secondhand video machine and arranged for herself such an impossible luxury. She'd had Wyatt move their only television set from the
living room up the stairs into her bedroom. He'd unboxed the VCR
and connected it to the television. Every other day Caroline, who
otherwise shuffled about the house in a robe and slippers, got dressed

and drove to Jefferson City to rent movies. The cases for these movies, with their extravagant drawings and photographs, were left lying about on the kitchen counter for Wyatt to consider. The movies she watched alone, two per night, behind the closed door of her bedroom. Then she fell asleep and, aided by medication, slept soundly and late into the next day.

Wyatt had a keen understanding of the opportunity this allowed. Late one night he took his shoes off, eased her door open, and carried the television and video machine piece by piece into the living room. The movie that had provoked him to take this risk was called *Time Bandits*. Its case contained a peculiar cartoon drawing of a pirate ship roosted on the top of a man's head. Very odd. But the movie was infinitely odder. It hardly made sense at all except as evidence that the fantasies that flitted through other people's heads were much more vivid and strange than his own.

The TV and video machine he returned to Caroline's bedroom. She didn't stir. But later, when she woke and resumed viewing *Time Bandits,* she found that the movie was not in the place where she'd left off. She brooded over this much of the day. "But how could that happen?" she asked Wyatt, doubtfully. She was aware of his deep interest in the movie's cassette box. "Did you do something?" she wondered. "Did you maybe sneak into my room and watch a little of the movie while I was sleeping?" He said no, more than a hundred times. Yet she seemed as if she'd be amused to know for certain that this had happened. "Come on. Let's hear it. What part of the movie did you see?" By then it was well after dark. She'd been going on like this most of the day. Exhausted, he admitted that he'd carried off the TV and video machine and watched the entire film, and her reaction was complicated. She looked dumbfounded and somewhat frightened, but also admiring. "That's a lot of planning and a lot of work," she said. "I honestly cannot believe you'd think up a plan like that." She gripped the matted bangs of her hair and pressed them down against her forehead. "I wouldn't have guessed it, Wyatt," she said and began wandering about the house, marveling at his transgression, and rooting through drawers and boxes and considering a variety of tools.

Eventually, she decided on an X-Acto knife. She had him remove his shoes and socks, and she held him by the ankle and cut him deeply across the bridge of each foot. A ferocious pain, a grisly, deep-to-the-bone burning. He'd have run away screaming if he could. Instead he squeezed his ankles and wept. It wasn't worth it: such unrelenting agony for a movie that didn't even make sense. Much of the night he lay on the kitchen floor moaning. When Caroline emerged from her room the next morning, she was much more like herself: slack-faced, irritable, insulted by everything he did. She said she wasn't going to put up with his carrying on. She packed a grocery bag with items from the cupboard and ordered him out to the tractor shed. He couldn't walk, of course. Even crawling on his hands and knees proved too painful. So he pulled himself along on his stomach as if he were scaling a mountain precipice. Out the door. Across the porch. Along the trampled front yard. Up the gravel drive leading to the tractor shed. It seemed to take forever, this journey. Through much of it she hovered over him, the grocery bag swinging at her side.

She left him in the shed. It was early October, cool and clear in the evenings, warm during the day. He found, stuffed beneath the workbench, several dusty blankets his father had once used on the occasions when he'd been exiled from the house. Wyatt wrapped himself in these blankets and searched through the grocery sack Caroline had left him. Orange soda. Ritz crackers. A bottle of aspirin. Two small Band-Aids not long enough to cover his wounds. He chewed several aspirin and sipped from the bottle of orange soda. It wasn't at all worth it, he decided for the hundredth time. Even more unfair, the X-Acto knife blade she'd used had been crusted with dirt and tar from cutting floor tiles. It would have been better, fairer, to have washed it first. In the deep throb of his wounds and in his shivering limbs, a message was being sent to him: *Wyatt, you are going to be sick.*

True enough. He shivered and retched and, late in the night, drenched his clothes in sweat and urine. In the expansive tractor shed, with its countless chassis and bald tires and milk crates of parts, he could cry out all he wanted. He couldn't sleep, however, even once his wounds had lost much of their sting and his feet had taken on a remarkable weight and thickness. Somehow he'd been granted elephant's feet. He was miserable, truly. But it didn't make any sense: the movie or the fact that she'd used a dirty knife blade. Or this: when he was seven years old, she'd taken him to the children's hospital in Kansas City so that surgeons could separate the fingers on both of his hands. He'd woken up in the recovery room, aching, nauseated, a boy in pain. All through the night and following day Caroline had sat with him, patting his head, wiping his lips when he spit up, wincing in misery every time he cried out.

The next morning a vehicle pulled up in the driveway. He could hear two people get out. One went to the door of the house and knocked. The other waited in the open bay of the shed—a silhouetted figure, a man who had his hands in the pockets of his coat and was rocking on the heels of his feet.

There were several moments of a prolonged and impending silence and then the creak of the house door and Caroline's husky voice. "No, sir. No. Not today," she insisted. "You can come back and look around another time," she said. "You there!" she shouted. "You stay out of that shed. You come again some other time!"

From deep within the piled center of the shed, Wyatt pulled himself forward, dragging his blankets and his swollen feet. He wouldn't have done so, wouldn't have called attention to himself, if she'd used a clean knife blade.

The man who'd been standing in the open bay caught his breath and stepped back. "Sweet Jesus," he said. "Are you . . . ? Wait a minute now. Terry! Hey, Terry! Get over here!"

The second man walked over and joined him. And then Caroline, barefoot, in her robe, with a tire iron she kept by the front door. "No, no, no," she said. "This does not have anything to do with you two. Get back in your truck, you hear? You come back again another time."

The man who'd been at the door stood and took in the sight of Wyatt. "Ms. Huddy," the man said. "Let me make sure I understand you. Are you refusing—"

"I'll call the law if you don't leave right this minute," she said. She raised her tire iron. "I'll swing on you if I have to."

He was a heavyset man, and he looked at her, his big, bald forehead creased in worry. He said, "Please do. Please do call the law. Let's have Sheriff Leahey come to the farm and sort this out. But if you decide to swing that tire iron, then understand that my friend, Ed, and I will be swinging back." He'd braced himself as if ready to lunge in her direction. His name, Wyatt would learn soon enough, was Terry Throckmorton. Captain Throckmorton. He and his friend, Ed McClintock, had been to the Huddy farm before and had purchased several antique iron tractor seats. Ed was a collector.

It seemed to take Caroline forever to make up her mind. One moment she was speechless in her indignation, the next she was screaming and making threats. Eventually she swung her tire iron, but before doing so she stepped back so that the curved end of the iron cut only through the air. Then she let out a great huffing sob. Was she crying? If so, Wyatt had never seen anything like it. She told Captain Throckmorton and Ed McClintock the story of their parents' deaths but with nearly all the dates and facts invented or rearranged.

"We're very sorry to hear it," Captain Throckmorton said.

But she claimed not to believe a word out of his mouth. She said she was going back into the house to find her father's shotgun and figure out how to load it and then she'd settle the matter once and for all. As soon as she stepped inside, Ed McClintock hurried and drove his pickup truck to the bay of the shed, and he and Captain Throckmorton helped Wyatt climb into the bed of the truck. Within minutes they were speeding out the gates of the farm.

They went first to the Jefferson City Police Station, where Sheriff Leahey took one look at Wyatt sprawled in the bed of the truck and summoned an ambulance. Sheriff Leahey had been out to the Huddy farm before and had past dealings with Caroline. He knew Wyatt by name. "Wyatt," he said. "How did this happen to you?"

And so Wyatt told him about the movie, *Time Bandits*, and the borrowing of Caroline's video machine and her choice of an unclean knife blade. As he spoke, the parked truck seemed to be listing to and fro, lulled by gentle waves. He could barely keep his eyelids open.

"Well, she's gone too far this time, hasn't she?" Sheriff Leahey said.

"Yes," Wyatt said from the tangle of dusty blankets in the back of Ed McClintock's truck. "Too far."

He spent a week recovering at St. Mary's Health Center. Afterward he moved into the Salvation Army depot and began his work on the loading dock. But he declined to press domestic violence charges against Caroline. Or even file for a restraining order. To this day he hadn't spoken to his sister. Which was not to say that he hadn't seen her. She came to the depot from time to time, and when she did, he made a point of staying out of sight behind the loading dock's canvas curtain. Surely Caroline knew he lived there, and yet she didn't seem to be searching for him. From his vantage point behind the curtain, she looked like any number of slumped bargain hunters. But different, too—more than a little clumsy, stuporous, drained of her anger. Harmless maybe.

During mess hall dinner Saturday evening, Wyatt observed Mr. Kindermann, whose habit was to sit silent and mostly unnoticed through each meal, rise from the director's table, and thread his way to the long serving counter at the center of the hall. He raised his hand in appeal for quiet and then announced, over the squall of voices, that they'd reached day six and were now halfway through the State Hospital Session.

At once a cheer went up. It had begun with the counselors, but more than a few campers, startled by the applause, had begun clapping and shouting in gruff imitation of what they'd just heard.

"For many of us it's an occasion worth celebrating," Mr. Kindermann said. He let his gaze travel the mess hall and alight on as many counselors as he could find: Carrie Reinkenmeyer, Daniel Hartpence, Kathleen Bram, Christopher Waterhouse—though his searching glance did not include Wyatt. "I do pay attention," he continued. "Some of your opinions have made their way to me. And so I know that you've been overwhelmed at times and challenged in ways you never expected. This is the seventh year we've welcomed campers from the state hospital, and each year we rediscover what a challenge it is. I don't kid myself. I know the demands are much harder for you, the counselors. But it's quite a challenge for those of us on the senior staff as well. We have more responsibility. We certainly worry more. The decisions we have to make seem harder. Or at least they feel harder to me." There was something about this last remark that made Wyatt and the others take pause—an intimacy perhaps, a privateness that they'd not yet heard from Mr. Kindermann. "And still we have another week to get through," he said. "Whatever this next week brings for us, I want you all to know that we see the hard work and sacrifices you're making. We're proud of you. We appreciate your efforts, more than you may realize."

There was more still. As a mark of Mr. Kindermann's appreciation, he would make possible a rare freedom. Once this evening's activity had ended and the campers had been put to bed, two counselors from each of the four cabins would meet at the camp office. Mr. Kindermann would hand over the keys to the camp van so that they could travel twelve miles to the Dairy Queen in Ellsinore. There they would buy treats for the entire staff. It would be Mr. Kindermann's great pleasure to pay for this outing.

Free ice cream? It shouldn't have lifted their spirits the way it did. They weren't children after all. But the promise of ice cream got them talking right away. Who would go to Ellsinore in the camp van? (Not Wyatt, since he had cabin watch that night.) What stops might they make along the way? What ice cream concoction would each of them order? To that end, a small notebook began to circulate, and throughout the evening's activity, a leisurely kickball tournament held in the open meadow, the notebook went back and forth among the counselors as each person inscribed or amended his or her order. It wasn't until after the evening activity had ended and they were shepherding their campers back to the cabins that one of the counselors, Ellen Swinderman, wondered if anyone had taken Linda Rucker's order. As it happened, no one had. In fact, they hadn't seen Linda Rucker at the scavenger hunt or, for that matter, at mess hall dinner.

No one thought to pursue this mystery. There were a hundred and four state hospital campers to bathe and get to bed. This was easily Wyatt's least favorite time of day. It required of him a sternness that felt like an elaborate bluff. In Cabin Two, amid the pandemonium of bare bodies and rank odors and casual bullying, he had to order and shove retarded men out of his way. Thomas Anwar Toomey had to be warned and warned again to extinguish his last cigarette and return to his bunk. In the mayhem of the sleeping barracks, Leonard Peirpont seemed especially hapless, especially pitiful. The decent thing would have been to sit awhile at the foot of Leonard's bunk and listen to a few of his disjointed remarks. No time for that. Wyatt had to be up and moving continuously back and forth between the two barracks and across the screened porch that connected them. It was on the floor of this porch where they'd set out mattresses for Dennis Dugan and Frederick Torbert, both of whom had been caught congregating in the back of the barracks at night with other men. On several occasions during the past few nights both Dennis and Frederick had been startled, traumatically so, by Christopher Waterhouse and his crashing pot lids. These pot lids had been tied together with yellow twine and were now hanging beside the porch door from a nail in the wall. They hung there as a kind of warning and, more than once, Wyatt, crossing the porch on his rounds, caught either Dennis or Frederick awake on his mattress and staring up at these hanging lids with an anxious regard.

At midnight Christopher Waterhouse appeared at the porch door with a paper bag containing Wyatt's hot fudge sundae with peanuts. Christopher had been one of the lucky eight who'd traveled by van to Ellsinore, and now he was back at Kindermann Forest bearing ice cream treats for those who'd stayed behind.

"Nicely done," he said to Wyatt through the screen mesh of the door. Apparently he meant the lack of noise and commotion in the sleeping barracks, as if this happy coincidence had been brought about by a magnificent effort from Wyatt. "Have you had to crash the cymbals on Dennis and Frederick?" he asked.

"No, no. They've been quiet."

"They're fake-sleeping right now," Christopher whispered. He opened the door wide enough to lean his head in and study them as they lay on their mattresses. "They're waiting for their chance."

"I guess so."

"No guessing about it, Wyatt. Come on now. You've earned this," he said, handing over the bag and a red plastic spoon. His expression was open, generous. He seemed entirely pleased to have this opportunity to stand on the cabin landing and watch Wyatt sample the sundae. "Go ahead," he said. "It's good stuff. We tried to keep it cold."

"I will. I'll just . . . wait till a little later."

"No you *won't*."

Wyatt turned back toward the darkened interior of the cabin. For a moment he thought he might pretend to hear a noise and investigate. Instead, he said, "I wear a retainer at night. To keep my teeth from going too crooked. I'm wearing it now."

"Well, don't be shy. Plop it out. Toss it in the bag here."

After some consideration, he did as Christopher Waterhouse suggested, plucked the retainer from the roof of his mouth, dropped it into the bag—a wet retainer, a thing as dreary and strangely formed as himself.

"Now try a little bit of this sundae."

Wyatt placed a spoonful delicately on his tongue. Even melted, it tasted like a rare prize.

"Well?" Christopher Waterhouse asked.

"Yes," Wyatt said.

"Yes what?"

"It's good stuff."

"I told you so," Christopher Waterhouse said. "Thanks for holding down the fort." He almost turned to walk away. "Hey," he said. "Here's a question I've been wanting to ask you for some time, Wyatt. Do you mind?"

"I don't mind," Wyatt said.

"You decided to come work here at Kindermann Forest, right? And you did it knowing that for the first two weeks you'd have to take care of people like Dennis and Frederick? Retarded people. You knew it and you decided to come here anyway?"

He took another modest bite of his hot fudge sundae. "I didn't know," Wyatt said. "I thought there'd be children."

"And you wanted to work with children?"

To hear Christopher Waterhouse speak this hope aloud made it seem all the more unlikely. "I thought . . . ," Wyatt said. "I thought that if we gave the kids a little bit of time they'd get used to me."

"That might be true," Christopher Waterhouse said. He seemed to be thinking the prospect through carefully. "Maybe all we have to do is wait till the kids get here and find out." Then he tilted his head in what seemed to be a sorrowful direction. *"But,"* he said, "I happen to know a few things. There's going to be some changes happening very soon at camp. Good changes, most of them. One of the things that's being talked about is moving a few people around once the State Hospital Session is over. You'd be one of them, Wyatt. You'd be moved over to the horse stables. You'd become a wrangler. Then they'd find or hire someone else to stay here in Cabin Two and look after the kids." He squinted apologetically. "What do you think about that?"

For the moment, Wyatt couldn't arrive at a conclusion. He was embarrassed to have Mr. Kindermann and Linda Rucker change the work assignments on his account. His first instinct was that it was probably for his own good.

"Do you even know anything about horses, Wyatt?"

"A little bit," he said.

"I'm not sure it's fair," Christopher Waterhouse said. "I'll have to think about it some more. I'll promise you this much, though. If I happen to be around people and they're talking about moving you to the horse stables, I'll say, 'Hold on a minute. Wyatt Huddy did a great job taking care of his state hospital campers, and now we need to give him a chance to work with the children.' I'll say that, if it's all right with you?"

Wyatt nodded, solemnly.

"But you're going to have to think about what it is that you want. What do you want, Wyatt?"

It nearly made him blush, this question. He wasn't used to such direct and intimate attention. The questions people put to one another. It amazed him. He made a small show of peering deep into the well of his paper sundae cup.

"You look ready to say something, Wyatt. Like you have something on your mind."

He did, of course. And, really, he should probably go ahead and discuss the matter. Wouldn't it be better to do so with Christopher Waterhouse, who'd been kinder to him than any of the other counselors?

"Well, that's all right then," Christopher said, after a prolonged and uneasy silence. "I have ice cream to deliver. You take care, Wyatt. I'll see you around." He stepped back from the screen door and into the blackness of the walkway.

Wyatt studied the empty landing where he'd been standing. Too late now. He'd come very close to discussing with Christopher a delicate subject. Not the matter of Evie Hicks, which was too terrible to admit. But another subject, almost equally troubling to Wyatt. It had to do with the meeting Mr. Kindermann had called in the camp office. About the disagreement over the IQ score of a retarded person. Was it seventy? Or was it one hundred? He'd certainly like to know.

Chapter Nine

Whatever the satisfactions of being camp nurse might be (and, surely, Harriet could think of several, if given a minute to concentrate), it wasn't an assignment that allowed much in the way of uninterrupted sleep. At some juncture of the night, in one or more of the four sleeping cabins, there came a point at which a camper's cough or rash or extremely odd behavior worried a counselor enough that he or she—most often a she, since the male counselors tended to let things slide—would usher the camper by flashlight out of the cabin and through the tunneling woods, up the gravel pathway to the infirmary door. Harriet, who slept in hospital scrubs and T-shirt, would rise to the occasion. Her remedies were simple enough: cough drops, calamine lotion, antihistamines and antacids, aspirin, unless the ailment was more serious and she'd have to unlock her medicine cabinet and retrieve an asthma inhaler or a calming middle-of-the-night dose of Valium. In almost every case the camper would be allowed to pass the rest of the night on an infirmary bed and the grateful counselor would shuffle back to the cabins.

Harriet would try to return to sleep. But always she was torn between the obligations of two rooms. First and foremost there was the narrow living quarters, where James slumbered away on a cot beside her single bed. All night he wore a pinch-mouthed, determined expression, as if he were being brave in the face of a scolding lecture. In this room she could lie close enough to her son to reach across the narrow aisle between their beds and hold his hand while he slept.

But in the next room, the much larger and weakly lit infirmary, there were always several or more state hospital campers turning in their bunks. Sometimes they called out in strange, reedy voices. Or they wheezed and belched and staggered to the bathroom, where, invariably, they performed a rushed and messy toilet. More troubling yet, the state hospital campers, while lying in their infirmary bunks, were always a few feet away from cabinets full of potent medications or razor-sharp instruments. Locked cabinets, certainly. But why did the cabinet doors have to be composed of glass panels large enough to smash a hand through?

And so Harriet became a back-and-forth sleeper: thirty minutes of light slumber beside James, until a worrisome cough or grunt or commotion in the next room would send her into the infirmary to sort out or clean up whatever mess had transpired in her absence. Then she'd settle down on one of the empty infirmary bunks and rest awhile—you couldn't exactly call it sleep—until the need to check on James moved her back into their living quarters. And so forth. And so on.

It would almost certainly wear her out, this routine. At some point—not tonight, hopefully—she would be too drained and groggy to trust herself. This was an unsettling thought, and at the moment— an obscure span of time somewhere between Saturday night and Sunday morning—Harriet, collapsed half-awake on an infirmary bunk, decided to ask Mr. Kindermann for an assistant at night. Or rather she'd demand an assistant. *Demand.* She'd no more than decided this than someone began tapping persistently on the infirmary door.

She checked her wristwatch: 5:32 A.M. Eventually she stood swaying and washed her face at the sink. She put her hand on the doorknob.

Outside Linda Rucker stood balanced on the infirmary step. She was cocooned inside an overlarge flannel shirt and gripped a cup of coffee in one hand. She seemed to be waiting, eyebrows raised, for a verdict from Harriet. Just beyond the infirmary yard, on the gravel roadway, sat an idling Chevrolet Nova packed to the ceiling with bedclothes, kitchenware, books, winter coats.

"Well?" Linda Rucker said.

"What time is it?" Harriet asked, even though she'd checked a moment ago. She was studying the Nova's vivid red parking lights glowing against a backdrop of blurred darkness.

"You don't know, do you?" Linda said.

"I . . ." She shrugged and rubbed the corners of her eyes. "I guess I don't."

"But I thought he made an announcement at dinner?"

"Mr. Kindermann? He did. But it was just about . . . free ice cream."

"Free ice cream?" Linda Rucker said. She'd stepped back onto the infirmary yard, rooted in her shirt pocket and found a cigarette. When she set fire to the tip, Harriet could see Linda's hands shaking. Her face—still a decidedly glum and unlovely face—was in the grip of a naked and agonized expression. "Free ice cream?" she repeated. "Well, no one's going to squabble about that, are they? But he was supposed to announce something else."

"What's that?"

"I've been let go," she said and grinned a hard, angry, impossible grin.

Let go? For a moment Harriet's confusion felt frozen in time. And then, all at once, it started to make sense—the odd timing of Linda's visit, the anguished expression, the packed Chevy Nova. She'd been too groggy to understand it at first, but each of these things carried the aura of a slowly unfolding crisis. "Why would he do that?" Harriet asked, incredulous.

"He seems to believe . . ." Linda shook her head and squeezed shut her eyes.

"What?"

"He thinks I have the hots for Christopher Waterhouse," Linda said. "He thinks I've let my . . . *feelings* for Christopher get in the way of doing my job. That I've formed a fixation."

"That's ridiculous."

"Yes. It is," Linda agreed, flatly.

"Do you think he's going senile? Or maybe suffered a stro—"

"No."

"But the decisions he makes. You can't make sense of them."

"He's doing exactly what he wants to do," Linda said. "It's easier for him now that Sandie's not around." With that she let out a long, deflated exhalation, half sigh, half sob. When Harriet stepped forward to steady her, to offer her comfort—but what kind of consoling gesture could you make to someone so closed off?—Linda stepped back and raised her hand, a clear appeal not to be touched. After a while, she said, "You haven't asked me if it's true."

"Well," Harriet said. "Is it true?"

"Is what true?"

"Do you have a fixation with Christopher Waterhouse?"

"I have a notion that I can't stop thinking about, a notion that he's not a good person."

"But do you have . . . feelings for him?"

"I do *not*," Linda insisted. She'd raised her voice so that it took on the terseness and hard sputter of a threat. All the more unnerving because with Linda Rucker, always glum, always restrained, you couldn't imagine what a further escalation of her anger might look like. "I'd be a fool if I did," she continued. "If I was a grown woman, running a summer camp and getting crushes on pretty lifeguards."

At this Harriet stepped down to the yard, bringing the infirmary door almost closed—enough to hear a commotion inside, but enough also to keep her resting patients from overhearing what Linda Rucker might say next. "All right," she said. "All right, Linda. Take it easy." She stood, arms folded, listening to the low idling of Linda's car. "And do you still have your suspicion? About Christopher?" she asked.

"I do," Linda said, a hard satisfaction in her voice. "But I've been up packing all night and making arrangements. And I'm upset about being let . . . about being fired, and now when I concentrate all I come up with are two things. You're not going to think much of either of them, Harriet."

"Go ahead," Harriet said. "Try me and let's see."

Linda Rucker pouted her thin lips and shrugged—a self-shielding gesture. She didn't expect to be believed. "On Monday," she said, "the first day of State Session, I went down to the pool at closing time, and I saw Christopher at work in the lifeguard stand. There were twenty or so campers who still had to be coaxed out of the water, and he climbed down from the chair and marched into the shallow end and he went straight to Evie Hicks. Pulled her up. Walked her out of the pool. One hand on her back, one on her elbow, very . . . professional. But of all the people in the pool he hurried over and chose Evie Hicks."

Between Harriet and Linda there was a look of commiseration. For Evie Hicks. To know her was to be worried on her behalf.

"The rest comes down to a feeling I have about Christopher. It's clear he thinks he's smarter and better than me. That's no surprise. I've been dealing with that attitude all my life. Maybe it's been the same for you. People can think they're better than you in all kinds of ways. Some of those ways aren't so bad. You can tolerate it, if you have to.

But I remember meeting Christopher Waterhouse for the first time and thinking to myself, Uh-oh, this guy expects me to be stupid, even though some part of him knows I'm not. He expects me to keep my mouth shut and be grateful for whatever attention he's willing to pay me." She let the cigarette, half-smoked, fall from her hand onto the grass, where she pawed at it with the toe of her tennis shoe. "It doesn't add up to much, does it? Most people in my position would have been smart enough not to make a fuss. This is the only real job I've had," Linda said. "Eighteen summers. Kitchen girl. Counselor. Unit leader. Program director. All that time I knew it wasn't going to last. I *knew* it. If a man like Mr. Kindermann owns a summer camp and wants to run in into the ground, well that's his business, isn't it? The stupidest thing is that, because of all the time I've spent out here in the off-season, I've got it in my head that it's *my* summer camp. In the middle of winter, when no one's around, it feels like it's *mine*. But I don't own it. I just know camp better than anyone else. And I know enough about the finances to understand that it's a money loser now and Schuller can only go a couple of more years. So I tell myself, Okay, all right. I'll stick around and be the one to watch over camp until it's shut down. I'll be the one to sell off the horses—if anyone would have them—and put the chain on the gate and walk away. But this is far worse, Harriet, because I'm not going to be around to do any of those things. I won't even know what happens."

"It'll be all right," Harriet said. "You're too tired right now. But you have your reasons and I'll . . . Do you know where you're going? You have someplace to stay, don't you?"

"Family," Linda said and rolled her eyes in a reluctant direction. "I have a sister who lives an hour or so from here, in Branson. We don't like each other much."

"I can let you know," Harriet said. "I can call you maybe."

And so Linda pulled a notepad from her pocket and copied out a name and number and passed it to Harriet. "I have to get out of here before Maureen and the kitchen girls roll in," she said. "It's too much, you understand? Explaining myself over and over again." She walked unsteadily to the Chevy Nova and climbed behind the wheel.

It wasn't a picturesque farewell. The car had been hastily packed, and all manner of debris—blankets, pillows, stuffed grocery bags and shoe boxes—kept spilling onto her shoulders and lap. She pushed them back, and finally, exasperated, she hung her head over the wheel and began sobbing—an odd, angry, masculine sob. She heaved her head and shoulders up and down, as if agreeing vehemently to some opinion or song coming over the car radio. Then she put the Nova in gear, and it lurched forward and sped along the camp road, bits of gravel popping beneath the tires, until she reached the front gate, turned left, and raced off toward Highway 52.

At breakfast that morning Schuller Kindermann sat at the head of the director's table chewing his scrambled eggs and waffles and wincing vaguely whenever the babbling noise of the mess hall rose to a clamorous level. There were brown finches hopping along the railroad ties just outside the mess hall's screen doors, and from time to time Schuller turned in his seat to admire them. He sipped his orange juice. Harriet, winding among the mess hall tables with her muffin tray of pills, would pause and study him. Any moment she expected him to rise and make his announcement. But throughout the whole of breakfast and two leisurely cups of coffee he did no such thing. Nor did he, after the meal, summon the senior staff to the camp office for a meeting. By late morning she could only conclude that he'd decided to let the news of Linda Rucker's departure circulate among the Kindermann Forest staff as rumor.

But who was supposed to spread this rumor? Had it been assumed that Harriet would do the talking? Or Christopher Waterhouse? The counselors all looked too drowsy and overburdened to carry the news.

An hour before lunch Reggie Boyd stopped by the infirmary yard and with his straw hat pulled down over his eyes asked Harriet if she'd heard anything about Linda Rucker leaving camp. Harriet chose her words carefully. Linda had been let go. She was staying with her sister in Branson. A very bare-boned account, yet it made Reggie Boyd bow his head demurely. "My goodness. That sure takes the cake, don't it?" he said, before thanking her and wandering away. Ten minutes later the mess hall doors swung open and down the steps toward the infirmary marched Maureen Boyd, red-faced, indignant. "Gone for good?" she asked. "Gone already? This is Schuller's doing. He's gone too far this time, hasn't he?" she demanded of Harriet. And with that Maureen strutted about the yard flexing her elbows and stomping the ground with her scuffed white work shoes. It was a pantomime of outrage Harriet had seen before among several of her backwoods North Carolina neighbors, older women mostly, who wanted to be thought of as feisty and truth-telling. Forces to be reckoned with. It was Maureen's belief that Linda Rucker had been let go for trying to oppose Schuller Kindermann's firing of fifteen counselors the week before. "He couldn't stand to have a woman speak against him, the bastard." In Maureen's opinion each member of the senior staff should threaten to quit unless Linda was rehired. Or, she said, barring that, the whole staff should stage a walkout during today's lunch at the mess hall.

None of this happened. Maureen, whose meager salary helped support two grown daughters and three grandbabies, sat a long while smoking and drinking coffee. "It's so god damn unfair," she said. Eventually she returned to work and, with her staff of freckled kitchen girls, served lunch, albeit ten minutes late.

Not one of the new counselors was outraged or offended; no one bothered to wear an expression of sadness on Linda Rucker's behalf. It seemed they'd never felt much in the way of loyalty to Linda. Her firing was, for them, a foreseeable event. Several of the female counselors who came to the infirmary claimed to know the reasons for Linda's dismissal. Carrie Reinkenmeyer knew. Kathleen Bram knew. She'd heard it from Marcy Bittman, who, in turn, had heard it from fellow lifeguard, Christopher Waterhouse.

They didn't mind repeating the story.

It began with Linda Rucker coming down to the pool every few hours during the first days of the State Session and watching, with a supervisor's alertness, the campers as they rode the surface of the pool on their inflated rings and kickboards. She'd check the maintenance schedule and then she'd stand awhile by the lifeguard chair talking with Christopher Waterhouse. "Well, I can see you're up to no good," she'd say. Or "Anybody ever tell you you're nothing but trouble?" It took a few of these remarks for Christopher to understand he was being teased and to reply in kind. "That's right," he'd answer. "Trouble's my middle name." They'd share a confidential chuckle. Marcy Bittman, walking the perimeter of the pool deck, overheard several such exchanges.

The next time Linda stopped by she said to him, "Not a bad job, getting paid to sit there and daydream. Don't you dare tell me what it is you daydream about, either. I don't need to know."

Christopher told her she was safe. He'd keep his daydreams to himself.

To be sure they talked about other things, too: pH levels and filter maintenance, but she had a way of steering the conversation toward a wisecrack or pun. One afternoon, just after lunch, she came to the pool, looked up at him in his chair, and said, "You must get bored stiff. Does that ever happen to you, Christopher? Do you ever get bored stiff?"

He looked at her and saw the glint of implication in her gaze and laughed. He told her that getting bored stiff was an occupational hazard for male lifeguards. But the good ones knew how to cross their legs and think about baseball.

His answer seemed to put her in an ecstatic mood. She couldn't stop laughing her slumped, tight-shouldered laugh. "That's a good one," she said. "Baseball. I'll remember that."

Later Christopher told Marcy Bittman he regretted this remark. It had complicated his dealings with Linda Rucker. During the school year he waited tables at an Italian restaurant in Cape Girardeau, and there were older female customers, most of them married with school-age kids, who expected a little flirtatious banter. But none of these women had been his supervisor. He should have remembered that.

The next afternoon, Wednesday, she stopped him outside the mess hall and said she had a true story she'd like to tell him. Would he like to hear it? Sure, he said. But she wouldn't reveal her story there at the mess hall. She said she'd be down to see him at the pool in a half hour.

An hour later she plodded down the pool steps and crossed the deck to his lifeguard chair. "You can't wait to hear, can you?" she said, as if waiting on her story had made him frantic or miserable. "All right. I'll quit torturing you. Here it is."

And then she told him that when she was a counselor, not so many years ago, she had a friendship with one of the maintenance men. A nice guy. Hard worker. But he was always . . . bored stiff. And so, together, they had come up with a solution. A friendly arrangement. She'd meet him behind the arts and crafts pavilion every day during Siesta. She'd unfasten his belt buckle and blue jeans. Then she'd help him relax. With her hand and a little bit of suntan lotion. A favor she was happy to perform. They usually only had ten minutes. And they had to be quiet, given the way sound carried through the woods. One problem, though. The maintenance man was very loud, especially at the moment when the favor she was performing got most . . . intense. So he'd do something funny. He'd take his John Deere cap off his head and bite down on the bill of the cap to keep from shouting out loud.

She wouldn't look Christopher in the eye. Instead she stood leaning awhile against the lifeguard stand. "Quite a story, isn't it?" she said, wistfully, and when Christopher, stunned silent in his lifeguard chair, failed to respond, she said, "Do you know what I'm going to do now? I'm gonna go up the stairs and then to the walkway. But instead of going left, to the meadow, I'm going the other way. Do you know that path?" As it happened, he did. She meant the path that lead to the archery pavilion, closed for the duration of the State Session. "When your break comes up in a few minutes," she said, "I think you should gather up a few things you might need—a towel and some lotion—and come join me." She didn't wait for an answer. She stepped away and announced, loudly, that she'd see him later, and as she crossed the deck, she swung her arm out in a big cheerful wave aimed at Marcy Bittman and several of the campers in the pool. At the top of the stairs Linda turned right, toward the archery pavilion, a path that would take her deeper into the woods.

At once Christopher climbed down from his chair and hurried over to Marcy Bittman's side of the pool and told her what had happened. They were both astonished.

More important, when his break came, he stayed right there at the pool, beside Marcy Bittman, marveling at the ordeal he'd been through.

He didn't see Linda Rucker again until the evening activity. One look from her and he knew: not just furious or disappointed or ashamed. He'd managed to offend the fiercest and most vulnerable part of her. In Linda Rucker he'd made a terrible enemy.

Could any of it be believed? The teasing? The bawdy joke? The lurid offer?

At the very least it was a story Harriet would have to weigh carefully. She'd have to view it with the same dispassionate concern she used to evaluate her patients' symptoms and complaints.

So, in this light, yes, such a thing could be believed. It could have happened. People were driven to do reckless and unseemly things. Harriet knew that.

But could Linda Rucker have said and done these things? Could she have stood beside the lifeguard chair and offered to masturbate Christopher Waterhouse with her hand and a dollop of suntan lotion?

No. Not likely. Or rather Harriet couldn't imagine a tone of voice or an expression that Linda might employ while making such an offer.

But Kathleen Bram and Carrie Reinkenmeyer and Marcy Bittman believed. They were grave and remarkably consistent in their telling of the story, and over the course of the afternoon most of the Kindermann Forest counseling staff stopped by the infirmary yard to hear the news. Certain details made them cringe. Suntan lotion, for instance. The girl counselors who heard this shivered their arms and wiggled their fingers as if they'd dipped their hands in something unsavory. "Oh, *my God*," they said. "She's so . . ."

Words failed them. But their appalled expressions made it clear. *Disgusting.* It disgusted them to hear what Linda Rucker had proposed. True, the counselors of Kindermann Forest had joked and gossiped about matters more lurid than masturbation. But Linda's offer was worse somehow—more blatant and unfair, more offensive.

Harriet stood back and listened to their complaints. She didn't offer a defense. What offended the counselors most, it seemed to her, was that the offer had come from Linda Rucker. *Disgusting* to think that the least attractive woman at Kindermann Forest had made a bid for the best-looking young man at camp.

In the mess hall that evening, after Harriet had finished passing out meds, she took a seat at the director's table and watched an unfazed Schuller Kindermann finish up his plate of chicken fingers, potato wedges, and sliced tomatoes. He seemed to be in the grip of an effusive mood, his manners lively, his conversation uncustomarily eager—the sort of tableside chitchat meant to lift the spirits of those around him.

To Harriet he said: "Excuse me, young lady. Would you steer more of those chicken fingers my way, if you please."

To Head Lifeguard Marcy Bittman: "You look tired enough to put your head down on the table and sleep. Hectic days. I know, I know. Come Saturday you'll be able to catch up on your sleep. I promise you that."

To a sullen Maureen Boyd: "Nicely done, Maureen. Especially the tomatoes. They're homegrown. I can taste that. But are they local?"

To James: "Did you know the largest tomato in the world was grown south of here in Arkansas? How many pounds do you think it weighed, James? Three pounds? Five? Would you believe it weighed seven pounds, three ounces? Because it did."

James wrinkled his slender nose. This wasn't, Harriet knew, a sign of the boy's skepticism; it was a wince of satisfaction at having a grown man, an important man, speak to him.

"Well, did you know this?" Schuller continued. "There's a giant tomato tree in China that produces tens of thousands of tomatoes each year?"

James nodded. "Yes," he said. "I know about that." And then he looked to his mother for confirmation. But what did Harriet know about giant tomato trees in China? And how to explain something almost as remarkable: Schuller's popularity with James and—according to Linda Rucker and Maureen Boyd—with all the youngest boys who came to camp, the seven- to ten-year-olds. They revered Schuller Kindermann, supposedly. But once they'd aged a few years, once they were beyond twelve or thirteen, they found him ridiculous.

At the end of the meal Schuller wished everyone gathered at the director's table a good evening and strolled across the meadow to his cottage. He had not mentioned, one way or the other, who would oversee the evening's activity: a campfire to be held in the southwest corner of the meadow, a campfire that would feature marshmallows and chocolate bars and a visit from an Indian brave and his loyal squaw, both on horseback.

The counselors were unsure how to proceed. Linda Rucker had always given them clear instructions for each evening event. Were *they* now responsible? Was it their job to prepare the campfire?

They needn't have worried. When they arrived at the meadow, they found a waist-high tepee of cedar logs erected and stuffed with newspaper. Ten minutes later Christopher Waterhouse drove up in the camp van and from its rear hatch produced two foldout tables, which he stocked with chocolate bars and marshmallows and thermoses of bug juice. From the edge of the crowd Harriet and James stood and watched the fire set ablaze. Everyone hunted for sticks upon which to spear their marshmallows. Counselor Michael Lauderback uncased his guitar and led the state hospital campers in a raucous and uneven version of "I've Been Working on the Railroad." Such awful crooning. Yet they were wildly happy to sing this song. Several campers who, until now, had spent their week dazed and flat-eyed and stumbling managed somehow to surface from beneath the heavy mantle of their medications and bark out a few words to the song. *Live . . . long . . . day,* they warbled, as if they were answering a chorus of voices that had traveled a very great distance to reach them.

At twilight two riders appeared on the horizon of the meadow and trotted their horses to within twenty yards of the fire. The Indian brave, a shirtless Wayne Kesterson in cutoff jeans and war paint across his chest and cheeks, folded his arms Indian-style and nodded sagely at their gathering. Beside him, Marcy Bittman, dressed in a buckskin-fringe skirt and blouse, beneath which they could see the outline of her black one-piece swimsuit, glared at them with a fervent gaze, thrusting her chin and breasts forward, an attempt, largely successful, to appear wild and fetching. Together Wayne and Marcy raised their hands as if swearing an oath and said: "We command all who have gathered here at the sacred fire to love the earth and lead honorable lives." Then they turned their trail horses and galloped off. The campers watched them go. All day long they'd been promised a visit from an Indian brave and squaw, and now those campers aware enough to understand what they'd just seen, the fulfillment of a promise, called after the horses. *Come back, come back, come back!*

Chapter Ten

I wouldn't buy an inch of cropland . . . *there,*" Leonard Peirpont said.

"Where?" Wyatt asked

"At the . . . Over at the . . ." But by then he'd lost the thread of his thoughts. With Leonard, you could see the gears slipping, the rift in concentration, the soft pursing and unpursing of his lips. "I wouldn't . . . ," he muttered.

"All right."

"Bolivar County," Leonard said. He seemed startled to have come up with the name. "I wouldn't go there. Not even if you paid me in a pile of silver dollar coins."

"What about a pile of gold coins?"

Leonard sat and brooded over the question, and then, unexpectedly, he grinned. It was odd, truly. Some part of Leonard seemed to know he was being teased. And yet, another part of him remained oblivious. "I wouldn't go there," he said. "Considering the way they'll treat you."

"And how do they treat you?"

"You know *full well*," he said, scowling through his glasses. "I don't have to tell you, do I?" His narrow professor's face turned an indignant red.

"All right. Take it easy, Leonard. Your move. Look here. Your move. Go ahead now," Wyatt said.

On the picnic table between them was a loaded checkerboard. Of all the activities at camp, this was Leonard's favorite, especially the jumping, one checker over another, his own or Wyatt's, regardless of direction or rules. He managed to clasp a red checker in his unsteady right hand. What happiness this brought him. At once he began jumping the checker forward and back and sideways.

It was Tuesday an hour after lunch, a ripely warm but by no means insufferable June afternoon. They'd chosen a shaded picnic table a dozen yards from The Sanctuary. Nearby Jerry Johnston and Thomas Anwar Toomey had found patches of earth to sit upon. Both men were occupied. Jerry had a bounty of paper scraps, which he pulled from the pockets of his overalls and sorted into various piles. But the piles, once completed, didn't appear to please him, and he'd shake his head and scramble all the scraps together and start over. Thomas Anwar had his cigarettes. At the moment he was squatting with his back against an elm tree, smoking and staring out at the afternoon with a look that was, for Thomas Anwar, close to satisfaction.

"Well, all right then," Wyatt said. He reset the checkerboard for Leonard. Then he called out to Jerry and Thomas Anwar. "I'll be right back," he said. "You two sit right here, you understand."

Neither of them bothered to look up at him.

"I'll be right back," he repeated, and then he rose from the table and took off at a brisk pace for The Sanctuary, turning around once, twice, three times and finding Leonard and Jerry and Thomas Anwar unchanged. Oblivious. He hurried through the swinging screen door of The Sanctuary. Inside, several camp dogs had crawled onto the couches and were stretched out sleeping, their dusty snouts buried in the crevices of the cushions. Otherwise The Sanctuary was vacant, the pay phone unattended. He slipped five quarters into the slot and dialed. While he waited he pulled back the window curtain for a view of the meadow and the picnic table where he'd been sitting.

The phone line clicked and hummed, and eventually Captain Throckmorton answered. "Wyatt," he said. "My goodness. *Wy-att*." There was a swell of relief in the captain's voice and, as always, a brand of good humor meant exclusively for Wyatt. "I've been wondering about you, Wyatt," the captain said. "I've been . . . How is it there? How are the children?"

So much to explain. Too much, really. He had to start at the beginning. He said he'd arrived at camp last Monday. Barbara McCauley had driven him down. But there were no children. Not yet. The children wouldn't arrive until next week. For now all the counselors here at Kindermann Forest had to take care of adults from the state hospital. Adults with problems.

"What kinds of problems, Wyatt?"

He looked out through the window at Leonard Peirpont, who sat hunched at the picnic table trying with his unsteady hands to fit his checkers into a neat stack. Leonard couldn't quite manage this simple task. *What an idiot,* Wyatt thought, tenderly. "All kinds of problems," he said. "Most of the people here are, you know, retarded."

There was from Captain Throckmorton a long, near-whistling sigh. After a while he said, "Oh my."

"The first two weeks here are for retarded people. Then the children come. That's the way it works."

"I didn't know that, Wyatt. If I had known, I'd have . . . I would have told you. You understand that, right?"

"Yes. I do."

"What have you . . . How have you been getting along?"

"It's hard work. Well, it's hard for all the counselors. Taking care of people who are like this."

"I'm sure it is."

"There's four more days until the state hospital buses come back and the campers leave. Then we get a day off. Then the children come."

"I see."

Wyatt stood holding the receiver to his ear, waiting. "So, yes, it's a lot of work," he said. There was a graceful way, surely, to steer the conversation in the direction it needed to go. He wished he knew how to do the steering. "I've been thinking about the horses here. About working with the horses."

"The horses?"

"Yes, that's right," he said. But he knew he'd been too vague. He concentrated. "There's some talk around here," he said. "People are saying that when the State Hospital Session ends, I'll be asked to stop being a counselor and become a wrangler instead. I wouldn't work with the children. I'd work with horses. I'd spend all day at the stables. I'd sleep there, too."

"At the stables?"

"Yes. That's what you do if you're a wrangler."

"Whose idea is this?" the captain asked. "Who is it that said you should become a wrangler?"

"The people in charge here. Mr. Kindermann maybe. I don't know."

"And do you want to be a wrangler? I mean, if it was up to you, would that be your choice?"

"I don't know."

"Well, let me ask you this, Wyatt. Have you done a good job this week, taking care of the people at camp? The retarded people?"

This seemed to Wyatt an unlikely, if not unfair, question. It wasn't an evaluation he should be asked to make. He leaned forward and pushed back the dusty and threadbare window curtains. Outside, in the brilliant light of the afternoon, Jerry Johnston was trying to rise to his feet. For a man of his roundness and size, this meant crawling to the picnic table and pulling himself up, one foot planted, then the other rising up in increments. "It's hard to say," Wyatt said. "It's hard to say one way or the other."

"And when you worked here at the depot. Did you do a good job then?"

"I'm not sure about that, either."

"Then let me make it clear. You did a very good job for us, Wyatt. Of all the people who work at the depot, you were the most thorough, the most dependable. And I'm willing to bet it's the same at Kindermann Forest. You've worked hard. I'm sure of it. You did what you were supposed to. Am I right about that?"

"Yes, maybe."

"So you did a good job, and that means you get to decide what your assignment should be. If it's working with the horses, if that's what you really want, then tell Mr. Kindermann. But if it's the children you want to work with—and I think it is, Wyatt, I think you'd like to spend your summer working with children rather than horses—then you need to go to Mr. Kindermann and tell him so."

"I don't know . . . I don't think that's the way people do it here."

"You can stand up for yourself and tell other people what it is you want."

"Yes, all right. But I'd have to say it a different way, wouldn't I? So that they wouldn't think . . . Because they might think I was making trouble." He turned his attention back out the window to the bright afternoon and the stretch of green meadow. Jerry Johnston had begun doing something odd. He was tottering about, drunkenly, throwing his head back one moment, as if to howl at the sky, and then hunching over suddenly, dangling his arms out as if he were an exhausted runner.

"It's okay to be direct with people. You can say, 'Look here, I did a good job and now I want to work with the children.'"

"Maybe so."

"You're allowed to make some trouble, Wyatt. It's perfectly all right to stand up for yourself and get angry sometimes. When people are being unfair to you, you can speak your mind."

Outside Jerry Johnston was standing up bolt straight and clutching at the buttons of his overalls. Then, as if a string had been suddenly cut, he collapsed heavily onto the ground.

Wyatt weighed the phone receiver in his hand. Far away, in Jefferson City, Captain Throckmorton was talking to him. . . . *Better to speak your mind than to . . .* The receiver was gray and chipped. It was rising in Wyatt's hand. After a moment of dumbstruck consideration, he placed it gently in the cradle.

He was a lurching and clumsy runner. He stumbled over furniture, bolted through the swinging screen door of The Sanctuary. It was still a lovely afternoon, sun-dappled and warm, a few distant strolling figures on the open meadow and a wave of happy voices rising from the pool in the woods—except now, near the picnic tables, there was Jerry Johnston's slumped form in the grass. Not motionless, not a still body, just a pear-shaped man in overalls lying on his side and rocking back and forth.

Wyatt hurried to him and bent down. *"Jerry,"* he said. "What'd you do? What happened?"

From Jerry a low gurgle. He'd gone red in the face. His fists were squeezed into tight paws.

Other people had begun to take notice: several counselors crossing the meadow turned toward the Sanctuary yard. Nearby, Leonard Peirpont looked up blinking from his stacks of checkers. Thomas Anwar Toomey crawled over from where he'd been smoking and gazed down upon his stricken friend. "No, no, no," Thomas Anwar said. "Not good! Not good!"

One of the kitchen girls appeared suddenly over Wyatt's shoulder.

She stared down at Jerry Johnston. "Oh shit!" she said and took off running for the infirmary.

"It hurts. It hurts. It hurts," Jerry moaned.

"Where?" Wyatt asked.

Jerry put a plump hand on the bib of his overalls. "Here," he said and patted his fingers atop his chest.

A simple gesture, but it made Wyatt cringe in dread. He could picture Jerry Johnston's heart, a swelled and probably misshapen vessel. It had deflated somehow or frozen midbeat. Jerry had dropped to the ground. While this had happened, Wyatt had been away on the phone claiming to be a responsible counselor.

Someone shouted, "Here she comes. She's coming now," meaning, of course, the camp nurse, Harriet Foster. There were several minutes, as long and as intimate as any Wyatt had known, in which he gripped Jerry Johnston's hand and listened to his anxious breathing.

The crowd had begun shouting for her, "Hurry, please. Hurry up, Harriet," until at last the throng of onlookers parted. How odd. They'd all wanted her here so badly—they'd longed for her—that once she'd arrived and knelt in the meadow grass beside Jerry, she seemed entirely too ordinary for this emergency. They wanted someone else. "All right, Jerry. All right," she said and, rather than brandish any tools from a canvas bag of instruments slung over her shoulder, she rested her hand on Jerry Johnston's forehead, then his cheek, and finally in the crook of his fat neck, as if he were a feverish child. "Don't breathe so fast," she said. "Slow it down, please."

"I can't," Jerry panted.

"Can't because it hurts? Or can't because you're scared?"

"I don't know," he said.

From her canvas bag she extracted a stethoscope and a blood pressure cuff, which she wrapped around Jerry Johnston's arm. "Tell me where it hurts," she said.

He patted his chest.

"Does it feel heavy? Does it feel like weight on top of you?"

He closed his eyes and shuddered.

"Does it burn?"

"Yes."

She pumped the blood pressure cuff and listened through her stethoscope, and then she looked up sharply and insisted that the crowd of onlookers back away and be quiet. Again she put her hands on Jerry Johnston's face and neck and listened through her stethoscope. She counted out loud to herself and bent down close to her patient, studying the features of his face—his eyes and nose and bulging tongue—and then leaned back on her heels and scrutinized him from a wary distance. At last she said, "I'd like you to sit up, Jerry. Would you do that?"

"No, no, I can't," he whimpered.

She turned her gaze from Jerry to Wyatt.

"What'd he have for lunch, Wyatt?" she asked.

"Hot dogs," Wyatt said. "Beans."

"How much?"

"A lot."

"How much is a lot?"

"Four hot dogs. Two plates of beans. Then some marshmallows he was saving."

"My goodness," she said. "Four hot dogs." She bowed her head, gratefully, and searched through the pockets of her jeans until she found a roll of antacid tablets. Into Jerry Johnston's wet mouth she placed two tablets and ordered him to chew.

"I can't," he grunted. "It hurts too much."

"Oh, but you can. Wyatt and I will sit beside you until the hurt goes away."

"But it won't go away," Jerry cried. Thick tears poured down his face. "I'm having a heart attack."

"No, no. You're having indigestion."

He turned his face away from them and cried harder.

"You ate too much for lunch, Jerry. If you sit up and swallow the tablets, I promise you'll feel better."

But he didn't appear any less anguished or afraid. He gazed up at Harriet and wept. "No heart attack," she promised. The crowd of onlookers pressed in around them. "No heart attack, Jerry," they said. "Sit up. Please. You can do it, Jerry." He lingered awhile under the warm light of their attention, and then, still weeping, he sat up, chewed and swallowed the antacid tablets. Wyatt and Harriet helped hoist him onto his feet for the journey to the infirmary—a plodding and laborious journey given that he required their constant support. He was still grief-stricken. "My heart," Jerry moaned as they marched him forward. "My heart." He could be distracted for a minute or two—*What's the best car to have, Jerry? What's on TV tonight?*—so that he'd walk ten or twenty paces reciting the virtues of Ford Mustangs and *The Dukes of Hazzard* before recalling the anguish of his heart attack. Then he'd slump backward and cry out, "No, no, no," and Wyatt and Harriet would catch him beneath the arms and bear the considerable weight of Jerry Johnston for a dozen yards or more until, at last, they'd crossed the meadow and climbed the infirmary step.

Inside, they guided Jerry, the infirmary's only patient, onto an empty bunk. A tremendous relief to drop the bulk of Jerry Johnston onto a mattress, to be unburdened. Afterward, they leaned against the bunk frame and tried to catch their breath.

"Sit up, Jerry," Harriet pleaded. She shuffled to the sink and filled a cup of water. "Sit up and drink some water." But he did the opposite: lay down and turned his face to the wall.

"Please," she said, wearily. When he didn't respond, she drank the water herself and lay down on a nearby bunk. Eyes closed, she draped a slender arm across her forehead, as if she were settling in for a long nap. "For goodness' sake," she said. "Sit down and rest a minute, Wyatt."

He wavered a moment and eased into a chair.

"You all right?" she asked.

"Yes," he said. "I'm all right." Which was mostly true. His difficulties, at the moment, were all minor. His back ached. He seemed to be sweating too much. And he wasn't used to young women, particularly attractive women, treating him with such familiarity. Such kindness. He wasn't at all sure that he liked it.

"I'll keep Jerry here till dinnertime," Harriet said, her eyes still closed. "He's just acting this way because he's scared. But he doesn't have anything to be scared of. Do you, Jerry?"

No answer from their patient except for a huffy, indignant snort.

Otherwise the infirmary was still and quiet and nicely cool. There were stripes of soft light bleeding though the window blinds.

"Wyatt," she said. "Every time I see you around camp, I always want to ask you . . . not ask . . . tell you. I always want to tell you." She propped her head up on her outstretched arm and peered at him. "I don't know if this will be worth anything to you, if it's even worth saying. But when I was in high school, back in North Carolina, there was a boy I knew. Only four years old. A boy with Apert syndrome. I took care of him sometimes. He had a twin brother. And what I know about that boy, Taylor, the one with Apert syndrome, was that he was as smart and normal as any other four-year-old. Smarter and more normal than his twin brother."

Wyatt sat perfectly still in his chair. For the time being he was too embarrassed, too aware of himself, to offer her a sensible reply.

"I thought I'd let you know about that," she said.

He nodded.

"Should I have let you know?" she asked. "Is it all right that I said something?"

"Yes," he said. "It's all right." He readied himself to stand and leave. "Thank you," he said.

Chapter Eleven

She stirred awake very early in the morning and found James standing at her bedside, flexing up and down on his tiptoes. He had one hand clenched on the crotch of his pajamas.

"Hold on now," she said. "Just a second. I need to find . . . Can you hold it?"

He nodded and tightened his grip. This was, for James, a typical morning dilemma: he needed badly to pee, and yet the infirmary bathroom was almost always occupied, usually by a very fat, half-dressed, retarded woman who'd failed to close the door and who could be seen propped atop the toilet like a roosting ostrich.

Harriet located her sandals. Then she led the boy out the door to the edge of the yard, to a dirt gulley that ran alongside the infirmary. A gauzy, break-of-day light was seeping through the dew-weighted cedar branches and clarifying, inch by inch, the yard and pathways and open meadow. No chirping birds or barking dogs yet. No lumbering campers, either. Without them the grounds of Kindermann Forest looked soft-edged and vulnerable.

James, poised at the edge of the gully, stood rocking to and fro and peeing with great accuracy, and when he was done he craned his face up to her, Harriet, his mother, and said, "I don't care if I ever see any of them again."

She didn't bother correcting him. Today was Thursday, day eleven of the State Hospital Session. It felt like a great accomplishment to have made it this far. Eleven days. Last night she'd heard the exhausted counselors of Kindermann Forest boast that they were in the home-stretch now. There were Thursday and Friday yet to conquer. It would all officially end Saturday morning, when three white state hospital buses rumbled into camp and reclaimed their one hundred and four patients. What a moment of relief that would be! To see the loaded buses pass from the gates of Kindermann Forest bound for the hospitals and group homes from which they'd come. The staff had already set their sights on such a moment. They were looking ahead and calculating each small milestone. Three more rise-and-shines. Two more working days in which, at nearly every moment, they'd be duty-bound to their campers. Two more evening activities. Two more clamorous bedtime routines. Two more dreadful showers.

For Harriet seven more rounds of medication to anxiously sort and distribute. Two more sleep-wrecked night shifts in the infirmary.

How nice it would be to stumble back to her bed for another hour's sleep. But there was no chance of that. From inside the infirmary came the sound of last night's patients stomping across the wood floor. James had found his digging spoons and was hunched down in the yard excavating tiny roads for his Matchbox cars.

A half hour before breakfast one of the counselors, Daniel Hartpence, brought Harriet her first patient of the day: Frederick Torbert. What could be said of Frederick that his appearance didn't already make clear? He had a broad chest and muscle-bloated arms and neck. (How could this be when Frederick, like several other brawny male campers, never seemed to exercise?) With his hard, jutting forehead and tiny black-marble eyes, he looked Neanderthal, which was precisely the way he behaved—ferocious and grunting and single-minded. One day last week, in the middle of mess hall lunch, he'd stood up, put his hands beneath the edge of his table, and flipped it over in one easy motion. Fortunately, no one had ended up beneath the overturned table, which was made of oak and weighed one hundred and sixty pounds. Just to move a mess hall table for sweeping required the wholesale exertions of four kitchen girls.

What brought Frederick to the infirmary was a thick splinter, several days old, lodged in the palm of his hand. As a source of pain and infection, it didn't seem to bother him. He sat beside Harriet on the picnic table in the infirmary yard, wiggling the beefy fingers of his injured hand. His unswerving gaze, softened from twice-daily doses of lithium, was focused on the crotch of Harriet's blue jean shorts.

Daniel Hartpence hovered over them, his legs half-cocked and ready to spring to Harriet's rescue. Or make a hasty retreat. "Did you know it's our turn to go see the ponies this afternoon?" Daniel announced brightly. "That'll sure be nice. Won't it, Frederick?"

From Frederick a bored grunt as Harriet tweezed the splinter from his palm.

"I know you've been looking forward to seeing the ponies," Daniel said.

"I bet he has," Harriet agreed. She smiled wanly. How halfhearted their banter sounded. But what else could they do? Around Frederick there was always the compulsion to make the sunniest of comments in order to displace whatever primitive thoughts might be gaining a perch inside his head.

She swabbed his wound with disinfectant and sealed it with a Band-Aid. "Is that better?" she asked. In answer he rose from the bench, opened his mouth in what might have been a loose grin. He held his enormous arms out to her. Apparently, he wanted a hug from Nurse Harriet.

A bad idea to accept this offer. But what horrible arrogance to refuse it. Harriet took a step toward his open arms, and at once he brought his hand down and rubbed the bandaged palm over the crotch of her shorts.

She stepped back right away. She'd learned to suffer these indignities with a minimal degree of fuss. No stomp of protest. No outward shudder of disgust. "All right," she said, as if his determined groping had been a mindless act. "I'll let you gentlemen get on with your day." She stood in the yard and watched Frederick Torbert being led away by a hushed and red-faced Daniel Hartpence.

Harriet went back to her post at the infirmary picnic table. A few moments later she shivered and crossed her legs. It unsettled her, the deliberateness of what Frederick Torbert had done. He'd wanted to reach out and touch her. He'd brooded over it while she worked on his hand. Then he'd done it. Not just a lack of boundaries. Or a lack of inhibitions. It wasn't Frederick Torbert's low IQ that gave him these longings or the boldness to act on them. If he weren't retarded, if by some medical procedure or godly miracle his IQ were made forty points higher, she'd still do all she could to avoid being left alone with him.

Then there was the matter of the phone call she'd promised Linda Rucker. It irked Harriet. What had seemed at the time like a kindly gesture had evolved somehow into the demands of an actual friendship. She brooded over her obligation much of the morning, and twenty minutes before lunch she roused herself and picked up the infirmary telephone and dialed the number of Linda Rucker's sister.

The line was answered by a wheezy voice: not that of Linda

Rucker but that of Linda Rucker's sister, who grunted heavily and shrieked out Linda's name, "Lin-duhhhhhhh! Lin-duhhhhhhhhh!" A long, low, crooning wail. Layered inside this wail, waiting to be excavated, were decades of grievance and compacted insult. "Lin-duhh-hhhhhhh!" the sister wailed one last time, and then, either bored or clumsy, she seemed to let the receiver drop from her hand and clatter down onto a table or countertop.

A steady plod, plod, plod of footsteps could be heard. The receiver was hoisted up. "Harriet?" Linda Rucker said, her voice clear and alert, lively compared to her sister's, but lacking a genuine spark of interest. She took in a long, near-whistling draw of breath. "Well," she sighed. "I guess you tracked me down, didn't you?"

"I did, yes."

"I thought you might call. One of these days."

"How are you, Linda?"

"I'm all right, I suppose. Considering."

"And have you . . . What have you been doing?"

"This and that," she said. "Settling in."

"And have you had time to look for a job?" Harriet asked. She'd not wanted to pose this question, but already it seemed they'd exhausted the safe topics.

"Oh, I've looked," Linda said. "I've found one, too."

Found one? That was good news, surely. A pleasant surprise. "Well, for goodness' sake. You're not wasting any time, are you?" Harriet said. It was a relief, really. Linda had found a job. And she was willing to talk about it, too, solitary and reticent Linda Rucker. She said she hadn't needed to look very hard. In fact on Sunday, as soon as she'd arrived at her sister's house, she had unloaded her car and gone straight out to look for work. In Branson, Missouri, an Ozark tourist town, there were scores of hotels and restaurants, hundreds of service jobs. She'd been hired right away at an enormous country buffet. Kitchen work. From 3:00 P.M. to 10:00 each evening Linda Rucker stood at a counter chopping vegetables and cheese for the buffet's famous mile-long food bar.

"It's fascinating work," Linda said dryly.

"But at least you have a start at something, don't you?"

"A start at what, though? It's just chopping and slicing."

"At least you're not lying around feeling sorry for yourself."

No answer to this. No offering to the contrary.

"Well," Harriet said. "You can always move on to something—"

"All right," Linda said. "Here's a question I don't really want to ask. Is Christopher Waterhouse the new program director?"

"Mmmm," Harriet said, as if this were an entirely new possibility to consider. "Well, that's the thing. No one's made an announcement, one way or the other."

"Is he acting like he is?"

"Sometimes, yes. Sometimes he does."

"Can I tell you something?" Linda asked. "I'm not proud of admitting this, Harriet. I *hate* him."

"I'm sure you do."

"I'd like to find a way to make him miserable."

"Well . . . ," Harriet said, vaguely.

"I'd like him to suffer."

"That's, you know . . ."

"I'm usually not like this. I'm a fair-minded person, mostly. But someone like Christopher Waterhouse, he doesn't feel awful about the things he does. He isn't disgusted with himself. So the only thing you could do with a person like that is tie him down and make him suffer, *physically*, I mean."

"Well . . . ," she said again.

"I'm not talking seriously here, Harriet. It's not like I'm making plans. I'm just saying that if someone or something were ready to make Christopher suffer, and all I had to do was give my approval to get it started, I'd do it. I'd think it over a little while and nod and say *go ahead*. There's nobody else in the whole world I feel that way about."

"All right," Harriet said. "All right."

"It's god damn awful knowing what's happening there at camp. It would've been better if you hadn't called."

"But you *asked* me to," Harriet said, incredulous.

"Did I?" There was a small wavering in Linda's voice that was both obliging and unconvinced. "I don't know about that . . . if it's true or not. But even if it is, I shouldn't have asked. It does me no good to hear these things right now. To know about camp. So I'm making a firm rule about this, Harriet. No more, please. No more news about camp."

"Fine, yes. No more news."

"Thank you," Linda Rucker said. This seemed to mark the end of their conversation, but at the last moment, she let out an indignant huff and said, "Even if things are starting to fall apart without me, I still don't want to know. It does me no good, you understand?"

"All right. I won't call again," Harriet said and hung up the phone.

No time, really, to reflect on this fraught conversation. She had medications to distribute, and a dirt-smeared five-year-old boy to wash and hurry across the yard and into the mess hall for a lunch of pizza squares and salad. For James this was a happy occasion. He took his place beside Schuller Kindermann at the director's table, and Harriet, balancing her muffin tray in one hand, roamed from table to table dispensing her potent medications. It was a task that required all of her concentration.

But afterward she was tired, a blanketing, unshakable tiredness that only a weekend of bed rest could cure. All morning she'd sipped Coca-Cola to remedy her fatigue. Just after lunch she did something she hadn't done in years: begged a cigarette and then stepped out the back door of the kitchen and smoked it among the stacks of milk crates and collapsed boxes. What a strange, woozy buzz it created in her head. Her breathing slowed. Her heartbeat raced. All the particulars of the kitchen's scrubby backyard seemed magnified by a degree or two. But her tiredness did not lift.

A few hours later, while sorting dinner medications in the infirmary yard, she put a hand to her forehead and fell asleep, probably for no more than ten minutes. She woke with her arms stretched across the enormous muffin tray. In the wells of the tray lolled dozens of bright capsules and tablets. Lithium, phenobarbital, Nembutal. Kneeling beside her on the bench, as if he'd materialized out of nothing, was James, calm and alert, his chin propped in his hands while he chewed, patiently, on something tiny and dark.

Raisins it turned out. But in those first moments of waking, she'd been given a terrible start.

The day wasn't conquered yet. There were duties—some of them usual, some unusual—for Harriet to perform. Nursing duties. She was a nurse, after all. (In her most hectic moments this sometimes struck her as the oddest of facts. *I am a nurse? How strange. How could this have happened to me?*) There were stacks of file charts into which she added her notations and initials. She changed urine-stained bedsheets. To anything that looked remotely like an insect bite or ivy rash she applied calamine lotion. The usual and the unusual. She rewrapped the Ace bandage on Mrs. Gilder's swollen ankle and then a few minutes later used a pair of hemostats to remove three pearl-white pajama buttons that Ms. Pauline Kopine had squirreled away in her right nostril. What a peculiar occupation, nursing, the way it veered back and forth between the honorable and the ridiculous.

But they were in the homestretch now, she reminded herself. And who knew? She might just have the necessary stamina to make it the rest of this day and another. But nothing more than that. Nothing left over.

At dinner she dealt out her medications and then sat for two plates of Maureen Boyd's benign but compulsively edible five-layer lasagna. She drank coffee and blinked away her weariness, and when she looked around, she noticed that many of the counselors were doing the same: gulping down long sips of coffee and then heaving their shoulders and stretching open their eyes as if to wake themselves from a dream. At the end of the meal Christopher Waterhouse bounded up to the long mess hall serving counter and raised his hand for quiet. He looked to be in a jubilant mood. He had an announcement to make. In thirty minutes everyone was to meet in the open meadow for the evening's activity: the Kindermann Forest Camp Carnival. "There will be *thrilling games,*" he said in an unpracticed barker's voice. *"Extravagant prizes. Spectacular feats of competition."*

It was a camp tradition that the evening activity be hawked like miracle-cure medicine. The counselors grinned knowingly. It seemed they'd come to enjoy these exaggerations, the teasing discrepancy between what the Kindermann Forest Camp Carnival was promised to be and the homely reality of how it would turn out.

Thirty minutes later, when Harriet arrived with James at the meadow, she and the counselors found seven milk crates containing the barest ingredients of carnival games: spoons and a carton of eggs; strips of cloth for a three-legged race; a clutch of water balloons. From this, apparently, they were meant to construct an evening of entertainment. No one could, of course. The state hospital campers were, by this late juncture of the day, tired, moody, easily distracted. The counselors lacked both the energy and the necessary will. They rolled their eyes and checked their watches and prayed for it to end. But they seemed to agree: you couldn't blame Christopher Waterhouse. He'd had too many responsibilities dumped in his lap; his daytime obligations as a lifeguard, and now the fresh demands of being the undeclared program director.

This was the attitude Harriet found so baffling: the tremendous leeway afforded to Christopher Waterhouse. Maybe Linda Rucker had some notion of it. In her phone call she'd pleaded not to know the ways camp had deteriorated. What could Harriet reasonably tell her anyway? *Kindermann Forest, without you, is shabby and disorganized. The evening activities are a tiresome joke. The blame for this seems to be Christopher Waterhouse's. By the way, no one misses you. No one seems to mind.*

For the rest of the evening the campers were set loose to sift through the crates of carnival games and roam the meadow as they pleased. As evening activities went, this one was shapeless and lazy. No games, thrilling or otherwise, were played. No feats of competition, either. The campers were free to scatter debris across the meadow or, in a few cases, to form chatty little cliques that looked, from a distance, as cheery and ordinary as any summer-party gathering. Others stood rooted in the grass, flailing their limbs about, rocking to and fro and turning their heads sharply to consider the darkening bowl of the sky or the overhead whir of insects. Rarely did a camper try to push beyond the grass boundaries and into the woods; they were more compliant now, or more exhausted, than they'd been the first day of camp.

A half hour before twilight Christopher Waterhouse came bouncing across the meadow in the camp van. Until that moment he'd barely been present at the carnival, though he'd been seen nearby, hurrying along the gravel paths or hefting boxes in and out of the mess hall; a young man with pressing duties and the authority to wander wherever he chose.

The van lumbered to a halt. He stepped out and hurried to the back of the vehicle, where he flung open the rear doors and set out several folding tables. Onto these tables he placed the evening snack: bug juice and vanilla wafers.

"Gather round!" he shouted. "Gather round! Our snack is served," he announced, and the campers, many of them dispersed across the meadow or sitting cross-legged in the grass, turned or rose and began to totter in his direction. Some of them were much more difficult to summon and needed to be goaded along by the counselors, directed with a firm hand—pushed, shoved, pulled by a shirtsleeve until they joined the thickening crowd at the rear of the van.

By then Christopher Waterhouse had stationed himself before the snack tables. He held up his hand for quiet. "Before we snack," he declared, "I'd like to know one thing. Who are the winners here?"

The campers stared back at him blankly.

"All right," he said with a patient nod. His expression was open and obliging. He looked ready to coax an honest answer from each of them. "Now listen up, please," he said while lifting a box from the bed of the van. "Our Kindermann Forest Camp Carnival is over. Or almost over. It's time now, don't you think, to reward the competition winners?" He plucked a brown paper lunch bag, one of many, from the box and held it up. "Will the winners of our camp carnival please raise their hands?"

At least half of the campers hoisted their hands aloft, and Christopher Waterhouse, who seemed charmed by their response, began flinging bags into the crowd, easy, looping tosses that landed upon or near their intended targets. For a few particular members of the crowd—camp favorites like Leonard Peirpont—he waded deep into the throng of bodies and placed the bags in their grasping hands. He pressed all the way to the outer edge of the gathering and handed a bag to Harriet's son, James.

Inside the bags were a hodgepodge of items scavenged from the camp office and mess hall: a plastic spoon, a dinner mint, a Kindermann Forest postcard, a camp brochure. Ridiculous items, or so Harriet thought, until she observed the campers, and James, too, sorting through the contents of their bags with blushes of pleasure.

"A few more left still," Christopher Waterhouse said, launching bags to various campers in the crowd. "For you and you and you and . . . you," he said, until all the prizes had been distributed and he held the upturned box over his head as proof. Then he pressed his way back and stood before the snack tables. "A reminder," he said. "You do know, don't you, that tomorrow night we have our final evening activity? It's big. It's spectacular. Even the name for it is big and spectacular." He wrinkled his brow, and in a pantomime of concentration he readied himself to pronounce the title. "The Kindermann Forest Talent Show Extravaganza and Farewell Dance," he said and grinned in relief at having got the name right. "Yes," he said. "That's right. Practice your special talent—your singing or magic tricks or whatever—and your dancing, too, because . . ." In the middle of this genial advice, he turned and spotted something in the bed of the van that required all of his attention. Whatever it was, it made him blink in surprise. "I can't believe it," he said. "My mind must be slipping gears." And he reached into the van and pulled out a straw hat, the floppy-brimmed kind the maintenance men used when mowing grass. "Look here. Look what I forgot. We have one more thing to do before we end our carnival. A grand ultimate prize to give away." He looked expectantly out at his audience and said, "Did you know that there's a town nearby called Ellsinore, and in Ellsinore there's a Dairy Queen? And when our counselors have done an especially good job, we load them in the van and take them to the Ellsinore Dairy Queen for ice cream. That's what we do, yes. They love it, too. It's their reward for a job well done." He'd balanced the straw hat, bottom side up, in the palm of his hand and held it out, as if raising a toast to his listeners. In the bowl of the hat was a nest of paper slips. He pulled them out and let them trickle through his fingers and fall back into the hat. "Your names," he explained to the campers. "One of you is going to go with me this evening to Ellsinore, to the Dairy Queen. I'll do the driving and the buying. You choose the ice cream and do the eating. That's a good deal, don't you think?" He waited, grinning, hat in hand, for something—a grunt of reply—from his audience. "Are we ready now to find out who the winner is?" he continued. "Do you understand? Are you ready?"

They were a difficult crowd to read. They'd pressed in tight around the rear of the van, elbowing for room and looking at Christopher shyly or warily out of the corners of their eyes. Perhaps a few of them *had* understood. A few of them might have been ready. But mostly they seemed to be looking past Christopher Waterhouse and focusing their attention on the foldout tables, where the cooler of bug juice and little bags of vanilla wafers awaited them.

"Here we go then," he said and lofted his right arm straight up in the air, then let the wrist dip and his hand free-fall in a perfect swan dive into the bowl of the hat. He fished about for a name, his lips and jaw set in a grimace of determination but his gaze light and winsome. Then he plucked a single slip of paper from the hat, read the name, wrinkled his nose. He seemed to be searching his memory. At last, he shrugged. "The winner is . . . ," he said.

Nearby, the wrangler Stephen Walburn began a drumroll against the rear fender of the van.

"And the winner is . . . ," Christopher Waterhouse repeated, this time in a proper announcer's baritone. The drumroll fell away. He glanced again at the slip of paper. "Evie Hicks," he said.

The moments that followed were cheerful and strange. "Evie Hicks," Christopher Waterhouse said, and right away the counselors applauded, and the campers, seeing their caretakers applaud, brought their hands together clumsily and with great energy; they loved to clap after all. The mood in the crowd seemed to be shifting toward gladness and relief: the counselors pleased to see the long evening draw almost to an end, the campers happy to lurch toward the tables and claim their snacks.

Harriet, in the rear of the crowd, tightened her hold on James's hand. She tilted her head to one side, still listening. *Evie Hicks.*

In spite of herself, she smiled—an anxious smile, yet there was a current of real satisfaction in it. She sometimes heard television comedians say outrageous and ugly things, and her reaction now was much the same: she smiled in disbelief at the boldness of the joke teller, though not the joke itself.

And at the same time, from a narrow back corridor of her mind, came a soft but keening exclamation of worry. *Oh, for goodness' sake.* Uttered in one quick, breathy exhalation, it was what her elderly female patients at Meadowmont Gardens Nursing Home, the Garden Ladies, said when the gossip they shared was especially dire. *Oh, for goodness' sake,* a signal of distress that portended not just sympathy and alarm but an open permission that the news be spread at once through the many corridors of Meadowmont Gardens. "Evie Hicks," Christopher Waterhouse said, and quietly, even distantly, in the back of Harriet's mind, a chorus of Garden Ladies sang out, *Oh, for goodness' sake.* It wasn't loud or shrill enough to drown out her clear thoughts. She wouldn't call herself distracted. Or panicked. Not yet. At least this lament, clear and persistent, did have one advantage: for the first time in days she felt properly awake.

Above the meadow—and the rolling valleys that surrounded it—stretched a sky of deepening dark blue, a sky in the last stage of dusk. Were Linda Rucker directing the Kindermann Forest Camp Carnival, they'd have finished and been back in the cabins by now. But here it was ten minutes till nine and the dusk-to-dawn lamps that girded the mess hall and infirmary were flickering on. The counselors were the first to realize it. The heavy, plum-colored sky. The glinting floodlights. *They were late.* And so, hurriedly, the crowd of campers was broken apart, corralled into dozens of small groups, each group pushed eastward toward the lip of the meadow. They had to eat their vanilla wafers while tottering along the gravel pathways into the woods, and once they reached the cabins they'd be rushed through the most unpleasant chores of the day: the use of toilets, the showering, the brushing of teeth and dressing into pajamas. All of this in the name of keeping the state hospital campers on schedule.

The real schedule, of course, the more pressing schedule, belonged to the counselors. They were more persistent—and more forceful— than usual. In their resolute expressions you could see how badly they wanted to be rid of their campers for the night. Before that could happen, the sleeping barracks would need to be set to order, the campers washed and ready for bed and more or less confined to their bunks. Once these goals had been accomplished, the counselors— except those unfortunate few assigned to cabin watch—would be set free until midnight to do as they pleased.

What they did in their off-hours, what *pleased* them, had become, thanks to the lively conversation of the infirmary yard, an open secret. Harriet was privy to what went on. For instance, she knew that Wayne Kesterson had brought a generous supply of marijuana to camp, and that he and Wrangler Stephen Walburn hoped the prospect of free pot would lure one or several girl counselors to their nightly campfire in the horse pasture. So far they'd been disappointed. But there'd been other successful pairings and partnerships. Kathleen Bram and Michael Lauderback spent their nighttime hours strolling hand in hand along the roads and gravel pathways of Kindermann Forest. During the workday they were coolly polite with one another, but to see them in the off-hours, to skirt by them on a darkened path and glimpse the intensity of their attraction, was a bracing and mostly unpleasant experience. And then there was the oddest configuration of all: among Carrie Reinkenmeyer and Daniel Hartpence and Emily

Boehler there appeared to be a burgeoning romance. Either that or they had formed the tightest clique at camp, a friendship so passionate that it included long eruptions of wild and exclusive laughter and an intense physical closeness. (They group-wrestled in the swimming pool, lounged upon one another on the Sanctuary couches, and often exchanged fierce, sloppy, half-jesting kisses to the cheek and neck.) If one of the three was scheduled to cabin watch, the other two stayed behind with their friend and helped out. If all three were free, they disappeared into the woods and went unaccounted for until midnight and beyond.

A strange place, summer camp. It was a small enough world that the shape of your private life could be widely known or guessed at. And still everyone managed to cling to their unwise behavior, their private intentions. The counselors. The campers. Harriet, too.

At the moment she wanted, intensely, to get her son washed and ready for bed. James was willing to oblige her, mostly. Like the campers, he had to chew his vanilla wafers while being towed across the meadow by an impatient caretaker. Inside the infirmary bathroom she stripped him naked and ran a warm washcloth over his face and body. She bullied him into brushing his teeth and dressed him in pajamas. Afterward Harriet carried him to their living quarters and arranged him in his bed. Back at their St. Louis home he would have required a storybook and a glass of water, but here at camp his only real concern, the only thing he insisted on, was that the door leading out of their living quarters into the yard be locked. The other door, to the infirmary itself, could be left unlocked and ajar, as long as his mother could be seen stationed at her work desk.

For James's sake, she took a seat at the desk and pretended to pour all her attention into the nearest open file. Yet there was a self-consciousness to everything she did: the way she rolled a pen between her fingers, the studious tilt of her head. She couldn't keep up this pretense for long.

At last she stood, pulled back the window curtain, and looked outside.

In the center of the meadow, at the rear of the camp van, was Christopher Waterhouse, from this distance a lanky and silhouetted figure moving in and out of the van's interior light. He'd accomplished a good deal in the hurried minutes Harriet had spent inside the infirmary. The remnants of the evening snack had been put away, the tables folded up, the milk crates and the game pieces—everything that constituted the Kindermann Forest Camp Carnival—stowed away in the bed of the van. He was moving out across the meadow now, bent over, trash bag in hand, plucking the first scraps of debris from the trampled and litter-strewn grass. This chore might take him ten minutes or less to complete.

Then he'd be on his way to the Ellsinore Dairy Queen with Evie Hicks.

Harriet let the window curtain swing shut. For several long minutes she did nothing but stand there dumbly while, from the back of her mind, the Garden Ladies insisted, *Oh, for goodness' sake, Harriet. For goodness' sake.*

Behind Harriet a bed frame creaked. A muted cough. A plaintive voice called out, "Here it comes. Ack ack ack."

There were patients in the infirmary to care for, a simple fact, but, under the circumstances, it had the force of a long-sought discovery. *Patients. Yes, of course. Two of them.* Stretched out on a tousled bunk, her head nested in a mound of borrowed pillows, was Miss Mary Ann Hornicker, the freckled, diabetic, and silent woman whom Harriet had met the first day of camp and who, over the last eleven days, for reasons complicated or simple, had come to adore Harriet. Miss Hornicker was propped up on one elbow studying her nurse as if Harriet might at any moment bestow on her the sweetest of blessings. Across the aisle lay Mrs. Nancy Klotter, who came to the infirmary once a day, sometimes more, with an invented condition. Could a person be both retarded and hypochondriac? Absolutely. There were other campers who could be counted in both categories, but Mrs. Klotter was, perhaps, the most committed to her imaginary ailments. "It's coming back again," she said now, sitting cross-legged on her bunk, a hand raised to ward off the return of her dry, unconvincing cough. "Ack, ack, ack," she gasped. "Ack, ack, ack."

Here at least was an opportunity for Harriet to lose herself in a few minor duties: a cup of tap water to soothe Mrs. Klotter's invented cough, a kind word for Miss Hornicker, a quick check of James (tucked perfectly in his bed but still awake), the night-lights in the bathroom and infirmary turned on, the overhead fluorescent lights dimmed, her muffin tray set out on her work desk and ready to be filled. And then what?

Then she opened the infirmary door and stepped onto the wood stairs. It was irrefutably nighttime now, the woods thickly dark, the air cooler and less muggy. A fractional moon glowed from behind the crowns of the tallest trees. From the vantage of the infirmary step, she could see the camp van lurching across the meadow. Its uneven headlights threw out a muddled brightness. Eventually it reached the roadway, the engine revving, gravel popping from beneath its tires, as it wheeled past the infirmary and made a sharp turn onto a narrow drive. Moments later it had disappeared behind the back corner of the mess hall.

A small cluster of people waited just inside the screened perimeter of the mess hall porch. The porch light had been turned on and, by benefit of its orange glow, Harriet could recognize each member of the group: the ragged and frightening Mulcrone sisters; their counselor, Veronica Yordy; and, atop a nearby mess hall dining table, half-sitting, half-sprawled, Evie Hicks.

It was easy enough to guess what was happening here: they were waiting for Christopher Waterhouse, waiting for the camp van to be unloaded and then driven around to the porch so that Evie could be loaded into the passenger seat for her ride to Ellsinore. They looked a little impatient, a little wilted, from the slow lapse of minutes. At least the Mulcrone sisters and Veronica Yordy did. (Veronica rocked on her heels and clapped her hands listlessly together. She was anxious, no doubt, to get Evie installed in the van and the Mulcrone sisters escorted to their cabin, washed and in their beds.) But Evie Hicks was a different case. She was slumped down studying the scratched surface of the mess hall table. You could mistake her slack posture and dawdling movements for teenage indolence, but Evie was the opposite of lazy. Her enthusiasms were myopic and absolute. Harriet had treated the girl for chapped lips and heat rash and given her medication three times a day. This much was clear: Evie was engrossed in whatever existed a few inches before her eyes. And she was altogether immune to the passage of time. One place, one time of day, was as good as any other to Evie. Of course it was a fool's game to try to guess what any of the state hospital campers might be thinking or feeling. But looking across the infirmary yard to the lit mess hall porch and Evie's light-haloed figure, Harriet was certain of one thing: the girl had no idea that she was waiting, much less what she was waiting for.

An engine groaned. From behind the mess hall came a widening spray of headlights. Then the camp van rumbled around the corner of the building, bouncing along the driveway and stopping—a bit too hastily, it seemed to Harriet—at the mess hall porch. The driver's door swung open. *"All aboard,"* Christopher Waterhouse called out.

The eagerness of these two words, *All aboard,* the inflated cheerfulness, made Harriet suddenly miserable. Without quite meaning to, she stepped back into the infirmary and closed the door. She looked around. A different world entirely here: the air chilled to seventy-five degrees and wrung of its dampness, the smell of Pine-Sol cleaner, the waxy glow of the bathroom night-light. From her shadowed bunk

Mary Ann Hornicker peered up wordlessly and adoringly at her favorite nurse. Mrs. Klotter resumed her cough. "Ack, ack, ack."

Harriet put her forehead against the closed infirmary door and squeezed shut her eyes.

A great shuddering wave of misgiving and dread washed over her. And resentment, too, at Christopher Waterhouse and Schuller Kindermann and Linda Rucker. Especially Linda Rucker, who, more than anyone, would expect that Harriet step forward and do something. But on what basis? On Linda's intuition, her *inkling* that Christopher Waterhouse harbored a perverse interest in Evie Hicks? On this basis Harriet was supposed to march across the roadway to the mess hall porch and make a persuasive case to Veronica Yordy. (If so, it had better be a brief and utterly convincing account, because among the advocates at camp for Christopher Waterhouse, Veronica and her best friend, Marcy Bittman, were surely the chummiest and most loyal.) Maureen Boyd might have been persuaded to join Harriet's cause, but she and the kitchen girls had gone home for the night. So what did this leave Harriet? The weakest and most ridiculous option of all: she could race to the director's cottage and make a frantic and useless appeal to her employer, the stubborn and foolish Schuller Kindermann.

Everyone to whom she might make an appeal was white. And somehow—though it wasn't charitable or exactly logical to think this way—their whiteness, their alikeness, and the safety of their large community made them easily fooled.

Fools. Incompetents. Knuckleheads. They'd put her in an impossible situation. Surely she'd earned the right to curse them in the ugliest possible terms, to shout in her mind, *Dumb Fucking Crackers. Idiots. Retards.* Cruel words. Desperate words. She hoped they might be enough to shock her into action.

In the end what got her going was so much milder. *Oh, for goodness' sake, Harriet. For goodness' sake,* the Garden Ladies called to her, and she lifted her head from the door and opened her eyes. She was waiting, as she always did, for something small and knowable to present itself in the middle of an emergency. Her hand found the doorknob. Smooth. Round. Cool to the touch. A doorknob. She turned the knob and in an instant was out the door and hurrying across the yard.

A vehicle was advancing down the road, bouncing along on its carriage in a way that seemed purposeful and jolly. She broke into a run and soon reached the gravelly edge of the roadway. The headlights, waxy and off-kilter, kept coming—fifty yards, twenty yards, then nearer. She stepped into the center of the road and put out her hand. In the glare it was hard to tell if the van was decreasing or maintaining its speed.

She held her ground, and eventually the driver slowed to accommodate her.

From behind the steering wheel, Christopher Waterhouse nodded to her and raised his eyebrows expectantly. His window was rolled down, his forearm balanced neatly on the window frame. The effort he'd made loading and unloading the van had left his T-shirt collar and underarms mooned in sweat, and the hair along his temples swept back damply against the side of his face. He was hunched forward in the driver's seat, the same stiff bearing of his shoulders and neck that he adopted in the high perch of his lifeguard chair.

"Nurse Harriet," he said, a term of address that had caught on with the Kindermann Forest staff. Not *Harriet,* but *Nurse Harriet.* Maybe the counselors considered it a mark of respect. Whenever they used it, they seemed to wait a moment afterward, as Christopher Waterhouse did now, for Harriet to blush in appreciation.

"Hey," she said. "I'm glad I was able to catch you before you left."

To judge from his open and encouraging expression, he seemed glad, too.

"Because I need to ask about something," she said. But this wasn't right. She shouldn't have said *ask*. It wasn't as if she was seeking permission. "I need to let you know about something," she amended herself.

"All right," he said, patiently. "Sure, go ahead."

"See, I've been trying to track Evie Hicks down all evening. Didn't see her at the camp carnival. And I couldn't find her at her cabin. Then I remembered. She's supposed to be going with you. To the Dairy Queen in Ellsinore."

"That's right," he said. He turned in his seat so that he could glance back at his passenger, Evie Hicks, who sat belted into the first of three benches. She wasn't able to collapse into her usual slack posture. The seat belts, one snugly across her stomach, the other diagonally between her full breasts, held her tight against the seat. Her head was tipped back, her mouth partly open, as if she were awaiting the services of a dentist.

"But she can't go," Harriet explained.

He wrinkled his brow in consideration of what she'd said. As meditations went, this one was thorough and good-natured. After a while he tipped his head forward, perhaps in agreement.

And who knew? Maybe this was all it took: a clear and polite request. Until now she'd never had what could reasonably be called a conversation with Christopher Waterhouse, though she'd said hello and thanked him each afternoon for the privilege of allowing James sole use of the swimming pool. If she was to judge Christopher on the basis of these interactions, then it was only fair to say that he'd been cheerful and accommodating. And on one occasion he'd been something more than that. On the second day of camp, when a female camper had snatched James up from his mess hall bench and held him to her hard chest with a terrible spastic energy, Christopher had jumped to his feet and pried the boy loose. On that occasion he'd been more than merely helpful. He'd been alert and brave.

"Hmmm," he said. "Why is that? Why can't she go with me?"

"Because she has a treatment I need to give her. Right away."

"A treatment for what?"

"A problem that ladies get sometimes. A kind of infection."

His comely and suntanned face blossomed with understanding. "Ohhhh," he said.

"She'll be feeling better in a day or two."

"Good," he said. He grinned and seemed to wait for a reciprocating smile from Harriet. "So I guess you'll have to give her the treatment when we get back from Ellsinore."

It made no sense. There was an odd little gap in logic between what she'd thought she made clear to him and his incongruent answer. Perhaps, at the bottom of it all, Christopher Waterhouse wasn't very bright. "No, no," she said. "It'll have to work the other way. You'll have to go to Ellsinore alone and bring the ice cream back for Evie."

Again she was struck by how calm and measured his reactions were. *Bring the ice cream back to Evie?* He seemed to think this an original and complicated notion. He needed to sit in his van awhile and ponder it. But after a few pensive moments he squinted his eyes and shook his head. "No," he said. "I don't think so. I'm going to have to say no to your idea, Nurse Harriet."

She couldn't quite help herself: she let out a startled *humpf* of disbelief. "What?" Harriet said. "What do you mean?"

"I'm saying I thought over your suggestion and I'm saying no." He placed his hand on the column shift lever and in one quick motion set the van into drive.

"Christopher," she said sternly. "What do you think you're doing?"

He shrugged. "I'm going to Ellsinore," he said.

And apparently he was. The tires of the van began crunching forward on the gravel, a very slow and gradual turning. It was no trouble at all for Harriet to plod along beside the van. *"Christopher?"* she insisted. She could see into the van's interior: the sallow dash lights and scuffed door paneling. Evie Hicks, reined tight to the seat, let her head loll to one side so that her gaze flitted dreamily along the windows of the van and settled briefly on Harriet.

"Stop the van," Harriet demanded. "Stop the van, Christopher." And when it was clear that he would not, she shouted, "I will examine this girl very carefully when she gets back!"

He stepped on the accelerator. The van, which had been rolling along as sluggishly as an old wagon, found its grip on the roadway and bounded forward beyond her reach.

She jogged after it. A ridiculous effort, really: there'd be no catching up. But still she ran stupidly and persistently along the edge of the open meadow. The van was hundreds of yards ahead of her now, its glinting taillights bobbing along the roadway. She pushed on, past the camp office and Schuller Kindermann's quaint cedar cottage, past The Sanctuary. The van lights seemed to be slowing—seemed to have stopped—at the entrance to Kindermann Forest. A moment or two of idleness, perhaps of decision. The van turned right onto County Road H.

It was astonishing to see this: a turn to the right, deliberate, unmistakable.

She stopped in her tracks, bent over, hands on her knees, gulping air.

Then she swiveled around and jogged back the way she came.

There was a flood of coppery light shining out the back window of The Sanctuary. She crossed into the grass and drew close. Inside, in the scuffed and dusty main room, around a Formica-topped kitchen table, the Lonesome Three had settled down for their nightly game of gin rummy. Two homely young women, one ungainly young man; each wedged in close to the table, appraising the neat arrangement of their cards. The Lonesome Three—mopish, aloof, segregated, available. The other counselors would be so much harder to locate at this time of night: by now they'd have slipped away to various safeholds within the forest to smoke dope and commingle and fall in love. Not so, the Lonesome Three.

She hurried toward the screen door at the front of The Sanctuary. To rouse the Lonesome Three from their game, she'd have to barge in wearing the stark expression of the overwrought. She'd issue stern orders if necessary. *Get up from the table! Something terrible is happening!*

None of this, fortunately, was necessary. As soon as she rounded the building another option presented itself: at a picnic table some twenty paces from The Sanctuary sat a lone figure, elbows propped on the tabletop, head bowed over an open book. Reading apparently, or trying to read under the diffuse glow of The Sanctuary's single outdoor floodlight. She stared at him dumbfounded. And then it made sense. *Of course.* There'd be another person not included in the after-hours revelry. Another counselor, large and capable.

"Wyatt," she called out to him. He looked up from his book, and she hoisted her hand aloft and waved. Certainly, she was panicked. But from the start there was a quality to everything she did—the eager rise of her hand, a high softness in her voice—that was the opposite of panicked, that was assured and intimate and designed, it seemed, to win him over. She rushed to the picnic table.

"Wyatt," she said. "Wyatt." She managed a deep breath, and then—odd under the circumstance—a polite little nod of greeting. "There's a serious problem," she said. "An emergency. Christopher Waterhouse is alone in the camp van with Evie Hicks. They shouldn't be alone together," she said. "It shouldn't be allowed to happen." By squinting and leaning forward, she could make out the title of the book Wyatt was reading, or trying to read. *Lives of the American Presi-*

dents. "Because Christopher can't be trusted," she said. "He can't be trusted, Wyatt. He lies. He arranges things the way he wants them. This evening he arranged the hat drawing so that Evie would win. So he and Evie would be alone together in the van." She studied him in the hope of a startled reaction, a crush of understanding. None came. Perhaps she needed to remember this: quiet, unassuming Wyatt Huddy wasn't the type to ask questions. It wasn't enough for her to imply what Christopher Waterhouse might do. She'd have to speak in terms explicit and ugly. "He'll molest her," she said. "He'll molest her. Or worse. He'll rape her." She watched him absorb this news: a tightening in his overbroad forehead, a sad pinch in the corner of his uneven mouth. She said she'd tried to stop this from happening. Just minutes ago, she'd halted the camp van in front of the infirmary and tried to reason with Christopher Waterhouse. But he couldn't be talked out of what he wanted to do. He'd driven away. And she'd run after the van. She'd seen it stop a moment at the front gate. Stop and turn right. The van turned *right*. Right onto County Road H. A left turn on County Road H would have taken the van to Highway 52. Highway 52 led to Ellsinore. But a right turn? All you got if you turned right was a few more miles of gravel road. Scrubby lots. Creek beds. Dwindling little side lanes that led to nowhere.

"Wyatt," she said and, before she could continue, she palmed the sweat off her brow and pushed back her tousled hair. The expression she was wearing felt wrong—too frantic and severe. Much better if she could relax her features and show Wyatt Huddy a composed face, maybe even an affectionate one. "What one of us should do," she offered. "What you should probably do . . ."

He rose to his feet, rigidly, gravely, as if his name had been called from a roster. "I'll take a walk," he said in a tight, diminished voice. "I'll see if I can find them."

"Thank you," she said. "Thank you, Wyatt."

In each of her encounters with Wyatt Huddy he'd never been able to raise his gaze to the level of her own. He'd never looked her in the eye. The same was true now. His gaze was averted and the emotion in his face was closely reined, nearly unreadable. She could say he looked pained. Or weighted with reluctance. Or proud that she had asked for his help. All three might be true. Before he turned to set out for the front gate, he stretched himself to his full height and drew a large breath of air into his chest. He flexed his hands open and shut. These small physical exertions were possibly the humblest acts of male bravado Harriet had ever seen. And she could tell they were being performed for her benefit, for her assurance. He wanted her to know that he was strong. He was able and ready. It shamed her to think how very little it had taken to win him over.

Then he bounded away, his strides long and clumsy and surprisingly quick. In just a few moments he'd moved beyond the soft luster of the Sanctuary floodlight, an indistinct shape, then an outline, and then less than that, an obscure stain of darkness where seconds earlier a person had been.

Chapter Twelve

At least he had the benefit of a night sky pierced by a million glossy little stars and the brightening presence of an unscreened moon—a pared-down but still prominent moon, fiercely white. It sent its reflected light out like a coded signal. Some things—the looming pin oak trees on either side of the road—had almost no ability to receive this light. Other things fared much better. The white gravel stones that shifted like loose snow beneath Wyatt's work boots were, it turned out, perfect receivers of moonlight.

In the unshadowed straightaways, with the full, gleaming breadth of the night sky bearing down, the roadway gave off a soft, pearly white blush of light. To Wyatt it seemed as if the lit corridor of County Road H had been unfurled across the sloping countryside for his benefit.

He pushed ahead. *Clompf. Clompf. Clompf.* He'd always been able to march along as fast as most people could jog. Plus he had the advantage of an excellent gravel road. Honestly and truly, a first-rate road. County Road H was broad and chalky white and lushly graded.

It appeared to have been built with the notion of teaching the jutting Ozark hillsides a lesson or two about orderliness and hard work.

If necessary, he'd follow County Road H all the way to its scattered and weedy end. He'd do it for Nurse Harriet Foster. And also, of course, for Evie Hicks. And yet he couldn't believe Evie was moments away from being molested, from being raped. Or rather he couldn't *imagine* that she was. To be convinced of such a thing he'd have to believe that in some people—people like Christopher Waterhouse— there existed an enormous gap between who they pretended to be in public and the selfish and ugly things they schemed to do in private. How awful it would be if this were true. And worse even to wonder if a similar gap might be present in all people, including those he most admired: Captain Throckmorton and Ed McClintock. Present in Nurse Harriet, too. Present in himself even.

From somewhere ahead, just over the next steep hill perhaps, came the bawl of a straining automobile engine. What a harsh, blustery clamor it made, though this clamor was no louder, really, than the keen of insects that seemed to pulse in steady waves from some dark epicenter of the forest. A minute passed. Then a vehicle slid into view and grew from an obscure trembling blur into a recognizable shape: a wobbly old pickup truck, its headlights off or out of order, piloted by a gaunt male driver. The truck stormed past Wyatt. In the instant or two before a fog of road dust enveloped him, Wyatt saw, in the open bed of the truck, two children, a boy and a girl, perched on ragged lawn chairs. They stared at him. He stared back. They were homely, square-faced children, who seemed to recognize Wyatt as a strolling member of their community. But this appreciation lasted no more than a second: they looked at him and vanished behind a tunneling whirl of dust.

He clamped a hand across his mouth and nose and stomped forward.

There were narrow brush-choked lanes angling off County Road

H and unwinding a dozen or more yards into the dark woods. Wyatt felt duty-bound to follow each thin lane—most of them little more than rutted tire tracks—even if it meant fumbling along in the pitch-blackness until he could make out the lane's obscure end point, usually a clutch of tree stumps or a shabby barbed-wire fence. One lane took him much farther: through a wide grove of tall sycamore trees, across a dry creek bed, up a gentle hill, where, in the distance, a fluttery orange lantern light could be seen glowing in the window of a log cabin. An inhabited cabin. It dawned on him then: he was trespassing on somebody's driveway.

He hurried back out to County Road H with a richer appreciation for what Harriet Foster had asked him to do. He'd have to stumble down each of these patchy little side lanes and driveways. There'd very likely be yard dogs, unleashed and growling, or outraged homeowners jolted from their beds and reaching for the nearest club or a loaded shotgun.

It was gratifying somehow to march along with this weighty sense of danger and responsibility. And that, really, was the funny part of it. Because for a short while, for five minutes maybe, or the time it took to march a quarter mile along County Road H, he convinced himself that the task he'd been assigned would require a very brave and determined exploration of the deep woods. Then he rounded a wide corner of the road and stopped in his tracks.

Right there, just a few yards off the gravel shoulder of County Road H, was the broad, boxy rear end of a stilled vehicle—the Kindermann Forest camp van.

You could hardly call the van hidden. It had been driven down a mild embankment and parked beside County Road H on a little slip of open meadow that was weedy and tire-rutted and bordered on three sides by a pitch-black frontier of cedar trees. This didn't appear to be an unusual place to park a vehicle. In the farm country where Wyatt had grown up—and also, it seemed, here in the Missouri Ozarks—you'd see, in the clarifying light of day, a car or pickup truck pulled off the road and onto a small clearing. The driver, you assumed, was napping or checking a survey map or had slipped away into the scrubby woods to fish in a nearby creek.

But at night the implications of a parked vehicle were different. Or seemed different.

The van's interior light had been turned on. There were lines of shadowed movement playing out on the rear windows, and though these windows were too thickly coated in road dust to see through, Wyatt could, by putting his hand against the rear quarter panel of the Kindermann Forest van, feel a tension uncoiling in the vehicle's undercarriage, a faint indication, maybe, of the gentle movements taking place within.

All his life he'd been taught to knock softly and wait. This seemed to be an occasion in which the usual rules could be overlooked. He put his shoulder against the van's sliding side door. His fingers closed around the latch. A few ounces of pressure and the latch unclicked. With a dry, grating screech the van door was swung open.

In his imaginings, in his vision of the world as it ought to be, he'd pieced together a half-vivid notion of what it would be like to love Evie Hicks. He knew, for instance, that they'd live together. They'd share an apartment in Jefferson City. Wyatt would work at the Salvation Army depot all day, and when he came home, he and Evie would have dinner and watch television and then, as if signaling a new juncture in their evening together, Evie would rise from the couch and go to the bedroom. There she'd dress in a nightgown and wait for him sitting upright on their bed. A few minutes later Wyatt would ease into the room and sit down beside her. (Would they be married? He wasn't at all sure. Maybe they would be, though the details of their engagement and wedding were nearly impossible to bring into focus.)

He'd turn down the bedroom lights, and then he'd reach across and put his hand on the underside of her full breast and hold it there for a long while, feeling the soft weight of it through the cotton of her nightgown. This act, which seemed to him enormously crucial and complicated, would inspire long minutes of intense happiness, hours of happiness. In the world as it ought to be, Evie would be aware enough to welcome the steady pressure of his hand and perhaps to feel a similar gladness.

But this, of course, was impossible. It was stupid even to dream this way—stupid and hurtful and unfair. Because there'd be no responding tenderness from Evie Hicks. Everything he might do to Evie—in the name of love or in the spirit of things far crueler—would be done against her will.

For proof of this all he needed to do was look inside the Kindermann Forest camp van.

There, within the shell of the van, under the coppery glow of the dome light, she'd been stripped naked and then put back under the harness of her seat belt. What he could see of her at first glance, her bare shoulders and arms and naked breasts—one flattened beneath a belt, one dangling free—was terrible and astonishing. Her knees were pinkly callused from all the crawling she did. Dark hair sprouted from the hollows beneath her armpits. A naked adult woman—or at least a naked Evie Hicks—was a pale and loosely formed creature.

This was an unexpected discovery, truly. He would have stood gawking at her in dumb wonder were it not for another remarkable sight: Christopher Waterhouse kneeling before Evie on the floor of the van. He'd pressed the side of his face adoringly against her thigh and slid his hands beneath her naked bottom. He was trying, it seemed, to raise her up straighter in her seat, to lift her hips and open wide her legs, which were flexing languidly, as if she were stirring in her sleep.

Once her legs were parted, he embraced Evie in a sudden, thrusting hug, writhed against her just a few moments—and stopped. Then he went back to the difficult business of raising Evie up in her seat and adjusting her flailing legs. How very calm, how very *patient,* his efforts appeared to be. Clearly he knew that the van door had been pushed open and that a person, an observer, was standing behind him. And yet his first craning look up at Wyatt revealed nothing in the way of shame or surprise. The only thing he seemed to want from Wyatt was a nodding admission that what was being done here—this raising and parting of Evie Hicks's legs—was a complicated and worthwhile endeavor.

"Stop it," Wyatt said in a hushed and unweighty voice. "Stop what you're doing. Right now."

It was enough to provoke in Christopher Waterhouse the slow stirrings of a second reaction: he blinked his eyes wetly and let his arms and shoulders go slack. Then he pulled his hands out from beneath Evie Hicks and began to crawl, awkwardly, out of the van. He lowered one foot on the grassy floor of the clearing, then the other. He raised himself up to full height. "Wyatt," he said. "Wyatt. We were having trouble here. We were having an *emergency.*" As he said this, he reached down and hoisted up his blue jeans and underwear, which were bundled around his thighs.

"An emergency?"

"She was choking on something. A piece of cracker or some candy. She was making an awful sound, Wyatt. I had to pull the van over and get her shirt off to pound on her back. So I could find out where the problem was."

To Wyatt it seemed that his first duty was to imagine such a thing: Evie choking, Christopher pulling the van over and crawling back to assist her, removing her T-shirt . . . but also her bra, her pants, her underwear, even her shoes and socks. These articles of clothing had been lined up on the van seat beside Evie, and the sight of her clothing, especially its neat arrangement, made him feel as if he'd been slapped powerfully by a cold hand. Slapped and slapped again. Only an idiot, only a retarded person, would believe such an excuse.

"I had to get her calmed down, Wyatt. She was acting wild. She was pulling off her—"

"She *wasn't*," Wyatt insisted. His hand was clenched around the van door latch. He let go and gripped Christopher Waterhouse by the shoulder with an equal prying strength.

"Hey, hey there . . . easy, Wyatt."

"Don't say things you know aren't true."

There was a fraught and astonished silence, in which it was possible to watch, moment by moment, a deep blush of appreciation bloom across Christopher's face. *Don't say things you know aren't true.* Yes, clearly, he understood the wisdom of this command. He admired Wyatt so very much. But this didn't keep Christopher Waterhouse from narrowing his eyes in concentration. Quietly, and after a prolonged deliberation, he said, "You have to understand, Wyatt. She doesn't mind what's happening."

It was hard to make sense of this. *She didn't mind.* But mind what exactly? The choking on a piece of candy? The argument that was taking place in her presence? These notions tangled and untangled themselves in Wyatt's mind. "What are you saying?" he asked.

"She likes it well enough. Being in the van. Having her clothes off. That's the truest thing I can tell you, Wyatt. Go ahead, take a look at her. A close look even. She doesn't mind."

Inside the van, Evie Hicks had ceased the slow pedaling of her legs and was slumped back against the seat. Her head was tipped toward the passenger window. True enough, there was nothing in the languid arrangement of her naked body that signaled a sense of alarm or unease. Her legs were half-parted. Her left hand, clumsy and unshy in its movements, flitted about—over her breasts and round belly, between her legs—and scratched where it pleased.

"Go ahead and sit inside the van with her awhile," Christopher Waterhouse said.

"No, no. I'm not going to—"

"She's not embarrassed. Why the hell should you be? Just talk to her, for Christ's sake. Say a few words. Put her at ease."

Wyatt stood rooted before the open door, his mind working furiously and arriving at nothing that resembled a coherent idea.

"*Jesus, Wyatt,*" Christopher exclaimed, not a curse or a cry of frustration, but an expression of fondness and wonder. "Think of it, man. Here's a chance to sit in a van and talk with a pretty naked girl. A girl who's not embarrassed. A girl who doesn't mind."

He could have withstood other tactics. But this warm cajoling from Christopher Waterhouse, so knowing and friendly, had an unraveling effect on Wyatt's defenses. He let go of Christopher's shoulder and braced himself inside the door of the van.

"How many chances like this are you going to have in your life?" Christopher Waterhouse asked. "A guy like you. With your condition. Just sit and talk for a minute or two. She already knows you're a gentleman, Wyatt."

Accordingly, Wyatt hoisted himself into the van, his head tucked low, his considerable weight rocking the vehicle on its chassis. The cramped interior of the van made him feel like a lurching giant. He squeezed past Evie Hicks. He sat beside her on the first bench, on top of her mounded clothing. At the same time Christopher Waterhouse began drawing the van door shut, a slow, whining pull, until it clicked into place and he double-tapped the van door window to let Wyatt know that his and Evie's privacy was now complete.

It was quiet enough inside the van to hear the bending of the springs in the bench, the swish of Evie Hicks's bare feet on the matted floor. There were movements outside as well. Christopher Waterhouse was climbing the embankment and padding noisily atop the thick gravel of County Road H. It seemed to Wyatt there was nothing else to do but lean a bit closer and examine the shadowed profile of Evie's face—the tendrils of brown hair that framed her ear and jaw-line. Beautiful hair. An entirely beautiful cheek and ear.

"Evie," he said. "Evie Hicks." He didn't expect an answer. "Evie," he said, more for his own encouragement. Then he reached out and with trembling fingertips touched very gently the underside of her breast. "Evie," he said tenderly. No spoken reply to this, but in her languid posture he sensed an unmistakable shift, a tightening of her bare limbs, an awareness, a turning away.

He took back his hand. Were Evie not present, he might have shouted at the top of his lungs, might have howled in shame. If he was alone, then surely he'd have clawed at the van upholstery with his bare hands or used his powerful legs to kick at the benches until they were bent down or snapped free from their moorings. He'd have made a wasteland of the van interior. As it was, he crawled forward to the door, swung it open, and stepped outside.

He found Christopher Waterhouse walking along the chalky white shoulder of County Road H. Christopher had traveled only a few dozen yards, and at the sound of Wyatt's swift approach, he turned and began what might have been an elaborate explanation. "I thought I'd leave you—" He'd half-raised his arms, and this allowed Wyatt to grasp him snugly around the chest and squeeze with all the urgent feeling he'd denied himself moments earlier in the van.

A rush of air escaped from Christopher's lungs. There was a snap-ping of delicate internal bones. He managed to swing out an arm and club Wyatt in the face. It hardly mattered. What did Wyatt know about fistfights? All his adult working life he'd grappled with large and dangerously heavy furniture. He tightened his arms around Christo-pher Waterhouse and again squeezed with all his might.

There was more soft popping along Christopher's rib cage and then a ragged and terrible series of breaths. "Uhhh, uhhh, uhhh," he cried. Released, he collapsed onto the chalky roadbed. His mouth moved, his lips formed breathy sounds. Wyatt had to bend down close to hear what was being said. "God damn you, Wyatt," Christopher moaned.

It wasn't hard to drag Christopher Waterhouse by the ankle across the gravelly surface of County Road H. He moaned and flailed his arms weakly, but there was nothing he could do to stop the journey he was on—across the roadbed, down the small embankment, back into the center of the clearing beside the Kindermann Forest camp van. By then he'd gone pale in the face. His particular agony was, for Wyatt, infuriating to watch: the way he strained for a single shallow breath, and then the cost of that breath, which made him shudder and writhe in agony.

Wyatt knelt down beside him and reached for whatever was handy: a big clump of grass, it turned out, which he pried from the earth. He held it inches from Christopher's face.

"You . . ." Christopher said, gasping, "ugly . . . fucking . . . re—"

Wyatt drove the clump of dirt and roots into Christopher's mouth, into his nose, into his clenched eyes. What a fit Christopher Waterhouse threw, twisting and retching and wagging his head violently back and forth. He raked at Wyatt's face with his clawed hands. The only way to stop this, it seemed, was to turn him onto his stomach and press his head down hard into the earth, to crawl onto his back, as a wrestler might, and hold his choking face to the ground.

Nothing accidental about this maneuver, nothing careless. It took time to accomplish. It required a tremendous effort to hold his hostage down and prevent him from drawing another breath.

What he was left with was sagging and loose-limbed and surprisingly difficult to move. To pull Christopher Waterhouse by the ankle was to have his other limbs—his unattended leg and arms—fold back and scrape the ground at unnatural angles. No good to try to drag him by the collar of his T-shirt, either; the collar stretched wide and long and the shirt threatened to unpeel from his body.

What a sight it must have made. What a woeful and clumsy spectacle. Worse even, the side door of the Kindermann Forest van was hanging wide open. Evie Hicks had been granted a privileged view of the struggle and its aftermath.

Wyatt, kneeling over his work, lifted his gaze up and nodded at her. With a raised hand, he pointed into the woods. He hoped the meaning was clear enough: he intended to crawl beneath the low-hanging cedar branches and drag Christopher Waterhouse, burden that he was, into the darkest corner of the forest. Did she understand why this needed to be done? Did she comprehend?

She was listing forward in her seat, her head low but her gaze open and aware. Hard to guess what her opinion might be—though it was fair to say that she was as interested in the slumped body at Wyatt's feet as she was in everything else: the twigs and pebbles and other earthly debris which all day long she knelt over and studied from the distance of just a few inches. She was amazed by everything she saw.

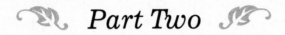

Part Two

St. Louis

2011

Chapter Thirteen

Some things were just too tricky to talk about. Certain *biases,* for example. You couldn't earn anyone's sympathy by describing the small insults a woman suffered when she reached the age of thirty-seven and remained—through no real effort or fault of her own—quite pretty. Apparently people got tired of it. At least with Marcy Bittman Lammers they did. Often she was aware of her friends—and new acquaintances, too—surveying her lively and delicate face (at the cusp of middle age still a pixieish face), her hazel eyes, her soft brown hair, her trim little body, and after a fickle moment, a bored moment really, shifting their attention elsewhere. Who knew why? People used to be captivated or made sweetly shy by her fine looks.

None of this for an instant stopped her from welcoming into her home the many friends and associates of her husband, Dr. Dean Lammers. She was honestly glad to do it. In fact she seemed to have a knack for placing her guests into conversational groups that generated a flood of cheerful talk. Yet when it came Marcy's turn to contribute to the conversation, she could sense people's interest starting to thin. If she talked on at any length—about a DVD movie she'd seen, about the family of handsome tree squirrels in her front yard—it would evaporate altogether.

It wasn't a terrible thing. She wouldn't call herself crushed by this lack of attention. Still, it was *interesting,* wasn't it? With Marcy no one seemed anymore to want to include her in talk that lasted more than a minute or went beyond any of the usual topics.

All afternoon and evening people had been stomping through Marcy and Dean Lammers's home in West St. Louis County. The idea was that this year they'd do an open house winter party. People could drop by anytime between 4:00 and 9:00 P.M. They could pile their coats and scarves in the little area off the foyer called the welcome room. Along the front hallway was one of five bathrooms, in case anyone should need it. In the great room there was a stoked fire and three open couches and a fully loaded wet bar. From there a person was likely to head downstairs, drink in hand, to the Lammerses' wide and lushly carpeted basement. There was a game room—pinball, Ping-Pong, foosball, shuffleboard—and a long serving counter bearing plattered holiday food. On the back wall of the basement was a flat-screen TV so large that one of Marcy's nephews had called it *gi-norm-ous.* The label stuck. This evening a crowd of some twenty guests had gathered around the gi-norm-ous television to watch the blustery final quarter of a snow-wrecked college football game. For now these guests were happy to linger awhile in the leather chairs. But at some point during the party they'd migrate, one by one or in pairs, up the stairs to the vast open kitchen with its gorgeously marbled counters and long windows full of wintry outdoor light. In the kitchen they'd take a seat at a hand-me-down oak breakfast table—the only underwhelming piece of furniture in the whole house—and have a talk with Dr. Dean Lammers.

For at least half the guests, Marcy's husband, Dr. Lammers, was their immediate supervisor—owner and director of a three-branch ophthalmology practice in greater St. Louis County. Eight interns—the attractive young men and women in the basement game room—called Dr. Lammers their attending ophthalmologist. To many of the other guests he was an essential client for the prescription drugs and medical equipment they peddled. By one means or another, they were beholden to him. So it was easy to assume these kitchen table chats with Dr. Lammers were a calculated obligation. But this most definitely wasn't the case. Dr. Lammers was widely and sincerely liked. People came to the table because they wanted to. And this, Marcy knew, was a rarer accomplishment than anyone realized: to be highly competent and at the same time to be a modest, funny, personable man.

But not perfect, of course. He was older than Marcy by twenty-one years—a round-faced, balding, bespectacled gentleman of fifty-eight. Despite Marcy's best efforts, Dr. Lammers was eighty-five pounds overweight. (One of the reasons he stationed himself at the kitchen table was to hide the full extent of his protruding belly.) It was true: they probably looked a little foolish strolling side by side: petite, pretty, younger-than-her-years Marcy Bittman Lammers and the older, overweight, stiff-jointed, and often hobbling Dr. Dean Lammers. They didn't make a logical couple. No doubt there were people—a few of them at this party—who liked to dwell on these differences, who liked maybe to imagine the two of them together in intimate and unflattering bedroom positions.

That would be cruel, certainly, but not so far off the mark. Tonight being Saturday (the second Saturday of the month no less), they'd convene in their bedroom after the party and clamber up onto their California king and assume a few of those positions. It wasn't an occasion Marcy looked forward to. Even so, she recognized the relative importance of this schedule: the second and fourth Saturdays of each month. Mark your calendars! People might think this a pathetic marital arrangement. The handsome young newlywed interns downstairs in the game room; easy to imagine them scoffing. But really, what the hell did they know? Let these newlywed interns grow middle-aged and older and stay married. It would be interesting to see what kinds of schedules they ended up keeping.

Still and all, she enjoyed opening the doors of her home for a holiday party. What happiness to order food and arrange the house, room by room, exactly as she pleased. She really wasn't a demanding hostess. It was perfectly fine with Marcy if, as they pushed toward late evening, the party atmosphere got a bit loud and lived-in. Perfectly all right if a handful of guests decided to stay until nine o'clock and beyond. In these waning minutes of the party Marcy could wander into the less trafficked corners of her home and pick up an abandoned party cup (though most people were awfully neat at parties these days). She could step out of her pumps a moment and wiggle her toes and stand before the second-floor bay windows and get a bit, well, moony. That was the term she and Dr. Lammers had arrived at after a fierce negotiation. *Getting a bit moony.* He could say, without ruffling anyone's feathers, "All right now, sweetie pie. Let's not get moony over any of this." By which, generally, he meant: *Let's not get lonesome.* Or: *Let's not get melancholy.* Or, more specifically, though it couldn't be spoken aloud: *Let's not waste any more time thinking about Christopher Waterhouse.*

As if she—or anyone—had such command over her emotions: to feel an unexpected ache and be able to steer it back from where it came. There was something about the waning moments of a holiday party—the house emptying of people and a charged stillness filling the rooms—that turned her into a conductor for certain feelings. Before she knew it the full weight of her longing was upon her.

She missed Christopher Waterhouse. She ached to commune. Mostly she'd gotten over the way he'd died, the particular and awful death he'd suffered. But in place of this shock she had, fifteen years after the fact, a much larger capacity to imagine the life-moments Christopher had missed out on. He would absolutely have loved this holiday party, the downstairs game room, the rowdy company of the young interns. The trick, of course, was to remember that he'd be nearly forty years old—a boyish forty, most likely, an alert, happy, physically vital man. Maybe he'd like the artichoke dip she'd made or the shuffleboard game, because these small pleasures, thousands of them over the course of life, were what you missed out on if you died when you were just twenty-two. No Sunday morning breakfasts on the patio. No Caribbean vacations. No movies, either. How awful to miss out on going to the movie theater. Sometimes she and Dr. Lammers saw such outstanding movies at the eighteen-screen cineplex, the kinds of movies in which opposite-minded people fell in love or showed unexpected kindness to homeless men or idiot savants. These were the movies that buoyed you up on a wave of good feeling and made you want to turn to the person next to you, even if it was a stranger, and say, "Oh, that was cute! That was just darling!"

For some reason she always imagined Christopher being a father (though not necessarily married). He'd have a handsome, good-natured teenage son. She could imagine the deep pleasures parenthood would bring Christopher Waterhouse, whereas, childless by choice, she'd not been able to do the same for herself or Dr. Lammers.

Really, if she let herself, she could get awfully moony over the path Christopher Waterhouse's life might have taken. She could bring a wave of sorrow down upon herself. Dr. Lammers would notice it right away. There'd be a shift then. They'd sense an off-kilter loyalty in one another, and they'd spend several days or more being wary and removed. For Marcy this would be almost unbearable: to even for a few days not have the steady pulse of Dr. Lammers's affection. She loved him so very much. Stranger yet, she could long for Christopher Waterhouse and somehow love her husband all the more. It wasn't normal, of course. She'd never heard of such a thing or seen it acted out in a movie. She could spend an evening aching privately for Christopher Waterhouse, and the very next morning, at the kitchen table, serving Dr. Lammers his coffee and low-fat Danish, she wanted to throw herself in his lap and squeeze him until they were both breathless. The warmth of him, the softness; it was a more nourishing pleasure than sex. (It was cleaner, too, thank you very much.) She wouldn't have been able to endure this unlikely divide—the longing for a dear dead friend, the affection for her husband—if she and Dr. Lammers hadn't reached a hard-won understanding.

This had happened the previous year during a very miserable period in Marcy's life. There'd been several months, maybe a whole winter, when she'd been nothing but moony. Moony every day. Every night. At last Dr. Lammers had sat her down and said, "Look here, Marcy darling. We have to get past this, don't we? You need to see someone and talk things over. Either that or the two of us need to take some time and consider the facts of what happened to Christopher Waterhouse, the *objective* evidence. We need to look at the evidence and reach a conclusion."

It was impossible that she would *see* someone. She wasn't in the business of talking to strangers.

So instead Dr. Lammers had proposed what he called a "fair-minded deal." He knew a very good legal researcher, a former paralegal for the state of Missouri, and he'd have her go back a decade and a half through the records and assemble all the evidence of Christopher Waterhouse's murder. The investigation. The prosecuting and defending attorneys' notes. The trial that hadn't really been a trial at all. Once Marcy and Dr. Lammers had a chance to look everything over, they'd make a decision.

Either they'd realize that a reasonable effort had been made to honor Christopher's life and bring his murderer to justice—Marcy might not like the *results* of this effort, but she'd have to accept what happened. She'd have to make peace with the way things had turned out—or they'd decide that the investigation and pretrial and the sentencing of Wyatt Huddy had diminished or been neglectful to Christopher Waterhouse. If this was the case, Dr. Lammers would spend a little money to try to set the record straight.

Set the record straight? But what did he mean exactly?

There were people, Dr. Lammers explained, who could be hired to help bring the story of Christopher's life and murder to the public's attention. An article might be published in a newspaper or magazine—a fond remembrance. There might just be a place and time to honor Christopher with a memorial.

It caught her by surprise, this suggestion; it nearly took her breath away. A *wonderful* idea. At once the possibilities for this memorial assembled themselves in her mind. Christopher's family could be invited up to St. Louis from their home in the Missouri Bootheel. All the counselors at Kindermann Forest who'd once thought so highly of Christopher could be tracked down and invited. They'd come together, all these years after his death, and honor him in a way that would be solemn and touching.

The picture of it was so clear in her imagination; she agreed right away to Dr. Lammers's "fair-minded deal." Even so, she knew it was a serious undertaking. Pledges were made. She and Dr. Lammers both vowed to honor the objective facts.

And as it turned out there were quite a few things—powerful things—that she didn't know about Christopher Waterhouse's murder. She'd been so young at the time. Maybe her reaction to his death hadn't been thoughtful or orderly. How could it have been? There was no time for clear thinking. One day she was a lifeguard at Kindermann Forest and the next she'd lost her dear friend and was sent home, where her mother, Coco Bittman, insisted that Marcy enjoy what remained of her summer break. She couldn't possibly. Her head was spinning. In the fall she'd been exquisitely relieved to pack up her things and drive back to college. Every once in a while her mother would send her a news clipping. A trial date had been set. A plea for change of venue denied.

One thing had caught her attention right away. In her dorm mailroom one afternoon she'd read a confounding sentence from an article in the *Springfield News-Leader*:

> Wyatt Huddy of Jefferson City, Missouri, age twenty-three, a camper during the Kindermann Forest State Session, awaits trial in Shannon County on second-degree murder charges.

Not a camper! A counselor, for goodness' sake! Wyatt Huddy had arrived the same day as Marcy and the other Kindermann Forest counselors. He'd been assigned a group of state hospital campers to care for. For two weeks he'd accompanied these campers to every event and activity. All day. Every day. He'd sat with them at every meal.

Two months later in the *St. Louis Post-Dispatch*, the same mistake.

> Wyatt Huddy, age twenty-three, a camper . . .

For Marcy this had been a source of sharp but fleeting irritation at the time. She remembered being amazed at the sloppiness. The professional world—or at least the world of journalists—was supposed to be more capable than that. In retrospect, she realized she should have done something right away. She should have contacted the other Kindermann Forest counselors and made a fuss.

Several months after Marcy and Dr. Lammers had agreed to their "fair-minded deal," the first packet of evidence arrived. Inside was a note from the paralegal. "Pay special attention to this," she'd written and clipped the note to a folder of affidavits that had been gathered by the defense on Wyatt Huddy's behalf.

Affidavit number one: a statement from Terry M. Throckmorton, a captain in the Salvation Army and the director of the depot and thrift store in Jefferson City, Missouri. He'd employed Wyatt Huddy for four and a half years, and during that time Wyatt had proved himself to be hardworking and honest—a very dependable employee. He was capable of independent work, as long as the directions for that work were clear and given to Wyatt incrementally, which was to say, one task at a time. Mostly he unloaded trucks and made simple repairs to furniture. He was not able to operate the cash register or reliably answer the telephone. It was very difficult for Wyatt to deal with more than one customer at a time. But he was consistent. In four and a half years he hadn't missed a single day of work. Of all the depot employees, Wyatt Huddy was the most deserving of a vacation. To that end Captain Terry Throckmorton had contacted Program Director Linda Rucker and inquired as to whether or not Wyatt Huddy might be allowed to attend the June 17–29, 1996, session at Kindermann Forest. Linda Rucker, in consultation with Camp Director Schuller Kindermann, gave her consent, and Wyatt Huddy was added to the list of campers. But this didn't mean that Wyatt was eager to go to Kindermann Forest. According to Captain Throckmorton, he had to be persuaded. He needed a certain amount of encouragement to leave the familiar world of the Jefferson City Salvation Army Depot.

Affidavit number two: a sullen and somewhat disjointed statement from Wyatt Huddy's sister, Caroline Huddy, explaining that she'd raised Wyatt after the death of their mother. He was neither a smart nor a reliable child. Often he was stubborn and slow, and these qualities, Caroline Huddy guessed, might have been signs of his diminished intelligence. She wasn't sure. He wouldn't have been involved in a murder, she believed, if he'd remained under her supervision at the family farm. But that hadn't happened. He'd been encouraged to leave their home and go to camp. She seemed to despise anyone who'd taken an interest, professional or otherwise, in the tragedy, including those who had helped solicit her statement.

Affidavit number three: a statement from Harriet Foster, R.N., explaining that, in accordance with her duties as camp nurse at Kindermann Forest, she had examined Wyatt Huddy, along with dozens of other state hospital campers, on the first day of the session, Monday, June 17, 1996. She had determined him to be healthy and able enough to meet the physical requirements of a two-week session at Kindermann Forest. This had been a quick examination, Nurse Foster noted. Her other encounters with Wyatt Huddy over the course of the two-week session were similarly brief, in most cases no longer than the few moments it took to dispense his medications. At no point did she have access to his complete medical history. Therefore she didn't know for certain the exact nature of his disability. But she did observe in Wyatt Huddy a lack of awareness and a difficulty understanding ordinary social cues. In this way, she could say that he seemed to have the same diminished IQ abilities as many of the other state hospital campers.

Affidavit number four: a statement from Kindermann Forest Program Director Linda Rucker explaining that she'd received a request from Captain Terry Throckmorton of the Salvation Army regarding Wyatt Huddy. She'd considered this request. She'd talked it over with Camp Director Schuller Kindermann. They'd both agreed to allow Wyatt Huddy to attend the June 17–29 State Hospital Session along with other disabled campers from the state hospital. They'd done so because Captain Throckmorton had assured her that Wyatt would be easy to manage. This turned out to be entirely true. In the broad and often unsettling range of disabled behavior, Wyatt Huddy's conduct had been calm and accommodating. Linda Rucker had seen ample evidence of these qualities because the counseling staff of Kindermann Forest—especially the male counselors—had been stretched thin, and most days she'd had to step in and act as de facto counselor for Wyatt Huddy and the other campers in his group, Leonard Peirpont, Jerry Johnston, Thomas Anwar Toomey. According to Linda Rucker, they were all likable and obedient campers, though Wyatt may have been the most even-tempered and cooperative. He was frequently helpful. In the course of the two-week session, Linda Rucker couldn't recall a single instance in which he'd been angry or upset or uncooperative. She could not imagine Wyatt being violent, unless deliberately or cruelly provoked.

What a startling experience it was for Marcy Bittman Lammers to hold these affidavits in her hands. Could she call it a conspiracy? Yes, she thought she could. At the very least it was an effort to disguise the facts. It was so very important that Dr. Lammers understand. Wyatt Huddy had been hired as a counselor. He'd been assigned campers. He'd attended every staff meeting. He wasn't retarded. But what was he then? Disfigured maybe. He had a queerly shaped head, a sloping face. Each afternoon he'd guided his campers, one by one, down the pool steps and then sat cross-legged on the deck while they tottered around the shallow end. He wouldn't take off his shoes and dangle his feet in the water. An odd young man—hulking and private. But he was as aware and as capable as any other member of the Kindermann Forest staff.

Not everything the paralegal sent them could be called a revelation, but each item was, in its own way, interesting to Marcy. The Kindermann

Forest camp van was a 1992 GMC Rally Wagon with 112,000 miles on the odometer. The air temperature the night and approximate time of the murder was seventy-eight degrees. The sky had been clear, the moon in its waxing crescent phase. Insignificant details maybe, but they stirred her imagination. Then came the coroner's report. Christopher Waterhouse's recovered body had weighed one hundred and eighty-three pounds. At least six of his ribs had been broken. Two of these broken ribs had punctured his lungs. His abrasions numbered in the dozens. He'd died of traumatic asphyxiation. There were details from the coroner's report that Dr. Lammers said he'd better keep to himself. (Though he did tell her that the attack on Christopher Waterhouse was mostly likely an act of rage, and not anything sexual.) At the very least Marcy wanted to know where and in what condition Christopher's body had been found. In a shallow creek bed, Dr. Lammers explained. A quarter mile deep into the forest. He'd been dropped into the creek and covered with large slabs of flagstone. Most likely he'd been dead prior to this makeshift burial.

How horrible it was to know this. Now she had to strictly guard her thoughts. If not, her anxious mind would pull back the screen of forest branches and see Christopher's pale and muddied body mounded with stones.

She was more cautious then about which documents she allowed herself to look at. Court petitions and pretrial motions? Yes, fine. No problem. The crime scene reports from Ellsinore Chief of Police David Pressy and from the Missouri State Highway Patrol? No thank you. Over the course of three months the evidence kept coming. It wasn't exactly an orderly progression. Several of the bureaus and departments to which the paralegal applied gave up their documents in miserly increments.

Sometimes Marcy wondered: Were they being purposefully

obstructed? She phoned and asked the paralegal if someone might be working behind the scenes to keep this evidence from reaching them.

No, no, the paralegal said. Any difficulties they'd encountered had to do with authorizations and filing procedures. The remedy for this was always the same: time and persistence. For example, the paralegal had needed to use a delicate brand of persuasion when it came to the case files belonging to Shannon County Prosecuting Attorney Henry Masner. And for good reason. Henry Masner had died in office three years earlier. Portions of his files were stored in the Shannon County Courthouse, the town hall basement, and Mr. Masner's home office. He was still, fortunately, an admired figure in Shannon County. On his behalf, the county's single records clerk, Mrs. Denita Medlock, was willing to do a respectful search of his files. She was seventy-nine years old. Her search took time.

But what riches Mrs. Medlock discovered. In one of Mr. Masner's files was a time allotment sheet that detailed the work hours he'd put in building a second-degree murder case against Wyatt Huddy. This would have been an almost inconsequential document, yet it revealed that during the spring of 1997 he'd had five meetings with Camp Nurse Harriet Foster at the Shannon County Courthouse. Five meetings! This meant that Harriet Foster had driven down from St. Louis on five separate occasions to speak with Mr. Masner, the attorney assigned to prosecute Wyatt Huddy. You had to wonder what topics had been discussed at these meetings. Or, the better question, what agenda Harriet Foster had been pushing.

It took six weeks for the records clerk Denita Medlock to uncover and pass along a document that answered this question: a typed statement from Harriet Foster seven pages long, signed and notarized and submitted in the early summer of 1997 to both the prosecuting and defending attorneys.

And what had she, Marcy Bittman, been doing while Harriet Foster met with attorneys and composed her elaborate statement? Marcy had been away at a private college in rural Illinois earning a degree in public relations. This was a very fortunate thing. She adored her school. And she loved the other young women who were her sisters at the sorority. But she was also a changed person. Most evenings she'd pack up her school textbooks and climb to the higher floors of the college library and find a window-side table from which to look out over the darkening campus. It was as if she were receiving, for the first time in her life, a strange, one-of-a-kind feeling. If she'd known how, she would have drawn a bleak picture or written a sad song for Christopher Waterhouse. But that was an absurd notion. She wasn't a singer or an artist. She'd always known herself to be an extremely positive person—a bright personality, happy-go-lucky, caring, purposeful, full of joy. And there she was those evenings at the library window receiving the first stirrings of a lonesome ache she'd later learn to call "getting moony."

According to her statement, Harriet Foster believed—was convinced, in fact—that Christopher had manipulated a prize drawing so that he would have a reasonable excuse to be alone with the state hospital camper Evie Hicks; so he might bring her into the camp van and drive her out beyond the confines of Kindermann Forest. His intention was to find a secluded area where he could molest or rape her. Wyatt Huddy had prevented this from happening.

The charge wasn't a complete shock to Marcy. (There'd been ugly rumors in the days following Wyatt's arrest.) But lurking just beneath the calm tone of this statement was an awful insinuation.

Yes, Harriet Foster admitted. What happened to Christopher Waterhouse was tragic. He'd died a violent and terrifying death. She'd been devastated to learn of it. More so, she'd been overwhelmed with remorse to realize she'd set the tragedy in motion by sending Wyatt Huddy out alone to search for the camp van.

But beneath Harriet Foster's supposed remorse, her apology—if that's what it was—lay another line of reasoning, unaddressed, unwritten. What Wyatt Huddy had done upon finding the camp van may not have been wise or justified. But it may have been necessary.

How wildly unfair this was. It was enraging, really, for Marcy to have to consider this accusation. To read the statement was to be lectured to in a tone that was deliberate and vaguely superior. Sentence by sentence, over the course of seven single-spaced pages, it all added up to a terrible and sprawling lie. (But—and this was hard to admit—she admired the statement, too. The patience it took to compose something this long and clear, the hours of hard work. It made you wonder: Where did a black nurse from the inner city learn to write this way?) If possible, she'd track Harriet Foster down and wave a mangled copy of the statement in her bewildered face. *Look here, God damn it. I know what you're up to. I know what you're trying to pull here.*

All of which made for a very satisfying fantasy, but here at the kitchen table, reading the statement for the second and third times, she was more inclined to scream. She didn't dare. Not in Dr. Lammers's cool presence. With Dr. Lammers all the evidence had to be dispassionately considered. The pages of Harriet Foster's statement needed to be set out before them on the table. *All right then,* they had to say and sip from their warm mugs of raspberry herbal tea. *Let's take a moment and break down the argument piece by piece.*

For instance . . .

Less than an hour before the murder, Harriet Foster claimed to have stopped Christopher Waterhouse and Evie Hicks in the camp van. She said she'd tried her best to convince Christopher to leave Evie Hicks with her and drive to the Ellsinore Dairy Queen alone. But he could not be persuaded. He'd been extremely patient and polite, but this was a pretense; he barely listened to her. His attention was elsewhere. He put the van in gear and drove off. She ran after him. At the camp gate he turned right instead of left, and she knew then, beyond any doubt, that he did not intend to take Evie Hicks to Ellsinore. Instead he was driving east along County Road H looking for an isolated place to park the van.

It was terrifying, she said, to realize his true intentions. There was no other counselor, no other staff member, whom Harriet could find to help her. She ran back to the infirmary. Desperate as she was, she made an appeal to one of the campers who happened to be staying that night in the infirmary: Wyatt Huddy, large, powerful, obedient.

But this made no sense at all. In her previous affidavit—and in the affidavits she'd no doubt helped gather from others—Harriet Foster had insisted Wyatt Huddy showed all the signs and symptoms of a retarded man. Now she was saying she'd chosen him to be her hero?

Another sip of tea. A shuffling of papers.

"Not likely," Marcy said, and Dr. Lammers nodded, perhaps in agreement.

When you got right down to it, there was very little that could pass for evidence in Harriet Foster's long statement. She saw this. Or she noticed that. *Christopher Waterhouse had rigged a prize drawing. He'd turned right on County Road H.* But could any of it be verified? According to Harriet Foster, two and half hours after Wyatt had gone off in search of Christopher, he'd come back to the infirmary in the camp van. Harriet had run out and thrown open the van door. And what had she seen? Wyatt Huddy scratched and disheveled and smeared with dirt. Evie Hicks strapped naked onto the bench of the van, her clothes piled beside her. She had the dazed look of someone who'd undergone a terrible ordeal. This was Harriet's evidence that Christopher had molested or raped her.

But really, Marcy insisted, it was important to look beyond Harriet's easy explanations. Why not suspect Wyatt Huddy of this attack? He'd already proved himself to be a murderer.

"Yes, that's right," Dr. Lammers said evenly. "It's a valid possibility."

Marcy was so very glad to hear him admit this. But honestly, she'd've liked to have noticed a shred of intensity in his reaction, a trace of passion, for goodness' sake. Without it, she worried that the cool sincerity of Harriet Foster's statement had had its effect.

They sifted through other documents. There were lesser topics to discuss. What had Marcy thought of the camp management? Linda Rucker? Very average, Marcy said. And what about Schuller Kindermann? Oh, there was something wonderful about Mr. Kindermann, she said, though she couldn't at the moment articulate what it was. Instead she rose and put a half dozen cinnamon scones in the toaster oven. She was bundling up and filing away documents when the oven buzzer went off.

Dr. Lammers, his scone lightly buttered and set before him, lifted a few broken crumbs to his lips. "Oh, that's very nice, Marcy," he said. "Thank you." Whatever he'd just tasted seemed to stir him toward other thoughts. "But you never noticed any funny stuff, sexually I mean, with Christopher?" he asked.

She didn't need to hesitate. "No," she said. "Absolutely not. We weren't what you would call . . ." There was a word she couldn't quite locate. "We weren't ever *dating*," she said. "We weren't girlfriend and boyfriend."

But really, when it came to sex, what counted as funny anyway? There were always a few messy and confidential things young men liked to do that couldn't easily be called *normal*. In these matters Marcy had some experience. She'd been thirty when she married Dr. Lammers. By then she'd had a number of relationships and had witnessed some noteworthy preferences and habits. For instance, she once lived with a sweet-tempered anesthesiologist in training who was a fan of the city's modern dance troupe and liked, in the privacy of their bedroom, to strip naked and dance for her. He liked to be seen. Dr. Lammers, too, had at least one interesting inclination. On the second and fourth Saturdays of each month he preferred Marcy to dress in nothing but red panties and wait for him beneath the covers of their bed. He liked to pull back those covers and say, with a bemused expression, "Ah yes, the doctor will see you now." A private little joke between them, certainly. But he seemed to relish reciting this line and indulging in an enthusiastic survey of her body. Wasn't that a little funny?

Less amusing was the fact that most of the young men Marcy dated had tried to lead her, wordlessly, into the realm of some new sexual practice. At least Christopher Waterhouse had come to her as a friend and, in the bright, romping light of the swimming pool deck, had been able to look her in the eye and speak honestly about what he needed. The problem, he said, was Linda Rucker. She'd been so intent and so very explicit about the sexual things she wanted him to do. A terrible picture had been created in his mind. It was warping his imagination. When he closed his eyes at night and tried to sleep, he saw Linda Rucker eager and unclothed and reaching for him. What he needed was an altogether different and more powerful image to take its place. He craved a strong reminder of what a beautiful woman looked like.

Was Marcy flattered? Was she glad to have been asked? No, not really. But she must have been willing. The young woman she'd been then—the cheerful, eager twenty-two-year-old Marcy Bittman— must have thought it over and decided to accommodate her friend. Late in the afternoon, once the campers had finished for the day, and Harriet Foster and her son had completed their private swim and gone away, after the deck was hosed down and the water tested, she and Christopher stepped into the pool house supply room and closed the door. The physical part of what happened in that room was entirely Christopher's doing. He had his lotion and a beach towel and his hand. It was Marcy's task—her burden, too—to remove her one-piece suit. He liked her to stand in a certain way. This was uncomfortable, but only mildly so. It wasn't as if he ogled or leered at her, but he did look up and *reference* her from time to time. And something else, too: he took her discarded swimsuit and pressed a particular section of it to his mouth and nose. So yes, maybe this act, the breathing in of her swimsuit, would qualify in Dr. Lammers's view as *funny stuff.* For Marcy it was simply an embarrassment. She wore that suit all day long. If she hadn't constantly been getting in and out of a chlorinated pool, she wouldn't have let Christopher anywhere near it.

They were together in the storeroom, in exactly this way, three times. Three afternoons in a row. It didn't take long for Christopher to finish and clean himself up. Less than five minutes, surely. And after he finished, he was so authentically grateful. *Thank you, Marcy,* he said, *thank you,* though not in a way that was exaggerated or loaded with expectation. She nodded and got dressed and helped lock up the pool. Then they went back to their respective cabins, and a half hour later, when they saw each other again at the mess hall for dinner, Christopher would grin and raise one eyebrow a bit, and the meaning of this expression would come through so clearly. *Yes*, he was saying, *what happened between us thirty minutes ago was a little odd, a little reckless, but I'm so glad to have gone through it with a trusted friend.*

All of which begged the question. Did she love him? Had she been lovesick for Christopher Waterhouse?

Her most truthful answer? No. Not love. Though maybe something akin to love or something that, at the very least, carried an equal urgency.

She recognized in Christopher a tendency she'd seen in no one else. Whenever he talked with the other counselors at Kindermann

Forest, a part of Christopher, an awareness, was flitting around outside the bounds of the conversation. If you looked very closely, you could see that this separate part of Christopher was trying to study the manners and expressions of the persons with whom he talked. And in the moments after the conversation ended, you could see those learned expressions being played out faintly on Christopher's face. He was schooling himself in how other people behaved and how they might feel.

This particular longing she understood completely: she'd always had a hunch that what lay at the center of certain people—Dr. Lammers and Harriet Foster, just to name a few—was better and brighter and wiser than what existed at the center of herself. In the company of these people, she was always leaning forward a bit, trying to learn the secrets of what made them vivid and worthwhile.

And to see the same tendency alive in Christopher Waterhouse? It was perhaps the most reassuring thing she'd ever witnessed.

It seemed to Marcy they were very busy people that year—the year of opening envelopes and weighing evidence. She had her cooking and health classes, and Dr. Lammers had his endless roster of patients and interns to be trained and the opening of the third laser vision eye care clinic. Despite their hectic lives, Dr. Lammers did something exceptional: he took Marcy to Barbados for five sun-burnished and blissful days. Truly they needed this time together, more than they needed the bright weather and the exquisite staff service at their resort. What mattered most was that they could lie in bed or sit for a long dinner and speak their opinions of things without having to be so god damn fair-minded, so neutral and altogether dull. In Barbados they were candid. They were close. And they brought some of that closeness and candor back home into their daily life in St. Louis. They breezed by for a few happy weeks while the packets of evidence arrived in the mail and accumulated in a teakwood tray on the kitchen counter.

The thought occurred to Marcy that she might sift through the envelopes on her own and weed out any documents that were distracting or inconsequential.

She never did, though, and a few weeks later, when she and Dr. Lammers sat down to the kitchen table, the first item to spill from the envelope was a thick criminal case file from Pemiscot County, Missouri. It bore Christopher Waterhouse's name.

They opened the file and read the title of the topmost document: a record of arrest dated September 23, 1995, some nine months before the start of the Kindermann Forest State Hospital Session. There were other documents in this file—charges and incidents and reports that appeared to date back to Christopher Waterhouse's early adolescence.

A terrible sense of alertness came over Marcy. She managed to bring her full teacup to her chest without spilling a drop. "Let's put this whole file aside for a moment," she said. "Let's put it aside and move on to something else. Can we do that, please?"

"Well, I don't—"

"Please, *Dean!*"

He looked up with an acute and wary brand of respect. After a moment, he nodded. They turned their attention to other envelopes and considered entirely different documents, most of them minor in importance. Petitions to delay. Petitions to seek a psychiatric evaluation of Wyatt Huddy. More significant, they found a memo from the prosecuting attorney, Henry Masner, to the defense attorney, Mackland Benders.

> —*Mackland*
>> *In regard to our earlier discussion.*
>> *We'll have it your way. I'm willing to drop second-degree charges*

and press for a diminished capacity conviction based on Wyatt Huddy's limited IQ.

I don't foresee the Waterhouse family objecting to this change. Their enthusiasm for my prosecution case, or for anything involving their son, is mild at best.

It gives me no satisfaction to prosecute Mr. Huddy on this charge. But necessary, I would think.

Strange to feel this pity from Henry Masner, three years dead, reach them in the form of this memo. They placed it among the constellation of other documents. Then they arranged and bundled up various stacks of papers, and heated two soft pretzels in the toaster oven and served them with honey mustard. With nothing else left to consider, they turned their attention back to Christopher Waterhouse's criminal case file.

He'd been charged in September 1995 with sexual assault upon a thirteen-year-old girl, a neighbor in his hometown of Caruthersville, Missouri. The record of arrest described an adult male perpetrator sneaking into the girl's home through a basement window, finding her second-floor bedroom, and performing an act of sodomy upon her. The victim claimed to recognize Christopher Waterhouse at the time of the attack. He'd been charged with first-degree sexual assault. After three days' incarceration, he was released on bail. His court date had been set for November 1996.

There were other reports in this file. A year earlier a girl Christopher had dated had made an unpleasant accusation: she'd been pressured during a college party to take part in a sex act involving multiple partners. No charges had come of this. She'd been distraught enough to contact the police and file a report, but she did not believe—or was not willing to believe—that what she'd been pressured to do qualified as sexual assault.

A month prior to this Christopher had been cited for drunkenness and lewd behavior in the parking lot of an all-night convenience store.

A year earlier he'd exposed himself to a group of teenage girls at a shopping mall.

The file included several reports that dated back to Christopher's years in junior high school. It seemed to Marcy that what these reports entailed might have been typical adolescent behavior—peering into neighbors' windows, running about naked at night—if the behavior hadn't been so frequent, the incidents so many.

Was there a calm way, a *fair-minded* way, to talk about what these files contained? If so, Marcy didn't know what it might be. Nor, it seemed, did Dr. Lammers. He'd been so fully engrossed in the final pages of the case file that, when he lifted his face up to her, his bespectacled eyes were pared down into a myopic squint.

"Well . . . ,"he said at last. "Well, Marcy . . ." He shook his head, and the obvious satisfaction he took in his bewilderment, his speechlessness, irked her. He was such a fussy, childish man, such an innocent. It was maddening, the way he seemed to savor the shock he'd just endured.

They waited patiently for each other to assemble their arguments. It was surprising, really. She was far more composed than she might have expected. She folded her hands and, in a voice that was level and instructive, said, "Do you know what I think, Dean? I think, if we try, we can consider all this with an open mind. We can put it in perspective alongside all the really good things, the outstanding things, we know about Christopher."

It wasn't as if she expected him to agree. But the intensity of his reaction: his face, in the span of a few moments, turned a mottled red. "Do you understand what we've just read?" he said with such incredulousness, such breathy astonishment. "All these awful things?"

For emphasis, he pinched a thick corner of Christopher's case file. "What's written down here is only the stuff he got caught doing. My God, Marcy. *Imagine* the things he got away with."

This was the last remark from Dr. Lammers that she was able to calmly absorb. After that she seemed to undergo a profound change: one moment coolly indignant, and the next wild and raving. It wasn't like her. She shrieked out some terrible things. Horrible things, really. It was astonishing that such hurtful notions were lurking somewhere in her mind.

They'd never had a fight remotely like this one. Dr. Lammers had never before stood so staunchly behind his supposed principles. He swore he'd never invest a dime of his money in honoring a person like Christopher Waterhouse. A person who happened to be a . . .

"What?" she demanded to know.

"A pervert," he said. "A pedophile."

With this they crossed over into some starker and more darkly cunning realm of their argument. She made herself perfectly clear: the choice of whether or not to honor Christopher wasn't Dr. Lammers's. It was hers. And she'd decided to go ahead with the memorial. She'd spend whatever money she thought necessary.

Dr. Lammers assured her she'd do no such thing. If she went ahead with the memorial, she'd be doing it with her own money. She'd also be doing it as a single woman, rather than as his wife.

Neither of them had ever before made such an open reference to divorce. But it was fine with Marcy. She said she'd pay for and organize Christopher's memorial as a divorced woman. She already had a lawyer in mind. In fact she'd done some preparation work with this lawyer. She knew some things for certain: she'd get the house they were standing in. At the very least Dr. Lammers would have to sell off one of his laser vision eye care clinics. As she made these pronouncements, she was gathering up her purse and coat in order, she told Dr. Lammers, to go out and pay a visit to her lawyer. Her limbs were shaking, her balance skewed. She could hardly navigate the maze of her own living room. Entirely stupid that she should crawl behind the wheel of an automobile and attempt to drive. She did though. It was a starkly gray Sunday afternoon in March. Of course she knew of no lawyer with whom she might consult. Instead she drove to the empty back parking lot of a Walgreens drugstore. For what must have been several hours she raged and wailed and became undone.

From the second-floor window she could see the last pair of holiday party guests descending the front steps and strolling arm in arm along the walkway to their car. A very nice couple, by the look of them, the young man stately and attractive, his wife in a lovely maroon coat, her brown hair uncovered and swaying prettily with each step she took. Her name was Abigail, if Marcy remembered correctly. Her husband, a sales rep for a laser eye technology company, was named Jason or Joshua. Earlier in the evening they'd stood by the fire in the great room and talked with Marcy, briefly, about the new soccer and softball complex set to open in their township at the start of summer.

Now, at the end of the driveway, they were easing open the doors of their sedan. It wasn't hard for Marcy to imagine how the remainder of the couple's night would unfold. They'd drive home and collapse onto their couch. Maybe they'd fix a drink and watch TV awhile. Or make love.

Or fall into an argument. Because that, too, was a feature of being married. At almost any time, or under the umbrella of any mood, a disruption could present itself. There were many kinds: an annoyance, a disappointment mild or severe, an icy, unspoken bitterness. It could go on for days. Or it could explode into a sudden raging misery in which everything in the marriage was turned inside out and made to look shabby and sick and intolerable. No matter how long you'd been married there was never a stage at which you moved beyond these pitfalls.

Thank heavens she and Dr. Lammers had had the good sense to sit down and negotiate those things that could not be tolerated in their marriage. For Marcy it wasn't bearable that her friend Christopher should be labeled with certain cruel names. He was to be spoken of with respect or not at all.

For Dr. Lammers's sake she'd agreed to keep her *moonyness* to herself. In a minute or two, when he climbed the stairs to the bedroom and found her at the bathroom sink or, more to his liking, beneath the covers of their bed, he hoped to be greeted by a face purged of sorrow and longing.

The other term of their negotiation was a bit harder to bear. No memorial for Christopher Waterhouse. Though what she chose to commemorate in her heart of hearts was her business, wasn't it?

Chapter Fourteen

For their strenuous efforts with the state hospital campers, each member of the Kindermann Forest counseling staff was paid, after taxes, two hundred and forty-seven dollars and twenty-three cents. The paychecks were handwritten and signed by Schuller Kindermann, though he did not distribute the checks. That duty fell to Head Cook Maureen Boyd, and the formalities of her assignment—standing at the mess hall serving counter, calling out the names, dispersing the checks—appeared to terrify her. Several times her voice went wheezy or silent. Her hand shook. As soon as the last check was doled out, she took a deep, bolstering breath and made her announcement.

It was true, she said. The remaining camp sessions had all been canceled. The children would not be coming. Their parents had been called and told to keep their sons and daughters at home. Or find another camp. Because the summer at Kindermann Forest was over. Finished. Everyone was dismissed—the kitchen and maintenance staff, the counselors, the wrangler and lifeguard. Dismissed. Officially so. This was their notification—right here, right now. She said she could not, in her wildest dreams, have guessed the summer would end this way.

The news settled over them in crushing increments. Eventually they understood. There was nothing else to do but gather their belongings from the sleeping cabins and arrange rides home. Their careers as summer camp counselors had lasted twelve days.

What a humbling experience it was to return home, to go back to being moody lodgers in their parents' houses. The first thing they did upon arriving was telephone the boyfriends and girlfriends they'd abandoned two weeks earlier. *Hey there. Listen, it's me. I'm back. All right now . . . hold on just a minute. Don't be that way.* Humiliating. They walked in the pressing summer heat to the drive-thru restaurants and day-care centers and begged to have their dull summer jobs back.

They'd been gone twelve days. It felt like an embarrassing, even laughably brief, stretch of time. Now they were back stocking groceries and mowing lawns and counting down the days of their summer break. Six weeks. Four weeks. Then—*thank God*—two weeks. In late August they were relieved to pack up their things and move back to college.

Or rent an apartment. Or join the U.S. Navy. Or get married. That was how the summer ended for Kathleen Bram and Michael Lauderback: a late September wedding at the First Baptist chapel in Kathleen's hometown of Swansea, Illinois. On the face of it, all their choices seemed unwise. They were both twenty years old. Neither had a college degree. Except for their twelve days at Kindermann Forest, they'd never lived away from home. At the time of the wedding Kathleen was three months pregnant. (Why shouldn't she be? They'd had eight consecutive nights of fumbling and revelatory sex on the floor of the Kindermann Forest arts and crafts pavilion.) And yet, despite these obstacles, they survived the difficult first few years of their marriage. Later, in their mid-twenties, they both began careers—occupational therapy for Kathleen, real estate for Michael—that sustained them very nicely. Theirs was an unlikely success: three more children over the next decade, a boisterous and secure family life, and a married partnership that was steady and unpretentious and deeply companionable. The new friends they made in the neighborhood and at church were a little puzzled—and envious. But you couldn't very well ask to know the secret of Kathleen and Michael's marriage. Happy couples were never able to explain their good fortune from the inside out.

Instead their friends asked how Kathleen and Michael had met.

"At summer camp," Kathleen said. "We were camp counselors."

"Really?" their friends exclaimed. *A summer camp.* It set their minds racing. They could picture it all so clearly: the quaint, tree-shaded sleeping cabins, the rowdy and adoring children, the sudden camaraderie between male and female counselors—the possibilities this entailed for tenderness, for love.

"How wonderful," their friends said. "A summer camp. What a wonderful place to meet and fall in love."

It was *wonderful.* For Kathleen and Michael it was. Their memories of Kindermann Forest always carried a special vibrancy. Call it an atmosphere. Call it an aura of goodwill. They could recall this goodwill arising from nearly everyone at camp—from the counselors and lifeguards, from the nurse, from the kitchen and maintenance staff. Even from the state hospital campers. That's right. This same goodwill was alive in the campers, too. Kathleen and Michael had talked about it over the years. At Kindermann Forest they'd been twenty years old and in love for the first and only time. They'd been lit from within. It might sound improbable, but the state hospital campers were aware of what was happening between Kathleen and Michael. The campers wanted, in their own way, to honor and be near it. They liked to stand close to Kathleen and Michael's unfolding tenderness and wag their heads in approval.

Too bad this aura of goodwill didn't extend to everyone at Kindermann Forest. It was fair to say that many of the counselors were beyond its reach. None of the Lonesome Three felt *honored* during their time at Kindermann Forest. They weren't entirely surprised when the camp season came to an early end. (To the Lonesome Three it seemed that every night at Kindermann Forest there was something reckless and carnal happening inside the perimeter of the woods. No real surprise that the summer should end in a homicide.) They packed up their things and shared a ride to St. Louis. There they nodded farewell and went back to their respective hometowns. In the fall they returned to college. They were dutiful—if less than popular—students, and after graduation they found entry-level business jobs and became dutiful—if less than popular—employees. They weren't the type to keep in touch with one another or any of the other Kindermann Forest counselors. At various times in their lives all of the Lonesome Three had short-lived and tepid romantic associations. One of them was married for less than a year. Otherwise the basic ingredients of their lives were very similar: an unremarkable job, a single-bedroom apartment, a pet that was often fickle in its affections. Were the Lonesome Three unhappy? They wouldn't have said so. Or at least they wouldn't have claimed to be *terribly* unhappy. Mostly they felt resentment at never having been welcomed into the fold of office co-workers or college roommates—or, for that matter, fellow camp counselors. The fault for this, they knew, was probably their own. It wasn't simply a matter of being unattractive; every day they encountered less than attractive people who had wide circles of friends, who had devoted lovers or grateful wives and husbands. No, the problem was a part of who they were. They seemed always to give off a faint but steady signal that kept other people at a distance. There was something within them—a strange disability that had them lurching on the inside—that couldn't easily be named or diagnosed. It couldn't be remedied, either. They were lonesome all their lives.

Kindermann Forest Counselor Wayne Kesterson went to jail for possessing five and a half ounces of homegrown marijuana. This wasn't an unforeseen event—all summer he'd carried inside him a worming sense of dread—but the terms of his incarceration were swift and startling. The judge decided that Wayne would serve his allotted forty days over the course of sixteen weekends. Weekends? At the sentencing Wayne tried to wrap his mind around this possibility: Monday through Friday he'd be a free-strolling member of society? Weekends he'd be a shuffling prisoner?

He wasn't far off the mark. Each Friday at 6:00 P.M. he checked into the St. Louis County Jail, donned an orange jumpsuit, and was placed, along with thirty other drug and alcohol offenders, in an enormous holding cell. Each man found a small portion of the concrete floor to call his own. They ate boloney and cheese sandwiches from paper trays and slept on foldout cots. There was moodiness and bad hygiene, but little outright violence. The minutes of each hour trickled by. Monday at 6:00 A.M. they were set free. It was then, stumbling out into the shrill morning light of the new workweek, that they realized how unfair their punishment was. There was no way to recapture what they'd missed out on over the weekend: the keg parties and dope smoking and courting of drunken women. No good at all to try to reenact these things on a Monday morning. There was no time for it anyway. They had to hurry home, shower, and race off to work.

For Wayne this meant rushing to St. Matthew's Catholic Hospital for the start of his 7:30 A.M. shift. His department was housekeeping, his assignment was wielding the large and powerful Tour Master 5200 electric floor polisher. He had plenty of time while buffing the long hospital corridors to reflect on the jail conversations he'd had over the weekend. The boasting. The bullshit. He could review it all in his mind and scoff. Nearly every man in the holding cell had elaborate plans to start a business, to enroll in college, to run for public office. At least Wayne wasn't trying to make himself look better in the eyes of other weekend prisoners. He was a floor polisher, for Christ's sake. He wasn't going to get an advanced degree or rise to the station of hospital director. It was achievement enough to hold down a steady job for a while.

Or, as it turned out, more than a while. A few years. It wasn't so bad, really. A floor polisher's salary was nearly twice that of a burger flipper or grocery store cashier. The benefits were good. In five years he'd saved enough for a down payment on a mobile home. He rented a grassy little lot in a trailer park. At work there was always a flood of young nurses strolling across his floors. He knew most of them by name. Over the years he dated more than a few of these nurses. Several became steady girlfriends. And even after the relationships ran their course he was on friendly enough terms with these nurses to go out for a drink or sell them a little pot now and then. It was only mildly surprising to realize he'd worked at St. Matthew's for a decade. By then he had a strong hunch he wasn't going to be a husband or father. That was probably for the best. He didn't have any strong inclinations to be someone's spouse or someone's daddy. He liked to come home and smoke and see what was on TV. Every once in a while he'd do something stupid: get a DWI and, rather than hire a lawyer, give up his driver's license. Stupid maybe. And a little embarrassing. What else could he do but learn to live with it? He was thirty-three years old, then thirty-five, then thirty-seven. He was the only long-term employee of St. Matthew's who came to work each morning on the public bus. But once he arrived people seemed glad to see him. *Morning, Wayne,* they liked to say. He was a fixture at St. Matthew's. So what if his life's work was floor polishing? He wasn't going to walk around feeling ashamed for doing a competent job. And the work itself wasn't so bad. He could grip the weighty handlebars of the Tour Master 5200 and slip away comfortably inside himself. An hour later he'd surface to find the long hospital corridor behind him gleaming in the light.

One afternoon in the chilly late winter of 2011, Wayne, on the bus ride home from work, lifted his gaze from a scavenged newspaper and studied one of his fellow passengers—an old man—sitting across the aisle. It was an odd sensation. Just to sit and look at this old man made Wayne fretful—a sharp, insinuating fretfulness. When he got home, he'd have to smoke and drink a stiff Coke and bourbon.

And then it dawned on him: the old man across the bus aisle was Mr. Stottlemeir. Terrence J. Stottlemeir. Years ago—could it be fifteen years?—at a summer camp called Kindermann Forest, Wayne had cared for Mr. Stottlemeir. He'd been Mr. Stottlemeir's counselor, though this was a misleading term because, really, the duties he'd performed for Mr. Stottlemeir—the showering and dressing and cleaning up after a bowel movement—had been the duties of a nurse's aide. For two mostly awful weeks Wayne had suffered in these duties: he'd been screamed at and ridiculed, slapped and cursed.

But this couldn't be the same Mr. Stottlemeir. That Mr. Stottlemeir had, in the summer of 1996, been old and impossibly cranky. By now he'd be more than ancient. He'd be dead. Also the Terrence J. Stottlemeir whom Wayne had cared for had been completely out of his mind. He'd had an unnerving habit of ratcheting his head back and forth and opening his crooked mouth. He'd raved. He'd slapped and clawed. Just to feed Mr. Stottlemeir his meals each day they'd had to dress him in a heavily buttoned garment that resembled a straitjacket. The old man sitting now across the bus aisle from Wayne looked to be in full command of his arms and of the taut bearing of his neck and shoulders. He raised two fingers. With a delicate, pinching grip, he adjusted the bridge of his glasses. He was maybe seventy years of age, perhaps seventy-five. Now and then a potent thought seemed to break the surface of his calm expression, and he furrowed his brow and scribbled a few letters or marks onto a writing tablet balanced on one knee. Then he lifted his pale face to the window and looked out again, thoughtfully, at the passing city blocks.

A short while later the bus stopped along Olive Road, at the Friendly Village Retirement Home, and the old man rose from his bus seat and along with a half dozen other elderly passengers filed to the front of the bus. Down the steps they went, donning mittens and scarves and treading carefully across the frozen pavement to the gated entranceway of the Friendly Village.

It was, for Wayne, an unsettling encounter, deeply so. For several days he couldn't think of anything else. It couldn't possibly have been Mr. Stottlemeir. And yet there was a quality to the old man's face, a refinement, a princeliness, that couldn't belong to anyone else. It was god damn unnerving. And the usual remedies—the smoking and watching of his favorite TV shows—did little to settle Wayne down. In the middle of the night it dawned on him: Mr. Stottlemeir hadn't been elderly in 1996. He'd been late middle-aged—fifty-five or sixty years old.

At work Wayne talked about the encounter to anyone who'd listen: his fellow floor polishers, the kitchen staff. He talked about the man who might have been Mr. Stottlemeir to the nurses of St. Matthew's. This turned out to be a wise tactic. Nurses knew things. They knew other nurses. For example, the nurses at St. Matthew's knew several nurses at the Friendly Village Retirement Home. The St. Matthew's nurses, stirred by Wayne's distress, called the Friendly Village Retirement Home and made an inquiry.

The old man on the bus *was* Terrence J. Stottlemeir. He was seventy-two years old. He'd been a long-term resident of the state hospital in Farmington. Six years ago an eager doctor at the state hospital had tried a series of new prescription medications on Mr. Stottlemeir. The first two medicines did nothing. The third one changed everything. In a matter of days Mr. Stottlemeir went from cursing and flailing his arms to padding along the state hospital corridors and studying, patiently, the framed prints of horse pastures and forest cottages. At the nurses' station he made a polite request for butterscotch pudding. More impressive, he could use the toilet on his own. He could feed himself. The things he said were mostly lucid and reasonable. It was clear to his attendants that Mr. Stottlemeir no longer required the services of a locked-down institution. Still though, he had to suffer confinement in the state hospital for two more years, until a diligent caseworker was able to secure for Mr. Stottlemeir a change of status: from ward of the state to Medicaid patient. He ended up at the Friendly Village Retirement Home, a stroke of real luck, since the home was new and staffed with well-paid and conscientious nurses. The food at the Friendly Village was said to be varied and delicious. He took advantage of the home's flower arranging and Jazzercise classes. On Fridays he went by bus with a group of other Friendly Village residents to the botanical garden to make pencil sketches of the acclaimed orchid collection.

Wayne Kesterson, of course, was amazed and grateful to receive this news. "Un-*fucking*-believable," he kept telling the St. Matthew's nurses. Not that he doubted the story. But he had to keep explaining it to himself in order for the truth to sink in: Mr. Stottlemeir had been idiotic and crazy for many years. Now, with the right medication, he'd come to his senses.

It was agonizing to wait for the bus after work on Friday. How awful it would be to see Mr. Stottlemeir again. But how disappointing it would be—crushing really—for Mr. Stottlemeir to be absent from the rows of passengers.

Fortunately or unfortunately, he was there, same row, same window-side bench. The seat beside him was open. Wayne took it. For a few wintry miles he could do nothing but rack his mind for an innocent observation to share. "Four more weeks of winter," he said at last. "I'll be glad to be done with it. How 'bout you?"

Mr. Stottlemeir tightened his regal expression. He seemed willing to acknowledge that someone had spoken to him, but for the time being he wasn't ready to reply.

"I work at St. Matthew's," Wayne said, more forcefully. "I'm in with the housekeeping crew. What I do is polish the floors."

Mr. Stottlemeir sat back a few inches in his seat. He turned his head and braved a quick glance at Wayne.

"In a hospital," Wayne said. "The floors have to be kept clean and shiny. It reassures people. So I polish. I clean up the messes. And I show up on time each morning."

"Yes," Mr. Stottlemeir said. "Yes, you do." His voice sounded raspy, unused.

"I do my work."

Outside there were knots of people shivering within a mud-splattered bus shelter. Every time they opened their mouths plumes of foggy breath escaped them.

"I pay my taxes, too," Wayne said. "Federal and state."

"Good for you," Mr. Stottlemeir said, weakly.

"But some people, they think that if you're not a brain surgeon then you're not worth talking to. You're a nobody. Or worse than that. A loser. A screwup." He waited. His hands were trembling. "They think you're a stinking puddle of piss."

From Mr. Stottlemeir came a slow and rather dreamy fluttering of the eyelids. He cocked his head to the side and concentrated on Wayne's remark. "No, no," Mr. Stottlemeir said. "They'd be wrong, if they said that. They'd be wrong, wouldn't they?"

Something about the politeness of this attention undid Wayne. One moment he was all right, the next he was pitched forward with his mouth hanging open, his face pressed against the forward seat, long, heaving breaths—all the way to the Friendly Village and beyond.

The tract of land formerly known as Kindermann Forest Summer Camp appeared on the commercial real estate market in February 1997. It made for an altogether impressive listing: one hundred and sixteen acres (some wooded, some cleared), an access throughway to Barker Lake, a fifty-meter swimming pool and shower house, four large sleeping cabins, an expansive kitchen and dining hall, an infirmary and camp office, two single-unit sleeping cottages, a stable and wrangler's quarters, two pavilions, five enclosed utility sheds. The price had been set at two and a half million dollars. According to the real estate agent, Schuller Kindermann preferred that the property be sold to individuals interested in operating an arts and crafts, nature, and Christian faith summer camp. He most definitely did not want the grounds and facilities turned into a commercial sports camp, of which there were already several in the Missouri Ozarks region. If necessary, he was willing to turn down offers.

For a long while there were no offers to turn down. During the summer of 1997 the camp was rented out for family reunions and company retreats. This turned out to be a wasted effort. The money collected didn't cover the liability insurance premiums. That fall the herd of sixteen trail horses was sold off, and Reggie Boyd, who lived in the director's cottage and watched over the property, was released from his duties. The metal gate at the entrance to Kindermann Forest was closed, wound with chain, and locked shut.

Seven years later a retired heart surgeon from Kansas City bought the grounds for five hundred and thirty-nine thousand dollars. He and his wife planned to refurbish the buildings and open a Bible study camp. It never came to pass.

By the summer of 2011 the buildings had begun to rupture. Wild shrubs sprang from every clear patch of lawn or yard. The open meadow of Kindermann Forest was lost to a drove of rangy young cedar trees. Inside the woods all four cabins were now banked beneath a crushing wave of tree limbs and bushes. Thick cords of ivy pried through the window screens into the dark inner chambers of the sleeping barracks.

At the swimming pool a lone sycamore tree had pushed its way up from one of a hundred cracks in the pool floor. It wasn't as impossible a place for a tree as one might think: all that dampness and uncontested sunlight.

Still though, what a remarkable sight: a twelve-foot sapling rising up from the shallow end of an abandoned pool. It grew fast and wild and strange.

Chapter Fifteen

On Saturday morning she loaded into the passenger seat of her Honda Accord a handsome new piece of rollaway luggage and drove it out past the elegant brick houses of her neighborhood and onto the wide and uncrowded lanes of Kingshighway Avenue. The traffic lights shone mostly in her favor. In five minutes' time she was rolling through a precinct of St. Louis know as The Hill, glancing now and then at the luggage belted into the seat beside her, and trailing behind a bread truck and a sprightly weekend bicyclist, past corner bars and shuttered restaurants, the bread truck and bicyclist turning right, and Harriet pushing ahead one more block and pulling up, at last, to the front security station of the Gateway Psychiatric Rehabilitation Center.

From behind the paneled windows of the station the weekend security officer rose to his feet and nodded in recognition of Harriet, or perhaps her green Honda. He waved her in.

Directly ahead, at the cusp of a circling blacktop lane, stood an immense and improbably beautiful brick and marble asylum built in the nineteenth century and topped by an elaborate pillared dome. You could see this building, aptly nicknamed the Dome Building, from numerous vantage points throughout South St. Louis. Sightseers always mistook it for a state or federal courthouse. Once they learned its true purpose, they were inclined to drive along the fenced perimeter of the Gateway Psychiatric campus and scan the Dome Building's six floors of windows in the hope of seeing an inmate's deranged face pressed against the glass.

Inevitably they were disappointed. But at least they still had their bleak notions of what a mental asylum interior might hold. All Harriet's best notions had long ago been dismantled or turned inside out. She parked her car and towed the luggage by its laddering handle across the lot toward a newer region of the Gateway Psychiatric campus: a low-set and sprawling administrative building that fronted a network of redbrick living cottages. (Never mind the Dome Building, which still housed more difficult cases. Harriet hadn't set foot inside it in nine years.) In the administration building lobby she donned her visitor's pass, went straight to the security screening lane, and set her purse and luggage atop a viewing counter. She was the first and, thus far, only visitor of the morning, and she had to jingle the contents of her purse a few times before the weekend security guards, Maurice and Laquisha, noticed her and filed out from their windowed office.

"We don't open till *nine* in the A.M.," Laquisha mock-scolded her. "What time your watch say, Nurse Harriet?"

"Nine-oh-one."

"Hell it does. Try eight-fifty-eight. You got us off to the races two whole minutes before we ready to go."

"Well, giddyup then," Harriet said.

For this bit of teasing she was treated to Laquisha and Maurice's sly indignation, their head-shaking disbelief and sharp, inclusive laughter. Even so, Harriet's purse was pulled open and the contents given a thorough sift. Her empty rollaway luggage was unzipped and the nylon lining pressed and pinched, as if Laquisha were shopping at Sears and had taken a fussy interest in the stitches and seams.

"Step up to the line, please," Maurice said, and once he'd powered the metal detector on, he motioned Harriet forward until she'd passed over the threshold of the machine, and he nodded his approval and said, "Thank you kindly, young lady," a flattery he used only with middle- and late-aged black women.

She was reunited with her purse and luggage, and off she went down a long corridor of doors and name plaques and bulletin boards until she passed through the width of the building and exited the doors at the other side. Here she followed a network of paved walkways until all at once she was in a village of sizable redbrick Gateway Living Cottages. Harriet's destination was Living Cottage No. 8. At the front entranceway she pressed the buzzer and waited to be let in.

On the whole what she'd seen over the years in the living cottages and the Dome Building and the administration corridors wasn't wildly different from the things she'd seen in the long hallways of the hospitals and nursing homes in which she'd worked. If she were looking for bleakness and desperate behavior, she could find it easily enough in any of these institutions. Yet there was brighter evidence, too. The facilities at Gateway and the determined staff were a grade or two above those of most hospitals and homes. Not perfect, of course. No institution was. You could wrinkle your nose at the dissembling that went into a name like *living cottage*. But if you were institutionalized in the state of Missouri, it would be your good fortune to wind up in a Gateway Living Cottage. Better than a prison cell, certainly. And far better, infinitely better, than what had come before the Living Cottages: the Lunatic Asylum, the Insane Asylum, the City Sanitarium.

The door to Living Cottage No. 8 eased open and Harriet was ushered into the Saturday morning rituals of what she'd come to think of as a large and varied family. They couldn't be obliged or understood all at once, this family. She had to press forward into the foyer and choose her encounters carefully.

First, a wave to the three on-duty care attendants—Mary Jo Savini, perched behind the staff station counter—and Franklin and Yvonne, who were out in the large common room guiding several residents through the rigors of morning cleanup.

Holding tight to the station counter was B. J. Tompkins, a resident to be avoided because of his constant and anguished claims against the city's utility services. With B.J. she averted her gaze and ignored his pleas ("That's what I'm tellin' you, lady. Come on, now. Come on now, lady"). His aim was to turn Harriet into the enemy spokesperson for the telephone or electric or sewer company.

"Come on now, lady!" B.J. shouted.

Harriet wasn't buying. She skirted past him into the common room and found an unclaimed sofa on which to sit. Again she raised her hand in greeting to the care attendants, Franklin and Yvonne, an undemanding little wave that meant she was present and ready, when they were, to be accompanied down the hall to the residents' living quarters.

Nearby, at the common room activity table, several listless and sleep-disheveled men were fumbling with paper and paintbrushes and colored bowls of water. They were middle-aged gentlemen, each marked with a telltale unevenness in his gaze, a result of antipsychotic medications that tended to pool in the blood at night and made waking to the new day a formidable challenge. It was hard to imagine a less eager group of watercolor artists. But worse, somehow, to try to envision what their sense of the rackety common room might feel like: the bloated sunlight in the cottage windows, the slow crawl of time.

Certainly there were more spirited men and women among the cottage's ten residents. One of these, sixty-two-year-old Lucy Rose Dwyer, a staff favorite, was seated close by in a sofa chair having a hushed conversation with an absent relative or former lover or childhood friend. One could never be certain. What was obvious, at least to Harriet and the living cottage staff, was that for the past sixteen months Lucy had been speaking to these friends via a deactivated cell phone.

"Oh, but he never did," Lucy insisted. "He *never, never* did." The lilt of her voice was pleading and vaguely southern. She cupped the phone to her chin at an odd angle. "He never did plant the sweet gum tree like he said he would. And should we be surprised? Should we, my darling . . . my dear one? No, no, no, no, no. Because he never would do what he was *supposed* to. For goodness' sake. The problem—and everyone knew it, too—was that he was just very, very small. A tiny little man. He liked to slip inside things. Remember? He liked to crawl right into your shirt pocket, my dear. *Zip-do-la*. And there he'd be, riding around in your pocket all day long . . ."

They were hard to resist, these monologues from Lucy Rose Dwyer. It was Lucy's good fortune maybe that her psychosis and personality combined to produce the kind of eccentric behavior people enjoyed: her wistful, one-sided conversations, her deactivated cell phone, her tiny shirt-pocket men.

". . . and he was happy as a little crab in its shell, wasn't he? As long as you didn't ask him to weed the garden on Sunday or wash behind his little ears . . ."

There'd been a time when Harriet had turned incidents like this into funny anecdotes. She'd trafficked these anecdotes to the outside world, to the hospital break room with her fellow nurses or out on the occasional date. After a while she lost her enthusiasm for it. Not because she thought it in bad taste. But because she'd come to realize that even her best reenactments lacked accuracy. You could mimic what was said easily enough, but you could never capture the longing that propelled these stories or the world-unto-itself conviction.

"We had to follow him everywhere," Lucy sighed. "Didn't we, my darling? I'm not saying it was fair. I'm just saying it was the job we got stuck with, you and me . . . my darling . . . my dear one."

One of the cottage's care attendants, lean, handsome, unperturbed Franklin, summoned Harriet from the couch and accompanied her down a short hallway to the last of several resident rooms. Any foray beyond the common room required an escort—though Franklin wasn't necessarily along for Harriet's protection. Visitors to the living cottages sometimes had odd notions of what might restore a friend or loved one to mental normalcy: a bit of smuggled wine or homegrown marijuana or, in rare cases, a bout of hurried sex atop the resident's single bed.

Franklin's job was to monitor room visits from a cool distance. He knocked on the open door of room ten and, before stepping aside and ushering Harriet in, he shouted out a canny greeting, "Hey-yo, there. Wyatt, my good man. Your lady friend has arrived."

In many ways the room resembled a modern college dorm room, though this dorm room was composed of four thirteen-foot redbrick walls and a single casement window too high and narrow to crawl through. Every furnishing in the room had been meticulously set to order: the chair and desk, the bookshelf, the polished night table bearing a remote control for the thirteen-inch television bracketed into the wall. The bed had been expertly made. Atop the taut covers were three tidy stacks of folded clothing. The arranger of this clothing and the keeper of the room, Wyatt Huddy, was sitting at the foot of the bed, arms folded, his head lowered and his eyes drawn almost shut. He might have been contemplating the gleaming tile floor or the satiny tops of his running shoes. Certainly, he was aware of Harriet, though he didn't speak her name or return her lively *good morning*. The signs of his gladness, his relief, were more subtle than that: his tightly squared shoulders slackened by a degree or two; the corners of his uneven mouth creased outward in what she'd long ago recognized as a grimace of intense satisfaction.

She steered the rollaway luggage right up to the tips of his running shoes, tapped him with it once, twice, three times. "Look at this here," she said. "It's got wheels. You pull it right along. Like so. It's luggage for people *on the move*."

He reached out and touched the dangling sales tags: $49.99. She'd left the tags on so he'd know he was worthy of brand-new.

"I got my clothes ready," he said.

"I see that. Where's your blue Windbreaker?"

"It's hung . . . It's hanging in the closet."

"Well, let's bring that along, too. You'll need it in the evenings when we go out walking."

She stepped back and watched him rise and retrieve the Windbreaker. "And your retainer," she said. "And toothbrush." He veered toward the bathroom and gathered both objects. "And your scorecards, too, Wyatt. Let's not forget those."

She was certain of this: he would place into the suitcase whatever she asked. He would do it without hesitation or question. It wasn't a matter of his being stupid; from the very beginning of his confinement she'd instilled in him a habit of strict compliance. He did as he was told. If he had a grievance with a resident or care attendant, he waited to speak his mind until Harriet visited—Tuesday or Thursday evenings, most Saturday mornings. To meet her standards of cleanliness, he rose a half hour before the 8:00 A.M. staff wake-up and wiped down every bare surface in the room with a damp cloth. He swept the floor. Then he made his bed to Harriet's exacting specifications. He performed these tasks six mornings a week. Sundays he slept until eight and then attended services in a chapel inside the administration building.

With these routines she believed she'd helped make the otherwise shapeless hours of his life a degree or two more bearable. And she'd played a part in diminishing him, too. He was a less imposing man that he'd been at Kindermann Forest. Part of this had to do with the way he'd aged; he was thirty-eight years old, and his uneven face, especially his forehead, was folded into thick creases. For a decade he'd worn specially fitted glasses to correct his nearsightedness. His hair was longer. (The extra length helped disguise the cranial incongruities of Apert syndrome.) Over the years he'd had a progression of surgeries for recurring infections in his gums and ear canals, and the rigors of these surgeries had left him thirty-five pounds lighter than he'd once been. He was no longer strapping or brawny. What was he then? Larger than average maybe, but not noticeably so. A stranger looking at Wyatt Huddy for the first time might think that he'd made an incomplete recovery from a dire accident: the looming forehead, the wide gap between his offset eyes, the sloping mouth. It would all have its effect. But so, too, would Wyatt's subdued demeanor, his bowed posture, the tight and wincing expression he wore, the deliberate way he watched the placement of his footsteps—a hesitant and resigned man, a man patiently awaiting the next instruction.

"Better push the closet and bathroom doors shut, Wyatt. Yes, like that. Thank you." She turned and called back to her escort in the hallway. "Franklin. Any way for you to do us a favor and lock up the room?"

"No, ma'am. The room stays unlocked."

"Even while he's away?"

"Yes, ma'am. Even while he's away."

She leaned in close to help Wyatt zip up the luggage. "How about the dresser drawers, Wyatt? Any money inside?"

"Yes, I think so."

"How much?"

"Sixty dollars, maybe."

"Well, put it in your wallet and bring it with you." Once he'd done this, she placed the luggage in his hand and ushered him out of the room. Before she pulled the door closed, she flipped off the light and took a last appraising look around. The dull gleam of the night table and desktop. A bookshelf lined with twenty or more jigsaw puzzle boxes. A very small library of books: a dictionary, a baseball almanac, a beginner's book of crossword puzzles, a scuffed and mostly unread edition of *Lives of the American Presidents.*

A supremely clean and well-ordered room—the kind of room, maybe, a person could return to without falling into despair.

She couldn't accompany Wyatt Huddy from Living Cottage No. 8 without first halting at the staff station counter and discussing with Living Cottage Manager Mary Jo Savini a list of Gateway furlough regulations. Each regulation needed to be read aloud, agreed to, and initialed. First, Harriet would take possession of Wyatt's prescription and nonprescription medications (Prilosec for acid reflux, Altoprev for cholesterol, Advil for the head and body ache). She would dispense these medications at the proper times and in the proper amounts. At eight o'clock each evening she would contact the on-duty living cottage manager and make a brief report of Wyatt Huddy's basic condition and state of mind. If he was excessively agitated or paranoid, she would immediately seek advice from a Gateway psychiatrist. Should he become violent, Harriet would call the St. Louis Police Department for assistance. She and Wyatt Huddy were not to travel more than fifty miles from the Gateway Psychiatric Rehabilitation campus. He was not to consume alcohol or illegal drugs. As stipulated, she would return Wyatt Huddy to Living Cottage No. 8 at the end of this weekend, Labor Day weekend, on Monday, September 5, 2011, by no later than two in the afternoon.

She signed and dated the bottom of the page.

To mark the occasion of Wyatt's departure, they were summoned to the common room activity table so that the care attendants Franklin and Yvonne could try to provoke the circle of spiritless watercolor artists into a round of applause. (They could not be roused, these gentlemen, though they did look up at Wyatt with their watery and uneven eyes.) B. J. Tompkins stomped over and flashed his mouthful of awful yellow teeth. "Ain't nothing. No matter. No how," he hissed. He caught sight of Harriet and bristled in agitation. "Come on now, lady!" he pleaded.

This was as much of a send-off as Harriet could stand. "Thank you," she sang out to the Living Cottage staff and corralled Wyatt and his rollaway luggage into the foyer, where they waited a few interminable seconds for the front door of Living Cottage No. 8 to be buzzed open. They stepped out into the glaring light of a warm September morning. Fortunately, Wyatt seemed to share her sense of urgency, and they hurried along the walkway and then passed through the long tunneling hallway of the administration building. The weekend security guards, Maurice and Laquisha, looked up from their station. "Look who we got here," Laquisha said. "You and your lady friend have a good weekend, Wyatt."

"We'll do our best," Harriet said, angling toward the doors. The term *lady friend* always troubled her vaguely. To her parents' generation, *lady friend* referred to woman who could be counted on for sex.

In the parking lot they loaded the luggage into the trunk and squeezed into the front seats. She guided her Honda out past the security station. An oblique nod of farewell from the station guard. *"Goodbye,"* Harriet whispered and steered her car beyond the limits of the Gateway campus. An auspicious moment: Wyatt Huddy had been successfully furloughed.

Yet this wasn't his first excursion out into the world. On several occasions he'd been escorted off-campus to visit the orthodontist or shuttled to the hospital for outpatient surgery. For the past year and a half he'd been allowed to pass through the facility's front gate and walk with Harriet into the surrounding Hill neighborhood. (They could go to lunch if they pleased, or shop at a nearby market, anything really, as long as Wyatt was back at Living Cottage No. 8 within ninety minutes.) In order to secure this privilege she'd had to petition the Gateway Psychiatric Physicians' Board. She'd been told to expect her first petitions to be denied. And they were. Denied. Denied. Denied. Granted. Encouraged, she set her sights on a more extravagant permission: a weekend furlough. Denied. Denied. Denied. Denied. Eventually she was asked to attend a committee meeting with the Psychiatric Physicians' Board. Certain questions were put to her. Did she have a safe and stable home life? Did she understand, did she *appreciate,* that if her petition was granted she'd be solely responsible for a man with an IQ of 67? A man with a history of violence?

Yes, absolutely, she said. She understood. She was ready for it. She'd been a nurse for nearly twenty years, she reminded the board. She'd seen some things in that time. She'd dealt with her share of emergencies.

Perhaps they approved of her answer. They were not an unreasonable group—four men, two women, each with a brand of career fatigue that seemed to have made them inwardly frail.

But there was one thing Harriet thought worth mentioning. It might not be fair, she said, to call it a *history* of violence. Wyatt Huddy had only been violent once. On one occasion. That was fifteen years ago.

The members of the board exchanged a wearied look. Then they offered her this revision: a past incident of violence, they said. An incident that resulted in the death of a camp counselor.

All right, she said. A past incident. That's more accurate, I think. Thank you.

And what would she and Wyatt Huddy do, what activities would they engage in, if the board granted them a weekend furlough?

They'd stay at her home mostly, she said. He doesn't like crowds. They'd go for a walk around Harriet's neighborhood. He'd listen to the baseball game and keep track of the stats on his scorecard. The things he liked doing at Living Cottage No. 8, he'd do in her home.

There was one other thing the Psychiatric Physicians' Board wanted to know. Where was all this leading, Harriet? they asked. They'd already granted Wyatt Huddy twice-monthly permission to stroll outside the Gateway campus. Now she was applying for a week-end furlough. What would she ask for next?

She thought it best not to disguise her intentions. The next thing, she said, is to get Wyatt Huddy released into my care. Yes, she said. Yes. That's what we'll do next. We'll prove to you he can be trusted to spend a weekend away. Then I'll file whatever petitions and state-ments I need to.

And just how long do you plan to care for Wyatt Huddy?

As long as he needs it, she said. As long as he lives.

Thank you for making that clear, they said. You can, if you like, resubmit your petition for a weekend furlough.

Thank you, she said. I will.

And she did. Denied. Denied. Granted.

She'd learned a few things over the years about bureaucrats, especially those who worked in the fields of criminal justice and mental health. As a species, they believed in incremental progress. They adored well-written documents. The good ones seemed to need from Harriet a delicate signal that proved she recognized their competency. The bad bureaucrats, the ones who operated inside a fog of self-doubt, needed more frequent and obvious encouragement.

In the months following Wyatt's arrest, the bureaucrats she'd encountered had all been middle-aged white men from rural Shan-non County, Missouri. Perhaps the real revelation, at least for twenty-seven-year-old Harriet Foster, was how eagerly and with what courtliness they had welcomed her into their musty offices. "My goodness, you're here! *Come in. Come in,* Miss Foster." They would haul out a leather armchair for her to sit in and hustle off to the office break room for a chilled can of Pepsi-Cola. Who'd have guessed that a personal visit from an alert and neatly dressed young black woman would be such a rich occasion for these gentlemen?

She'd been offered some good advice during these office visits. The best guidance had come from the opposing council: Shannon County Prosecuting Attorney Henry Masner. Professionally speaking, Mr. Masner was not persuaded by her version of the events leading to Christopher Waterhouse's death. But he was vehement about how a court document should be worded and filed. And he held a pitying regard for Wyatt's court-appointed defense attorney, the rheumy-eyed and often frazzled Mackland Benders. Henry Masner was of the opinion that Mackland Benders's pretrial efforts were scattered and incomplete. Now is the time, he warned Harriet, to make sure Mackland Benders gets his house in order.

To that end she'd written an affidavit describing her professional opinion of Wyatt Huddy's diminished intelligence. She'd also helped solicit similar affidavits from a few inclined individuals—from Linda Rucker and from Wyatt's former employer, Captain Terry Throckmorton of the Salvation Army. These were delicate negotiations. She'd needed Linda and Terry Throckmorton to recognize a version of events in which Wyatt Huddy had come to Kindermann Forest as a camper. (It wasn't at all unlikely, she told them. They needed first to understand how Wyatt's role at Kindermann Forest would affect the charges brought against him. In this light, they could picture him as a camper, couldn't they? They could see him as indistinguishable among the hundred and four retarded adults from the state hospital.) She'd had to help in the shaping and sometimes in the precise wording of these documents. But her duties didn't end there. She still had to arrange for the authors to sign the documents in the presence of a notary public.

Hard to know if these affidavits would have stood up in a court of a law. They were never put to the test, never read by anyone other than the case lawyers and court clerks of Shannon County. Even so, she didn't regret the meticulous effort she'd put into creating and securing these documents.

Except maybe in one instance. In the fall of 1996, five months after Wyatt had been arrested and held for trial in the Shannon County jail, Harriet had made a trip to Jefferson City, Missouri. She'd set out in her car on a ringingly clear Friday morning in November, and just two hours later she was threading her way along the neat avenues of the state capital. It was a comely and quaint and serious town, with its pale marbled state buildings and the wide, curving embrace of the Missouri River. By comparison the outskirts of Jefferson City looked a bit scrubby and unexceptional. She found a winding gravel driveway that led off Highway 54 and followed it to the loading dock of the Jefferson City Salvation Army Depot.

She'd guessed there would be a discrepancy between Captain Throckmorton's winsome phone voice and the impression he'd make in person. But *my* what a difference. He emerged from his depot office carrying his round belly like a basket of clutched laundry. His large head was bald and gleaming, and buttressed at the back of the neck with a ladder of plump wrinkles. A funny-looking man maybe, but in his calm face there was a flush of something unexpected: an old-fashioned, discreet handsomeness.

In their phone conversations it had been clear to Harriet that, of all the people she'd contacted regarding Wyatt's arrest and trial, only Captain Throckmorton shared her agony over the prospect of a murder conviction and lengthy prison sentence. He'd been quick to grasp the alternative: not guilty by reason of diminished IQ. "Yes," he'd said. "I see how it might have happened that way with Wyatt. He might not have been *capable* of understanding."

She'd been relieved to hear this. Still, she had to make it clear to Captain Throckmorton that there'd been a mix-up. Some people, she'd explained, were under the impression that Wyatt had come to camp as a counselor. Whereas she and Captain Throckmorton both knew that he'd been sent to Kindermann Forest as a camper.

There'd been a weighted pause on the telephone. At last Captain Throckmorton had said, "I remember it like you do, Miss Foster. I sent Wyatt Huddy away with the understanding he'd be a *camper* at Kindermann Forest."

In the depot office she sat in an armchair and read the statement Captain Throckmorton had prepared. Carefully worded, expertly typed, it needed only to be signed in the presence of a notary public.

They had lunch at a sandwich shop several blocks from the state capitol. Waiting for them at a table was Captain Throckmorton's friend and roommate, Ed McClintock, who stood and greeted Harriet formally and shyly, then lowered himself back into his chair. Ed McClintock had a broomy mustache and a glinting sidelong gaze, which Harriet found difficult to read. "Beware the jalapeño cheese dip," he declared ominously. But when the waitress came, he ordered the dip along with a poor boy sandwich minus the tomatoes. "Make my poor boy a little poorer, if you please," he said.

They were joined a few minutes later by a wiry little woman named Rachel Young. Rachel worked as a part-time clerk for the Department of Motor Vehicles, but she had other interests and proficiencies, including certification as a notary public. She'd brought along her notary stamp in a felt-lined wood box, which she passed around for her lunch partners to inspect. "If called upon," she said dryly, "I can use either the stamp or the box as a weapon."

It dawned on Harriet that they'd convened at the sandwich shop for a greater purpose than lunch. They were here to plan the next stage of her visit to Jefferson City: a trip to the Huddy farm to try to solicit a statement from Wyatt's sister, Caroline.

"If it were up to me," Ed McClintock said, "I'd bring along a policeman's stick and a pair of handcuffs." He let his wry, sidelong gaze settle on Captain Throckmorton for a moment. "But I've been *overruled.*"

"Not entirely," the captain said. "Show the ladies your weapon of choice, Ed."

From a weighty ring of keys attached to his belt loop Ed McClintock unfastened a palm-size canister of pepper spray, bright purple and covered in plump cartoon daisies. It had been found, Captain Throckmorton explained, in one of the depot donation bins.

As a group they seemed to be cheered by the fact of this bright pepper spray canister—though afterward all their talk regarding a confrontation with Caroline Huddy was practical and sobering. Captain Throckmorton and Ed McClintock had a few provisional schemes that might persuade her to offer a statement. But beyond that, what were they to do? What if Caroline Huddy came after them with a shotgun? Pepper-spray her and run, they decided. What if she called the police? No chance of that. Her phone service had been out for many months. She'd long ago stopped paying her utilities.

Rachel Young had known Caroline Huddy in high school and still saw her in the Jefferson City shops from time to time. In high school they'd called Caroline Huddy Viking Girl because of her size and her rampaging personality.

"She's been a miserable person all her life," Captain Throckmorton said. "I try to keep that in mind. The state she's in. Her inner pain. Still though, I consider the things she's done to Wyatt unforgivable."

"What things would those be?" Harriet asked.

It was a strange and grievous experience to be told of the injuries inflicted to Wyatt's feet and the long hours he'd spent suffering in the family shed before rescue. Worse somehow to hear of it in a Jefferson City sandwich shop, with its peppermint-striped wallpaper and cheery lunchtime crowd. There was no way for Harriet to locate herself in this silly shop, no proper direction to turn her anger and disgust. Instead she listened to Captain Throckmorton's account and afterward shielded her eyes with her unsteady hand.

They drove in a procession of three cars out through the quaint neighborhoods of Jefferson City and across the Missouri River. East of the river the land was hilly and open, the farmhouses handsome and sided by long sloping fields of cut hay. None of this tidiness, however, could be found a mile or two off the blacktop highway. To reach this interior land they had to travel slowly along dirt roads whose crumbling edges gave way to sudden ditches and sprawls of litter. The Huddy farm had a rusted swing gate that had fallen back into the bushes. The house was two-storied and weathered and set in the middle of a sun-flooded clearing. Twenty yards away, along a well-trod dirt path, was an immense tin metal tractor shed.

They made no effort to hide the clamor of their arrival: the squawking car doors, the stomp of their footsteps across the cedar-board front porch. Captain Throckmorton knocked on the door and knocked again. "Caroline Huddy!" he called out. No answer. And no sounds or movement from the inner precincts of the house. After several minutes of waiting he shrugged and turned the doorknob.

"Wait a minute now," Rachel Young said. She'd been wavering on the lip of the porch and had turned to them with a blanched expression. "I'll stay here," she said. "When the document's ready, you holler and I'll come on in with my stamp."

They gave her a sympathetic nod. Captain Throckmorton pushed open the door.

Inside they discovered a living room thronged with debris: piles of scuffed secondhand furniture, great mounds of wadded-up plastic bags and bundled clothing. Pathways had been cleared from one room to the next. In the kitchen a large dormant portable generator had been set up on cinder blocks near an open window. A bright orange extension cord ran out from the generator, across the floor, and into the hallway.

They followed the cord up a cluttered staircase to the second-floor landing and finally to a closed bedroom door. "Anyone home?" Captain Throckmorton inquired. "Caroline? Caroline Huddy?" Propped against the doorframe was a twin-barrel shotgun, which Ed McClintock hoisted up with one hand. He snapped open the chambers and removed both shells and set the gun back in its place. Then he eased open the bedroom door.

Caroline Huddy was propped up waiting for them in a bed full of scavenged sofa cushions. There was nothing haphazard about the arrangement of these cushions; they'd been stacked in careful layers at the rear of the bed so that they rose up thronelike and supported her broad back. Each of her plump forearms had its own plaid cushion. Arrayed across the quilt were dozens of essential items in sealed Ziploc bags: candy and nuts and various breakfast cereals, tissues, lip balms, remote controls for the television and VCR.

She looked up at them from the encampment of her bed. The best that could be said of her, physically, was that she had clear hazel eyes edged with vivid black lashes. (No mascara on those lashes; their thickness and length and curled ends appeared to be natural gifts.) Otherwise her features were blunt and heavy, her face hinged with an overlarge jaw—an old-time boxer's jaw—and her mouth set in one long, thin, inexpressive line. It was hard to see any clear resemblance to Wyatt, except maybe in the general stockiness of her build and in the size and roughness of Caroline Huddy's resting hands.

"Did I invite *any* of you into my house?" Caroline Huddy asked. "Did I?" she insisted. "*Any* of you?" Each time she uttered the word *any*, in her wispy, unused voice, she stared directly at Harriet.

"We had no choice but to let ourselves in," Captain Throckmorton said. "I apologize for that. But we're here to talk over some important matters."

She sat up straighter against her wall of layered cushions. Again she lifted her gaze and studied each of her three visitors: Captain

Throckmorton, Ed McClintock, Harriet. There was a murky, hard-to-determine quality in Caroline Huddy's posture and blunt expression, but if Harriet had to guess, she would say she was seeing a woman marginally pleased to have uninvited guests in the doorway of her bedroom, a woman ready to be included in the serious talk.

"There are decisions to be made," Captain Throckmorton said. "Regarding your brother, Wyatt."

Caroline huffed air through her broad nose and then, patiently, lowered and raised her thick eyelashes.

"You're aware of what happened to Wyatt last summer at Kindermann Forest?"

"I know you sent him off to camp," she said. "And I know he squeezed the stuffing out of some dumb son-of-a-bitch counselor." All this she recited matter-of-factly; her words might have been barbed, but the delivery was dispassionate.

"Yes," Captain Throckmorton said. "I did send him off. And there was a tragedy at camp. You probably also know that Wyatt is being prosecuted in Shannon County, Missouri, and the prosecution will go forward one of two ways. That's what our friend here, Harriet Foster, has come to talk to you about."

Harriet stepped forward. It would be a mistake, she knew, a grievous insult, to sit on the edge of Caroline Huddy's bed. Fortunately, there was a seamstress's stool in the corner of the room. "May I use the stool?" she asked and, having received permission from Caroline Huddy in the form of an indifferent shrug, Harriet took the stool and sat at the bedside.

"I'm a friend of Wyatt," Harriet began. "I worked as the camp nurse last summer at Kindermann Forest."

"A friend?"

"That's right. A good friend, I hope."

Caroline Huddy gazed at her somberly. "You Negro girls will go with anyone, won't you?" It was voiced with such mildness, this remark, as if it, too, were a kind of uninvited guest, poised on the threshold, wondering shyly if it could come in. "I bet you don't like the word *Negro,* do you?" Caroline Huddy asked. "There's another name I could use."

At this Ed McClintock let out a gruff sigh and stepped back out of the room. They could hear his creaking footsteps on the landing, then the stairs.

"People use all sorts of names," Harriet said. "Here are two names I'm willing to accept from you. You can call me Ms. Foster or Nurse Harriet. Anything else and we're going to have trouble."

There was from Caroline Huddy a softening of her blunt expression. "All right then, *Nurse Harriet,*" she said. For the time being she seemed pleased to have made this concession. More so, there was an even stronger sense of what Harriet had first noticed upon entering the bedroom: Caroline Huddy was eager for camaraderie. How very odd and impossible this was. She seemed to want to say the most poisonous things. And she wanted someone—anyone, a black nurse even—to be her dearest friend.

"What I want to tell you," Harriet explained, "is that your brother, Wyatt, will be tried sometime next summer. The prosecutor wants to seek a second-degree murder conviction, which means—"

"He'll be put in the electric chair."

"No, no. They won't be seeking a death sentence. But they will ask the jury for life in prison. There's another way to go about it, though. We can make it clear to the judge that instead of prison Wyatt should be put in a state hospital or group home. He shouldn't stand trial at all because of his diminished intelligence."

"Diminished intelligence," Caroline Huddy repeated. She seemed to think it a marvelous term.

"Because he's mentally retarded."

"Wyatt?" she said. "Retarded? He may look that way, Nurse Harriet. But it's a condition he has."

"I know about the condition. Some people with Apert syndrome have a normal IQ. And others suffer from mental retardation. It's much better for Wyatt if we make it clear to the judge that because of his diminished intelligence he didn't know what he was doing at the time of the murder."

"Didn't know?" Caroline Huddy said. She shook her head in dumb wonder. "He squeezed a man to death without knowing?"

"In my car I have a typewriter. It's electric. I'm guessing that Captain Throckmorton or Ed McClintock can start up the generator in your kitchen. I can sit here by your bedside and type a statement that explains how you saw plenty of signs of Wyatt's diminished intelligence when he was growing up. When it's done, we'll call up a woman we have waiting on your front porch, a notary public named Rachel Young. You'll sign the statement in her presence and she'll put her notary stamp on it."

"Rachel Young? I won't sign anything in front of that bitch."

"There's no time to find anyone else. It'll have to be Rachel."

Caroline Huddy sighed wistfully. "Too bad for you then. My answer is no."

"A statement from you could make the difference for Wyatt," Harriet said. "The difference between a lifetime in prison, which we both know would be awful, and a life being cared for in a state mental health facility. If he went to a state facility, he'd have a chance of getting out someday. I'd like you to think about that a minute, please, Caroline."

To this Caroline Huddy tipped back her head and narrowed her features in mock deliberation. While she performed this act, they could hear Ed McClintock climbing the stairs again. A moment later he was in the bedroom doorway holding an object behind his back.

"I've thought it all through," Caroline Huddy announced. "And my answer— Are you ready, *Nurse Harriet*? My answer is still no. No and no again. There's a reason for it, too. I'm saying no because there's a big difference between retarded and stupid. Wyatt's always been stupid. And if you do a stupid thing, Nurse Harriet, then you pay the price."

"Have you paid the price? For the stupid things—"

"Shut your face," Caroline Huddy said. "You don't know a damn thing about what I've done."

"Excuse me, ladies," Ed McClintock said. He'd taken a few steps forward into the bedroom. To Caroline Huddy he tipped his head in a tepid nod. "Look here, Caroline," he said, and from behind his back he produced what looked to be a steering wheel, thin and over-large and chipped along its outer edges. "When I was passing through your living room, I happened to see this little gem. From an Oliver 70 series farm tractor. A model from the nineteen forties, or maybe fifties. I'm not sure. You know I collect old tractor seats and steering wheels, and so I thought—"

"Put your twenty dollars on my dresser and get out of my room."

"I will," he said. "But I think it's only fair to mention that this steering wheel is a real gem to me. To another collector it might only be worth twenty dollars. To me, though, it's worth more." He freed his wallet from his back pocket and held it open so that Caroline Huddy could see the layered bills in its fold. "The fairest price I can think of, for me personally, is all the money I've got here in my wallet. That would be two hundred dollars even."

She was, for the time being, frozen in a state of surprise that looked entirely genuine.

"I'll go ahead and put this two hundred dollars on the dresser for you, Caroline," Ed McClintock said. "I'll do it once you and Ms. Foster have sorted through your *difficulties* . . . once the statement's been typed up and Rachel's had a chance to put her stamp on it."

It was hard to imagine what a smile from Caroline Huddy might look like, but here it was: a sudden creasing of her long, thin mouth, and a blossoming in her cheeks that was almost girlish. "You're as

worse as the rest of them," she said. "You come into my house thinking you're better, but you're worse. Truly you are. Someone should
report you," she said gamely.

"Nothing to report," Ed McClintock said. "All I'm doing is paying
fair money for an item that's important to me."

"Hell you are," she said. "God damn hell you are." She appeared to
be on the verge of a strange, eruptive laughter. "Ha. Ha. Ha. Ed," she
said. "Know what I should do? I should call out the authorities on you."

"Go ahead," he said. "Should I fetch you the telephone?"

"I should throw that money right back in your fat face."

"Maybe you should," he said. There was an acute, mocking humor
in his sidelong gaze. "Then you can sit up here and wait for the next
collector to come by and offer you two hundred dollars. That'd be
something, wouldn't it?"

"Well it might . . . It would. God *damn* it."

"It sure would. Because I looked through your kitchen cupboards
downstairs, Caroline. Ain't a damn thing in them. Everything you
have to get by on is right here on your bed." He stood back and surveyed her Ziploc bags of cereals and nuts—her various luxuries.

"You go straight to god damn hell, you bastard. You don't know
a thing. You don't know *anything*, you fucker." Caroline Huddy was
beyond herself then, rocking back and forth against her cushions, crying out half-strangled phrases that were crude and bitter one moment
and loaded with self-pity the next. She said she'd been treated badly
all her life. Everyone in Jeff City knew it, too. She'd had a sick mother,
a worthless father. And Wyatt. She'd done the best she could with
Wyatt, spoiled him, loved him too much.

"The god damn shame of it is this," she said. "I've taken care of
people all my life and now there's no one round to take care of me."
She wagged her head back and forth, amazed that she'd spoken this
truth aloud. Her face was covered with a film of tears and mucus,
which she wiped at with the underside of her forearm. "God damn it.

God damn it. *God damn it,*" she cursed. Then she gave a slow nod of acceptance and a long, deep steadying breath. "Run and get your god damn typewriter," she said to Harriet. "I'll tell the judge about Wyatt being *dim-witted.*"

"About his diminished intelligence," Harriet corrected her.

"Yes, God damn it. About his diminished intelligence. His mental retardation. But I'll do it in my own words, you understand? You'll type it out just like I say it."

It took time for Harriet to retrieve the typewriter from her car, more time for Captain Throckmorton and Ed McClintock to find a canister of gasoline and prime the generator in the kitchen. There were long minutes when Harriet waited at the bedside for a steady current of electricity to power the typewriter on her lap. It wasn't a matter of feeling awkward. She'd grown accustomed to that. It was the prospect of being the lone witness to Caroline Huddy's life in this bedroom: the way she sat propped up in her bed, blinking her long eyelashes, looking out the window and reaching into a bag, now and then, for a handful of cornflakes. A gaze out the window. A handful of cornflakes. A blinking consideration of the stacked boxes and bags on her dresser and bookshelves. The sum and substance of her life. Horrible to imagine it going on like this day after day.

Yet Caroline Huddy seemed to have developed a supreme patience for it. She chewed her cornflakes and let her gaze drift across the room and settle on Harriet. "Hey, Nurse Harriet," she said. "Let me ask you something. The times you've gone to see Wyatt locked up in jail, does he look sorry? Sorry for what he's done?"

"Yes, he does. Very sorry."

She parted her thin lips. Her unlikely smile presented itself. "All right then. Let me ask you this. The counselor boy that Wyatt squeezed to death. Did you know him?"

"I did."

"Did you know him well?"

"Well enough to know what kind of person he was."

"And what kind of person was he?"

"The very worst kind."

"Really?" Caroline Huddy said. Clearly, she'd not expected this reply. The surprise of it, the novelty, made her overlarge jaw hang open. "The very worst kind?" she repeated. She needed some private time, apparently, to sort through this riddle, and so she turned again and surveyed the view outside her window. Her hand burrowed into the bag of cornflakes. After a while she grew absolutely still. Then she turned back to Harriet with a face purged of its anger and gruff confidence. Caroline Huddy's voice wavered. "Worse than me?" she asked.

It might have been the most sincere and pleading inquiry Harriet had ever heard. She sat and considered her answer. "Yes," Harriet said. "He was worse." After all, she still needed an affidavit from the one remaining member of Wyatt's family.

But her private, unspoken answer would not have been so different. Yes, Christopher Waterhouse was worse, she might say. Worse because he seemed to Harriet to be entirely self-satisfied, an untroubled young man with a terrible selfishness and a sharp eye for the next opportunity. Caroline Huddy, on the other hand, was full of misery. Not regret. She wasn't sorry. Neither of them was. But at least Caroline Huddy was miserable.

Moments later the typewriter thrummed to life. Harriet rolled in a fresh piece of paper and recorded, as faithfully as possible, Caroline Huddy's terse remembrances and opinions. Rachel Young was called up to witness the signing of the statement. And once this was accomplished, the only reason for being at the Huddy farm dissolved and they were all—Harriet and Rachel and Ed McClintock and Captain Throckmorton—eager to be gone. The generator was shut down, the typewriter packed away. A stack of twenty-dollar bills was left on the bedroom dresser.

All the while Caroline Huddy, who'd crawled out from beneath the quilts of her bed—she could walk well enough it seemed, or at least shamble along the cleared pathways of her house—was calling out curses and insults and other provocations meant to snare them in an argument and delay their departure, if only by a minute or two.

No one bothered to answer her. They would not be delayed. Hurriedly, they climbed into their cars and away they went, out along the crumbling dirt roads to the prettier blacktop lanes and finally a convenience store parking lot where Harriet climbed from her car to say goodbye. But how exactly to thank Captain Throckmorton and Ed McClintock for their help? "Thank you," she said and patted their hefty shoulders, though this gesture seemed only to embarrass them. She would have to find a better way, she told herself, when they met up again for the trial next summer. But the trial didn't happen. She never saw or spoke to either man again.

Halfway to St. Louis she stopped at a rest area and couldn't resist pulling Caroline Huddy's affidavit from its manila folder.

> *I raised Wyatt up after the death of our beloved mother, Florence Huddy. He was not a smart or reliable child. His attention wandered. He had to be told again and again and again what work to do and what was right and what was wrong. I always knew Wyatt to be slow and stubborn, and some people say this falls in line with having a diminished intelligence. I'm not trained in this area. I can't say. But maybe so. In my opinion he was fine and could be controlled here in the relaxing environment of our farm. But once he left and was under the supervision of others, he ran into a lot of trouble. As for the tragedy, who knows how much he understood or didn't understand? I always taught him to behave better. It's also my opinion that queers and Negro nurses should keep with their own kind and quit putting their noses in other people's business.*
>
> *Sincerely, Caroline Huddy*

Chapter Sixteen

She owned a nicer home than might be expected of an unmarried black nurse: a two-story redbrick, built for the upper middle class in the nineteen forties, rigorously constructed, Bavarian in its details, and now, almost seven decades later, made elegant by time and the upward spiraling of Boston ivy. Three gorgeous elm trees shaded the backyard. There were stained-glass windows in the kitchen and master bedroom, two richly manteled fireplaces, a dumbwaiter, a roomy and mostly dry basement. She'd been fortunate on two accounts. The previous owners—an elderly black married couple, proprietors of a nearby hardware store—had been meticulous caretakers of the property. But when she'd bought the home, eleven years earlier, the neighborhood was skirting toward a neglected state. A few windows in nearby houses had been sealed with plastic. There was windblown litter in the streets. Worrying signs, to be sure. She'd acquired the house for just sixty-four thousand and braced herself for further decline. Almost at once the opposite happened. Other bargain hunters—black, white, Asian, gay—began buying up properties along her street. In a short while the neighborhood had stabilized, and each year since then it had incrementally improved. If she had to, she could sell the house now for more than twice what she'd paid for it.

Her guest for the weekend, Wyatt Huddy, seemed impressed without knowing a shred of this history. "Harriet?" he said while towing his luggage along the neat little sidewalk to the front steps. He lifted his head in order to follow the sprawl of ivy all the way up to the eaves of the second floor. "This is your house," he said, as if trying to convince himself. "Harriet, are you . . . ?"

Most likely he'd wanted to know if she was rich. It wasn't politeness that kept him from asking. He'd been hushed by the arched church door entranceway, with its cast-iron knocker, hushed again by the warm burnished woodwork of the interior hallway, the tiled kitchen, the living room with its plump oak mantel. She escorted him from room to room and watched him absorb each detail: a sharp, craning glance from his tilted head, a huff of surprise or quick grimace of satisfaction. How nice to feel that the home she'd perfected over the years was so *appreciated.* Then again, what did Wyatt Huddy have as points of comparison? When measured against the Huddy farm or Living Cottage No. 8, it must seem like she lived in a cut-from-a-storybook palace.

She took him to the guest room and placed his rollaway luggage on a sea chest, showed him the bathroom and the portable radio, which he could use to listen to the Cardinals game that evening. Then, though she'd meant to save the surprise for later, she led him to a narrow door off the kitchen and down a flight of steps to a basement that was lit by dusty bare bulbs. The surprise was in the far corner: a long and wide tarp-covered platform. She pulled back the tarp.

Not just a model railroad layout; that would be neither accurate nor fair. On the platform was an expansive reproduction of a bygone midwestern town, a settlement of some twenty faux-wood buildings—from the nineteen thirties maybe, but also timeless—set among rolling hills and mossy green pastureland and circled by three interweaving track lines. A very energetic town, by the look of it. A throng of customers, tiny but ecstatic, crowded around a produce truck. Little men heaved pickaxes on the gravel shoulders of the tracks. At the baseball park an Irish setter had raced out onto center field, where it took a joyful, frozen leap. All of it, of course—the figures, the buildings, the lush landscape—was too painstaking and pure to have ever existed in real life.

The layout had been a gift for James and had arrived four years after the closing of Kindermann Forest, when the boy was nine years old. It had come from Schuller Kindermann, who'd telephoned one morning to announce to Harriet that he'd sold his St. Louis town house and was moving to a retirement community in nearby Webster Groves. He was then eighty-two years old. His brother, Sandie, had recently passed away. Most of their town house possessions had been let go in an estate sale. But Schuller had a very special model railroad layout he'd like to pass on to James. "Would that be all right with you, Nurse Harriet?" he'd asked, a steady tremor of apprehension in his voice. They'd not seen or spoken to one another in several years. Perhaps he was worried she'd refuse his offer. Or resurrect a past grievance. But why on earth would she do either of those things? "Yes," she'd said. "Thank you. That would be very nice, Mr. Kindermann." He'd let forth a sigh of relief and said he'd send some boys over on Saturday morning. She had better, he suggested, make a little room in her basement.

She couldn't remember now what exactly she'd expected—a delivery boy maybe, hauling a large box of wire train track down into her basement? Instead there'd been a rented U-Haul truck and a team of three very earnest boy-men hired from a local hobby shop. Her basement doorway hadn't been wide enough. The boy-men needed to dismantle one of the basement window wells and pass the platform through in eight separate sections. Then, over the course of the day, they reassembled the layout, glued and painted the seams, reconnected the wiring, tested the lights inside the little buildings, the track, the locomotives, and set out the tiny human and animal figurines. The finished platform occupied a third of Harriet's basement. She might have been outraged if the layout hadn't been so absurdly beautiful. James was overwhelmed: a miniaturized world all to himself. For years he regarded the layout with quiet adoration. No single item Harriet had given the boy had produced such awe and lasting pleasure.

As she expected, Wyatt Huddy was astonished. But his clear, grinning surprise was tempered by his need to inspect the layout up close. He knelt on one knee at the edge of the platform and touched, very gently, the round red and white Rx sign mounted above the drugstore. He asked to know who'd built the layout. Was it James? Had James put this together all by himself?

It had come to James, she explained, as a gift. From Schuller Kindermann. This fact appeared to complicate Wyatt's satisfaction: a gift from Schuller Kindermann, who had died seven years after moving to his retirement community, died of a stroke at the prosperous age of eighty-nine. This made the layout an heirloom, an artifact handed down from a man whose lifework as a summer camp owner Wyatt had helped bring to an early end.

"Was it made especially for James?" Wyatt asked.

"I don't think so, no. I think Mr. Kindermann and his brother made it especially for themselves. When he got old and moved to a nursing home, Mr. Kindermann decided to pass it along to James. It's beautiful, isn't it?"

"It is. Very beautiful."

Over the years she'd led dozens of guests down to her basement and pulled back the tarp. She'd enjoyed the variety of surprised reactions. One evening she'd revealed the layout to a rowdy group of women nurses who'd gathered at her house for after-work margaritas. The sight of the layout had made them gasp and put their hands to their mouths. Where had it come from? they wanted to know. Harriet explained how the layout had been a gift created by a pair of elderly brothers, bachelor brothers, never married, never even dated, as far as anyone knew. *"Amazing,"* her friend Patty Donahue said. She sipped her drink and grinned. "So this is what grown men do when they've given up all hope. When there's no chance they'll ever get laid."

There was a sudden peal of laughter from the other nurses—a bark of laughter, exuberant, righteous, feminine. They stepped closer to the platform, took another look at the tidy little features of the layout, and raised their margarita glasses in salute.

After lunch Wyatt Huddy helped her rake grass trimmings and tree branches from her backyard. They loaded debris into recycling bins, and he hauled them out to the back alleyway. How pleased he looked, how satisfied, to help her with these chores. He was equally content to walk with her along the tree-shaded sidewalks of her neighborhood, out to the main thoroughfare. It was her good fortune to live in an area of the city known for its boutique shops and art cinema and ethnic restaurants, known also for its generous mixing of races and for its tolerance of street musicians, loiterers, eccentric personalities. Few people stared at them as they walked along.

Already she'd developed a steady sense of his presence, a step behind her, head lowered, no sound from him except the low scuff of his sneakers on the pavement. Her constant companion.

More constant than her son, James. This wasn't a complaint, not exactly. She was wholly grateful to be his mother. But what a richer and more demanding experience it had been to be the guardian of his childhood. James was twenty years old now, and she'd like to say that he'd been successfully launched into adulthood. And who knew? Maybe it was true. He lived an independent life. He made fiberglass sculpture and played bass in an indie-rock band and worked as a parking valet, a courier, a Web designer, a part-time vendor of jewelry and obscure T-shirts. She suspected he smoked too much pot. All of these activities he conducted three hundred miles away in Chicago. He'd moved there for no better reason than to share an apartment with friends. That was two years ago. Since then he'd finished one semester of college. He'd had several serious relationships with girls. *Several relationships.* It sounded reassuring. But Harriet could phrase it differently. She could say he'd been co-opted by several young women, a certain kind of young woman: dreadlocked, tattooed, either African American or Caucasian, free spirits, or so it seemed. With James these women, girls really, saw an opportunity to claim an inward and obliging young man and enlist him in their service. Eventually he got tired of it and stood up for himself.

In these matters Harriet kept her opinions mostly to herself. How could she not? She'd been involved in her own romantic relationships over the years. When it came to men, she hadn't denied herself. Her work life provided certain opportunities: a hospital security guard, a former patient or two, a male nurse, and even, for a few weeks, a cardiologist. At their best these relationships had reassured her on several fronts. Men still noticed her. At least some men did. She might not have been a striking middle-aged woman. Admittedly, she'd grown thick around the middle. Twenty years of nursing had left her feet uneven and achy, her back a little stooped. Most days she wore a thick support belt to help hoist patients from their beds. Like a lot of other veteran nurses, she teetered a bit when she walked. But the men she dated didn't seem to notice or mind. They liked her company. In the past she'd worried she might have harbored a secret preference for white men. Yet the strength of her affections didn't seem to bear this out. She'd dated and slept with a modest but satisfying variety:

African American, Jewish, Jamaican, Italian. She'd had no crippling need, as some of her friends did, to marry these men or occupy the same address.

Throughout these relationships, and over the course of fifteen years, there'd been James to consider, and beyond James, always in the background, always waiting for her in a locked-down state institution, Wyatt Huddy. She'd only told a few close friends about Wyatt. Among her fellow nurses, Harriet didn't announce her intentions. She never said, *Is it Tuesday afternoon already? Well then, I'm off to the Gateway Psychiatric Rehabilitation Center to see my poor, dear friend, Wyatt Huddy.* At the Gateway campus she was known to the security officers and care attendants as Wyatt Huddy's advocate, his devoted lady friend. They approved of her commitment. Over time they'd come to treat Harriet with a fussy brand of respect.

But they didn't know her reasons. And they had an unreliable memory when it came to the extent of Harriet's devotion. At various times during Wyatt's incarceration, her attendance had been less than perfect. In the summer of 2005, for instance, she'd been occupied with James. He was a stealthy and moody fourteen-year-old boy. Was he sliding into delinquency? Not really. But she wasn't sure of anything at the time. And she'd been involved that summer with a high school history teacher, a lively and impulsive man who liked to travel to other cities during his summer break. Harriet couldn't help herself: on her weekends off she'd gone with him to Minneapolis and New Orleans and, once even, all the way to Clearwater, Florida. As for Wyatt, the best she could do was call Living Cottage No. 8 and check in with him. *Are you doing all right, Wyatt? Are you getting along okay?* He assured her he was. *Good,* she said. *Look here. I'm not going to be able to make it out next Saturday, or for a little while after that. I'm really busy with things, Wyatt. But that'll change once I get everything . . . you know, in order. All right then. I'll be out and see you as soon as I can.*

Yes, he said. Yes, thank you, Harriet.

Then she rushed off with the history teacher—a very able lover—to the Le Pavillon Hotel in New Orleans. At various moments throughout the weekend her heart panged with guilt—for James, mostly. She'd had to send him away to her aunt Marie's for another weekend. That wasn't fair, was it? As for Wyatt, his steadfast and complacent tone sometimes irritated her. *Yes, thank you, Harriet.* Such a dutiful man. It was important to remember though: he was capable of acting on his own. She shouldn't hold herself responsible for *everything*. At Kindermann Forest she'd sent him out to find the camp van and to interrupt Christopher Waterhouse. The rest of it—the broken ribs, the traumatic asphyxiation—had been Wyatt's doing.

Several more weeks slipped by. Her obligations toward Wyatt weighed on her. It seemed that she'd gone a long time without visiting—a month maybe, or nearly so. One morning at work she'd pulled a calendar from her purse and marked the number of days. It was awful to see it tallied up. Forty-three days had passed since she'd visited the Gateway Psychiatric Rehabilitation Center. *Forty-three days.* It pained her to imagine the effect on Wyatt. Each of those days he'd been clinging to his routine and waiting for her.

She'd hurried to her car after work and driven straight to the Gateway campus. The care attendants in Living Cottage No. 8 had been glad to usher her in. *Wyatt*, they'd called out. *Wyatt. Your lady friend is here.*

He'd been seated at the common room table with a jigsaw puzzle set out before him. At the sight of her, he'd sat back in his chair. His odd mouth had creased open. Across his face had bloomed an intense expression—not anger, not aloofness. Either of those would have been easier for Harriet to take. No, this was a trickier reaction to handle. It had made her eyes prick. She'd had to sit down quickly in the nearest chair.

"Nurse Harriet," he'd said. His face had reddened, a blush of gratitude. Clearly, he couldn't help himself; he was so very glad, so very relieved, to see her.

For dinner that evening Harriet served baked catfish and French fries along with baby carrots she'd slow-cooked in a Crock-Pot. Her guest lowered his head over his plate and ate in neat little bites while wiping the corners of his mouth with a paper napkin. He hardly said a word. As soon as he finished, he stood and, as he'd been taught at Gateway Living Cottage No. 8, rinsed his plate and silverware in water and set them out beside the kitchen sink. He settled back into his chair at the kitchen table.

"Wyatt," Harriet said. "If you're eating a meal someone made for you, and you think it's good, you can say so. You can say something like 'This is good catfish, Harriet.'"

He stretched open his eyes and peered at her from behind the thick lenses of his glasses. "Yes," he said. "That's right. That's a good thing to know, Harriet." There was nothing playful or sarcastic in his remark. On the contrary, he looked very pleased to have been offered this advice.

"I'd like to ask you something," she said. "How's it feel to be away from the living cottage?"

"Good."

"Good? That doesn't tell me a whole lot. How is it good?"

He required some time to consider the possibilities. "Well, it's good to be away from some of the living cottage people . . . B.J. and Miss Gladys. And it's good to go outside and walk around."

"And what else? I'd like to know what's on your mind. Your opinions of things."

He sat up straighter in his chair and nodded to himself. "That was a good catfish dinner, Harriet."

"Thank you for saying so. Would you like to cook dinner sometime?"

"Me?" he asked. "Oh, no, no, no. I couldn't do that."

"But would you like to learn to cook? Or learn to do something else?"

"I might," he said. "I don't know."

"Or go visit some other city?"

"Yes, maybe," he said doubtfully.

"You know what I think about, Wyatt?" she said.

And he did know, clearly. Because his back and shoulders stiffened and he put his hands on the table edge, bracing himself for her apology. He'd endured at least a dozen apologies from Harriet over the years in various circumstances and in different locations. Certain anniversaries made her apologize. During his incarceration she'd tried to express her remorse each time he'd been placed in a different jail or holding cell. At the Gateway Psychiatric Rehabilitation Center she'd apologized each time he'd had to adjust to a new room or living cottage.

She said, "I think about how your life would have turned out different if you hadn't gone to Kindermann Forest and if I hadn't sent you out to look for the camp van. I'm sure you would have had a very different life, Wyatt. Who knows? Maybe you'd have learned to cook or gone to school or met someone and got married. A lot of different things might have happened to you. It could have been a much, much better life."

He sat frowning at what he'd just heard. He shook his head. "It wouldn't have been that kind of life," he said.

"What kind?"

"Not a *much better* life."

She was taken aback for a moment—by the sharpness of his assessment, by its essential truth. After all these years she could still be fooled by his off-center face and awkward manners. At times she could still make the mistake of thinking him simpleminded, naïve. "But you don't know for sure," she insisted, weakly.

"I do know. I'd have stayed right there at the depot in Jeff City. And I'd have been by myself." He touched the corner of his glasses and nodded. "I'm that kind of person," he said.

At eight o'clock that evening Harriet called the on-duty manager of Living Cottage No. 8 and reported that she and Wyatt Huddy had gathered branches and grass trimmings from her backyard, gone for a walk, and had dinner together. He'd shown every indication of enjoying these activities. His state of mind was calm. She said that, in the ten hours he'd been her guest, Wyatt had been at all times pleasant and cooperative.

"And where is Wyatt now?" the cottage manager asked. "What's he doing while we're speaking?"

"He's upstairs in the guest room," Harriet explained. "I've got the radio turned on for him. He's listening to the Cardinals play the Dodgers. He's got his game cards out and he's doing his thing."

"His thing?"

"He's keeping track of each play—the strikes and hits and errors and so forth." Through the phone line she could hear the cottage manager typing these comments into a computer—a scuttling click, click, click.

"That sounds like a nice way to spend the evening," the cottage manager said. "Thank you. We'll talk again tomorrow, Ms. Foster."

"Yes, we will," Harriet said. "Tomorrow. Goodbye."

In nearly all her dealings with the Gateway staff, Harriet had to rein in the urge to speak forcefully on Wyatt's behalf. She'd figured out a long time ago that any argument she might wage would be both futile and unnecessary.

Still though, to the officious cottage manager, Harriet wanted to say, Look here now. You have a job to do. We both know that. But we also know that Wyatt Huddy has never acted out—never lost control, never screamed or made threats. More important, he's never harmed a staff member or living cottage resident. And he never *would*. Harriet could vouch for him. She could *promise*. If necessary, she'd put up everything she owned as collateral. She was prepared to offer a personal guarantee.

All of this she was ready to do from the vantage point of her handsome kitchen—more than a hundred miles from the weedy ruins of Kindermann Forest Summer Camp, more than fifteen years removed from the night Christopher Waterhouse had loaded Evie Hicks into the camp van and taken her for a ride along County Road H.

Chapter Seventeen

On that night, June 27, 1996, at Kindermann Forest, she'd not been able to offer any guarantees.

She'd stood outside The Sanctuary, under a dome of hazy floodlight, and pushed the sweat back from her bangs. "What one of us should do," she'd said to Wyatt. "What you should probably do . . ."

Fortunately, he'd understood. He rose from the picnic table and flexed his arms to show her how capable he was. "I'll take a walk," he said. "I'll see if I can find them."

How very grateful she was to hear this. "Thank you," she said. "Thank you, Wyatt." She stood there weary and shaken and watched him march off into the darkness.

Inside her chest a tightly coiled knot of feeling was beginning to unwind—a slackening of her panic. Her determination, too. She could feel it draining away, the persuasiveness she'd needed to enlist Wyatt Huddy to her cause, the strength it took to make large decisions. Small decisions were still within her reach. She noticed Wyatt's open book on the picnic table and decided to scoop it up and tuck the book under her arm. She had modest plans to safe-keep *Lives of the American Presidents* until it could be returned to its grateful owner.

Across the open meadow the lighted windows of the infirmary seemed to wink at her. She wanted—ached really—to be back at her work desk, back among the open medical files, the hum and chilly breath of the air conditioner. The telephone, too. Perhaps she'd make use of the phone. The police could be called. Not *could*, she warned herself, *must*.

She broke into a loping jog along the grassy border of the roadway. Once she'd drawn closer, she could see the infirmary door hanging open. Poised on the lighted threshold to the infirmary was a figure, a person, leaning out the doorway a moment and scanning the darkness, then withdrawing back inside.

The person was state hospital camper Mary Ann Hornicker. Mute and retarded, Mary Ann was able to convey a complicated sense of crisis just by bouncing up and down on her small feet and clutching the hemline of her billowy pajama top.

Harriet sprinted across the infirmary yard. *Easy does it,* she chided herself. It was important to remember that this would most likely be a small crisis—wet bedsheets maybe, or something messier on the bathroom floor.

She took a deep, steadying breath and, upon entering the infirmary, headed straight for her living quarters.

The covers on James's empty cot had been thrown back, hastily it seemed to Harriet. No sign of the boy huddled beneath the cot or squeezed under Harriet's bed. Stunned, she wheeled back toward the infirmary. In Mary Ann Hornicker's wide-eyed and freckled face, Harriet saw the flicker of something—an awareness, a cringing sense of obligation. Mary Ann Hornicker must have seen James cross into the infirmary and step out the front door—step or been frightened. Perhaps he'd been chased.

It was too much for Harriet. Too much to bear the thought of her son wailing in anguish, running out into the darkness, toward graver dangers. Just to imagine it made her wild and belligerent.

"What did you . . . WHAT DID YOU DO?" she screamed at Mary Ann Hornicker and at the other infirmary patient, Nancy Klotter, who was burrowed into her bunk, a sheet drawn up over her head. "Did you SCARE him?" Harriet shouted.

They would not, either of them, engage with her.

"DID YOU SCARE HIM?" she screamed.

No answer from Mary Ann Hornicker or Nancy Klotter. Or rather, no intelligible answer. Nancy Klotter, under the tent of her bedsheet, pretended to writhe and moan from some terrible quaking sickness. Mary Ann Hornicker took a few unsteady steps forward. She unsealed her lips. Her plump throat convulsed. The round and unremarkable features of her face began to tighten and crease until they'd contorted into a mask of violent straining. From her open mouth came a dry clicking of teeth, a homely croak.

Aggrieved, Harriet stumbled out into the infirmary yard and ran unthinkingly toward the mess hall. "James?" she called out. "James?" In the hall she flipped on as many wall switches as she could find. The fluorescent lights flared. The heavy tables, the long serving counter, the gas range and ovens all blinked into view.

But it made no sense to look here. James had never shown interest in the mess hall or kitchen. He wasn't the type to rise in the night for a snack. She made herself stop and concentrate. The possibilities she overturned were heartbreaking and grim.

She threw open the mess hall doors and took off running down the gravel pathway. As she ran, she scanned the open meadow, lush and rolling and edged with dark, spindly tree shadows. No movement at all on the wide surface of the meadow. No strolling people. No loping dogs even. Two paths led into the woods: one to the sleeping cabins, the other to the swimming pool. A pair of adult figures—

love-struck counselors by the look of them—were slipping away hand in hand down the swimming pool path.

She nearly called out to them. But what a time-consuming chore to try to explain herself, to shout her message across the darkened meadow. *My son is missing. He is everything to me.* She'd have to make it clear to this couple. *Whatever you're feeling for one another right now, it does not compare to the way I cherish my son.*

She took the path to the sleeping cabins and entered the woods. Her breaths were loud and grunting, the tree-shrouded pathway obscenely dark. But she was able to track her footsteps on the white gravel. At the second fork in the pathway she clambered up a wood walkway and arrived at a concrete landing. She pounded her open hand against the screen door of Cabin Two.

Gibby Tumminello, the assigned night watch counselor, came to the door.

"James," she said out of breath. "My son, James." How much *feeling* there was squeezed into these three words. "He's run off. He's gone missing." Her wrecked expression seemed to have made it clear to Gibby: she wasn't talking about a boyhood lark. This was a crisis.

"I want you to do two things," she said. "I want you to help me search the whole cabin for James. Every room. Every inch. And I want you to make sure that the worst troublemakers you have— Dennis Dugan and Frederick Torbert—are here in the cabin. I want to be sure they're accounted for."

Gibby gave her a wide-eyed nod. Under normal circumstances, he was a feckless and deeply immature young man, too full of boyish humor to warrant much attention from the girl counselors. But he seemed to grasp at once the gravity of Harriet's request. "Will do," he said. "Will do, Nurse Harriet." He grabbed a flashlight and darted into the right-side sleeping barracks.

She didn't have to go far to find Dennis Dugan and Frederick Torbert. They'd been moved, along with their bunk mattresses, out onto the floor of the screened porch: Dennis, his mouth crooked open, sleeping on his side like a collapsed drunk, Frederick Torbert awake and staring up at Harriet from beneath the ridge of his jutting forehead. Earlier in the day he'd reached out with his bandaged hand and rubbed the crotch of her blue jean shorts. Maybe she was paranoid. But it was easy now to believe he was staring at her and turning the memory of that illicit touch over and over in his mind like a shiny penny. He raised himself up with his brawny arms.

"Lay back down, Frederick," she hissed at him. "Lay back down, God damn it."

After a moment of silent calculation, he did what he was told. Perhaps it had been the look on Harriet's face, the scowling authority brought on by this particular emergency.

She stepped across the porch and entered the left-side barracks, a long, stuffy wreck of a room crammed with off-center bunk beds. A terrible salty-sweet body odor had filled the barracks, arising, she was sure, from the filthy underwear and socks and sweat-soaked T-shirts that were mounded wall to wall across the floor. What a nightmare, this laundry. Two days from now it would have to be stuffed into duffel bags and dragged reeking back onto the state hospital buses. Nearly all of the Cabin Two male campers had fallen into an exhausted sleep, their odd faces gone slack and unguarded. "James," she whispered urgently. "James." She stepped over an outstretched arm and searched, row by row, all the way to the far corner of the barracks. None of her worst imaginings proved true. The huddled form in the corner of the cabin was a listing duffel bag and not a boy. The mound in the bed beside a sleeping camper was wet towels and not a child. Still, it shook her to the core to have imagined, if only for a second, such obscene possibilities. She stumbled back to the front porch. By then Gibby Tumminello had completed his search of the right-side barracks and the Cabin Two bathroom and come up empty-handed.

The next stage of her search must have looked to an outsider like a pure expression of panic or the most crippling kind of indecision. She ran to the screen door of men's Cabin One, peered inside, but did not go in. A notion came to her, and she set off running along the pathway, out of the woods, up the sloping hill of the meadow toward The Sanctuary. There might be other off-duty counselors—in addition to the Lonesome Three—lounging on the Sanctuary couches. She would storm inside and demand they form a search party.

But halfway across the open meadow she spotted a strong light brightening the window of Schuller Kindermann's cottage. The presence of this light derailed her hasty plans. She was suddenly indignant. It was outrageous, really. None of what was happening tonight—the crisis with Evie Hicks and Christopher Waterhouse, the crisis with James—would have occurred if Schuller Kindermann hadn't been so disastrously wrong in his decisions. Again and again he'd proved himself to be an incompetent leader. An absent leader. If she had any real hope of help, it would have to come from outside camp. She'd have to call the Ellsinore Police. She would place this call from the camp office. But first she would pound on Schuller's cottage door and inform him of the twin emergencies. She'd let him know what a fool he was.

She bounded up the pine board steps of his porch. Her hand was raised and ready to knock. She looked through the screen door window and nearly collapsed in relief.

Inside the cottage, sitting on stools before a brightly lit drafting table, were Schuller Kindermann and her son, James.

"Oh, for goodness' sake," she said and placed her sweating face against the door screen. She wasn't heard—could not have been heard above the cottage's clanky window fan.

At the drafting table Schuller and James had both folded their arms across their chests and tilted their heads forward in a deep and silent consideration of the materials set out before them: papers and rulers and thin colored pencils. They could hardly have been less alike, the old man and the boy, except in the directness and the intensity of their concentration. By the look of them, you'd think the world depended on their next move—the selection of a pencil, the drawing of a simple line.

She was able, despite the weary trembling in her legs and a sudden rawness in her voice, to enter Schuller Kindermann's cottage and speak her son's name. She knelt down and drew him into her arms. "I've been out looking for you," she said and squeezed his lean little body with a fierceness that might have been vengeful. But she didn't sob into the boy's ear. She didn't scold. For now she held him and coaxed forth his explanation.

What had happened was simple enough. An hour earlier he'd stood on his cot in their living quarters and through the window watched his mother wave down the Kindermann Forest van and confront Christopher Waterhouse. The van pulled away. His mother ran after it. James, who didn't want to be left alone in the infirmary with Nancy Klotter and Mary Ann Hornicker, went after her. Did Nancy and Mary Ann chase after you? Harriet asked. Did they scare you? They didn't, he said. What did they do then? Nothing, he said and shrugged. But when pressed, he revealed that Mary Ann Hornicker had tried to bring him a cup of water. When he stepped into the infirmary yard, both women tried to get him to put on his socks and shoes. He wouldn't allow it. He took off in his pajamas and bare feet and ran along the grassy edge of the meadow after his mother, ran until he lost sight of her. Then he saw the bright lamplight in Mr. Kindermann's window and went to the cottage door and knocked.

What could Harriet say to this? What rule had been broken? Had she ever told the boy that, when she took off running and left him in the company of state hospital patients, he was supposed to stay put?

So it was an awful misunderstanding. A frightening mess. But at least James had had the good sense to seek refuge in the director's cottage. In Schuller Kindermann he'd found a willing host. Materials for a craft project had been set out on the table. Together they'd been drafting the outline of a long and mighty suspension bridge.

"James," she said, "you climb back up on the stool and keep working on your bridge. Mr. Kindermann and I need to talk over some things. If you need anything, you just call out and ask for it, all right?"

He looked altogether surprised by his mother's calm demeanor, her new leniency. Up he went onto the stool, happy to oblige her.

She motioned Schuller Kindermann to stand with her by the cottage screen door. He did so without protest. His steps were mannered and deliberate. A vague half grin appeared on his patient face. Perhaps he thought he was about to be lectured to by an overwrought mother.

"Mr. Kindermann," she said. What a vivid little moment this was. The way he looked at her, so tolerant and alert. She nearly reached out and put a steadying hand on his shoulder.

In her coolest and most instructive voice she explained that an emergency was happening at camp tonight. One of the state hospital campers, a young woman named Evie Hicks, had been put into the camp van and taken outside of Kindermann Forest. The person driving the van, the person who'd taken her, was Christopher Waterhouse. He'd done so in order to molest or rape Evie Hicks. Listen, she said. Listen. She wanted to make it absolutely clear to Mr. Kindermann. She wasn't speculating about Christopher Waterhouse's intentions. This wasn't a matter of camp gossip. Christopher meant to molest or rape Evie Hicks. All of this was happening right now. All of this was—

At the drafting table James had swiveled around on his stool. "Mr. Kindermann," he said. "Can there be ladders on the bridge? Ladders hanging down from the sides?"

Schuller Kindermann squeezed shut his eyes a moment. "Ladders?" he said. "Yes, I don't see why not. Go ahead and draw them in if you like."

"They'll hang down almost all the way to the water," James said.

Harriet waited. All of this was happening now, she said. Evie Hicks was out in the camp van with Christopher Waterhouse. This shouldn't have been allowed to happen, she said. Christopher Waterhouse shouldn't have been made the new program director. Linda Rucker shouldn't have been fired. The original Kindermann Forest counselors shouldn't have been let go for swimming naked at night. All terrible decisions, she said. All of them your decisions, Mr. Kindermann. There's no one in charge at camp, she said. There's no one to stop the very worst people—people like Christopher Waterhouse—from doing what they want.

She could have continued on if she liked. It was startling to realize there wasn't going to be an interruption, a shout of denial, even a scowl of outrage from Schuller Kindermann. Instead he was listening to her with an interest that could best be described as polite, even *kindly*. His hard opinions, his stubbornness, seemed to have dissolved away into nothing.

"I understand," he said. "I've been listening, Nurse Harriet. You've made it perfectly clear. You don't appreciate my . . . decisions. Is there anything else you have to say?"

"Yes," she said. "You also need to know that I sent Wyatt Huddy out to look for the camp van on County Road H."

"Remind me again," Schuller said. "Who is Wyatt Huddy?"

"One of the counselors."

"Which one?"

How best to identify Wyatt? She might say, *The one who is large and strong.* Or *The one who, with just a little encouragement, just a few affectionate gestures, can be persuaded to do what I want.* She said, "The one with the distorted face."

Schuller nodded. "Yes," he said. "I remember now."

"He shouldn't be the only one out there, Mr. Kindermann. We need help from the outside. From the police," she said. "The police in Ellsinore should be called out to camp."

He stood and weighed this suggestion while rocking back and forth on the heels of his loafers. "The Ellsinore Police," he said. "You think they'd be able to help us?" He shook his head, mildly. "Maybe we should just wait awhile. Sometimes these problems work themselves out."

"Not this problem," she said. "It's a call that has to be made. I'll do it if you like."

He shrugged. "Well, I'm too . . . tired to be making phone calls tonight," he said. He turned and surveyed the tidy arrangement of furniture in his cottage. He raised his eyebrows wearily. "If a phone call is going to get made tonight, you're the one who's going to be handling it."

"Fine," she said.

"And when the Ellsinore police chief comes to camp, you'll speak to him. Can you do that, Nurse Harriet? Can you be the . . . director of this emergency?"

"I can. Yes."

"Well, that's good to know," he said. "But tell me this, please. If you had a place like Kindermann Forest, if you were the director . . . what kind of camp do you think it would be?"

She could do nothing but stare at him perplexed. "I don't know, Mr. Kindermann," she said. "I'm sure it would be a hard place to manage. But the first thing, I guess, is that I'd try and make it as safe a place as possible."

He gave her answer a cool nod of appreciation. "Well," he said. "I always had it in my mind that I'd make a camp for children who liked to sit someplace quiet and make beautiful things. A camp for a boy like your son, James. That was my idea. But it hardly ever works out that way. You can't pick and choose which kids come to your camp.

You get all sorts. All kinds of campers. All kinds of counselors." He shook his head, dismayed. "You can't control it as well as you hoped," Schuller said. "After a while, it all gets away from you. It all goes . . ." He held out his thin arms. "Beyond your reach."

She hoisted James onto her back and carried him in a stooping walk across the meadow toward the infirmary. He wasn't often awake this late at night, and from his high perch on her back she could feel him turning about and raising his head to take in his surroundings: the clear, star-crowned, temperate night.

She plodded along. Her son's bare feet bounced against her hips. In time they reached the infirmary yard and climbed the steps. It was easy to believe in the first few moments of their arrival that her two patients, Nancy Klotter and Mary Ann Hornicker, had fled into the night. She stood with James still clinging to her back and squinted into the shadowed darkness of the infirmary. In the back of the room were two mounded forms: Nancy and Mary Ann. Both women had crawled onto bunks and pulled their blankets up over their heads. From the veils of these blankets, they peered out at Harriet, awaiting her wrath.

In the living quarters she placed James in his cot and tried to explain, without scolding, the panic she'd felt when he ran off. "It's a terrible feeling not to know where you are, James." Could he, at five years old, fathom this feeling? Maybe not the exact dread that she'd felt, but some version of this fear had sent him running after her in the first place.

She fetched a damp cloth and rubbed down his ankles and bare feet. Tomorrow he'd pay a price for his wandering in scratches and chigger bites. He'd be tired, too. Already his gaze was weighted and slow. He lay back on his bunk and considered his mother. In a short while his eyes fluttered and he turned his face to the pillow.

She went to the infirmary cabinet and found the list of emergency phone numbers. She put the telephone receiver to her ear. A simple matter, really, of dialing a number and offering a few instructions— and yet she couldn't bring herself to do it. Instead she moved out onto the infirmary steps and listened for the sound of an approaching automobile. After a few quiet minutes the sound she was waiting for began as a low hum in the distance. Hundreds of yards up the camp roadway there was a flicker of brightness and then, soon enough, the full wash of approaching headlights. A vehicle was rolling along the camp roadway at an almost inchmeal pace.

She stood there on the steps, and the thing she'd been waiting for, the Kindermann Forest camp van, pulled close and stopped before the infirmary. From the van's stilled engine came a wet clicking and beyond that, from the far corners of the woods, a steady thrum of insects.

The driver's door creaked open. Wyatt Huddy slipped out and leaned back wearily against the side of the van.

She stepped down into the infirmary yard. "Wyatt . . . ?" she said. Through the windows of the van she could see various shapes still and dark. Otherwise it was hard to determine what the interior might hold. "Wyatt . . . ?" she tried again. "What happened?"

He placed a hand to his forehead and wiped away a smear of sweat. After a moment he cleared his throat and said, "I'm not used to . . ."

"What?"

"Driving at night. The only time I've driven is in the daytime."

"You did all right," she said. "You made it back. Wyatt, what happened?"

In answer he stood straighter against the van and pointed to the passenger door on its opposite side.

Around the van she went, to the sliding door. She turned the latch, swung it open. There, strapped into the first bench of the van, was Evie Hicks, stripped naked and roused into a flailing state of panic by the sudden loud squawk of the van door. She shook her head wildly back and forth and pedaled her bare legs. This was for Harriet an altogether traumatic sight. She'd spent a frantic portion of the night stumbling bewildered across the grounds of Kindermann Forest trying to prevent an *imagined* attack on Evie Hicks. Far, far worse now to be presented with the evidence of that attack: the girl's startled expression, her bare body straining against the seat belts.

It took time to settle Evie down. From Harriet it required not just a calming voice but a willingness to keep her distance. She sat on the running board by the open door and stared out into the darkened meadow. Eventually she said, "All right, Evie. All right now. It's getting late, isn't it? We should see about getting you out of this old van, shouldn't we?" She reached out and put her hand on the girl's shoulder. At once there was a quick pulling away, an awareness.

And so Harriet sat awhile longer, and the next time she reached out and touched Evie's shoulder the reaction was less severe. This allowed Harriet certain privileges. She leaned over the girl and gathered up her clothes and underwear. Then she unfastened the seat belt and guided Evie out the door and onto the roadway.

A few careful steps and they were moving across the infirmary yard. What a sight this was, what a singular vision: a naked Evie Hicks plodding in her usual pigeon-toed shuffle across the moon-brightened grass. Not beautiful exactly. Not alluring, either. Not under these terrible circumstances. But with the stark whiteness of her skin and the loose assembly of her long-legged body, she looked rare and otherworldly, as if she'd stepped out from behind the curtain of a blindingly strange play.

Inside the infirmary they went straight to the bathroom, where Harriet turned on the overhead light and began her careful inspection of Evie Hicks's body. No bruises on the girl's arms or neck or chest. She'd not been hit or scratched. If her skin bore any marks at all, they were the minor indentations of the seat upholstery and safety belts.

A more delicate inspection needed to be made, but the girl would not part her legs for Nurse Harriet. "Evie," Harriet said. "Evie, please. Let me take a look." In response Evie squeezed her thighs together. No matter her position—standing at the sink, sitting on the toilet—she could not be persuaded.

It was one of the more pitifully sad refusals Harriet had ever witnessed. She dressed the girl in an infirmary nightgown, led her to a bunk, took her temperature and blood pressure, and wiped her face with a cool cloth. At least there was one consolation: whatever Evie had endured tonight, she would not become pregnant. For the past eleven days, Harriet, in her morning round of medications, had made sure that each female state hospital camper with a birth control prescription had received her pill. Each woman. Every morning. Evie Hicks included. Without fail. All the while there was a brown paper bag somewhere in Schuller Kindermann's office—one he'd opened or not—full of throat lozenges.

She was aware of her other two patients, Mary Ann Hornicker and Nancy Klotter, watching her from their bunks at the rear of the infirmary. "Ladies," she said. "We should try and get some sleep. It's been a very . . . We've had a very hard night." These were, Harriet hoped, soothing words, if not quite the apology Mary Ann and Nancy deserved. Once she saw that they were settled and on the pathway to sleep, she stepped out the infirmary door and found Wyatt Huddy waiting for her at the picnic table.

Certainly he looked tired. He had the stooped posture of someone who'd been humbled by a tremendous physical effort. His head hung a degree lower than usual. He flexed his large shoulders and placed his forearms out across the table. Gingerly, he opened and closed his hands.

He had reason to do this: there were thick, red scratches across those forearms. She took a seat at the table and held his wrist and considered his injuries. They were the kinds of markings she'd expected to find on Evie Hicks: long, angry abrasions caused by a clawed hand. And there were other markings as well: a red welt on the side of his face, a lengthy tapered scratch across his collarbone. Was she startled? Was she shocked? Not quite. The events of the night had dulled her capacity to be taken by surprise.

"You were in a fight," she said. "A fight with Christopher. I can guess that much, Wyatt. But the rest I don't know."

He sat with his head lowered. He made no acknowledgment that he'd been spoken to, but at least he hadn't pulled his arms free from her grasp.

"I don't know the circumstances," she continued. "And I *have* to know, Wyatt. I've had an awful night and I can't do another thing until I know."

He began to stir, a slow back and forth tilting of his head. He sealed and unsealed his lips, raised his face to her, without looking her in the eye. For several moments he did nothing but try to arrange the distorted features of his face into an accommodating expression. Then he let forth a long, huffing sigh and said, "All right, all right, Harriet."

He said he'd gone out looking for the camp van. And after a while he'd found it off the side of the road. Not so far from Kindermann Forest. Evie was inside, buckled into the seat. Without clothes. And Christopher was there with her. Touching her between the legs. Putting his face there, too. Pushing himself against her.

She made herself ask the difficult questions. "Did Christopher have his clothes on? Was he having intercourse with Evie? Do you know what that means, Wyatt? Intercourse?"

He said that Christopher had his clothes on. But they were undid. Unfastened. As for the word *intercourse*, Wyatt said he knew what it meant. It might have been the thing Christopher was doing to Evie Hicks. Or maybe not. Either way Wyatt had made Christopher stop.

"And then?"

Across Wyatt's uneven face came a clenched tightness, a kind of grief. "I got mad. Christopher, too. There was a fight. It went on for a while."

"But you're all right, aren't you?" she asked. "You have some scratches, but nothing worse than that?"

"Just scratches."

"And Christopher?"

"Same thing. Scratches and bumps."

"And what did Christopher do after the fight?"

A long pause. "He was still mad. He said he didn't want to come back to camp. He said he was quitting his job."

"Quitting?"

"Yes."

"But where is he now, Wyatt? Because if he's out there, then we should call the police. So they can find him. So he doesn't attack someone else. Another girl."

"He won't do that," Wyatt said. "He's gone off on his own."

"Off where?"

"Off to be alone."

Off to be alone? She could picture it as well as feel it. Not just a lone body, but the wave of dread people would feel when the news came to them. Lives were going to be overturned. It would be no simple matter to set them right again.

"But . . . where?" she asked. She held him hard by the wrists. "Where did he go?"

From Wyatt there was a moment of calm reflection. "Into the woods," he said.

How much better would it have been if she'd called the Ellsinore Police? Some things would surely have been easier. They could have told the authorities about Evie Hicks's assault *before* rather than *after*.

That, clearly, would have been the better choice. But the call hadn't been made. Instead Harriet retired to her living quarters and lay on her bed turning and agonizing and sometimes even sleeping for short stretches of time. In the morning she rose and pressed on with the last full day of the State Hospital Session.

She wasn't the only one. The Kindermann Forest counselors were up at seven-thirty urging their campers to wash and brush their teeth and hurry to breakfast. In the mess hall there was the usual clamor and chaos, but something else also—a renewed liveliness and sense of relief among the counselors, this being the last full day.

By midmorning certain questions began to circulate; mainly, where the hell was Christopher Waterhouse? His fellow lifeguard, Marcy Bittman, had to work the pool all morning by herself. It wasn't safe, she insisted, to have just one guard on duty. She knew for a fact it was a violation of YMCA lifeguard safety regulations. She managed as well as she could through the morning, and after lunch, with no sign of Christopher, she closed and locked the gate and declared the pool off-limits.

Fortunately there were other activities to occupy the campers: canoeing and arts and crafts or a visit to the horse stables. There were also preparations to be made for the evening activity: the Kindermann Forest Talent Show Extravaganza and Farewell Dance. Some counselors took the assignment more seriously than others. Ellen Swinderman stitched together grass skirts for her four campers and spent the afternoon coaxing her ladies to sing "I'm in Love with a Wonderful Guy" from *South Pacific*. But for most of the counselors it was easier to rely on things the state hospital campers already knew, the sudden and often incomprehensible sight gags and pantomimes they'd been performing since they arrived. And if not that, then always and forever, "I've Been Working on the Railroad" sung in any register, in any odd accent or with any garbled voice.

It wasn't until after dinner that it dawned on the counselors: Where would the talent show take place? Who would decorate? Who would set up the microphone and sound system? Not Christopher Waterhouse. He was still missing. Out sick, they guessed. Sick or hungover. Lying low.

His absence didn't dampen their enthusiasm too much. At seven-thirty they convened in the mess hall and began moving the heavy tables off to the side of the room. A three-piece stereo system was carried across the meadow from The Sanctuary and installed along the mess hall serving counter. In spite of their best efforts, no one could locate a microphone. But it hardly mattered. When had the state hospital campers ever needed a microphone to be heard?

Once the Kindermann Forest Talent Show Extravaganza and Farewell Dance began, it was clear to the staff that they'd embarked on one of the better evening activities. Perhaps the best one of all. They hadn't expected it to mean so much. But what an obvious rush of good feeling it brought the campers to march up in front of the mess hall counter and perform their acts. Not just a good feeling. Pride. How justifiably proud they were of themselves. It didn't at all matter that the song they planned to perform had just been sung by the previous group. When their time came, they stomped up to the mess hall counter bursting with eagerness. *I've been working on the railroad. All the livelong day.* What a sight to behold! Portly Jerry Johnston, crooning high and sweet. Thomas Anwar Toomey, his thin, haggard body shaking right along with his wavering voice. Leonard Peirpont, holding fast to the counter's edge and singing for all he was worth. And their counselor, shy, somber Wyatt Huddy, watching from the sidelines and nodding his respect.

After the last group had performed, the stereo was turned on. The campers needed no prompting; they took to the floor gripping one another or their counselors hard and close and swaying with an energy that was raw and contagious. Who would have guessed how much they loved to dance? *One more song,* they begged. *One more, please. One more.*

At ten-thirty they all stumbled back down to the sleeping cabins. The campers hadn't been allowed to stay out this late before, and as a result their bedtime routine suffered. Few of them could be bullied into a shower or made to brush their teeth. Instead they stomped into the sleeping barracks and tossed and turned in their bunks. The counselors stood on the cabin porches watching them and feeling a surge of astonishment. They'd managed somehow to reach the end of the State Hospital Session. All that was left tomorrow morning was a breakfast of cereal and fruit and the shuttling of the campers and their bags back onto the state hospital buses. After that the Kindermann Forest counselors would have forty-eight hours to rest and do their laundry and await the arrival of children who were blessedly healthy and normal.

But there were other things happening beyond the borders of Kindermann Forest, too. Early Saturday morning a pickup truck pulled off County Road H onto a clearing of rutted grass known to local hunters and fishermen as a staging ground from which they could set forth into the woods. A man stepped out from the truck along with his dog, a boxy and energetic black Lab retriever. They set off along a thin path into the woods. The man had a notion to try his luck fishing some of the deep sinkholes along the creek that led to Barker Lake. Too bad his dog wouldn't cooperate, wouldn't follow along quietly at his heels, wouldn't even keep to the path. And what an awful shrieking howl the dog let out. It was impossible to fish with such a clamor. The man had no choice but to follow the dog through the brush and down a steep creek bed until they arrived at a mound of flagstones. He pulled back a few stones and made a discovery.

Not just the fact of a violent death; the pricey sneakers and blue jeans and haircut made it clear the body wasn't local. The man dragged his whining dog back through the forest. At the clearing he climbed into his pickup truck and drove to the Ellsinore Police Station. He told the sheriff he'd just found the body of a summer camp counselor.

An hour later a caravan of three white state hospital buses rumbled past the front gate of Kindermann Forest and made their way along the camp road before rolling to a halt in the open meadow. The bus doors swung open. Out marched a regiment of uniformed attendants. They paused in the bright sunlight and considered the crowd of campers and counselors waiting for them in the meadow. It was a sobering moment for the attendants; their hundred and four state hospital patients were returned to them. The hard work of it couldn't be avoided any longer. Soon they began hefting bags of reeking laundry into the rear hatches of the buses and walking among the throngs of waiting patients, checking off names from a list.

Down the steps of a bus came a stout and ferocious woman, Nurse B. Colette Dunbar. She'd already worked herself into a state of scowling anxiety. "Leonard?" she huffed. "Leonard Peirpont?" She stomped across the grass and pushed her way into the thickest folds of the crowd. Eventually she found him propped against an elm tree. "Leonard," she said, incredulous. "Look at you. Look at you, Leonard." She leaned close and inspected his arms and elbows, the nape of neck, his handsome face. No injuries. No rashes. He'd not changed at all in the twelve days he'd been away. *"Leonard,"* she said, overcome by the welcome sight of him.

In time and with great effort the buses were loaded, the state hospital patients ushered to their seats. The diesel engines roared. With a heavy lurch the caravan embarked from the meadow and rolled along the camp roadway until at last they passed through the gates of Kindermann Forest and were gone forever.

In their absence an odd and clarifying quiet: the camp dogs could be heard yelping along the edge of the forest. The mess hall screen door let out a long, slow squawk. And beneath these sounds the kind of silence that fills a tunnel after the passing of a hurtling freight train.

For a moment the counselors were too stunned and exhausted to move. It felt like a weighty absence, as if they'd just said farewell to the dearest of friends.

Chapter Eighteen

On Sunday evening at 8:00 P.M. Harriet phoned the on-duty manager of Living Cottage No. 8 and reported that she and Wyatt Huddy had gone grocery shopping in the morning and in the afternoon had attended an employee barbecue sponsored by the hospital where Harriet worked.

"A barbecue?" the cottage manager marveled. "That must have been nice. How did Wyatt do? With the other people, I mean. Did he interact?"

"Yes, he did," Harriet said. "He talked with a few people." By this she meant that he'd edged up close to a circle of her friends, lowered his head, and said, "Thank you for inviting me. My name is Wyatt Huddy." Her nurse friends had been charmed by his shyness. (And no doubt they'd wondered, too, what disability might be the cause of his awkwardness and disfigured face.) Throughout much of the barbecue he'd sat in a foldout chair next to a portable radio and scored each inning of the Cardinals–Dodgers game. Had he enjoyed himself? She guessed that he had, though it probably wasn't the social interaction at the barbecue that had brought him contentment. It was the chance to sit outside on a beautiful summer day and be surrounded by a lively crowd.

"As far as you know, Ms. Foster, has Wyatt been eating and sleeping well this weekend?"

"Very well, yes."

"I'm glad to hear that. Can we talk just a minute about tomorrow, please?"

"All right."

"I'd recommend that you speak with Wyatt tonight and let him know the plans for tomorrow. The exact plans—when you'll need to pack up and leave your house. Let him know the check-in time here at Gateway. It'll be easier for him, you understand, if he can anticipate how the day will unfold."

"I'll do that, yes."

"They go by quick, these weekend furloughs. We'll see you both back here tomorrow at the living cottage."

"Yes. Tomorrow afternoon. See you then."

She turned off the lights in the kitchen and climbed the stairs to the second floor. In the guest room she found Wyatt sitting crosslegged on the bed. He'd taken his shower and shaved and had dressed in cotton pajamas. With his stiff, black glasses and damp hair combed back from his forehead, he looked prim and bashful and vaguely handsome.

"You look comfortable," she said. "I'm guessing you like sleeping in this bed?"

His only reply was to stare at her patiently. With Wyatt she could make all the homey observations she liked. Few of them would result in an actual conversation.

"So I thought we should talk a minute about the plans for tomorrow. What we need to do. And when we need to do it."

"Yes," he said. "Okay, Harriet."

"We'll get up and have breakfast," she said. "I have a friend named Sarah Mitchell, who'll drop by and visit for a little while. She'll come at ten in the morning. After she's gone we'll have lunch and go for a walk. Then we'll need to pack up your things and head back to Gateway."

He seemed to be picturing this sequence in his mind. A visit from a friend. A lunch. A walk. Then the return to Gateway.

"Your check-in time is two o'clock, but I think we should get there a half hour early. To show them we respect the rules."

"The rules," he said. "Yes, all right."

"I want you to understand something, Wyatt. This weekend furlough is just the start. We'll go back to Gateway tomorrow and show them we can be trusted. Then we'll ask for more. I'll file a request to get you furloughed for a weekend in October. After that we can look forward to Thanksgiving. We'll ask for five days at Thanksgiving. At Christmas we'll ask for a week and half. Each time you'll come here and stay with me, and each time we'll follow the rules. I'll keep at it, Wyatt. I'll keep asking for furloughs, and as long as we do things right, they'll keep giving them to us." She eased down onto the foot of the bed. "When next spring rolls around," she said, "I'm going to ask the physicians' board to release you into my care. Release you permanently. They'll say no at first—once or twice or maybe three times. But soon enough, they'll say yes. You'll be out of Gateway for good. And when you leave Gateway, you can come here and live with me. I'd be glad to have you, Wyatt."

He turned suddenly and gave the furnishings of her guest room— the dresser and wallpaper and window curtains—a fresh consideration. "I'd stay here in this room?" he asked.

"Yes, you would. You'd stay here. We'd find you a part-time job somewhere. You'd go to work. The rest of the time you could do what you pleased. You could come and go as you like."

"We'd live together in this house," he said as if testing the soundness of the idea. He lowered his head and for several long moments seemed frozen in his concentration. Then he said, "Would we live together like married people do, Harriet?"

What stunned her most was that he'd found the courage to ask such a question. There'd been occasions throughout the years when her affection for him had spilled over the boundaries of friendship into something else. Had she been flirting with him? No, not exactly. But sometimes, when he'd been at his lowest, she'd used an imploring look to raise his spirits. She hadn't been shy about reaching out to touch him when the moment seemed right. All along she'd believed he'd been unaware of the implications.

Somewhere in the inner workings of the mattress a metal coil chimed softly. She could hear the slow whoosh of air passing through the floor vent. Each of these small sounds seemed to be making a fierce demand on her attention.

"I wouldn't know how . . ." she said vaguely. "But there are ways . . . There are times when . . ." She shook her head, at a loss.

Then she stood and crossed the room and turned off the overhead light. The result wasn't darkness; there was still a strong dusky glow filtering through the window curtains. She kicked off her shoes and pulled back the bedcovers. "Here," she whispered. "Crawl beneath the covers, Wyatt." He did as she asked—without hesitating, without the awkwardness or trepidation that might have ruined the moment.

Harriet slipped beneath the covers and embraced him. It was a precarious thing to do: to lie close beside him and try to explain with her body something so complicated and so fraught with potential misunderstanding. The best she could hope for was that he harbored only modest expectations. Not a married life together; she couldn't bear that. She wasn't patient or accepting enough to be tethered to him day and night. But if he wanted sometimes to lie in bed with a woman, with Harriet, then she wasn't going to deny him comfort.

She pressed her face against his neck and welcomed the pressure of his warm hands on her hips and eventually her breasts. What occurred between them—what was occurring now—wasn't the reckless variety of sex that all those years ago at Kindermann Forest had been an unrelenting current passing through the counselors and campers. Instead, she and Wyatt were slow-motion lovers. His body was firm and strong. There were rich pleasures to be had here: to be the first person to lay his body bare and attend to it, lovingly, with her hands. How grateful and astonished he was. It didn't at all matter to Harriet that he wasn't yet a practiced enough lover for intercourse. The real pleasure, the deeper pleasure, was to witness him trembling and shy. Afterward they folded themselves together. She kissed his cheek and placed a hand on his beating heart. It amazed and gladdened her. What had seemed audacious to Harriet at the outset was now warm and tender—elemental.

By seven-thirty the next morning they were up and washed and finished with breakfast. Outside, the dawn light was falling in velvety strips across the fenced backyard. How welcoming it looked: an altogether beautiful Labor Day morning. They took their steaming cups of coffee out to the yard and settled into wrought-iron patio chairs.

For a half hour or more she could do nothing but sip her coffee and watch the yard fill with light. Outwardly she was calm. Inwardly a potent collision of feeling kept her from speaking. Where to begin? She was glad, even grateful, for what she and Wyatt had shared last night. And yet she'd not been entirely honest with him. Certain information she'd kept to herself. Each time she glanced at him now, she fought back the need to apologize.

Better to say it as simply and clearly as she could. "Wyatt," she said. "My friend Sarah Mitchell will stop by this morning. Sarah is a professor at the University of Missouri. A professor in the education department. She teaches teachers. She's an expert on how to give tests. All kinds of tests." Harriet waited. On the opposite side of the patio table Wyatt had lifted his gaze to her. He seemed to be holding his breath. "What Professor Mitchell is especially good at," she said, "is a particular kind of test. An IQ test."

He set his coffee cup on the patio table and pulled the glasses from his face. With the hem of his T-shirt in his hand, he began scrubbing away at the lenses.

"Professor Mitchell and I know each other a little. I helped her gather health data for a project she was doing a while back. But she doesn't know you, Wyatt. Not at all. Not a single thing about you. I've asked Professor Mitchell to do me an important favor this morning. I've asked her to come to my house and give you a—"

"A test," Wyatt said. "A *test*." The word seemed to unnerve him. He clenched and unclenched his jaw as he scrubbed away at his glasses.

What else could she do but try to explain? She said she'd thought long and hard about it, and she'd come to the conclusion that this was a test he needed to take. He'd been a silent witness to most of the preparations she and his defense lawyer had made, and he knew about the affidavits that Harriet had gathered on his behalf. He'd heard most of them read aloud. And the first time he'd taken an IQ test for a court-appointed psychiatrist he'd done so under special instructions from Harriet. She'd told him that when the psychiatrists asked him to give as many answers as he could, Wyatt should only give one or two. No more than that. All of these measures had been necessary in order to get him sentenced to a state hospital facility. "But they've taken their toll," she said. "Over the years I can tell you've grown unsure of your abilities. And that's a shame," she said. "Because I know for certain you don't have a diminished IQ."

He frowned severely and squared his shoulders as if he'd just been gravely insulted. "It's not fair to say that, Harriet." His voice was heavy and low. "You're not the one who'll be taking the test."

"I understand that. You can say no if you like. You can refuse. But I think you should take the test. It's something that would put your mind at rest."

"No," he said. "No, it wouldn't."

"Why on earth wouldn't it? Why not?"

"Either way. If I pass the test. Or not. Either way, there's something to feel bad about."

"That makes no sense to me, Wyatt."

He glared out at the yard. What a face he showed her—lopsided and trembling and pinched with raw feeling. "There are times," he said, "when I like to think I *was* confused. Confused or . . . retarded. There are times when I like to believe I didn't understand what I was doing. Back then. When I did what I did to Christopher. When I killed him."

"That was a special circumstance," she said. "You were upset at what you saw Christopher doing in the van. Because he was an awful person."

It was a line of reasoning that didn't seem to have the power to persuade him. He shrugged.

"You don't believe he was awful?"

"I do," he said.

"So?"

"I did an awful thing, too." He held up a hand and stretched open his fingers, which were stubby and blunt and still bore the faint scars of having been separated by a scalpel. "I touched Evie Hicks," he said. "I was alone with her in the van and I touched Evie." He cupped his hand and placed his fingertips on the right side of his chest. "Here," he said. "I touched her here."

She did her absolute best to stay calm, to maintain a neutral expression. "You touched Evie on her chest? On her breast?"

He nodded mournfully. Then he gasped loudly and wetly though one side of his mouth.

"When did this happen, Wyatt?"

"It happened before I did what I did. Before I killed Christopher."

"Before? I don't understand."

"Some things were said to me. That Evie wouldn't mind. That I should spend some time alone with her. Because a person like me—with my condition—I wouldn't get another chance to be alone with a girl."

For a decade or more her feelings toward Christopher Waterhouse had been resigned, some days even ambivalent. He was dust and bones after all. Fortunately so. But what a surge of rage and anguish shot through her now. If she could, she'd dig up and set fire to those dusty bones. Or she'd launch a campaign—letters and newspaper ads, billboards for Christ's sake—to let the world know how petty and cruel and worthless he'd been. "*God damn* him," she said through clenched teeth. She shook her head steadily back and forth. "*Wrong. Wrong. Wrong,*"she hissed. "That shouldn't have been said to you, Wyatt. The things Christopher Waterhouse did were bad enough," she said. "But the things he said to people—not just you, but other people at camp—were a kind of poison. God damn him for saying those things." She pinched the bridge of her nose and concentrated. "So," she said. "Wyatt. You reached out and touched Evie Hicks . . . on the breast. And then?"

"She knew what I was doing. She didn't like it."

"Did you touch her anywhere else? I'm asking this because . . . If it's worse than that, if it went farther . . . It would be better, for your sake, to tell me everything that went on. I'm not going to hate you. I'd understand. I've made mistakes, too. Did you touch Evie on her bottom? Or between her legs?"

"No."

"Did you— Wyatt. Did you take any of your clothes off?"

"I didn't. I touched her one time. Then I stopped. Then I got angry at myself. After that I went looking for Christopher."

It was somehow enough, this terse explanation. *He touched Evie Hicks. He got angry with himself. Then he killed Christopher Waterhouse.* Harriet believed she'd just heard an accurate account of what had happened.

"Listen," she said. "Listen, Wyatt. The mistake you made doesn't compare to what Christopher Waterhouse did to Evie. That was far worse. And would have been even more awful if you hadn't found the van and stopped him. You understand that, don't you? *Damn it,* Wyatt. I need a response. You can't just hang your head and ignore what I'm saying. What Christopher did was worse, wasn't it?"

He lifted his head and nodded. "Yes, it was worse."

"Listen. We're all flawed. We all make mistakes. But most of us, thankfully, aren't willing to harm another person. The idea is too upsetting. Inside us an important shift occurs. We stop ourselves. That's what you did, Wyatt. You thought of the harm that would come to Evie Hicks. You stopped. You will always be a good person," she said.

He sat perfectly still in his chair. After a while he slipped his glasses back on his face.

"Take the test," she said. "It's something you need to know about yourself."

He gave her an exasperated look and turned away. This, she knew, was his last gesture of protest before he consented.

"I wish you'd told me about the test before now," he said. "I might have practiced a few things. If I'd known this was coming."

A few minutes after ten the iron knocker at the front door sounded. Harriet ushered Professor Mitchell into the front hallway. She was a thin, energetic woman in her mid-fifties. A large carry bag was slung across her shoulder. "What a wonderful house, Harriet," she said. "Thank you for inviting me over." Behind these gracious remarks there was an efficient appraisal being made. She looked ready to get on with the task at hand.

To her credit Professor Mitchell didn't pause for a second when taken to the kitchen and introduced to Wyatt. She wished him a good morning and shook his hand before taking her place at the table. From her carry bag she began extracting the components of her test: laminated picture cards, puzzle pieces, colored blocks, pencils, and sheets of paper with half-completed drawings.

"I don't know your reasons for wanting this test," Professor Mitchell said. "But I can tell you this. An IQ test is useful for a few things. Mostly to help students with disabilities get the help they need. For almost everything else it's no use at all. No real predictor of what a person is able to achieve. I hope you'll keep that in mind, Wyatt. Are you ready to begin?"

He gripped the seat of his chair with both hands and nodded woefully.

For the duration of the test, an hour and ten minutes, Harriet waited in the living room. She had a vague notion that she might accomplish a few minor chores while she waited. The chairs and sofa might be vigorously cleaned. Or the magazine rack set to order. She made several false starts at these chores, but in the end she kept easing back into her reading chair and eavesdropping on Professor Mitchell's instructions. *Can you use the blocks and make this design here?* And later . . . *Can you think of another object that might be made from this line, Wyatt? Good, yes, that works. Can you think of another? All right. And another? All right. How about one more? That's all right then. Let's move on to the next picture.*

Eventually there was ten long minutes of silence, and then Professor Mitchell called out, "Harriet, would you come in now, please?"

Chapter Nineteen

Wyatt," Professor Mitchell said. "If it's all right with you, I'd like to go ahead and discuss the results of the test."

He tried to wet his lips and shape a few simple words: *Yes. All right.* No use. All he could do, in the end, was nod in consent.

In some private chamber of his mind he heard the word *mercy* spoken aloud. *Mercy,* intoned with great reverence and clarity. He lowered his face to the table as if he'd been instructed to say grace. From the corner of his eye he could see Harriet wavering in the entranceway. She took a few hurried steps across the kitchen floor and stood behind the chair he was sitting in. Both of her hands settled onto his shoulders. After a few moments he felt her lean down and embrace him from behind.

"Are we ready?" Professor Mitchell said.

"We're ready," Harriet said on his behalf.

"All right then," Professor Mitchell said. "I hope you won't be disappointed to know, Wyatt, that according to the test we just performed, a test that is useful in some ways and not very useful in many others, you have an IQ that lands squarely in the medium range. We have a term for this. We say a medium-range IQ. The number earned from today's test is ninety-seven. If we tested you again next week, it might be a few points lower or a few points higher. That's why it's fairer and more accurate to refer to the range of the IQ rather than the specific score."

He could feel Harriet's arms clasped across his chest, squeezing him mightily. She said, "Medium range is another way of saying average, Wyatt. An average IQ."

He gave a slow, stunned nod. "What would it be . . . ,"he said and faltered. "What would the score be for someone who's . . . retarded?"

"There are different ranges for that," Professor Mitchell said. "The mild retardation range is anywhere from fifty to sixty-nine. The range for moderate and severe retardation would be lower than that."

"I've heard," he said. "Some people have told me that if you have a score that's lower than a hundred, then it means you're retarded."

Professor Mitchell fixed him with a steady and patient stare. "Those people would be mistaken."

He tried to rise from his seat, thought better of it, and sat back down. "Thank you," he said. "Thank you, Professor Mitchell."

"You're very welcome, Wyatt," she said. She slung her bag across her shoulder and made ready to leave. "I hope you're not upset by these results."

Harriet and Wyatt both answered her. "No, no," they said.

"It's just that you look, both of you, like you're in a state of shock."

A kind of shock, maybe. In the minutes after Professor Mitchell's departure, he was too startled to linger inside Harriet Foster's handsome redbrick home. He crossed through the living room and stepped out the front door onto the sidewalk. When he turned, he found Harriet at his side.

"A walk?" he asked. It seemed to Wyatt that he'd been promised a last walk around the neighborhood.

A bright and expansive midday was unfolding itself across the lanes and small front yards. They walked along at a brisk pace. Around them they could hear the side doors of minivans sliding shut, the squeaks of swing sets rising up from beyond backyard fences. Block after block they went, past the grocers and apartment buildings and school playgrounds. How strange that he couldn't quite gauge the distance they'd traveled or the length of time they'd been out walking. When they passed a bank clock, they saw it was already half past noon.

They had no choice but to turn around and hurry back along the same lanes and tree-shaded sidewalks. Strolling beside him, Harriet asked, "Are you happy, Wyatt? Are you pleased to know?"

"Yes. I'm glad to know."

"It's one thing—one large important thing—that you don't have to spend time wondering about anymore. So it's a relief, isn't it?"

"It is," he said. "I have an average-range IQ."

"Yes, you do, Wyatt. It's a proven fact."

As soon as they returned to the house, he climbed the stairs to the guest room and packed his belongings into the rollaway suitcase. He made his bed according to Harriet's strict standards. Then he carried the suitcase down the stairs and into the kitchen, where he sat for a hurried lunch of grilled cheese sandwiches and tomato soup.

The kitchen wall clock read a quarter past one. Harriet caught him glancing at it.

She said, "We'll need to go in a few minutes, Wyatt. Get yourself ready for that." She reached across the table and took his hand. "Are you ready?"

"Yes."

He turned to the kitchen window. Outside, in the fenced backyard, the branches of Harriet's prized elm trees were being lifted by a languid summer breeze.

"What are you thinking about, Wyatt?" she asked. "What are you thinking about with that average-range IQ of yours?"

What could he say? He'd never been able to translate his most private thoughts into spoken words. It was a trait he'd shared with the state hospital campers of Kindermann Forest. But in other ways he was different. He was not of their tribe. He'd like to believe that in the deepest and wisest part of himself he'd known this all along.

"You have a beautiful house, Harriet."

"Thank you."

"I'm lucky to be here," he said.

Acknowledgments

My sincere thanks to the University of Missouri, St. Louis, for a 2007–08 Research Board Award that allowed me to focus solely on *The Inverted Forest*. I'm also grateful for two fellowships at The MacDowell Colony. Debbie Logan, Patrick Harned, Joe Betz, and Jean Dalton Young contributed to the research. Davie MacTaggart should have been thanked for the last book. Rebecca Pastor and Zachary Lazar were essential first readers for *The Inverted Forest*. Jen Jen Chang, also a first reader, is my essential partner.

Thanks to Mary Troy and to the exceptional students in our University of Missouri–St. Louis, MFA program.

I'm hugely fortunate to have Lisa Bankoff at ICM and Colin Harrison at Scribner on my side.

Last, my love and thanks to Anna Dalton and Aimee Dalton, beyond measure, beyond words. The next book will be for you.

About the Author

John Dalton is the author of the novel *Heaven Lake,* winner of the Barnes & Noble 2004 Discover Award in fiction and the Sue Kaufman Prize from the American Academy of Arts and Letters. He is a graduate of the Iowa Writers' Workshop and is currently a member of the English faculty at the University of Missouri–St. Louis, where he teaches in the MFA Writing Program. John lives with his wife and two daughters in St. Louis.